WAR DRUMS

THE PALMETTO TRILOGY

CALL TO ARMS
WAR DRUMS
WITH HONOR

WAR DRUMS

LIVIA HALLAM
with JAMES REASONER

CUMBERLAND HOUSE
NASHVILLE, TENNESSEE

WAR DRUMS
PUBLISHED BY CUMBERLAND HOUSE PUBLISHING, INC.
431 Harding Industrial Drive
Nashville, Tennessee 37211

Cover design by Gore Studio, Inc., Nashville, Tennessee

Library of Congress Cataloging-in-Publication Data

Hallam, Livia, 1957–
    War drums / Livia Hallam, with James Reasoner.
        p.   cm. — (Palmetto trilogy)
    ISBN-13: 978-1-68162-932-2 (pbk. : alk. paper)

    1. South Carolina—History—Civil War, 1861–1865—Fiction. 2. Domestic fiction.
I. Reasoner, James. II. Title. III. Series.
PS3573.A787W37 2006
813'.54—dc22   2006021834

Printed in the United States of America

1 2 3 4 5 6 7 8 9 10—10 09 08 07 06

To Paul Washburn,

the best father and father-in-law
a pair of writers could have

WAR DRUMS

Nassau, the Bahamas

AUGUST 1861

ALLARD TYLER'S FIRST SIGHT of the island—Captain Barnaby
Yorke informed him it was New Providence Island—was as a
green smudge low to the water. It grew in size as the *Ghost*, a
Confederate privateer out of Charleston, South Carolina, approached,
as did the larger island to the west, which was called Andros Island.
New Providence, though smaller, was where the settlement of Nassau
was situated, and its appearance was provident indeed for the battered
Confederate schooner and her equally shot-up crew.

Allard was a slender, hard-muscled young man with a shock of
brown hair and a short brown beard grown since he had been at sea.
His leg was sore and stiff from a wound caused by a large splinter of
wood slamming into it after a shell burst, as was his side where a Yankee bayonet had raked it during hand-to-hand fighting in a fierce battle with two Federal ships off the Florida coast. Captain Yorke had
doused both injuries liberally with whiskey before bandaging them,
so Allard thought they would heal without festering. The liquor had
burned like hellfire, especially on the wound in his thigh, but it was
worth it not to have his leg rot off.

Three members of the crew, including the helmsman, had been
killed in the fighting that had seen the *Ghost* sink a Federal frigate and
damage an enemy sloop. Several other men were wounded, but the
captain believed they would all survive. Four wounded Yankees were

locked up belowdecks. They would be turned over to the British governor at Nassau and ultimately sent home from there. Members of the boarding party who had been killed had been given honorable burials at sea, and the prisoners could testify to that. "We're not pirates," Yorke had told them sternly, "and I'd appreciate it if you'd tell your superiors that much when you get home."

The ship's engine was out of commission. Yorke estimated it would take at least a week to repair it. Even then, there would be quite a bit of work needed to put it back into shape. That work would have to wait until they returned to Charleston and the shipyard that was owned by Allard's father, Malachi Tyler. The rest of the damage could be handled in Nassau.

As they drew near the island, Allard stood at the railing, watching the land and the settlement take shape. New Providence was low and rolling, with no large hills. Palm trees grew thickly in places, and the open areas were covered with saw grass. The settlement sprawled along the shore with only a narrow strip of beach here and there between the buildings and the water. Quite a few large ships were docked here, all of them flying the Union Jack. Nassau was an important stop on the British trade routes. It was an old settlement, founded by the Spaniards centuries earlier. Allard saw the sun reflecting off whitewashed adobe walls. The red-tile roofs were bright and colorful. The frame buildings were equally bright. They had been painted seemingly every hue in the rainbow. Here and there were larger, more impressive buildings constructed of brick or hewn stone. He saw a couple of bell towers that marked the churches. Although Nassau was considerably smaller than his hometown of Charleston, Allard thought it was a beautiful city with an exotic and intriguing air to it. He heard music playing somewhere as the *Ghost* eased up to one of the docks and sailors leaped ashore to make the ship fast.

When the gangplank was in place, Allard and Yorke limped down it to greet a ruddy-faced man who awaited them. He shook hands with them and introduced himself as Cyril Judkins, the harbormaster.

"Cap'n Barnaby Yorke, master of the *Ghost*," Yorke introduced himself. "And this is my third mate, Mr. Allard Tyler, who also happens to be the son o' this vessel's owner."

"Your father is Malachi Tyler?" Judkins asked.

"That's right," Allard replied. "Do you know my father, sir?"

"I know of him. He built this ship?"

Yorke said, "That he did."

"It's a bloody shame to get a ship built by Malachi Tyler all shot up this way."

Yorke grinned. "Truer words were never spoken. I thought we'd heave to for a while and get her patched up."

"That can certainly be arranged," Judkins said. "I take it you encountered a Union vessel?"

"Several of them, includin' a frigate that's now on the bottom, over Bimini way."

Judkins's eyebrows arched. "This little schooner sank a Union frigate in battle?"

"Sometimes it ain't the size o' the ship that matters, Mr. Judkins. It's what's in the hearts o' the men sailin' her."

Judkins nodded slowly. The British were a seagoing race. He knew exactly what Yorke was talking about.

"Do any of your men require medical attention?"

"A few should probably see a sawbones, if you've got one who's any good around here."

"We have a fine doctor, an American, in fact. Dr. Richard Henry Savage. His office is just down Bay Street here a short distance."

Yorke and Judkins continued talking for several minutes while Allard turned his attention to the town. On the highest elevation in sight was an oddly shaped building that resembled a ship. Near it was a large frame mansion painted a striking shade of pink.

Judkins saw him eying the structures and said, "That's Government House, the center of the colonial government and the residence of Governor Haworth. And beside it is Fort Fincastle, built by the Spaniards when they occupied these islands." Judkins turned back to

Yorke. "Speaking of Governor Haworth, when it was reported to him that a Confederate schooner was approaching the harbor, he asked me to pass along an invitation to its captain for dinner this evening." The Englishman glanced over at Allard. "And I'll take the liberty of extending the invitation to Mr. Tyler, as well. I'm sure Governor Haworth would like to meet both of you."

"Tell the governor we're pleased to accept," Yorke said. "Ain't we, lad?"

"Cap'n, we're rather bloody and filthy and ragged," Allard pointed out.

Yorke dropped a hand on his shoulder. "Come on along with me to see the doc, and then I know a place where we can get a shave and a bath and all the pamperin' we need to make us presentable again." He winked at Judkins. "I been to Nassau before, you see. I'm hopin' Graciela's is still where it used to be."

Judkins's rather prominent ears turned red, but he nodded and said, "Ah . . . yes, it is. Or so I hear. I wouldn't know from personal experience, mind you."

"O' course not." Yorke steered Allard toward Bay Street. "Come on, lad. By this evenin', you'll feel like a new man!"

ALLARD THOUGHT it would be going too far to say that he felt like a new man that evening, but he did feel considerably better. Cleaner, too, and better-dressed.

Dr. Savage had commended Yorke for the job he had done of caring for the injured men, including the Yankee prisoners. All the physician had needed to do was put clean dressings on all the wounds. The most seriously wounded men would be staying at his infirmary while they recuperated.

After the visit to the doctor's office, Yorke had taken Allard to a large house on a palm-shaded side street. From the looks of the place, some rich businessman or important colonial official might live there. In actuality, the mistress of the place was a beautiful, middle-aged woman Yorke called Doña Graciela. She lived there with a dozen young women, all of them lovely, ranging from a dark-skinned island lass to a lithe redhead with a delightful Irish lilt in her voice to a fair-haired girl with a brisk New England accent. Several of them greeted Yorke warmly, remembering him from his previous visits to the island.

He had clapped Allard on the shoulder and said to them, "Take good care o' my young friend here," and just like that, Allard had found himself surrounded by eager young lovelies garbed in scandalously skimpy clothing. Since he was slightly wounded, he was too weak to protest as they took him to a luxuriously appointed upstairs room, drew a hot bath for him, shaved him, washed him, and dressed him in a fine lightweight cotton suit. They would have done more than that, surely, but although he enjoyed their company and the care they were giving him, he was unstirred by their beauty.

There was only one woman for him. Even though she was far away, he would never escape the hold that Diana Pinckston had on him. He was glad that he had asked her to marry him as soon as the *Ghost* returned from this voyage. Knowing that Diana was waiting for him and that they would spend the rest of their lives together made it easy for him to resist the charms of Doña Graciela's girls.

After leaving Graciela's, the two men walked along palm-lined streets then turned to climb a flight of stairs apparently carved from the stone of a shallow cliff. "Queen Anne's Staircase," Yorke explained. Like Allard, he had been bathed and dressed in fresh clothes, his long gray hair was clean, and his salt-and-pepper beard was neatly trimmed. "Been here ever since the Spaniards built that fort up yonder. Why anybody would want to build a fort that looks like a warship on a mountain, I couldn't tell you, but that's the crazy Spaniards for you."

This hill hardly qualified as a mountain, Allard thought, but the fort did look a bit like a frigate. When he and Yorke reached the top of the stairs, they followed a tree-lined path that led to Government House.

A bald-headed man with prominent white side whiskers came to the door of the pink mansion. He wore the livery of a British butler and greeted them with a solemn, "Come in, gentlemen. Governor Haworth is expecting you."

Allard and Yorke had both been given broad-brimmed planter's hats at Doña Graciela's. The butler took the headgear and then led them through the foyer and down a hall with a gleaming hardwood floor. Government House had a lot of windows, and it was filled with the light of the setting sun and a fresh island breeze. They entered a large room with french doors that led to a terrace overlooking the harbor. Fans turned lazily on the ceiling, keeping the flower-scented air in motion. It seemed to Allard that he could hear music nearly everywhere he went in Nassau, and this place was no different. The strains of a merry song drifted up from somewhere in the settlement below.

The man waiting for them wore a light-colored suit like a native, but his ruddy face and erect carriage identified him as an Englishman. He had a waxed mustache and a thick brush of iron-gray hair. The man turned away from the windows as the butler announced, "Your guests are here, Governor."

The aristocratic-looking man smiled and came toward them with an outstretched hand. "Governor William Haworth, gentlemen," he introduced himself. "I'm afraid I've been in the islands long enough that we don't often stand on ceremony around here."

"Fine with me, Governor," Yorke said as he shook hands with the official. "I'm Cap'n Barnaby Yorke, and where I come from, we don't cotton much to formality, either." He jerked a thumb toward Allard. "This is Mr. Allard Tyler."

Allard shook hands with Haworth. After which, the governor asked, "Would you care for a drink? I have some rather good sherry."

Yorke licked his lips. "Sounds mighty fine to me, sir."

Haworth poured the drinks himself and handed them around. Nearby, a couple of island women were setting a table covered with a delicate white tablecloth.

"Dinner will be ready soon," Haworth announced. "In the meantime, I hear that you had quite an adventure at sea. Would you care to tell me all about it?"

Allard left the yarn-spinning to Yorke. The captain was better at it. His attention wandered a little as Yorke and Haworth talked, and he glanced out the windows again toward the terrace. To his surprise he saw a woman.

With her back to Allard, she stood at the railing of the terrace, her hands resting lightly on it as she looked out at the sea. The sun had dropped behind the horizon a few minutes earlier, but the western sky was still brilliant with a reddish orange glow that painted the high, fragile clouds with its soft luminance. The light gave the woman's blond hair reddish highlights. She was not overly tall, but she was well shaped in the low-cut, full-skirted gown she wore. The gown left her shoulders bare, and Allard thought her skin was beautiful in the richly fading sunset glow.

"I say, Mr. Tyler," Governor Haworth said, breaking into Allard's study of the woman. "Would you mind stepping out onto the terrace and telling my daughter that dinner is ready? She'll be joining us this evening."

Allard managed to turn around and nod. "Yes, of course, sir," he replied. His voice sounded odd in his ears, like it was too loud for these surroundings. Any words spoken here should be hushed, as if they were in a cathedral.

What was wrong with him? Why were those thoughts in his head? The light, the faint music, the island breeze caressing his face as he stepped onto the terrace. It was all perfect somehow, a moment of beauty frozen in time, the sort of moment that came along too seldom in a man's life.

"Miss Haworth?" he said, hating to intrude on her thoughts and disturb the perfection of the moment.

Yet as she turned, the moment grew even more perfect as he saw how lovely she was.

She smiled at him. "You must be Mr. Tyler." She held out her hand. "I'm Winifred Haworth. So pleased to meet you."

He took her smooth cool hand, and her smile grew sweeter and her blue eyes sparkled as he struggled to find his voice and introduce himself. She laughed softly and put him at ease. He held her hand, for some reason not wanting to let it go. She didn't try to pull away. Instead she moved closer, reached out her other hand, and rested it lightly on his sleeve.

The soft music seemed to grow louder, and the orange glow paled in the sky. As he stood looking into the eyes of Winifred Haworth, Allard Tyler told himself to think of Charleston, of Diana, of the beautiful woman who would soon be his wife.

PART ONE

"There prevails here [Charleston]
a finer manner of life."
—*Johann David Schoepf*

CHAPTER ONE

Wedding Plans

S O MUCH TO DO, Diana Pinckston thought as she stood in front of the full-length mirror with a claw-footed stand in her bedroom in the Tyler mansion. So much to do to get ready for the wedding . . . and so little time.

Of course, she reminded herself, she didn't really know how long she had to get ready. Allard was with Captain Yorke on the *Ghost,* and there wouldn't be any wedding until he returned. Still, Diana wanted to have everything ready as much as possible so there wouldn't be any needless delay once he was back. No time for Allard to get cold feet, that was what Allard's sister, Lucinda, would say.

Lucinda had a pretty low opinion not only of him but of all men. Diana supposed she couldn't blame her future sister-in-law for feeling that way. She might be rather bitter and cynical too if she had gone through the same ordeal Lucinda had.

But, in a way, it was Lucinda's own fault. She was the one who had carried on shamelessly with Cam Gilmore and then found herself in the family way. She had to have Aunt Susie, an old slave woman, take care of the problem. If Lucinda had shown some restraint, such a thing never would have happened.

Diana turned first one way and then the other, studying her reflection in the mirror. She wore a light green gown that went well with her long red hair. She was trying to decide whether to add the garment to her trousseau.

Seemingly of their own accord, her eyes went to the beautiful mahogany wardrobe on the other side of the room. Her wedding dress was in there, specially made by the finest seamstress in Charleston, which meant that she was also the finest seamstress in the Confederacy. Diana liked to take the gown out of the wardrobe and just gaze at it, picturing herself in it, standing next to Allard at the altar in the church as they were joined together for all time in holy matrimony.

Diana's mother had paid for the wedding dress, saying that her daughter had to have only the best for her special day. Diana supposed that her mother was trying to mend the fences that had been broken between them when her mother left her husband and Diana's father, Maj. Stafford Pinckston.

The major was somewhere in Virginia now, serving with the artillery as the gallant Confederate army tried to repel the invading barbaric horde from the North. It was highly likely that he would be unable to return to Charleston for his daughter's wedding, and that sent a pang of regret through Diana. He would understand, she told herself. Even though her father couldn't be there, she had to marry Allard—*while you've got the chance.*

She wasn't sure if the mocking voice she heard in the back of her mind was her own or Lucinda's.

"What do you think, Miss Diana?"

Diana caught her breath sharply. She had been so wrapped up in her thoughts that she had almost forgotten she wasn't alone. Ellie, one of the housemaids, had been helping her.

"I don't know," Diana said. "Help me take it off."

Ellie unfastened the tiny pearl buttons that ran down the back of the dress, and Diana shrugged out of the garment, leaving her clad in petticoats and corset, her breasts bare. Allard had seen her breasts once, she reminded herself, in one shameful yet exhilarating moment when they had let their passion for each other get the best of them. Diana felt her face burning as she remembered, and she looked forward to what they would do once they were married.

A knock sounded on the door while Ellie was hanging up the

gown. "Diana?" a woman's voice called through the panel. "We have to talk about the flowers for the wedding, dear."

Diana recognized the voice of her future mother-in-law, Katherine Tyler. In recent months, Katherine had been as much a mother to Diana as her own mother, Tamara Pinckston, had been. More so, in fact, since Diana had been living here and Tamara was on the other side of Charleston, staying with her own parents, where she had run after deserting her husband.

"I'll be right down, Mrs. Tyler," Diana said through the door. She turned and saw that Ellie was bringing her a camisole and one of her everyday dresses, a nice one made of cotton and dyed a dark gray. Ellie was a fine maid with a gift for anticipating the wishes of those she served.

"You can make up your mind about that other dress later, Miss Diana," she said as she helped Diana into the gray gown. "Ain't no hurry on that. Lawd, I don't know why Miss Katherine's goin' on already 'bout the flowers."

Diana turned quickly toward her. "Why do you say that?" she demanded. "Have you heard something about Master Allard? About the *Ghost*?"

Ellie stepped back, a startled expression on her young, pretty face. "I ain't heard a thing, miss, about Marse Allard or that boat. Why'd you think I had?"

"You just sounded like you knew something, like maybe Mr. Tyler had gotten a message from them, and you overheard him talking about it."

Ellie shook her head vehemently. "No, ma'am, nothin' like that."

"Then why did you say there was plenty of time?"

"I just figured . . . well, I didn't think Marse Allard and Cap'n Yorke would be back for a while yet. They gots lots to do, sinkin' them Yankee ships and all."

"Oh." Diana relaxed a little. "I thought you might have heard something in particular about them."

"I wish I had, Miss Diana, so's I could ease your mind. I surely do."

Diana wished that something would ease her mind, but she knew that only one thing could accomplish that: the safe return from the sea of the man she loved.

When she was dressed, she went downstairs and found Katherine in the parlor, talking to Lucinda. Allard's sister was quite beautiful, one of the loveliest young women in Charleston, with masses of blonde curls and smooth, fair skin. But she was downright pale these days, Diana thought, and had never really regained her color after Aunt Susie's ministrations. It took skillful applications of cosmetics to conceal the dark circles that sometimes appeared under Lucinda's eyes. Luckily for her, she had such skill.

"There you are, dear," Katherine said. Short and tending toward stoutness in middle age, Katherine retained some of the beauty of her youth. Her hair was as thick and curly as her daughter's, but it was beginning to be touched with gray. She fluttered around the house like a bird and tended to laugh too much, sometimes at inappropriate moments, but she had a good heart, and Diana loved her.

Still, Katherine could be exasperating on occasion. Such as now, when she said, "We have to start making arrangements for the floral displays. These things can't be left until the last minute."

"I realize that, Mrs. Tyler," Diana said, "but we can't really decide on anything when we don't know exactly when the wedding will be, can we?"

"That was your mistake, right there," Katherine said tartly. "You and Allard should have allowed enough time for him to get back and gone ahead and set a date. I'll swan, I don't understand the helter-skelter way you young folks do things these days. Weddings don't plan themselves, you know."

"There's a war going on, Mother," Lucinda volunteered from the armchair where she sat and did her needlework. "That makes it difficult to be sure of anything. It could be winter before Allard gets back."

"Oh, I hope not," Katherine said. "There won't be any good flowers blooming in the winter."

Flowers were the last thing on Diana's mind at the moment. She hoped it wouldn't be winter before Allard got back, because she couldn't stand the thought of not seeing him again for another three or four months. He had already been gone for more than a month, and she missed him fiercely.

"I'll tell you what," she said as she sat on the divan next to Katherine. "We'll go to the flower market tomorrow and talk to the people there about what they expect to have available over the next few weeks."

"That would be nice, dear. Thank you. And when that wandering son of mine comes home this time, don't you dare let him get away!"

"I won't," Diana promised. She glanced toward Lucinda and saw the veiled smile on the older girl's lips and the glitter in her eyes. Lucinda was mocking her, mocking the love she felt for Allard and the faith she had in him. For a moment, Diana wanted to go over there and slap her. But she couldn't do that, of course. All she could do was smile and hope that Lucinda could see the confidence she had in Allard.

And hope that that confidence was not misplaced.

SUCH FOOLS, Lucinda thought as she looked at her mother and Diana prattling on about the wedding. A wedding that would probably never take place, because even if her little brother didn't get himself killed on the ocean fighting the Yankees, he would probably find himself some lusty, dusky island girl and forget all about pale, puling Diana Pinckston.

Lucinda's fingers trembled a little as she worked with needle and thread on the cloth in her lap. She liked having something to keep her mind off . . . *things* . . . but it was getting more and more difficult all the time to manage the needlework. Her nerves were in too bad a shape, and she couldn't always make her fingers do what she wanted them to.

As if to prove that point, she suddenly stabbed the needle into the tip of her middle finger on her left hand. She emitted a slight sound at the pain and shifted in the chair.

Katherine looked around in alarm, distracted from her endless, mindless wedding talk. "Oh, dear," she said. "Are you all right, Lucinda? Did you prick yourself?"

Lucinda held up her left hand and used her right to squeeze the stricken finger. A drop of bright red blood appeared on the fingertip, hanging there for a moment before Lucinda raised the finger to her mouth and sucked the blood away.

"Yes, Mother," she said. "I did."

"You should put something on it—"

"I'll be fine." Lucinda set the needlework aside on the small table next to her chair. "I don't want to get any blood on this fabric, though."

Katherine laughed for no apparent reason. "You should go upstairs and put a dressing on it."

"Yes, I can do that." Lucinda rose to her feet. "You two go ahead with what you're doing. Don't mind me."

"Get one of the maids to help you if you need to," Katherine called after her daughter as she left the room.

That's exactly what she would do, Lucinda thought as she climbed the stairs. She would get one of the maids to help her. And she knew just the one she needed. She turned her head and called, "Ellie!"

The slave came out of the hall that led to the kitchen and followed Lucinda up the stairs.

"You wanted me for somethin', Miss Lucinda?" she asked as she caught up.

Lucinda paused when she reached the top of the stairs. Turning, she said quietly, "You know what I want."

"No, missy, I—"

"Don't play stupid with me," Lucinda grated. "You can act like a dumb little darky all you want to, but I know it isn't true. Now you go and get me what I need."

Ellie took a deep breath, her nostrils flaring. "It ain't that easy."

"Of course it is. The stuff isn't hard to get."

"Your daddy don't like havin' it in the house. He catches me bringin' it in, he's liable to whip me."

"My father never whipped a slave in his life, and you know it. Besides, he's not even here. He's down at the shipyard." Lucinda's tone took on added urgency. "Now go and fetch it!"

Ellie sighed. "All right. But if I get in trouble, I's tellin'—"

Lucinda's right hand came up quickly and caught hold of Ellie's chin. The fingers dug in and twisted. Ellie came up on her toes and her head went back, her eyes widening in pain.

Lucinda put her face inches away from the housemaid's and hissed, "I said my father doesn't whip slaves! I don't mind doing it, though. Not a bit. I'll take a cat-o'-nine-tails and strip that black hide of yours right off, you little bitch." She gave Ellie's chin a shove that made her stagger back a step. "Do you understand me?"

Ellie didn't answer for a couple of seconds. She worked her jaw back and forth and finally said, "Yes'm, Miss Lucinda, I understand. I'll go get what you need."

"I'll be in my room," Lucinda said. And she turned and walked down the hall without looking back at the maid, confident that Ellie would do as she was told.

ELLIE MOVED easily through the streets of Charleston, keeping her eyes downcast respectfully whenever she passed a white person. She was headed toward the docks on the eastern side of the city, not far above White Point. Before she reached the docks themselves, though, she ducked down a side street and entered a squalid building with the word "Apothecary" written in crudely formed letters on the dirty glass of its front window. As a slave, of course, Ellie wasn't supposed to be able to know what the letters spelled, but in fact she could read quite well and thought that she could have done a better job of painting that sign.

The window was so grimy it didn't let much light into the shop. No one was there, but a bell hung over the door jangled when Ellie went in, so she wasn't surprised when a man came through some ratty curtains that masked a door behind a counter leading to the rear of the building. He was white and in his fifties. His mostly bald head stuck forward grotesquely from his shoulders. Wings of white hair swept backward behind his ears. "What is it?" he asked in a sullen voice. "What is it you want, girl?"

Ellie licked her lips and swallowed. "My master done sent me to get his potion for him," she answered.

"What potion is that?" the apothecary snapped. "Who's your master?"

"Marse Jabez Wardell." Ellie drew out her natural drawl until it was a servile exaggeration. "I gets a potion here fo' him ev'ry couple o' weeks. You 'member, Marse Clark."

There was no Jabez Wardell. Ellie had made up the name the first time she had come down here, because Lucinda didn't want anyone to know for whom Ellie was running this sordid errand. Ellie knew that Miss Lucinda talked big, but she also knew that her mistress was scared of her father and didn't want him to know what was going on with his daughter. There was a lot that had happened under his roof that Marse Malachi had no idea about, Ellie thought wryly.

The apothecary pushed up his spectacles from the end of his long, skinny nose. "Yes, yes, o' course, you're Mr. Wardell's girl." He turned to the dusty bottles on the shelves behind him. "Let me see, let me see."

Ellie had no idea if the man knew that Jabez Wardell was fictional. She didn't care. The apothecary probably didn't, either, as long as he was paid. Ellie slipped a hand into the pocket of her dress and closed it around the coin Lucinda had given her. She had a stack of such coins hidden in her quarters, but they were only to be used when Lucinda sent her out like this.

The man took down one of the bottles and turned back to the counter. "Here you go, girl. This here is Mr. Wardell's potion. You got the money for it?"

Ellie took out the coin and slid it across the counter.

The apothecary clapped his hand down on hers, trapping it. He pressed down hard enough that the edges of the coin bit into Ellie's palm. "You're a toothsome little wench," he said. "Why don't you come in the back with me?"

"I . . . I can't. I don't get back in a hurry with this here potion, Marse Wardell, he's gonna whip me."

"You sure, gal? I got other potions here, things that'll make you feel mighty good."

Ellie jerked her hand free and grabbed the bottle from the counter. "I gots to go!" she said desperately as she turned toward the door. The apothecary just chuckled as she hurried out of the dim, dusty shop.

She was still trembling a little from the encounter by the time she returned to the Tyler mansion. She hoped Miss Katherine hadn't missed her. Sooner or later, sneaking around like this for Miss Lucinda was going to get her in bad trouble. Ellie was sure of it.

Today, though, she was able to slip into the house through the back door, apparently with no one the wiser. She went up the rear stairs and along the corridor to Lucinda's room. A soft rap on the door was answered with a curt, "Come in."

She was lying down when Ellie entered the room. Sitting up, she held out a shaking hand. "Give it to me," she demanded.

Ellie took the small brown bottle from the pocket of her dress.

"Take the cork out," Lucinda added. "I'm too shaky to manage it."

Ellie began working the cork from the neck of the bottle. As it came free, the bottle slipped a little in her fingers, and she almost dropped it.

"No!" Lucinda gasped.

"I got it," Ellie said as her grip tightened on the bottle. "I got it, missy."

"Give it to me!"

Ellie handed over the bottle. Lucinda took it, lifted it to her lips, and swallowed some of the liquid. As she lowered the bottle, she closed her eyes and a long sigh swelled from within her. Slowly, her hands stopped shaking. With a languorous smile spreading across her face, she raised the bottle and took another nip of the opium.

Quickly, Ellie stepped forward and took the bottle from Lucinda, knowing from experience that within moments her mistress would lean back, stretch like a cat, then fall asleep as the potent drug coursed through her body. There was nothing illegal about the stuff, of course, but Marse Malachi didn't like it and didn't want it in his house. Especially not like this, when it wasn't even disguised as a tonic for dyspepsia or female complaint or anything like that. This was the raw drug, the same thing that the waterfront whores used. Which was appropriate, given Lucinda's morals—or lack thereof.

Ellie pushed the cork back into the bottle and reflected on how foolish white folks were sometimes. Lucinda hadn't known what Ellie brought her; this bottle could have just as easily contained poison. But Miss Lucinda had snatched it and guzzled it down without ever hesitating. She was lucky that Ellie was a good girl and wouldn't ever hurt anybody, not even a high-toned alley cat like the blonde woman who now snored softly in the big, luxurious four-poster bed.

Ellie put the bottle in the bottom drawer of the nightstand next to the bed, under some of the needlework that Lucinda fiddled with incessantly. That was their agreed-upon hiding place. Ellie just hoped that she would make this bottle last longer than she had the last one. That apothecary, old Marse Clark, leered at her every time she came in, but today was the first day he had been bold enough to touch her. There was no telling what he might do next time. No telling. But whatever it was, Ellie was sure she wouldn't like it.

Quietly, she slipped out of the room and closed the door behind her, leaving Lucinda to sleep off her drugged stupor. You wouldn't think that somebody like her—young, white, beautiful, rich—would have such bad problems that she would need to deaden herself to the rest of the world. Obviously, though, that was the case. Ellie knew the reason why, but she still didn't understand it.

Most times, she thought she never would understand white folks.

WHEN MALACHI TYLER strode into his home that evening, he was met by Thomas, the elderly butler, who took his hat, coat, and walking stick. Katherine was waiting in the foyer as well. She came up on her toes as Malachi bent to give her a quick kiss. He tried not to frown as he both smelled and tasted brandy. Katherine liked to take a little nip now and then, and Malachi tried not to interfere as long as she maintained the household properly. But he was a man who despised weakness, not only in himself, but also in others, and sometimes it was difficult not to say anything to his wife.

There was something to be said for keeping the peace, though, so he forced a smile onto his face and asked her how her day had been.

"Why, it was just fine, Malachi," Katherine began. "Diana and I spent most of it working on the preparations for the wedding between her and that wayward son of ours." She laughed as she linked her arm with his, and they walked down the hall toward the dining room. Malachi could already smell the food.

He was a compact, sharp-eyed man, mostly bald with a fringe of graying rusty hair remaining on his head. Born into a family of sailors, the sea had always seemed strangely foreign to him. He had never had any desire to go out on the waves himself. But somehow, despite that, designing and building ships had always come naturally to him. And with the money he had inherited from his father, he had turned the Tyler shipyard into one of the leading enterprises of its kind in Charleston—indeed, in South Carolina and the entire South itself. Now it was engaged in turning out vessels for the Confederate navy. That cause might not make the shipyard as much money, but Malachi still supported it wholeheartedly.

"I received a letter from James Bulloch today," he commented as they entered the dining room. "You remember him."

She shook her head. "I'm afraid I don't."

"He's a naval expert and former captain of several ships. Bulloch's in England now, trying to acquire vessels—or have them built—for the Confederacy." Malachi took his place at the head of the table and continued. "He's having a ship built at the Birkenhead Ironworks, the yard that's owned by the Lairds. From the way Bulloch described this vessel in such glowing terms, I suspect that he's trying to goad me into building something to match it. He doesn't know about the *Ghost*." Malachi leaned back in his chair and grinned. "But I intend to tell him when I reply to his letter."

"Why, Malachi Tyler," Katherine said with a laugh. "You sound almost proud of yourself."

"Not of myself. Of that schooner. It's a fine ship." His face darkened slightly. "Yorke had better bring it back safe and sound."

"Along with our son?"

"Well, yes, of course. That goes without saying."

It still galled Malachi that Allard had defied him and gone off adventuring with that old reprobate, Barnaby Yorke. No doubt Yorke was filling Allard's head with lurid, gruesome tales about that other old pirate—Black Nick Tyler—Malachi's father and Allard's grandfather. Malachi had done his best to keep the unsavory truth about Nicholas Tyler from Allard, but in the end he had failed. And Allard, with his impulsive nature and hunger for glory and excitement, had jumped at the chance to sail with his grandfather's old first mate and partner in piracy, Yorke.

The boy was a damned fool. He could have stayed at the Citadel, the prestigious military academy in Charleston where he had been a cadet and had been well on his way to becoming an officer, if that was what he wanted. Or he could have come into the family business and worked with him at the shipyard. Allard was smart as a whip—when he wanted to be. Unfortunately he had succumbed to the lure of adventure, and now he was somewhere on the Atlantic, sailing with Yorke and searching for Yankee ships to either seize or sink.

Sometimes, Malachi thought, he wished he had kicked that boy's hind end until some sense finally made it from there to his brain.

He didn't want Katherine to start mooning about Allard's being gone and ruin their dinner, so he said, "Where are Lucinda and Diana?" His daughter and future daughter-in-law usually ate with them, and the two beautiful young women certainly brightened up the table.

"Ellie said Lucinda's not feeling well."

Malachi frowned. "Did you go up to check on her?"

"Ellie said she was sleeping."

Katherine relied altogether too much on the slaves, he thought. She should have looked into this matter herself. All too often Lucinda remained in her room, claiming to feel unwell, and it had been like that for months. Malachi thought they ought to have the doctor in to take a look at her, but Katherine insisted it was nothing to worry about.

"What about Diana?"

"She took the carriage and went to have dinner with her mother and grandparents. Tamara sent a note inviting Diana to join them."

Malachi nodded. "I see. So it's just the two of us tonight."

"That's right." Katherine's smile was rather rueful. "It seems odd, doesn't it?"

"Not to me. Reminds me of when we were first married." Malachi lifted his wine glass. "We had a lot of good times back then . . . Katie."

"Oh, my goodness, Malachi!" She laughed. "You haven't called me Katie for the longest time."

"Perhaps I should have. After dinner, would you care to go for a stroll in the gardens?"

"Why, I'd love that. But what's gotten into you tonight?"

He just smiled and shook his head. He didn't know the answer to that question. Lately he'd had the feeling that things were slipping away from him, despite the fact that there was a war on and he was extremely busy at the shipyard. But his daughter was withdrawn and his son was at sea. And even when Allard came back, the boy would be marrying and beginning to make a life of his own. All of that combined to make Malachi feel old, he supposed. He wanted something of his youth back.

And if a moonlit walk with his wife through the gardens, under the magnolia trees, would help, then he supposed that was what he would do.

"To us," Katherine said impulsively as she lifted her wine glass at the other end of the table.

Malachi smiled, nodded, and raised his glass. "To us," he repeated.

CHAPTER TWO

Dinner at the Oaks

IANA SWAYED BACK AND forth slightly as the carriage rocked along the cobblestone streets. She was lost in thought, wondering what this evening would bring. Any time her mother was involved, one could never predict what would happen. Tamara Edith Rutherford Pinckston was nothing if not volatile. She had proven that by the ease with which she had deserted her husband of almost twenty years and returned home to live with her parents.

Diana also had to wonder what her grandparents thought about that. A wife's abandoning her husband carried a certain stigma. Tamara's actions had no doubt caused a considerable amount of gossip among Charleston's elite, and Francis and Evelyn Rutherford must have heard some of the whispering, even though their friends would try to keep most of it behind their backs. Diana's grandparents had opposed the marriage in the first place, believing that Stafford Pinckston was not good enough for their daughter even though he came from a fine old family. The Pinckston family had fallen on hard times financially, though, and not much of their fortune was left. Pinckston actually had to rely on his *wages*, of all things, and while a position as professor of artillery and mathematics at the Citadel carried with it some respectability, it was never going to make a man rich.

Tamara had been young and in love, though, which meant she could be as stubborn as any farm mule. She had married Stafford, expecting that their love for each other would smooth over any obstacles. And of course, much to her disillusionment, that had proven not to be the case. From the start, there had been a great deal of tension in the marriage, and not even the arrival of Diana a couple of years later had done much to ease it. There had been no more babies, due to Tamara's delicate physical condition, and where more children might have kept her busy, the lack of them gave her time to think about all the areas in which her life had fallen short of her expectations.

Diana leaned back against the cushioned seat and thought about how she had been drawn to Allard Tyler ever since they were children. After being friends for as far back as she could remember, their friendship had finally blossomed into love and impending marriage. Actually, she thought, they had probably been in love long before either of them even knew it. All that had been required was enough time for that realization to sink in. And the fact that a war had come along and made them both think seriously about the future had probably had something to do with it too.

Charleston was gripped by a festive air this evening, as it had been pretty much since the Ordinance of Secession had passed the previous December, separating the state of South Carolina from the Union. The sense of something truly momentous happening had deepened with the firing on the *Star of the West,* the Union vessel that had tried to bring reinforcements and supplies to the Federal garrison on Fort Sumter in Charleston Harbor. The Yankee ship had been turned back by cannon fire from batteries manned largely by Citadel cadets, among them Allard and his best friend Robert Gilmore.

Then, in the spring, had come the actual bombardment of the massive masonry fort itself, followed by the Yankees' surrender. War fever had gripped Charleston, and so far that grip had not lessened. The Yankees had thrown a blockade around the harbor to keep supplies out of the city, but that had done little to dampen the enthusiasm of Charleston's inhabitants. In July they had heard the news of the great Confederate victory at Manassas, where the Union troops that had marched so arrogantly into Virginia were routed and forced to scamper back to their camps across the Potomac in Washington, D.C. That was only the first military triumph of many to come, everyone in Charleston was certain.

Over the past few months, troops had poured into the city and established camps where they were being trained to fight the Yankees. From the window of the carriage, Diana could see the stirring sweep of scores of campfires being kindled in the dusk. Soldiers clad mostly in gray and butternut, but with a scattering of other colors such as bright red and blue, strolled along the streets, their drilling done for the day. Some of them, seeing the fine carriage passing by with a beautiful young woman riding in it, snatched their caps off their heads and waved them in the air as they grinned and called greetings to her. Diana didn't respond directly, of course; it would have been improper to do so. But she did allow herself a slight smile as she gazed at all those fine young Southern men.

Finally, with a clip-clop of hooves from the team of sturdy horses pulling the carriage, the carriage reached the Rutherford mansion, known as the Oaks, and turned in through a gate in the hedge that surrounded it. The long drive circled in front of the big, stately house with its impressive columns. As the vehicle came to a stop and Diana climbed out, assisted by an elderly slave, she could hear in the distance the sound of music coming from the nearest of the army camps. The tune lent a merry air to the soft summer night.

Her grandparents were waiting for her at the entryway. Francis Rutherford was a tall, stiffly erect man with white hair and a beard. He spoke in deep, impressive tones. When Diana was a little girl, she had thought on more than one occasion that, when God spoke, He probably sounded something like her grandfather.

Diana's grandmother Evelyn was the source of Diana's red hair. Her curls were still red, although Diana suspected they had a bit of help in maintaining that shade.

Evelyn put her arms around her granddaughter and hugged her, saying, "My dear, you look lovelier than ever. Come in, come in. How are you?"

"I'm fine, Grandmother," Diana replied with a bright smile. "Where's Mother?"

"She should be down momentarily," her grandfather rumbled. "In fact, here she comes now."

Diana turned and saw her mother descending the long, curving staircase to the entrance hall. Tamara's hand trailed along the brilliantly polished banister. She wore a pale yellow gown with large hoop skirts.

There was no denying that Tamara Pinckston was a stunningly beautiful woman. She was tall and stately, with a magnificent figure that needed less assistance than most in achieving a waspish waist. Her darkly auburn hair was thick and lovely. Growing up, Diana had often felt like a faded flower next to her mother. She knew now that that wasn't the case and that she was attractive too, but still, she felt that no one could truly compare with Tamara when it came to looks.

"Hello, darling." Her smile was cool as she greeted her daughter. "I'm so glad you could join us this evening."

"I'm glad to be here," Diana answered her, feeling slightly awkward. "Thank you for inviting me." She suppressed a feeling of irritation that prickled at her. Her mother acted like the lady of this manor when in truth she was an interloper. She should have been across town in the old Pinckston mansion where she belonged. It might not be as impressive as the Oaks, but it was Tamara's home, the home she had made with her husband. It had been Diana's home, too, for her entire life . . . until, in a fit of pique, Tamara had left, prompting her husband to join the Confederate army and go off to fight the Yankees. Rather than live in the big empty house alone, Diana had moved in with the Tylers. She was grateful for their hospitality, but a part of her resented her mother for causing the situation in the first place.

Of course, it didn't really matter, she told herself as her mother reached the bottom of the stairs and Diana moved forward to embrace her. Soon enough, she and Allard would be married and starting a life of their own together.

Francis Rutherford ushered the three women in his life into the dining room, where the long table was covered with a cloth of snowy Irish linen and set with the finest crystal, china, and silver. Light from the cut-glass chandeliers played over the table and made the settings sparkle. Francis held the chairs for his wife, daughter, and grand-daughter in turn, and then the servants began bringing in the food.

Diana's grandfather inquired politely about the Tylers. "They're fine," she said. "Mrs. Tyler is all excited about the preparations for the wedding."

She thought she saw the line of her mother's mouth tighten a little, but she couldn't be sure about that.

"Any word from that young man of yours?" Francis asked. "Or is he still at sea, battling those Yankee bas—." He stopped short at a frown of disapproval from his wife and corrected himself. "Those Yankee scoundrels."

"He and Captain Yorke are still privateering, I suppose you'd say," Diana replied. "I hope they won't be gone much longer, but I really don't know how long they'll be at sea."

"I remember Captain Yorke," Evelyn said. "My word, but he cut quite a handsome, dashing figure in his younger days. All the ladies in Charleston were a-twitter over him . . . some of the married ones as well as the unmarried ones," she added with a smile and a tilt of her head. "I recall that there was some talk about him and Katie Tyler—"

"That's enough gossip, Evelyn," her husband cut in. "You don't want to impugn the integrity of our friends."

"Certainly not. And I didn't say that Katie and Captain Yorke were ever actually *involved*. I just meant that she was known to cast a few admiring glances in his direction." Evelyn sipped from her wine glass. "If the truth be known, I probably glanced in his direction a time or two myself."

"Mother!" Tamara remonstrated. "You simply delight in acting scandalous, don't you?"

"Someone has to, dear," Evelyn said with a deceptively sweet smile.

"Ladies, ladies," Francis said, unruffled by the exchange. By this time he was accustomed to playing peacemaker between his wife and daughter. To change the subject, he said to Diana, "Do you ever hear anything from that young man who was a friend of Allard's? What was his name? Gilmore?"

"Yes, Robert Gilmore," she said. "He's in the Hampton Legion, where Father was until the army reassigned the artillery."

This time Tamara's lips definitely thinned at the mention of her husband. Diana chose to ignore her.

"Robert has command of his own company now," she continued. "His commanding officer was killed at Manassas, and Robert was promoted in his place."

Francis shook his head. "It's terrible to hear about any of our young men losing their lives, even in a victory like Manassas. But I'm glad that young Gilmore survived and is doing well. What about your father?"

"Francis," Evelyn said warningly before Diana could reply, "we said we weren't going to discuss Stafford tonight."

"Damn it, he's an officer in the Confederate army, and therefore worthy of at least a little respect. Besides, he's Diana's father, and you can't expect her to forget about that."

"Yes, but—"

"It's all right," Tamara broke in. "Don't avoid mentioning Stafford on my account. I've made my peace with what happened."

Well, wasn't that wonderful, Diana thought. Her mother had made peace with what happened. It was too bad that *she* hadn't.

Even though she knew she ought to suppress the impulse, the angry words that sprang to her lips slipped out before she could stop them. "What happened, Mother, was that you left Father . . . and me . . . because he didn't make enough money to suit you."

"That's not true!" Tamara responded. "There's a lot more to it than that. Things you don't know about, Diana. And it's not your place to talk to me that way."

"I just don't think what you did to Father was right."

Evelyn said sternly, "Your mother did what she felt she had to do, Diana." She was defending Tamara now.

"Perhaps we shouldn't discuss the war at all," Francis suggested.

They hadn't been discussing the war, Diana thought. They had been discussing her father. But she didn't want to argue, either. She had spent entirely too much time already engaging in pointless, one-sided, mental arguments with her mother. She knew she would never win a real argument because Tamara was utterly incapable of entertaining the notion that she might be wrong about anything.

"That's fine," Tamara said in response to her father's suggestion. "We'll talk about the wedding instead."

Diana frowned a little. She wasn't sure she liked that idea any better.

"After we've eaten," Francis said firmly. "The cooks have gone to the trouble of preparing an excellent meal, and we should enjoy it."

For the next hour, talk was kept to a minimum and consisted mostly of inconsequential comments about Charleston society. Diana knew all the people her mother and grandparents mentioned, but she didn't care about any of them.

When the meal was over, Francis lolled back in his chair. Diana felt a momentary surge of pity for him. This was the time of the evening when he should have been able to retire to his study with some male companions for brandy and cigars and whatever else went on at such times. Bawdy jokes, she suspected. Instead he was stuck here with three females, all of whom he loved, but none of whom got along particularly well together. Poor Grandfather Rutherford, she thought.

Tamara wasted no time getting back to where the discussion had left off. "Now, about the wedding," she began.

"There's no point in worrying about it now, Mother," Diana said before she could go on. "The date hasn't been set, and it won't be until Allard returns from his voyage."

"It was very impractical of the two of you to make such an arrangement," Tamara chided, unknowingly echoing Katherine Tyler from earlier in the day. "Weddings require a great deal of planning and preparation. They simply can't be thrown together at the last minute."

"There shouldn't be any hurry," Diana pointed out. "Once Allard returns, he won't be leaving again. He's going to stay in Charleston and work with his father at the shipyard. So we can take as long as we need to get ready for the wedding."

Evelyn smiled. "Perhaps your mother is worried that you and Allard might be in a hurry for other reasons, dear."

"Mother!" Tamara snapped. "What are you implying?"

Diana felt her face growing warm. She said, "Grandmother, I can assure you there's no reason to worry about anything along those lines."

"Well, one never knows," Evelyn said with a casual wave of her hand.

Francis tossed back the wine in his glass and held it out for one of the black-liveried servants to refill.

"At any rate," Tamara said through teeth that clenched momentarily, "I think it would be best, Diana, if you were to move in here so that we can get ready for this wedding, whenever it takes place, in a proper fashion."

The suggestion took Diana so much by surprise that, for a moment, all she could do was stare across the table at her mother. Leave the Tyler household and move in here? Impossible!

When she was able to speak, she said, "I could never do that, Mother. For one thing, Mrs. Tyler is doing a fine job with the wedding preparations."

Evelyn leaned forward. "But it's not *her* job, dear. Traditionally, the bride's mother is in charge of the nuptials. Of course, in this case, the bride's grandmother should have a hand in it too."

Diana shook her head. She couldn't imagine her mother and grandmother being in charge of the wedding. They would be at each other's throats constantly. She said, "Mother, I appreciate your arranging for me to have that beautiful wedding gown. I really do. But that's enough for you to do—"

"Nonsense," Tamara said. "Don't you know, Diana, that the sheer fact you're living with the Tylers instead of here is already causing a scandal in Charleston?"

"Really?" Diana replied as coolly as she could. "I haven't heard anything about it."

"Well, of course not. No one is going to discuss it in front of you. But I assure you, they're talking about it behind your back."

"And why should I care about that?"

"Because you're deliberately humiliating me!" Tamara flared. "You never should have moved in with the Tylers. It was . . . it was indecent!"

"They offered me a home!"

"You had a home here!"

"No," Diana said in a voice that shook with anger despite being pitched quietly. "I had a home with you and Father. But you destroyed that by walking out on us."

Tamara flinched as if her daughter had slapped her. She sat back in her chair and looked across the table at Diana for a moment before saying, "I never walked out on you, Diana. I left your father. It's . . . different."

"Really? Because I felt as abandoned as he did. If I were a man, I probably would have gone off to war too. It might have made me feel better to shoot a few of those damned Yankees."

"Diana!" The exclamation came simultaneously from both her mother and her grandmother. They might not see eye to eye on many things, but at this moment they seemed united in their disapproval of Diana. Her grandfather, however, appeared to be hiding a grin.

In the tense silence that followed, Francis grew more serious until he said, "I must admit, Diana, it doesn't look too good for you to be living under the same roof as the boy you're planning to marry. Now, we all know that nothing improper is going on, but still, appearances *do* matter."

"Yes, but Allard's not even there," Diana pointed out. "The only other young person in the house is Allard's sister, Lucinda."

Tamara sniffed. "A bad influence if ever there was one. Why, if you even had a hint of some of the stories I've heard about *her* . . ."

Diana kept her face carefully expressionless. Her mother might have heard gossip about Lucinda Tyler, but Diana had witnessed with her own eyes the evidence of Lucinda's shameful behavior. She couldn't point that out, though, because it would only damage her own argument.

"And, eventually, Allard will be back," Evelyn pointed out. "Why not make things easier by staying with us before he returns?"

"And that way Katherine Tyler will have to keep her hands off my daughter's wedding," Tamara added.

That was it more than anything else, Diana thought. Her mother didn't really care that much about any gossip. She was just jealous because she wasn't in charge of the wedding plans. She wanted to be the center of attention, as always, and felt resentful because she wasn't.

And the next best thing to being a bride, of course, was being the mother of a bride.

Diana took her napkin out of her lap, wadded it, and threw it on the white linen tablecloth. "I won't do it," she said flatly. "I won't live here. I'm staying at the Tylers."

Tamara glared at her. "You'll do as I say. You're still a child."

Diana came to her feet. "You'll have to lock me in a room to keep me here."

"Then maybe that's just what we'll do," Tamara shot back as she stood up and leaned forward intently, resting her hands on the table.

"Stop it!" Francis said. The legs of his chair scraped on the fine hardwood floor as he thrust it back and stood. "I won't have my daughter and my granddaughter shouting at each other like a couple of field hands!"

"Francis!" Evelyn gasped.

He turned to one of the servants and snapped an order. "Have the carriage brought around for my granddaughter."

"Yes suh, Marse Francis," the man replied and then hurried to do his master's bidding.

"Papa, you can't let her leave," Tamara said, suddenly sounding like a child accustomed to getting her way . . . which, in reality, she pretty much was.

"Everyone's upset and nothing's going to be settled tonight," Francis said. "Diana, your mother and your grandmother make some excellent points. I want you to promise me that you'll give careful consideration to what they had to say."

Diana hesitated, not wanting to promise any such thing, but for her grandfather's sake she finally nodded. "All right," she said. "I'll think about it."

Francis smiled. "That's fair." He looked at his wife and daughter. "Isn't it, ladies?"

"I don't know why you're taking her side," Tamara said with a pout. "She's my daughter, and she ought to do what I tell her to do."

"Perhaps you'd better look at her again," Francis suggested gently. "Diana's not a little girl anymore, Tamara. She's a young woman with a mind of her own. And right now, that mind is made up."

It certainly is, Diana thought.

"If you want her to change it," her grandfather went on, "you have to give her some time to think about what you've said. She'll come around and see that you're right." He turned to Diana, reached out and rested a hand lightly on her arm. "Darling, just remember that you're welcome here any time and that we'd love to have you with us."

She moved closer to him and impulsively hugged him. "Thank you, Grandfather," she whispered.

"Now, we said practically the same thing," Evelyn protested, "and the girl almost bit our heads off! I just don't understand it." She leveled a disapproving gaze on Tamara. "Clearly, the job you did of raising your daughter was deficient, my dear."

"You're a fine one to talk," Tamara snapped back at her.

The servant returned to the dining room and announced, "The carriage is ready, Marse Francis."

He pressed his lips to Diana's forehead in a quick kiss. "Go while you still can, girl," he urged. "But remember what I told you."

"I will." She gave him a smile and was gone, pausing in the entrance hall only long enough to let one of the housemaids help her into the hat and light jacket she had worn earlier.

Fearing that her mother and her grandmother might pursue her and try to convince her to change her mind, she didn't really relax until she was in the carriage and the vehicle was rolling away from the Oaks. Then and only then did she sigh in relief.

But that sense of relief didn't last long before it was replaced with anger. How dare they do such a thing? The time to think about propriety had been before her mother left her father. Worrying about scandal and gossip now was just pointless.

Diana tried to calm herself by thinking about how she and Allard would soon be together again. And once they were, nothing would ever part them until the time came for one or the other of them to say farewell and go on to heaven. And even after that, they would still be together in their hearts until that glorious day when their spirits were reunited. She closed her eyes and felt her anger seeping away as the carriage rocked along.

When she opened them again, the carriage was going past one of the army camps. Now that night had fallen, the scores of fires seemed even brighter, spread out like stars on a carpet of sable. It was a stirring sight, and as she saw it, Diana thought that surely with such a glorious army being assembled, the war would soon be over. The Yankees were weak and pathetic and couldn't stand against the Confederacy. Why, the war might even be over by the time Allard returned to Charleston. His voyage might be the last one, not just for him, but also for all the gallant young men who had sailed on the *Ghost*.

That was such an encouraging thought that she wished she could see Allard right then, just so she could share it with him.

CHAPTER THREE

Winifred

ONE THING CHARLESTON HAD in abundance was beautiful young women. Given his family's prominent position in the city's society, Allard Tyler had been acquainted with many of them. But he wasn't sure he had ever known a young woman quite as *intriguing* as Winifred Haworth.

For one thing, there was the way she spoke. There was something about those soft, British-accented tones that he found positively appealing. Allard was accustomed to nearly everyone speaking with a Southern drawl, although in a port city such as Charleston, one heard accents of all kinds as ships from around the world docked there.

Winifred's laugh was like music too. And as Allard sat across from her at Governor Haworth's table, enjoying a fine meal that featured several kinds of fish and seafood, he couldn't help but laugh with her and return the smiles she gave him.

Yet guilt gnawed at his vitals like a hungry rat.

He shouldn't be smiling and laughing, and he knew it. He shouldn't be admiring Winifred Haworth's stunning blonde loveliness. After all, he reminded himself, he was engaged. Back in Charleston, another beautiful young woman waited for him. He worried that he was being disloyal to Diana by enjoying Winifred's company.

But was he really, he asked himself. Or was he merely being polite, being a good dinner companion? He couldn't very well just sit there scowling and ignoring their hostess, now could he? Governor Haworth had mentioned that his wife had died, so Winifred was the mistress of Government House. Both of them had been courteous enough to have him and Barnaby Yorke to dinner, so he couldn't be rude to them.

Forgive me, Diana, he thought. It's only a smile, a laugh. They mean nothing.

"So tell me, Captain," the governor said as a servant refilled his wine glass, "all about your privateering activities."

"Well, we've traded shot and shell with more than our share of Yankee ships," Yorke began. "Captured a few of them and sent three to the bottom, including a frigate."

"Your ship is a schooner, is that correct?"

Yorke nodded. "Aye, sir, and a sweeter ship you'll never find. The man who designed and built her, young Allard's father, Malachi, is a right smart man when it comes to such vessels. You might even call him a genius."

How surprised would his father be, Allard thought, to hear Barnaby Yorke describe him as a genius? Malachi Tyler seldom missed an opportunity to insult the captain, and yet here was Yorke praising the man who heartily disliked him. That generousness and even-handedness made Yorke rise even higher in Allard's estimation.

"I wouldn't have thought you'd have enough firepower to sink a frigate," Governor Haworth mused.

"Well . . . ," Yorke smiled. "Rammin' her and knockin' a big hole in her bow may have had something to do with it."

"I see. No wonder you need to do some repair work on your vessel while you're here. If there's any way I or anyone else in Nassau can assist you, Captain, please let me know."

"I'm obliged for your kindness, Governor."

Haworth took a sip of his wine. "You understand, of course, that as a representative of the British government, there are limits to what I can do officially. My government has yet to recognize yours. But I'm a man of considerable influence, and I'm willing to bring as much of it to bear for the cause of the Confederacy as I can."

"And that's greatly appreciated," Yorke responded with a nod.

Winifred steepled her hands in front of her and said to Allard, "So your father builds ships?"

"That's right, Miss Haworth," he said. "He owns the Tyler shipyard in Charleston."

"He must be very wealthy, then. And I suppose you are too."

Yorke leaned forward and said, "Don't praise him so much it goes to his head, miss. Right now he's just a lowly third mate, and that's all he is."

Winifred laughed. "I beg your pardon, Captain, but Mr. Tyler doesn't have the look of a subordinate officer. I suspect that one day he'll be the master and commander of his own ship."

"You could be right about that," Yorke allowed. "Command comes naturally to some lads. We'll have to wait and see about Allard here."

Allard felt a little uncomfortable to have them discussing him that way, almost as if he weren't sitting there. But before he could say anything, the butler came into the dining room, waddled over to Haworth, and bent to whisper something in the governor's ear. A look of irritation flashed over Haworth's ruddy face.

"He's here now?" he asked the butler.

"Yes sir. I asked him to wait in the library."

"Very well." Haworth took his napkin from his lap and set it on the table next to his empty plate. "I suppose I'll have to see him. Tell him I'll join him in a few minutes."

The butler bowed. "Yes sir."

To Allard and Yorke, Haworth said, "If you gentlemen will excuse me . . . government business, you know. Such things are never done."

"That's why captaining a sailing ship is more than enough for me," Yorke said with a chuckle. "A ship of state interests me not at all."

"I'll have brandy and cigars brought to you," Haworth promised as he got to his feet. "Winifred, why don't you and Mr. Tyler step onto the terrace and enjoy the evening air?"

"That sounds very nice," Winifred agreed with a smile, the full force of which was directed toward Allard.

He didn't see any way he could refuse the invitation without being impolite, so he stood and stepped quickly around the table to hold her chair for her. She stood, but instead of moving toward the french doors that led onto the terrace, she hesitated. Allard realized after a second that she was waiting for him to take her arm.

As he linked arms with her, he glanced over his shoulder and saw Yorke watching them. The captain had a gleam in his eye. He appeared to be enjoying Allard's attempts to be polite without being *too* friendly toward the governor's daughter.

Lord, he thought suddenly, what if Captain Yorke goes back to Charleston and tells Diana about how Winifred flirted so shamelessly with him? Surely he wouldn't do that. Maybe it would be better, Allard decided, if he told Diana about Winifred himself. That way it wouldn't look like he was trying to hide anything from her. Being open and honest, that was the way to go.

Winifred opened the doors, and they stepped onto the terrace. Night had fallen, so the spectacular colors that had been in the sky earlier as the sun set were gone now. But the air was still warm and fragrant, the lights of Nassau were spread out before them at the bottom of the hill, and the soft strains of music still drifted up the slope.

"It's a lovely evening, isn't it?" Winifred asked as they paused at the terrace railing.

"It certainly is." Allard was all too aware of her bare arm linked with his. He could feel the warmth of her flesh even through the sleeves of his coat and light jacket. The subtle scent of her perfume was as intoxicating as the wine he'd drunk at dinner. More intoxicating, really. To get his mind off that, he asked, "Can you always hear music from the town?"

"Nearly always. The islanders are full of the joy of life, and they express it through their songs as well as their laughter. Ever since my father and I have lived here, I've gone to sleep every night listening to that music."

"I imagine you sleep quite well."

"Very well. Nothing ever bothers me . . . except sometimes the mosquitoes."

It was probably a mistake, Allard decided, to start thinking about how well Winifred Haworth slept, because that made him think of what she might wear to bed, and that was a wholly inappropriate subject for consideration, of course.

After a moment of silence, during which he couldn't think of anything to say—pesky images of Winifred in lace and a diaphanous gown kept intruding into his mind—she said, "So tell me all about your life in Charleston, Mr. Tyler. Since your father owns a shipyard, I'm surprised that you're not working there."

At last, he thought with relief, something safe and not the least bit provocative to discuss. "My father would have liked nothing better," he began. "He's always had it in mind that I would eventually take over the yard, and I suppose that someday I probably will. But not just yet. I want to see a bit of the world first."

"Ah, you're gripped by wanderlust."

"I don't know that I'd go so far as to describe it that strongly . . . but why not." Allard had to chuckle. "Wanderlust it is. Besides, the sea is in my blood. My grandfather was a ship's captain. In fact, he fought as a privateer in the War of 1812—"

He stopped short, realizing that he probably shouldn't have said that. It was Winifred's countrymen, after all, whom Black Nick Tyler had battled during his war.

She must have read his mind, because she said with a smile, "Don't trouble yourself, Mr. Tyler. That was a long time ago. The fact that our grandfathers may have crossed swords has nothing to do with us."

"No, I suppose not," he said, relieved again. "Thank you for your understanding. I meant no offense."

"And none was taken. Go on, tell me more about yourself."

She was extremely easy to talk to. Without really thinking about what he was doing, he disengaged his arm from hers, leaned his other forearm on the terrace railing, and half turned so he was facing her. "For the past couple of years I was a cadet at the Citadel in Charleston. That's the state military academy of South Carolina."

"I've heard of the Citadel," she murmured. "It's said that fine officers and finer gentlemen are educated there."

"I hope that's true in my case. Unfortunately, the war came along, and I didn't feel like I could stay there to complete my studies. I had to do something to help the Confederacy right away. My best friend and fellow cadet, Robert Gilmore, felt the same way. We both resigned from the academy. Robert joined Hampton's Legion, commanded by Colonel Wade Hampton, and I made arrangements to sail on the *Ghost* as third mate."

"Why not first mate, since you're the son of the ship's owner?"

"Because the *Ghost* already had a good first mate and a second mate, too, for that matter," Allard said. "Captain Yorke isn't the sort of man who would sign someone on as first mate unless he was qualified for the job."

"Someday you'll be a captain yourself, just like my father said."

He shrugged. "That's doubtful. This is . . . my final voyage."

Winifred looked surprised, her pale eyebrows arching over her deep blue eyes. "Your final voyage?" she repeated. "Why? I was under the impression you liked sailing and being a privateer."

"Oh, I do," Allard admitted, "but there's something I love a great deal more. Someone, I should say. You see, I'm engaged to be married when I get back to Charleston."

"Really?" He couldn't tell if her tone had cooled a bit. "So you have a fiancée? Your childhood sweetheart, no doubt?"

"We've known each other since we were children," Allard said. "Her family and mine have been friends for years. But it's only in the past year that we've truly realized how we feel about each other."

Winifred smiled again. "What's her name?"

"Diana. Diana Pinckston."

"And is she beautiful? No, don't tell me. Of course she is. She would have to be."

"She's the most beautiful woman in the world . . . present company excepted, of course," he added hastily.

Winifred laughed. "Oh, it's all right, Allard. You don't have to except me from that comparison. I think it's sweet that you see Donna as the most beautiful woman in the world."

"Diana," he corrected her.

"Yes, of course. Diana." She clasped one of his hands in both of hers. "Well, tell me about her."

"She's a year younger than I am, and she has red hair and fair skin and lovely hazel eyes. I wish I had a picture in a locket or something like that to show you . . ."

"It's all right," Winifred assured him. "I can see her, just from your description of her. How does she feel about your going away on this voyage?"

"Well . . . it would have been all right with her if I had stayed in Charleston and married her, of course. But I had already given my word to Captain Yorke that I would sail with him. This is our second voyage together. I was on board the *Ghost* the first time she sailed out of Charleston. So Diana understood why I had to come, even though she might not have liked it all that much."

Winifred squeezed his hands. "If I was engaged to a fine young man such as you, Allard, I'm not sure I would ever let you out of my sight. Some other woman might try to steal you away."

He laughed. "There's no chance of that happening."

She looked at him intently for a moment, so intently that it suddenly made him a bit nervous. But then she added, "What are you going to do after you and Diana are married? You can't plan to return to the Citadel, surely."

"No, that part of my life is over," Allard said. "I'll work with my father at the shipyard."

"That will make him happy, I suspect."

"Oh, yes. It's what he's wanted all along."

"But what about what *you* want?"

He frowned. "I'm sorry. I don't understand."

"I mean no offense," she said, "but it seems to me that everyone is getting exactly what they want—except you. Your father gets you to work with him, and Diana gets you to be her husband."

"I *want* to be married to her. I want that more than anything else in the world."

"But it's not the *only* thing you want," Winifred insisted. "Forgive me for being bold, but I could tell by listening to your voice when you talked about seeing the world that your wanderlust isn't going to be satisfied with a couple of voyages. And admit it, Allard. There's a part of you that believes someday *you* could be the master of your own ship rather than being stuck in an office somewhere building ships for other men to sail."

She leaned toward him as she spoke, and his eyes couldn't help but be drawn to the creamy swell of her breasts in the low-cut gown and the tantalizing valley between them. He quickly forced his gaze away from those feminine charms.

"We, uh, all have to make compromises," he said clumsily. "Sometimes we have to give up some of the things we want for the greater good."

"Whose greater good?" Winifred asked. "Yours, or that of other people?"

He couldn't answer that, but he didn't have to, because at that moment, the french doors opened behind them and Captain Yorke strolled onto the terrace, a cigar clenched between his teeth and a snifter of brandy in his hand. He took a deep breath and said, "Ah, I've missed the smell of the tropics at night!"

Allard turned toward him, grateful for the interruption. Winifred smiled, but the expression seemed a bit forced.

"I hope I'm not intruding on you young people," Yorke went on.

"Not at all, Captain," Winifred told him. "I take it my father is still occupied with his business?"

Yorke took the cigar out of his mouth. "I suppose so. He hasn't returned."

"As he said, the duties of his office are never done." Winifred paused. "Allard was just telling me that this is going to be his last voyage with you."

"Aye, he'll be a landlubber from here on out." Yorke replaced the cigar in his mouth and used his free hand to slap Allard on the shoulder. "I hate to lose a good third mate, but I suppose we'll just have to make do."

"I'm sure you'd prefer that he continue to sail with you."

"I wouldn't presume to tell a young man what to do," Yorke said. "Especially not a young man in love."

"You've met the young woman?"

"Oh, aye. The lad's done right well by himself too. Diana is a fine lass."

"Of course she is," Winifred said. "Allard wouldn't be engaged to her if she wasn't."

Again, they were talking about him as if he wasn't there, he thought. Movement inside the dining room caught his eye, and Allard looked past Yorke to see that Governor Haworth had returned. The governor was not alone, however. He had a man with him who was dressed in an expensive, tight-fitting suit and tall black boots. The stranger was handsome, with olive skin and thick black hair. Allard thought him a Spaniard, though he might have come from South America or one of the Caribbean islands. Something about him made it difficult to pin down his exact heritage. Haworth led the man onto the terrace as the three people turned toward them.

"Captain Yorke, Mr. Tyler," he said, "allow me to present Señor Augustin Valencia."

"The pleasure is mine, señors," Valencia said in a softly accented voice. It didn't sound exactly Spanish or even Portuguese to Allard, but perhaps somewhere in between. Valencia bowed, a very Latin-looking move, and then extended his hand, much like an American. Allard had the feeling that he had been around so much, to so many different places, that he had picked up habits from several nationalities.

Given that, it came as no surprise when Haworth said, "Señor Valencia is intimately connected with the shipping industry. He has connections with several different lines and with various importing and exporting enterprises."

"Sounds like you're something of a trouble fixer," Yorke commented as he shook hands.

Valencia shrugged elegantly. "I prefer to think of myself as a smoother of the way, Captain. When the seas of commerce are raging, I make them tranquil again."

"Wish you could do that with real waves," Yorke said. "I'd sign you on to my crew in the blink of an eye if you could get rid of the storms."

Valencia smiled. "Unfortunately," he responded, "some things are beyond my power." He turned and shook hands with Allard. "Mr. Tyler. I know the name . . ."

"My father is Malachi Tyler," Allard supplied.

"Ah, yes! He has a reputation as perhaps the finest builder of ships in the American South."

"No maybe about it," Allard said. "And the Tyler shipyard is the best in America, period."

"Loyalty," Valencia said with a smile and a nod. "I like that in a man. No quality is more of a true indicator of character than loyalty."

With the introductions finished, Valencia turned to Winifred and took her hand. He bent to kiss the back of it, another move that made him seem Latin to Allard.

"Did you conclude your business with my father, Señor Valencia?" she asked.

"Most satisfactorily," he murmured. "But I will not bother you with the boring details, Señorita Haworth."

"Would you like some brandy?" the governor asked, still being a good host.

"Thank you, but no. I must be going." Valencia smiled at Allard and Yorke. "I just wanted to meet these illustrious visitors to the island. You will be in Nassau for a while, señors?"

"Long enough to get our ship patched up well enough to get us back to Charleston," Yorke answered.

"Perhaps our paths will cross again then." Valencia bowed once more. "Governor. Señors. And the lovely Señorita Haworth . . . I bid you good evening."

He turned and left the terrace, making his way through the dining room and out of the house without looking back.

"Señor Valencia is quite the gentleman," Haworth commented. "He was visiting me on behalf of some of the shipping companies he works with."

"No need to explain your business to us, Governor," Yorke said. "We don't aim to go pokin' our noses where they don't belong."

"I wasn't worried about that." Haworth turned to his daughter. "I hope you haven't talked young Mr. Tyler's ear off, darling. I know it's rare for you to meet someone close to your own age. At least someone who doesn't have black or brown skin, eh?"

Winifred showed no response to her father's gibe. Instead, she said, "I'm a bit tired. I believe I'll be retiring for the evening."

"It was a pleasure sharing your company, Miss Haworth," Allard said, and the statement was true in its way. Although being near Winifred had made him uncomfortably nervous at times, he *had* enjoyed talking to her. She was certainly beautiful and charming; there was no denying that. Simply recognizing that as a fact wasn't being disloyal to Diana in any way, he told himself.

Winifred put out her hand, shaking first with Yorke and then with Allard. He worried for a second that she might expect him to kiss it as Valencia had done, but she seemed perfectly content with a handshake from him.

He told himself that shouldn't disappoint him. But it did, a little.

Winifred said, "Good night, Father," and Haworth bent to kiss her on the forehead.

"Good night, dear. Sleep well."

She gave them smiles all around and left the terrace. When she was gone, Haworth asked, "Do you gentlemen have a place to spend the night?"

"Our cabins on board the *Ghost*'ll do fine for that," Yorke said.

"There are one or two hotels in town," Haworth said. "Not to mention places such as Doña Graciela's."

Yorke grinned. "I'm familiar with Graciela's place, Governor. To tell you the truth, that's where the lad and I went to get cleaned up earlier, before we came here."

Haworth threw back his head and laughed. "From a house of ill repute to the governor's mansion, eh? I must say, I'm sure it's not the first time such a journey has been made." He pumped Yorke's hand. "It was splendid meeting you, Captain. Remember what I said. Anything I can do to help you."

"I'll bear that in mind, sir," Yorke promised.

The governor turned to Allard. "And that offer extends to you as well, Mr. Tyler."

"Thank you, sir."

"I'm glad you came with Captain Yorke tonight. I know Winifred enjoyed getting to know you. Out here, so far from home, with so few proper young people around to befriend her, I'm sure she gets lonely. I hope you'll visit again while your ship is in port."

There was nothing Allard could do but smile, nod, and say, "It will be my pleasure, sir," even though he thought that it might not be such a good idea.

Not the way Winifred Haworth smiled and laughed. Not the way his eyes had been drawn to the smooth, enticing mounds of her bosom.

They finished saying their good-byes to Haworth and left the mansion. They were halfway down Queen Anne's Staircase before Allard realized that, while they were talking on the terrace, Winifred had stopped calling him Mr. Tyler and started calling him Allard, without his even noticing.

CHAPTER FOUR

Knives in the Night

QUITE THE beauty, ain't she?" Yorke asked as they reached the bottom of the hewn stairway and turned toward the docks on their way back to the *Ghost*.

"Who?"

Yorke laughed. "Don't act the innocent, lad. You know good an' well who I'm talkin' about." He jerked a thumb toward the top of the hill.

"Winifred is . . . attractive," Allard responded. He felt his face beginning to warm and wished that the captain hadn't brought up the subject. His thoughts were already confused enough.

"She's more than that, and you know it. I've sailed the seven seas for more than forty years and never saw a prettier gal . . . or one more obvious about what she wants."

"And what is that?" Allard asked.

"You, my boy."

Allard stopped short. "You must be mistaken," he said. "She was just being . . . a good hostess."

"Aye, it's a mighty fine hostess who makes sure that her guest gets such a good view of her bosoms. I was a guest, too, and you didn't catch her showin' 'em to me, now did you?"

Allard's face was flaming now. "She wasn't . . . she didn't . . . I mean, I'm sure it wasn't intentional—"

"Lord, you really are a babe in the woods, aren't you?" Yorke jerked his head toward the waterfront. "Come on, let's get back to the *Ghost.*"

After they had walked a few more steps, Allard said, "She *was* flirting with me, wasn't she?"

"She was indeed. And I don't suppose anyone could blame her. After all, you're a reasonably presentable young fella when you're cleaned up and shaved, and Graciela's gals did a good job on you this afternoon. Your ma raised you to be well mannered—no surprise there, knowin' Katie—and most importantly . . . you're rich."

Allard frowned. He never really thought about the fact that his family had money. He supposed that meant *he* had money too. But he certainly never dwelled on that.

"I don't understand why that would matter," he said. "Winifred and her father seem well-to-do."

"The man's in the foreign service. He doesn't make much from his position here, even though he wields some power as governor. No, the money that lines his pockets comes from the business advantages he gets as governor. I'd wager he knows every cargo that comes in and out of this port, and he's probably bein' paid off by half a dozen companies to make it easier for them to do business."

Allard's eyes widened. "Are you saying that Governor Haworth is dishonest?"

"I'm sayin' that a powerful man who does favors for his friends usually gets those favors repaid sooner or later. Whether or not such behavior is crooked, I couldn't say. But I do know it's the way the world works most o' the time." Yorke rubbed at his short salt-and-pepper beard. "That fella Valencia now, I'd say there's a good chance he walks on the shady side o' the street more often than not. And he's involved with Haworth, so that tells you something."

Allard shook his head. "It's just hard to believe, that's all. The governor seems so polite and cultured. He's *British,* for goodness sake!"

Yorke chuckled. "There are just as many black-hearted thieves in England as you'll find anywhere else, lad."

After a few more steps, Allard asked, "Do you think Winifred knows what her father is up to?"

"Again, there's no tellin'. She seems like a smart gal, though. And a determined one, judgin' from the way she was goin' after you."

"You're right," Allard admitted with a sigh. "That's why I told her that I'm engaged to Diana. I didn't want her getting any wrong ideas in her head."

"And she treated you different after you told her that, didn't she?"

"Well . . . maybe a little. She didn't really seem all that put off by it, though."

"Maybe she's one o' those gals who likes a challenge," Yorke mused. "Some women look at a man they're not supposed to have, and that makes 'em want him all the more."

This conversation was making Allard feel more and more uneasy. "Maybe we'd better get the *Ghost* patched up and get back to Charleston as quickly as we can."

Yorke clapped a hand on his shoulder. "I think that would be a fine idea, lad."

They had barely taken another step when a rush of footsteps sounded behind them.

Yorke wheeled around and Allard followed suit. He spotted several men rushing toward them out of the night. In the shadowy street, it was impossible to tell exactly how many there were. But there was no doubt in Allard's mind that he and Yorke were being attacked. Enough stray beams of moonlight penetrated the fronds of the palm trees that lined the street for him to see the flicker of knives as well as the bludgeons carried by some of the men. And as if to punctuate that conclusion, he heard a man growl, "It's them, all right! Get the bastards!"

Allard was unarmed. The revolver that his father had given him before he left Charleston was in his cabin on the schooner. He didn't know if Yorke had any weapons or not. Quickly, though, Yorke proved that he was indeed armed by yanking a short-barreled pepperbox pistol from under his coat and firing it practically in the face of one of the onrushing men. The man screamed as the bullets thudded into him and flung him backward.

Music was playing somewhere nearby. It seemed to get louder as the blast of the shot and the scream echoed through the night, as if the musicians were determined not to acknowledge the violence. Allard ducked instinctively as a club whipped toward his head. He lashed out with a leg, hoping to land the kick in the attacker's groin.

His boot thudded into the man's thigh instead, but the impact was enough to knock the club wielder off his feet. Another man swept in immediately, though, and he slashed at Allard with a long, heavy knife. Fear made Allard's heart pound wildly as he jerked aside, barely avoiding the blade. Pain throbbed in his leg and his side. He was too recently wounded to be in a desperate struggle like this. But the only alternative was to die, so he fought. These men didn't intend to merely rob him and Yorke or give them a beating. The attackers were out for blood.

Allard grabbed at the wrist of the man with the knife and got hold of it somehow in the darkness. He twisted as hard as he could, trying to make the man drop his weapon. The man grunted in pain but hung on. He swung his other fist at Allard and scraped his knuckles painfully along the side of the young man's head. Allard thrust a foot out, got it between the man's calves, and heaved. The wrestling move, practiced and perfected with Robert during their younger days, sent the attacker tumbling to the cobblestones.

One of the others rushing in tripped over the thrown man, taking the two of them out of the fight for a moment or so. Allard twisted around in time to see Yorke rip a cudgel out of an attacker's hand and turn it to his own benefit, flailing back and forth and opening up a space in the knot of men around him.

Allard leaped on the back of one man, taking him by surprise and getting an arm around the man's neck. He clamped down hard in an attempt to choke the man into senselessness. The man jerked his head back, though, smashing it into Allard's face. Allard felt blood spurt hotly from his nose as his grip loosened and he fell. He rolled on the pavement and came over onto his back in time to see one of the men swinging a kick at his head. He threw his hands up, grabbed the foot, and pulled. The man went over backward.

Allard scrambled up. The night was confusion and chaos around him. Drums pounded in the darkness, or maybe it was just his own pulse hammering in his head. Hands grabbed him from behind, pinning his arms. Another man rushed at him from the front, brandishing a knife. Allard swung his feet up, planted them in the chest of the oncoming man, and shoved. That not only deflected the man with the knife, but it also sent Allard and the man holding him flying backward. They slammed down on the cobblestones, the impact knocking them apart.

Allard was having trouble getting his breath now. Blood still ran from his nose. A shape loomed in front of him as he climbed unsteadily to his feet, and he threw a punch without thinking about it. Before the blow could land, a hamlike hand closed around his fist, stopping the punch in midair.

"Damn it, boy, it's me!"

It took a few seconds for the words to penetrate his battle-frenzied mind. Then he realized with a shock that the voice was that of Barnaby Yorke. "Cap'n?" he said numbly.

"Aye. The varmints are runnin' away like the rats they are."

Yorke released Allard's hand and pointed. He saw the shadowy shapes of several fleeing men as they scurried along the street toward the waterfront, passing through rectangles of lamplight that fell from the open windows and doors of the taverns they passed along the way. Three or four other men lay scattered in the street nearby, moaning from the punishment they had taken. Obviously, Allard and Yorke had put up more of a fight than the attackers had expected.

Yorke grasped Allard's arms. "Let's get back to the ship, lad," he said urgently. "The constabulary will show up sooner or later to see what all the commotion was, and if we're arrested, the governor might help us or he might not, dependin' on what he thinks will benefit him the most."

Allard didn't want a run-in with the local law, either. He didn't offer any protest or resistance as Yorke hustled him away from the scene of the attack. But the pain in his leg made him limp rather badly.

"Did one of those scoundrels cut you?" Yorke asked.

Allard shook his head. His nose throbbed too. "No, it just hurts because of that other wound. I shouldn't have been hopping around on it, I guess."

"If you hadn't hopped pretty lively, you'd have ended up with your head stove in or your throat cut from ear to ear."

"Then you agree they were trying to kill us, not just trying to rob us or anything like that."

"I've been set upon by thieves in all four corners of the globe, lad, and these weren't your common cutpurses. Oh, they would have taken our valuables, all right, but only after they'd made sure we were dead."

"But why?" Allard asked with a plaintive note in his voice. "Who would want to have us killed?"

"Well, the plain fact o' the matter is, I've made an enemy or two in my time. Could be that someone with a score to settle spotted us and hired some waterfront toughs to get rid of us. But the blame might also lie at the feet o' the Yankees."

That idea took Allard by surprise. "The Yankees?" he repeated.

"Aye. Make no mistake about it. They know that the British are sympathetic to the Confederacy, and they know that it's easy enough to reach Nassau from South Carolina. If supplies are to come in past the blockade, chances are that a lot of them will come through here first. Same with the cargoes headed for England and the rest o' Europe from the South. So there's a good chance the Yankees have agents here to disrupt that traffic as much as they can, and gettin' rid of the captain and one o' the mates from the ship that recently sunk a Union frigate would be a good start on that."

"You're talking about spies," Allard said.

"Aye, that I am."

Allard shook his head. As if worrying about Winifred Haworth and his unwanted reaction to her wasn't enough, now he was coming to realize that he might have landed in a nest of spies and all the dangers that went with that. Nassau was an undeniably beautiful place, but at the moment, Allard really missed being home. And Charleston had never seemed farther away.

THEY MADE it back to the ship without any more trouble, and when they got there, Yorke took Allard into his own cabin and had him wash the blood off his face. Allard winced as he dabbed at his nose with the wet cloth.

"Might be busted," Yorke commented. "Let me take a closer look."

The captain lifted a hand, and before Allard knew what was happening, Yorke took hold of his nose and wrenched hard on it. Allard howled as the pain exploded in his head, threatening to take off the top of it.

"If it was broken, which I doubt, it's straightened up now," Yorke said with a satisfied nod. "It'll swell up and bruise like a rainbow, but you ought to be able to breathe through it. Take a sniff and see."

The pain had subsided only a little, but he forced himself to take a deep breath anyway. He didn't want Yorke doing anything else to his nose. "Seems to work all right," he announced after a couple of breaths.

"Good. Now you'd better go get some sleep."

Allard hesitated at the door of the cabin. "Cap'n, are we going to do anything about those men who attacked us?"

"What would you have us do?" Yorke asked. "A few of 'em were hurt bad enough that they'll be laid up for a while, and the others all ran off into the night, where we'd never find them. I'd say the damage we done will have to be punishment enough."

"It wouldn't do any good to go to the authorities?"

"We can't prove what happened or tell the law who to look for." Yorke shrugged. "And it's been my experience that the less the authorities know about a fellow's business, the better off he is in the long run."

Allard nodded. "That makes sense. Good night, Cap'n."

"Good night, lad. Try not to roll over on that beezer o' yours. It'll hurt like the devil if you do."

With a wry grunt, Allard left the captain's cabin and headed for his own.

His sleep was restless that night because of his various aches and pains as well as the haunting images of both Diana and Winifred that continually floated past his mind's eye. He finally dozed and remained asleep for a while, but he was still quite tired and achy when he rolled out of his bunk the next morning.

He winced and grimaced as he caught a glimpse of himself in the looking glass that hung on the wall above the tiny basin. Just as Yorke had predicted, his nose was swollen and looked like a small, lumpy potato. And it was bruised to an alarming mixture of purple, black, and yellow. The bruising extended to Allard's eyes as well, which were surrounded by such dark circles that he reminded himself of a raccoon. All in all, his reflection was just about the ugliest sight he had seen in quite a while, so he resolved not to look at himself again until the swelling had gone down and the bruises had faded.

Yorke guffawed when Allard dragged into the mess a short time later. "I knew you'd have a good one, lad, but I didn't expect it to be quite so spectacular."

Allard could only grimace a kind of half smile. He sat down to eat, but even that was painful.

For the next few days, Yorke kept Allard so busy that he didn't have time to brood about his appearance or his aches and pains. The *Ghost* had suffered a great deal of damage during the battle with the Yankee frigate and the cargo sloop that had served as bait for the trap in which the privateers had almost been caught. But none of the holes in the hull were below the waterline, so the schooner didn't need to be put in dry dock for repairs.

The engines had also caught fire during the fight, but that blaze had been extinguished before it could spread to the rest of the ship. The *Ghost* would have to return to the Tyler shipyard before the machinery could be put completely right again. For the voyage home, the crew would have to rely on the sails, which meant that masts and spars blown off during the fighting had to be replaced. A temporary helm had been rigged to take the place of the one destroyed in the battle, but now a better one needed to be put in place.

Once the *Ghost* was back in Charleston, there would be time to repaint and varnish and make the schooner look like it had never been in battle. For now, though, the cosmetic repairs could wait, as long as the vessel was shipshape enough to make the return voyage to South Carolina.

Yorke gave Allard the responsibility of supervising most of the repair work. "Think of it as practice for when you're runnin' that shipyard back in Charleston," the captain advised.

Allard sighed. He knew from experience that he much preferred sailing a ship to working on one. Still, a promise was a promise, and he had made pledges to both Diana and his father. He intended to keep his word. But despite his best intentions, his mind kept straying back to the evening on the terrace at Government House and Winifred's observation that everyone seemed to be getting what they wanted . . . except him.

After a week had passed, Allard's nose, while still tender and a little bruised, looked pretty much like itself again. His leg was still stiff and sore, but not nearly as bad as it had been. And the scrape on his side from the Yankee bayonet was healing up nicely. He was glad he had recovered as much as he had, because on the afternoon of his eighth day in Nassau, he looked up from the deck, where a sailor was nailing down some new planking on the bridge, and saw Governor Haworth and his daughter strolling along the street by the docks. Allard caught his breath and hoped that the two of them would continue on past the wharf where the *Ghost* was tied up, but sure enough, they turned and walked alongside the schooner.

Haworth wore a tan suit and a broad-brimmed planter's hat. Winifred was in an orchid gown with ribbons of the same shade in her elaborately curled hair. She also carried a parasol. She looked up and saw Allard standing on the bridge, and a smile spread across her face as she lifted a hand and waved to him.

He managed to smile too as he returned the wave. Leaving the sailor to the task of repairing the bridge, he climbed down to the main deck and went over to the gangplank connecting the ship to the dock.

"Good afternoon," he called to them, trying not to look only at Winifred. "Welcome to the *Ghost*."

"Permission to come aboard?" Haworth asked.

"Of course, sir."

They ascended the gangplank, and when they reached the top, Haworth shook hands with Allard. Winifred gave him her hand as well, and as she did, her eyes widened. "Heavens, what happened to you, Allard? You look like you've been engaging in fisticuffs."

They would never believe him if he said that he had run into a hatch or something like that, so he fell back on the truth . . . to a certain extent. "Cap'n Yorke and I were set upon by thieves on our way back here from Government House last week. We had to fight our way clear of them."

"Good Lord!" Haworth exclaimed. "Did you report the incident to the constabulary?"

"There didn't seem to be any point to that," Allard replied with a shrug. "The thieves were gone, and they didn't actually steal anything."

"How terrible!" Winifred said. "That you were attacked, I mean, not that the robbers were unsuccessful."

"Were either of you seriously injured?" Haworth asked.

"Other than my nose, only our dignity was harmed," Allard said. "And in both cases, I think we're recovering." He smiled. "You should have seen me a few days ago. On the other hand, it's probably a good thing that you didn't. Someone that ugly shouldn't be in a place as beautiful as Nassau."

"Well, you certainly have my apologies, Mr. Tyler. As the governor of this island, I take full responsibility for everything that happens here. We've done our best to rid the place of cutthroats, but what can I say?" Haworth shrugged and shook his head. "Nassau was once a haven for pirates. Perhaps there are still more of them around than we'd like to think."

Allard didn't mention that his own grandfather had been accused more than once of being a pirate. With a name like Black Nick Tyler, he must have been a brigand at least part of the time.

"Where's Captain Yorke?" Haworth went on after a moment.

"Down below, supervising some of the work there. Shall I fetch him, Governor?"

"No, that's not necessary. Winifred and I were just out for a walk and thought we would stop by to see how your repairs were going."

"We hope to be ready to sail in another two or three days," Allard said.

"That soon?" Haworth sounded surprised. "I thought you would be here at least another week."

"No, the work has gone well. We'll be starting back to Charleston before you know it."

Winifred nudged her father with an elbow. Allard noticed the little movement but pretended not to.

Haworth cleared his throat. "In that case, I insist that you and Captain Yorke join us for dinner again before you leave. The other evening we spent together was so pleasant that I won't allow you to sail until we've had a chance to repeat it." He chuckled. "And I'm the governor, you know. I can do that."

Allard had no doubt that he could. The harbormaster, Cyril Judkins, wouldn't allow the schooner to leave if Haworth ordered otherwise. So even though he didn't think the governor would actually do such a thing, the possibility made Allard believe it would be better to accept the invitation.

"I think that would be all right with Cap'n Yorke," he said. "Although I really shouldn't speak for him."

"If you'll pass along the invitation, I'm sure he'll agree. Let's make it for tomorrow night, shall we? Around eight?"

There was no way out of it. Allard looked at the eager smile on Winifred's face and felt a pang of trepidation, but it was too late for excuses.

"We'll be there," he promised, then added, "Unless Cap'n Yorke decides that we can't make it."

"I'm confident that won't happen." Haworth touched a finger to the brim of his planter's hat. "Good day to you, Mr. Tyler."

"Good day, sir."

Winifred didn't turn immediately to follow her father down the gangplank. She stepped closer to Allard instead and laid her free hand on his forearm, where the sleeve of his shirt was rolled up and the tanned skin was bare. Her fingers were cool and smooth today, instead of warm, as they had been on that first night.

"I'm so glad you'll be coming to visit us again, Allard," she said. "I feel that we didn't finish our previous conversation. There were things left unsaid . . . and undone."

He swallowed hard. "I'm looking forward to it," which wasn't completely a lie. A part of him pleasantly anticipated spending more time with Winifred Haworth.

She left then, joining her father on the dock, but not before turning back for a moment to give Allard one more smile and wave, which he returned with much enthusiasm.

"What did they want?" Yorke asked from behind him, startling Allard a little.

"Oh, there you are, Cap'n. Governor Haworth and his daughter were just here."

"I saw 'em," Yorke said. His hands were greasy from the engine. He pulled a rag from his pocket and began to wipe them.

"They invited us to dinner tomorrow night, around eight."

Yorke grunted. "They walked all the way down here from the hill just for that? Seems like Haworth could've sent somebody with the invitation."

"Well, they said they were just out for a stroll, and then the governor asked when we would be leaving, and I told him we'd probably sail in another two or three days. That's when he invited us to dinner again."

"I see," Yorke said, nodding slowly. "Did they notice the batterin' your face took since they saw you last?"

"As a matter of fact, they did. I had to tell them what happened, Cap'n. There was nothing else I could do."

"No, I s'pose not. Did they seem surprised?"

Allard frowned. "Why, of course they seemed surprised. They didn't have any idea what had—" He stopped short as he realized what Yorke was implying. "You don't think Governor Haworth sent those men after us!"

"I don't think anything," Yorke said. "But I would be interested to know whether or not today was the first he'd heard of it."

"He was shocked and apologetic. I have to believe that he was completely surprised, Cap'n."

"Maybe so, maybe so. You accepted the invitation?"

"Yes sir. I didn't think I could gracefully decline. But I did tell them that I would have to check with you and that it was possible we might be unable to attend due to some reason unknown to me." Allard hesitated. "*Are* we going, Cap'n?"

"You said it yourself, lad. Wouldn't be polite not to." Yorke stuffed the rag back in his pocket and slapped a hand against Allard's shoulder. "A word of advice, though . . . this time you'd better take along that revolver o' yours."

"In case someone attacks us again, you mean?"

"Aye." Yorke grinned. "Or in case Miss Winifred gets a mite too frisky with you and won't take no for an answer!"

CHAPTER FIVE

Government House

T HE NEXT DAY, the crew was putting the finishing touches on the repairs. Barnaby Yorke was confident that the *Ghost* would be able to sail within twenty-four hours. And that was very good news to Allard.

That afternoon, Señor Augustin Valencia appeared at the dock. Allard was on deck and saw him approaching the schooner. Valencia paused, nodded, and spoke pleasantly to several men he passed along the way. Obviously, he was well known on the waterfront. That made sense. He worked with shipping companies, so he had to be well acquainted with everyone who frequented the docks.

Allard didn't figure that Valencia was actually bound for the *Ghost* but just walking in the general direction of the privateer, so he was a little surprised when the man paused at the bottom of the gangplank and called up, "May I come aboard, Señor Tyler?"

"Sure, come ahead," Allard told him.

Valencia wore a white suit and a straw hat and carried a black walking stick with a silver handle. When he came closer, Allard saw that the handle was fashioned in the shape of a woman's head and torso, complete with bare breasts. He thought it one of the most decadent things he had ever seen.

Valencia raised the stick in a salute of sorts when he reached the deck, giving Allard an even better look at the lewd decoration. "How are you, Señor Tyler?" he asked. "I heard that you had some slight trouble on the night of our meeting."

"That story has gotten around, has it?"

"Despite its cosmopolitan air, Nassau is still a relatively small settlement," Valencia responded with a smile. "Everyone knows everyone else's business . . . or at least they think they do. You were not injured?"

Allard shook his head. "Not badly."

"Most excellent news. Might I inquire as to the whereabouts of the good Captain Yorke?"

"He's in his cabin, I believe. Would you like for me to fetch him?"

"Please. I wish to discuss a business proposition with him."

"Well, in that case, why don't you come with me?" Allard suggested. "If the cap'n's going to talk business, I'm sure he'd rather do it in his cabin than on deck."

"That will be fine. Gracias, Señor Tyler."

Allard grunted. "Follow me. It's this way."

He led Valencia through a hatch and along a companionway to the captain's quarters. Yorke called, "Come in," in response to Allard's tap on the door.

He swung the door open and announced, "Señor Valencia to see you, Cap'n."

Yorke looked up from his writing in the ship's log. He set the pen back in its inkwell, closed the book, and stood up. "Come in, señor," he invited. "What brings you to the *Ghost*?"

"You are soon to sail for Charleston, are you not?" Valencia asked.

Yorke nodded. "Aye. Tomorrow, unless something happens to delay us."

"Then I have a business proposition that may be of interest to you, Captain."

Valencia glanced over his shoulder at Allard, and the young man took that as a cue to leave. He started to back out through the open door, but Yorke raised a hand to stop him.

"Hold on a minute, Allard," he said. "Maybe you'd better stay."

"Cap'n, I'm only the third mate. This is none of my business."

"You're the son o' the man who owns this ship," Yorke pointed out. "I'd say that makes it your business. Besides, I'm thinkin' of givin' you more responsibility for this voyage."

That took Allard by surprise. Why would Yorke be placing even more responsibility on him when his seagoing career would be over once the schooner docked at Charleston? Maybe the captain was trying to lure him into more voyages, despite the promises he had made to Diana and his father. If that was Yorke's intent, he was going to be disappointed, Allard vowed. But for the time being, if that was the way Yorke wanted to play it, Allard would go along with him. Besides, he had seen the glance Valencia gave him when Yorke suggested that he stay for the discussion. Valencia hadn't been too pleased by the idea, and since Allard felt an instinctive dislike for the man for some reason, the prospect of annoying him held a certain appeal.

"All right," he said. "Whatever you want, Cap'n."

Yorke smiled and then gave his full attention to Valencia. "Now, what can I do for you, señor?"

"You have space in your hold, do you not?"

"Aye. The *Ghost* isn't really a cargo ship, but we have room to carry some goods."

Loot from any Yankee ships they seized, that was what he meant, Allard thought. But at the moment they weren't carrying anything like that.

"There is a certain cargo that I would be interested in having you deliver to Charleston for me," Valencia said. "Do you think this would be possible?"

"Depends on what it is and how much room you'd need for it," Yorke replied.

"There are fifty crates in the shipment, each approximately six feet long, two feet wide, and two feet deep." Valencia hesitated. "Would it be absolutely necessary for you to know what these crates contain, Captain?"

"Absolutely," Yorke said in a flat voice. "I don't carry any cargo without knowin' what it is."

Valencia glanced at Allard again, who returned the look expressionlessly. Inwardly, he was enjoying Valencia's discomfort, although he felt a little guilty for doing so.

"It would really be best if as few people as possible know about this."

"Mr. Tyler's supervising the cargo for the trip back to Charleston," Yorke said. "I've made up my mind about that."

"Very well." Valencia didn't look happy about it, but he had no choice. "The crates contain rifles for the Confederate army."

"From England?"

"France."

Yorke nodded. "Should've said right off you were talkin' about arms for the Confederacy. I can't say no to that, Señor Valencia."

The man smiled. "I am very glad to hear that, Captain. When can my men start bringing them aboard?"

"Any time you like, as long as they're all stowed away before we're ready to sail tomorrow. Mr. Tyler and I won't be here tonight, mind you, but my first mate can handle things if you're still loadin'."

"Let me guess," Valencia murmured. "You and Señor Tyler are returning to Government House to have dinner with Governor Haworth and his lovely daughter."

"That's right," Yorke said with a smile. "The governor wouldn't hear of us leavin' until he'd had us to dinner again."

"Governor Haworth is a kind and generous host." Valencia's dark eyes cut over toward Allard. They were hard with anger, but Allard pretended not to see that. "Please give him and Señorita Winifred my compliments."

"We'll be glad to. Won't we, Allard?"

"Of course," Allard said.

"Now there is the matter of your fee for this service," Valencia began. "Contingent, of course, upon safe delivery of the cargo to Charleston."

"Half from you," Yorke said, "and a letter authorizing whoever takes delivery of the cargo to pay the other half."

Valencia frowned. "I do not know if these terms will be acceptable to my associates in South Carolina, and of course, given the circumstances, I cannot communicate easily with them. The blockade and all, you know."

"The terms will have to be all right if they want those guns," Yorke said bluntly. "You can work out the details and square everything with them later. That's your business, not mine."

Valencia sighed. "Very well. Half on departure, half on delivery." He named a figure. "Will that be acceptable?"

"I ain't one for hagglin'." Yorke stuck his hand out. "We've got a deal."

They sealed the deal with the handshake, and then Valencia turned to Allard. "Señor Tyler, you will take good care of my cargo?"

"Of course," Allard said. He gripped the hand that Valencia held out to him.

"Very well, then." Valencia gave a little bow. "I bid you gentlemen good day."

Allard escorted him off the ship, and Yorke followed them to the deck. As they stood at the rail, watching Valencia walk confidently across the waterfront, Yorke said, "I don't much like that gent. He's a little too slick for me."

"He seems to like you all right, Cap'n," Allard said. "It's me he doesn't like, although I'm not sure why."

"Well, you don't have to be friends with a fella to take his money for doin' a job." Yorke rested both hands on the railing and laughed. "Looks like we're blockade-runners now, as well as bein' privateers!"

YORKE WENT to Doña Graciela's again for a bath and a shave prior to his dinner engagement at Government House. At least, that was the reason he claimed he was going. Allard suspected that the captain had more in mind than good grooming, since Yorke had paid several visits already to Graciela's place while they were in Nassau. But that was none of his affair. If he hadn't been engaged to Diana, he might have gone there too.

As it was, he cleaned up in his cabin, standing in front of the looking glass as he carefully trimmed his beard. His hair had grown rather long, but he didn't attempt to cut it. Thankfully, the bruising around his eyes was gone and his nose looked normal. Painful though it had been, the nose being yanked on that way by Captain Yorke had probably been good for it. Otherwise it might have been crooked now. Allard prodded it gently with a fingertip. A little tenderness remained, but he figured it would be fine as long as he didn't get punched in the face or anything like that. And he certainly didn't intend to get in a fistfight at the governor's mansion.

Of course, one never knew what might happen . . .

The suits they had worn to the previous dinner had been soiled during the street fight, but Yorke had sent them out to be laundered during the intervening days. Allard dressed in his now, taking special care with the silk cravat he tied around his neck. He wanted to look presentable, but he told himself it had nothing to do with wanting to make an impression on Winifred Haworth. It was simply a sign of respect for him to look as nice as possible.

He settled his planter's hat in place, took one last glance at the looking glass, and nodded in satisfaction. He turned toward the door of his cabin but then stopped short, remembering something. Opening the sea chest at the foot of his bunk, he took out a polished wooden case.

When he opened it, light from the lamp gleamed on the silver-plated pistol and the heavy-bladed knife it contained. The weapons had been gifts from his father. Allard took the pistol out of the case and hefted it. It was a Colt Navy .36 caliber with a revolving cylinder that held six rounds. The pistol had been manufactured in England at Col. Samuel Colt's factory there.

Allard loaded five of the six chambers in the cylinder and then eased the hammer down on the empty chamber. Yorke had taught him that trick, saying that he would be a lot less likely to accidentally blow off a toe—or something even more vital—if he carried the revolver that way. He lifted the tails of his coat, reached behind him, and tucked the pistol into the waistband of his trousers. That might not be the most comfortable way to carry it, but at least it was concealed well at the small of his back.

If anyone jumped them this time, on the way to or from the governor's mansion, they would get a surprise. Five .36-caliber surprises, to be exact.

With the reassuring weight of the gun in his waistband, Allard left the *Ghost* and headed for Doña Graciela's, where he had agreed to meet Yorke. He knew his way around Nassau fairly well now and had no trouble finding the place. Doña Graciela herself answered the door and welcomed Allard.

"*Capitan* Yorke will join you shortly, Señor Tyler," she told him. She rested a hand on his arm. "In the meantime, is there anything I or my ladies can do for you?"

Allard swallowed, well aware of the woman's ample bosom in her low-cut gown. Even though she was at least twenty years older than him, Doña Graciela was an undeniably beautiful woman with thick curls as black as a raven's wing and a voluptuous figure poured into a tight-fitting, revealing gown. Allard glanced past her into the house's parlor, where several lovely young women in various stages of undress lounged on the heavy, overstuffed furniture.

"I, uh . . . no, thank you, I . . . I'm fine," he managed to say. He felt the warmth of the blood suffusing his face as he recalled all the attention some of those girls had paid him on his first visit here. Nothing had happened, of course, but still, this was one more thing that he hoped Diana never found out about.

"A drink, perhaps?" Graciela murmured. "A cup of wine?"

Allard's head jerked in a nod. "Yes, please. Thank you."

The woman made a languid motion with one hand, and a beautiful redhead, wearing a gauzy wrapper that left little to one's imagination, rose from a couch, poured the drink for Allard at a nearby sideboard, and brought it over to him. As she handed the cup to him, he struggled to keep from staring at the rosy roundness clearly visible through her filmy garment. He wished too that she hadn't had red hair, because that reminded him all the more of Diana and made him feel guiltier, even though he hadn't done anything to feel guilty *for.*

He lifted the cup to his lips and gulped down half the wine. The redheaded girl smiled, obviously amused by his discomfiture.

"Ah, there you are, lad." Yorke's booming voice came from the staircase, and Allard had never been happier to hear it. He turned toward the stairs, putting the redhead behind him so he couldn't see her anymore.

"Ready to go, Cap'n?" Allard asked as he set the cup on a small, spindly legged table.

Yorke reached the bottom of the stairs. "Aye, that I am, if you are."

"Oh, yes, I'm ready."

Before he could move, a soft hand rested on his shoulder and someone leaned warmly against him from behind. He recognized the redhead's Irish accent as she breathed into his ear, "Come back t' see me sometime when ye aren't in such a rush to leave, darlin'." Allard felt his eyes widen and his back stiffen in shock as the young woman's tongue licked his ear.

Laughter erupted from the other girls in the parlor.

Yorke grasped his arm and pulled him toward the door. "Come along, lad, before you die of heart failure or have an attack of apoplexy." With his other hand he touched a finger to the brim of his hat and addressed his hostess. "Thank you for all your kindnesses, Graciela, and that goes for all the young ladies too."

"I hope you visit us again the next time you are in Nassau, Barnaby."

Yorke grinned. "Oh, I think you can count on that."

Then, thankfully, the two men were outside and in the fresh air, away from the musky smells of perfume that pervaded the house. Allard drew in a deep breath and blew it out in a long sigh.

"Those gals think you're just adorable," Yorke told him with a chuckle as they walked through yet another spectacularly beautiful twilight. "Ah, to be young again. I think I'm a mite jealous of you, Allard."

"Don't be," Allard told him. "I don't think I've ever been so embarrassed in my life."

"There are times to be embarrassed," Yorke said, "and times to just enjoy what life brings you. If you're lucky, lad, as you grow older, you'll learn to tell the difference."

Allard didn't know what to say to that. He wasn't sure he would ever learn to enjoy having beautiful young ladies of ill repute fawning over him. At least, not without feeling hellaciously guilty about enjoying it so much. He forced those thoughts out of his mind and told himself to be alert instead. This time, if there were trouble, it wouldn't take him by surprise.

They didn't encounter any problems by the time they reached the foot of Queen Anne's Staircase, and the climb to the top of the hill on the carved stone steps passed without incident.

The same elderly butler met them at the door of Government House and ushered them into the dining room. Haworth was waiting there for them, and unlike the last time, Winifred was in the dining room with her father when Allard and Yorke arrived, rather than making her entrance from the terrace.

The governor shook hands with both of them. "I'm glad you could make it, gentlemen."

Winifred offered her hand as well. As Allard took it, he was seized for an instant by the impulse to bend over and kiss it, as Valencia had done that other night. Instead he simply clasped it for a moment and politely said, "You look lovely, Miss Haworth."

That was no exaggeration. The bodice of Winifred's light blue gown hugged her figure and then swept out into a stylish hoop. The garment's neckline left her shoulders bare, as was commonplace on this island where the weather stayed warm just about the entire year 'round. Winifred's blonde curls brushed her shoulders, inviting a man to run his fingers through them. Allard steeled himself to resist that unspoken invitation.

They sat down to dinner, and the evening passed in a blur of pleasant conversation, good food, and fine wine. Allard relaxed as the time went by. He had been worried about nothing, he told himself. Winifred acted pleasant toward him, but there was certainly nothing improper about her behavior, no hint that she had any romantic interest in him. She was just a good hostess treating a guest with the necessary graciousness. Allard decided that he had been wrong about her. She wasn't attracted to him at all. That was a relief.

"It's good to see that you've recuperated from your injuries, Mr. Tyler," Haworth commented.

"Yes, I think I'll be fine . . . as long as I don't get into any more brawls," Allard added.

"I spoke to the head of the local constabulary about that regrettable incident. He seemed to think that you were set upon by simple thieves, probably some waterfront toughs. He was going to ask around and see if he could get a hint as to who it might have been, but I don't believe he's been able to come up with anything."

Yorke waved a hand. "Doesn't matter now. We're fine, Allard and me, and tomorrow we'll be sailin'." He paused. "Which reminds me, that friend o' yours came to see us on the *Ghost*."

Haworth frowned slightly and said, "Friend of mine? I'm sure I don't know who you mean."

"Señor Valencia."

"Ah!" Haworth shrugged. "I wouldn't call the man a friend. He asked for my assistance in facilitating a few matters of commerce. As governor, of course, I do my best to see that trade flows smoothly in and out of Nassau."

In other words, thought Allard, Haworth and Valencia were associates, maybe even business partners, but they didn't particularly like each other. That matched up with the impression he had formed of the situation at the time of the first dinner with the governor.

"What did Valencia want?" Haworth went on.

"He had a business proposition, some cargo he wanted delivered to Charleston."

"And did you agree to carry that cargo for him?" Before Yorke could answer, Haworth continued quickly, "Forgive me, Captain. That was an impolite question. Your business dealings are none of my affair."

"Oh, I don't know about that."

Haworth's mouth tightened. "What do you mean?"

"Like you said," Yorke replied easily, "you're the governor here in Nassau. You've got a right to know what's goin' on."

"Yes, I suppose you could look at it that way. Still, I meant no offense."

"None taken. And for what it's worth, we're carryin' that cargo to Charleston for Señor Valencia. Rifles for the Confederacy . . . although I reckon they'll pass through the hands of a middleman first. That's where Valencia and his partners, whoever they are, will make their profit."

Haworth smiled thinly. "There's always a profit to be made somewhere, isn't there?"

"If there wasn't, the world would pretty much quit turnin', I suspect."

What Allard suspected was that there was more than one layer of meaning to this conversation. Haworth and Valencia might be partners in the gun-smuggling enterprise—or they might be rivals. Allard didn't know and didn't really care as long as none of the intrigue kept him from returning to Charleston and Diana. Once he was there, none of this would be his concern anymore. He would likely never again set foot on New Providence Island after the *Ghost* sailed.

When the meal was over, Haworth leaned back in his chair and said to his daughter, "If you'll excuse us, Winifred, dear, the gentlemen and I will repair to my study for a few moments of after-dinner reflection."

She laughed. "Go ahead, Father. Drink your brandy, smoke your cigars, and tell your bawdy stories. But don't think for a moment that I don't know what you and Captain Yorke and Mr. Tyler will be up to."

"Women are much too perceptive, gentlemen," Haworth said with a laugh and a shake of his head. "You can't put anything past them, not even the young and innocent ones like my daughter."

Winifred's cheeks dimpled as she smiled mockingly at him. She demurely rose from her chair, prompting the men to stand up quickly as well. "I suppose I'll have to enjoy the evening air on the terrace alone," she said.

Allard caught himself just before he volunteered to join her. That wouldn't have been a good idea, and besides, the twinkle in Winifred's eyes told him she was just joking, that she really didn't mind the men going off to Haworth's study.

Still, as they strolled out of the dining room, he couldn't help but glance back. Winifred had already stepped out to the terrace and stood at the railing. Something about her pulled at him and made him want to join her. But he turned away quickly and followed Haworth and Yorke down a short hall to a book-lined study. The governor broke out the brandy and cigars while Allard studied the titles of the leather-bound volumes on the shelves. Most of them appeared to be classics and histories ranging from the ancient world to the more recent.

For the next half hour or so, the men smoked and drank, and Yorke and Haworth discussed the war. It was clear that the Englishman's sympathies lay strongly with the South.

"As soon as my government grants official recognition to the Confederacy, I can do even more to further your cause, gentlemen," he said. "Our countries are inextricably tied together as trading partners, and it's foolish to delay. We *need* your cotton."

"The Yankees will have something to say about whether or not we can send it to you," Yorke commented.

"Yes, of course, the blockade. Well, Nassau is a neutral port. Any Confederate ship that wishes to run the blockade, like your *Ghost,* will always be welcome here. Under the current circumstances, British ships can't carry supplies or munitions or the like directly to Southern ports, but those cargoes can be brought here, transferred to Confederate ships, and taken back to your homeland."

"Through the blockade."

Haworth smiled thinly. "Admittedly, the enterprise won't be without danger. But anything that's worth the doing is worth a bit of risk, eh?"

"I've always found that to be true," Yorke agreed with a nod.

Allard didn't say much. In the presence of these two older, more experienced men of the world, he felt like a babe in the woods, as Yorke had once called him. He was content to sip his brandy, take an occasional puff on his cigar, and listen with great interest to the conversation.

That wasn't enough for Haworth, however. The governor turned to him and asked, "What about you, Mr. Tyler? What can you tell me about the war and the Confederacy's gallant effort to rid itself of the unwelcome domination of the Yankees?"

"Well, sir, I think it's a noble cause," Allard said.

"Do you think the South can win?"

"Of course we can," Allard declared without hesitation. "I was a student at the Citadel for two years, and I know what fine officers and courageous soldiers we can put in the field."

"Men can't win a war alone, no matter how brave they are," Haworth pointed out. "The North has more resources, a greater manufacturing capability—"

"And that won't win a war by itself, either," Allard said a bit hotly, forgetting for the moment that he was interrupting an important man. "In the end, wars are won by the hearts of the men fighting them. Our hearts are strong, and the Lord is on our side."

Haworth puffed on his cigar and blew out a cloud of whitish gray smoke. "That's all well and good, but a valiant heart fights a lot better if the man within whose breast it beats is well armed, well equipped, and well fed." He poked the glowing tip of his cigar in Allard's direction. "That's why your government and mine need to come to an official arrangement as soon as they possibly can."

Allard couldn't argue with that sentiment. In fact, he didn't have to continue the discussion at all. At that moment, a blood-curdling scream rang through Government House, coming from the direction of the dining room, the terrace—and Winifred Haworth.

CHAPTER SIX

Sunk!

ALTHOUGH ALL THREE MEN reacted instantly, Allard was the closest to the door and the first one through it. He was in the lead as they ran down the hallway toward the dining room.

Allard flung the door open and burst into the dining room. He spotted Winifred on the terrace, shrinking back from the railing with her hands pressed to her face. She had screamed only once, but her posture and attitude testified plainly that she was still fearful.

"Winifred, what is it?" Allard asked as he lunged through the open french doors, his hand poised to grasp the Colt. "What's wrong?"

She jerked at the sound of his voice and turned quickly toward him. Her eyes were wide. "Oh, Allard!" she cried.

And then, to his surprise, she threw herself at him and wrapped her arms around his neck, hugging him desperately.

Acting out of instinct, he put his arms around her as well. The soft mounds of her breasts pressed against his chest. They rose and fell rapidly as she panted to catch her breath.

"Winifred! What the deuce is going on?" Haworth demanded as he and Yorke arrived. "What was the meaning of that scream?"

She took a deep, ragged breath and lifted her head. "I saw . . . I saw someone," she said as she turned slightly in Allard's arms to point toward the tree-shrouded grounds that fell away down the hill beyond the terrace railing. "Someone sneaking up on the house like a thief . . . or a murderer!"

Haworth grimaced. "Is that all?"

"Is that all?" Winifred repeated indignantly. "Whoever it was could have killed us in our sleep!"

"I know you still have some fear of the natives, Winifred," Haworth said with forced patience, "but I assure you, they don't intend to assassinate us. What happened to this man you saw?"

"When I screamed, he ran off. He turned and ran back through the trees. He's gone now."

"Then I believe it would be safe for you to let go of my daughter, Mr. Tyler," the governor said dryly.

Allard did so, releasing Winifred and stepping back quickly, even though she tried to cling to him. His heart was pounding—from the surprise of hearing the scream, from the run down the hall from Haworth's study, and from having the soft, warm bundle that was Winifred molded against him for several moments.

She glared at her father. "What are you going to do? You can't just allow that man, whoever he was, to skulk around out there."

"I'm sure he's long gone by now," Haworth said. "But to ease your mind I'll have the servants search the grounds." He turned to the butler, who had come onto the terrace behind everyone else, and gave the orders. Then he said to Allard and Yorke, "Gentlemen, I believe we can return to the study now and finish our conversation."

"And leave me out here unprotected," Winifred said before anyone could move. "I insist that Mr. Tyler remain here to keep me company."

"You could bid our guests good night and retire to your room for the evening," Haworth pointed out, his voice hardening.

"But I choose not to do that," she said stubbornly. "It's a beautiful evening, lurker or no lurker, and I want to enjoy it."

"You can't impose on a guest—"

Once again Allard interrupted the governor. "It's no imposition, sir," he said. "I'd be glad to keep Miss Haworth company for a while."

Haworth was still carrying the stub of his cigar. He put it in his mouth, chewed on it for a second, then said, "That's up to you, Mr. Tyler. If you're certain . . ."

Allard nodded. "I'm sure I don't mind."

"Very well, then. Come along, Captain."

Yorke said, "I'll see you in a spell, lad. We don't need to stay out too late, since we're sailin' in the morning."

"Aye sir."

The two older men left the terrace and went through the dining room. Allard turned toward the railing, his eyes eagerly searching the shadows under the trees for any sign of movement. It had occurred to him that the intruder might have some connection to the attempt on his and Yorke's lives a week earlier. Allard almost hoped the man, whoever he was, came back tonight. If he could capture the intruder, he might get an answer to the question of who wanted him and the captain dead. On the other hand, the man Winifred had seen might have been a simple thief who had nothing to do with anything except a desire to rob Government House.

Allard didn't see anything, and after a moment, several servants moved into the woods, carrying lanterns and shotguns. They began working their way down the slope, searching for the intruder.

"They won't find him," Allard predicted. "Like your father said, I'll wager the man's long gone. Probably back in some dive on the waterfront, muttering in his beer about what went wrong."

"I was so frightened," Winifred said as she moved up close beside him. "I . . . I know I was being silly, but all I could think about was how those men attacked you and Captain Yorke, and I know some of the natives resent my father because he represents the Crown, and . . . and I just panicked, I suppose. I'm sorry, Allard."

He was back to being Allard again, instead of Mr. Tyler, now that they were alone. And there was practically no distance between them. Even with the heat of the day lingering into the evening, he could feel the warmth emanating from her body.

"That's all right, Miss Haworth," he began as he turned toward her. "You can be forgiven for being frightened. I would have been too."

She laughed. "Oh, no. I doubt that. A strong, competent man such as you wouldn't be frightened of a mere intruder. I saw the look on your face when you came running out here. You were ready to fight against any odds to protect me."

That was true enough, Allard thought. He was a South Carolinian, born and bred, which meant, above all, he was a gentleman. He would have faced any enemy if it involved protecting a lady. Any lady, not just Winifred Haworth.

He would have said as much, but Winifred didn't give him a chance. Instead she whispered, "You're so brave, Allard," and came up on her toes to press her lips against his in an urgent, passionate kiss.

Without thinking about what he was doing, he put his right arm around her waist. He didn't really draw her to him; it was more like she sagged against him, once more molding her body to his as she had done a few minutes earlier. She wasn't prompted by fear this time, however. Her passion and desire leaped through him like a gigantic spark, galvanizing his muscles and setting afire every nerve in his body. Her lips were hot and sweet, tender yet demanding, and as she kissed him, they parted in sensual invitation.

For a moment he felt like a man in the grip of an undertow, pulled down, down, down into the depths. He was drowning, but instead of water filling his lungs, it was fire filling his senses, running riot, and overwhelming him with the taste and smell and feel of this eager woman in his arms. Just as it was easy for a man sinking deep beneath the surface to give up and relinquish himself to his fate, it would have been so simple at that instant to surrender to Winifred Haworth and give her exactly what she wanted.

But if he did that, a small voice in the back of his mind insisted, he could never live with himself, could never look at himself in the mirror. More important, he knew he would never be able to look into Diana's eyes without feeling unworthy of her goodness, her love.

He placed a hand on her shoulder, trying to ignore how smooth and warm and sleek her bare skin was, and pulled away from her. She made a slight noise of disappointment and loss as his lips left hers.

"What is it, Allard?" she whispered urgently. "What's wrong?"

"I . . . I can't do this," he said.

"Do what? It was only a kiss. I'm grateful. You came running when you thought I was in danger, and for that you deserve a reward."

"No," he said. "No. My reward is simply the fact that you're safe."

She smiled and shook her head. "Oh, that's not nearly enough. That's not nearly all you're going to get, Allard."

"I told you, I'm engaged. I have a fiancée back in Charleston—"

"I don't care about that."

All he could do for a moment was stare at her with a shocked frown on his face. Finally he said, "You don't care?"

"No, not at all. Your fiancée is in Charleston, just as you said, and you're here. You can do whatever you please, and she'll never know the difference." Her voice lowered huskily. "And I mean that, Allard, *you can do whatever you please.*"

There it was. She was offering herself to him. And all he could think to say was, "I . . . I have to sail for home tomorrow."

"That leaves us tonight. Who knows how long my father and Captain Yorke will be in the study, smoking and drinking? We can go up to my room right now—"

With an effort that was almost violent, Allard turned away. He grabbed hold of the terrace railing with both hands and clung to it. "No," he said shakily, keeping the image of Diana in his mind. That strengthened him, and his words were a little steadier as he continued, "I'm sorry. I just can't do that. It's nothing to do with you, it's just—"

"I know," she broke in, and her voice was icy now. "Your heart belongs to another. You're as bad as those simpering fools in a Brontë novel!"

He turned his head to look at her, a little angry now himself. "You've no right—"

"I'm terribly embarrassed," she said. "I ought to tell my father that you made improper advances to me. He'd have you horsewhipped. It's no more than you deserve."

"Are you mad? I didn't touch you until you—"

Again she interrupted him. Her face contorted and tears began to course down her cheeks as she said miserably, "Forgive me, Allard. I . . . I know I'm a shameless woman. You're correct. I had no right to throw myself at you. Can you ever forgive me?"

"Of course," he said, not so much because he meant it as because he sensed her mood was so volatile. There was no telling what she might do given a chance to do anything. He hoped he could humor her until this mood had passed. But of course, he could only go so far in humoring her. The next best thing was to remove himself.

"I'm going to retire for the evening now, as my father suggested," she said. "I hope you'll think kindly of me—"

"Of course."

"And if you ever return to Nassau, you *will* come to visit me?"

"Certainly." It seemed like an easy enough promise to make, since he never intended to return.

"All right, then. We'll just pretend that the . . . awkward moments . . . never happened." She turned her cheek toward him. "Just kiss me good night, will you?"

He bent and brushed his lips quickly across her cheek. "Good night, Winifred."

"Good-bye, Allard," she whispered.

She turned and left the terrace, sweeping elegantly through the dining room without looking back. He stayed by the railing, one hand clenching firmly on to it. He tried to tell himself that he wasn't hanging on to keep himself from following her . . . but deep down, he was afraid that was exactly what he was doing.

WHEN YORKE found him on the terrace a short time later, Allard had recovered somewhat from the disturbing incident. The captain asked, "Any sign of whoever was lurkin' around earlier?"

Allard had seen the servants return to the house empty-handed. He shook his head and said, "No, they didn't find him."

"I'm not surprised."

Allard shot a quick glance in Yorke's direction. "What do you mean by that, Cap'n?"

Keeping his voice pitched low and quiet, Yorke said, "I'm not convinced there really was anybody sneakin' around."

"But Winifred said——." Understanding dawned on Allard. "Oh. You think she made the whole thing up, just to get some attention."

"I think she *could* have made it up, just to get some attention from *you*. That young woman's got designs on you, lad."

Allard knew that now, having seen the proof of it at extremely close range. He just nodded and said, "It doesn't matter. We're leaving tomorrow."

"Aye, and likely a good thing too." Yorke clapped a hand on Allard's shoulder. "The governor will be here in a few minutes to bid us good night. Don't know about you, but I'm ready to put this place behind us for a while."

"Amen," Allard murmured. Charleston was going to look better than ever to him—and so was Diana.

Haworth came out onto the terrace shortly and showed them out of Government House himself, shaking hands with them at the front door. "I think we'll be seeing a lot of each other over the coming months, Captain," he told Yorke. "You're always welcome here, and I don't just mean in Nassau. I mean in my home as well. And that goes for you too, of course, Mr. Tyler."

"Thank you, sir," Allard said.

As they descended Queen Anne's Staircase, Allard thought there was a hint of danger mixed in with the warm breeze and the sweet fragrance of flowers and the strains of music from the town. But where that feeling of menace came from, he couldn't really say. Nothing happened as he and Yorke walked back to the docks and boarded the *Ghost*.

Valencia's men had shown up in the late afternoon with three wagons loaded down with the crates that the schooner would deliver to Charleston. They had been brought aboard and stowed away safely.

When Yorke checked with the first mate, the officer told him that the evening had been quiet, no trouble.

"Nobody skulkin' around, tryin' to get to that cargo in our hold?"

"No sir," the first mate answered. "Were you expecting a problem?"

"Best to always expect problems," Yorke muttered. "That way you ain't surprised when they come knockin' on your door."

The rest of the night passed quietly, though, despite Yorke's seeming pessimism. Allard's sleep was troubled, probably because of what had happened with Winifred. He kept seeing her face in his dreams, whether he wanted to or not. He was still torn between being honest with Diana and telling her everything that had happened in Nassau or being discreet and shielding her from the truth so she wouldn't be hurt unnecessarily.

And when you came right down to it, he reminded himself, he *hadn't* been unfaithful to her. He had resisted Winifred's advances, and in truth, the temptation hadn't even been all that great. Of course Winifred was lovely, and he had reacted to her as any man would if he'd found himself holding such a beautiful, sensuous young woman in his arms. But not for a second had he considered giving in to her wiles. Still, he was leaning toward not mentioning anything about Winifred to Diana, just to be on the safe side.

Valencia appeared on the dock early the next morning, nattily dressed as always and carrying the black cane with the lewd silver handle. He came aboard at Yorke's invitation and handed over his portion of the fee they had agreed to the day before.

"I'm putting a great deal of faith in you, Captain," he said. "I trust that you will not let me down."

"We'll get them guns to Charleston, come hell or high water," Yorke promised. "Or we'll die tryin'."

"Dying serves no one," Valencia pointed out. "Only success. Good luck, Captain."

Yorke shook hands with him. "We're obliged for the good wishes, Señor Valencia."

The man left, and the work of getting ready to sail continued. The schooner's engines had been repaired enough so they could be run for short periods of time. The *Ghost* would leave Nassau under steam, but once clear of the harbor, the sails would be raised, and she would ride a fair wind home to South Carolina.

Allard felt excitement course through him when the deck vibrated faintly under his feet as the engines were fired up. He was on the rebuilt bridge with Yorke and the helmsman. On the main deck, crewmen untied the thick hawsers that held the ship in place and tossed them to workers on the dock. Like a living thing, the schooner trembled slightly as she found herself once more in the grip of the eternal sea.

Some of the island women came down to the docks to wave farewell to the sailors who had visited them during the past couple of weeks. Yorke had been good about letting the crew go ashore for entertainment and relaxation, and the sailors had taken advantage of the opportunity to get to know some of the women of Nassau. Allard thought he even spotted a few of the girls from Doña Graciela's, but he wasn't sure about that.

One thing he *was* sure of was that there was no sign of the governor or his daughter as the *Ghost* slipped away. When the vessel reached the outer edges of the harbor and the sails were raised to catch the wind, Allard looked back at the pink hilltop mansion and the bizarrely shaped Fort Fincastle and raised a hand briefly in farewell, even though he knew that no one up there could see him at this distance. He made the gesture anyway, because it felt like the right thing to do.

Then he turned and put New Providence Island behind him. He was on his way home.

NASSAU WAS a little more than five hundred miles from Charleston. Under full steam and following as direct a course as possible, a ship like the *Ghost* could make the voyage in three or four days. But with the efficiency of the engines sharply limited and the possibility that they would have to dodge Yankee craft plying the waters off the Florida coast, Yorke estimated that it would be more like a week, perhaps a few days longer, before the ship reached its home port.

Allard didn't really care. He was anxious to get back to Diana, of course, but at the same time he loved being on the water. The sea breeze and the salt spray were like tonics to him, easing a mind that might have been troubled otherwise.

The lack of steam power meant that the captain had to curtail their privateering activities, but two days out from Nassau, as the *Ghost* tacked around the western tip of Grand Bahama Island, an opportunity presented itself that Yorke couldn't resist. He called Allard to the bridge and pressed a telescope into his hands, saying, "Take a look, lad."

Allard brought the glass to his eye. After a moment he found the sails of a cutter several miles distant. The ship, about two-thirds the size of the *Ghost,* flew a Union flag from its mainmast.

"That's a Yankee revenue cutter," Yorke said with relish. "Just two guns and no engines. We can take her."

Allard lowered the glass. "I thought we were trying to get back to Charleston with as little trouble as possible. Those cutters are fast."

"Aye, but so are we! And with the help of our engines, we can run her down."

"Is it wise to push the engines?" Allard asked with a frown. "We don't know yet how well the repairs will hold up." He knew he shouldn't be arguing with the captain, of course. It was up to Yorke to decide what they would do. But as the son of the shipbuilder and owner, Allard felt a duty to speak up too.

"We won't have to use the engines very much," Yorke insisted. "And a cutter like that would make a nice little prize to take back to Charleston with us." He clenched a fist. "Come on, lad! You're Black Nick Tyler's own flesh and blood, aren't you? He'd never pass up this chance."

Allard felt a surge of excitement. "Aye, Cap'n. Let's take her."

"Now you're talkin'!" Yorke barked orders, the helmsman spun the wheel to change the schooner's course, and the chase was on.

The Yankee captain saw the *Ghost* coming, of course, and ordered all sail put on. Everything being equal, it would have been a good race. But once the *Ghost* had some steam up and the engines added their power to that of the wind, the schooner began to close in quickly.

The small cannon mounted at the cutter's stern geysered smoke as a shot was loosed at the pursuing schooner. The ball fell woefully short, however, and Allard realized that the shot had been as much a symbolic act of defiance as anything. A short time later, the cutter was in range of the larger gun on the *Ghost*'s bow, and Yorke ordered the gunner to put a shot just to port of the Federal vessel. The big gun belched smoke, and as the ball threw up a large splash just off the cutter's port bow, Yorke called to the gunner, "Bracket 'em!"

The next shot landed just to starboard of the cutter, and the message was obvious. Yorke could put the next ball right in the middle of the smaller craft if he so chose.

"They're heavin' to!" Yorke said as he slapped Allard on the back. "They know we'll blow 'em out of the water if they don't surrender."

The captain of the cutter ordered the colors struck. The Union flag came down. The cutter lowered its sails and waited to be boarded.

Yorke hove to as well and sent a boarding party across in the schooner's small boat. The Yankee captain formally surrendered and was brought back to the *Ghost* to meet with Yorke. The man's face was red with anger and frustration, but he was civil enough as he negotiated the release of his men.

"We're not far from Grand Bahama Island," the Yankee pointed out. "Let us take our boat, and we can row there."

"Aye, that's agreeable to me," Yorke said with a nod. "I'm not interested in prisoners, Cap'n, only in your ship. I intend to put a prize crew on her and sail her back to Charleston."

"Do it and be damned," the Yankee snapped, losing his patience. "You Rebels will get your comeuppance sooner or later."

"We'll see," Yorke said, tolerant in victory. "It looks like you're gettin' yours now."

It didn't take long to put a skeleton crew aboard the cutter, which was named the *Albert Ross*. The Federals rowed off to the east in their small boat, heading for Grand Bahama Island and the settlement of Freeport. The *Ghost* and the *Ross* turned north-northwest, toward the coastline of the Confederacy.

Flushed with that success, Yorke spent a great deal of time on the bridge with the spyglass held to his eye as he searched the sea for Yankee threats and/or potential victims. Allard hoped they wouldn't run across any more Union vessels until they reached the waters just outside Charleston Harbor, where the blockaders cruised. The *Ghost* was still crippled to a certain extent, plus they had a valuable cargo stored in the hold that had to be delivered. That was important both for the remainder of the fee they would collect and for the benefits the Confederacy would reap from the rifles. It seemed a little foolish to Allard for them to go looking for trouble.

Captain Yorke was in command, though, he reminded himself. The captain knew what he was doing. He had sailed with old Black Nick, after all.

Two days after the capture of the Yankee revenue cutter, the lookout spotted another ship. Yorke and Allard were not on the bridge at the time, but they heard the strident shouts and made their way there as quickly as possible. Yorke opened his telescope to its full length and squinted through the glass as he scanned the waves. Allard came up next to the captain in time to hear him mutter, "Damn."

"What is it, Cap'n?" Allard asked, feeling a tingle of apprehension.

Yorke lowered the glass. "A Yankee cruiser," he said, "and it's steamin' this way."

Allard felt his heart begin to slug more heavily in his chest. They would be heavily outgunned by the Union vessel, and with its full engine power, it was considerably faster than the *Ghost* too.

"What are we going to do?" he asked.

"Hard aport!" Yorke called to the helmsman by way of answer. To

Allard he said, "All we can do is run for the coast and hope to give the Yankee bastard the slip along the way."

Allard nodded tensely. They were somewhere off the Georgia coast, which was lined with offshore islands cut by narrow sounds and channels. If they could reach that mazelike region before the cruiser caught up to them, there was at least a chance they could get away.

They *had* to get away, he thought. Diana was waiting for him, waiting to become his wife so that they could spend the rest of their lives together. Some damned Yankees couldn't ruin all of that.

The crew on the *Ross* also spotted the Yankee cutter and headed back out to sea as the *Ghost* tacked toward the coast, which was still miles away and not yet visible. If the cutter saw them, it wouldn't be able to follow them both.

Yorke peered through the spyglass again and grunted a curse. "They spotted us, all right," he said, "and they've changed course to try to cut us off."

So it was a race again, just as it had been when the schooner was trying to run down the Yankee cutter. Now, though, the *Ghost* was the pursued, instead of the pursuer. And the stakes were higher. If the captain of the Federal cruiser recognized his prey as a Confederate privateer, he would likely try to sink the *Ghost* instead of capturing her. In their self-righteous arrogance, the Yankees regarded privateers as outright pirates, Allard knew.

He moved to the railing around the bridge. The *Ghost* had every inch of sail rigged, and a brisk wind filled the canvas so that the schooner seemed almost to leap through the water. It would have been a glorious sensation had the circumstances not been so grim. And even though the sleek ship's speed seemed breathtakingly fast, Allard knew the Yankee cruiser could make even more knots with its steam power. He tried to figure the angles involved and knew that it was going to be very close. The *Ghost* still had a chance to reach a possible haven before the cruiser intercepted it. It was a slim chance, but better than none.

Everything they could do was already being done, so Allard felt a growing sense of frustration as the afternoon slipped by and the race continued. With so much riding on the outcome, he wanted to take a hand in this deadly game himself, but there was nothing he could do.

After a while Yorke called the engineer to the bridge and told him to get some steam up. "Pour all the coal to the engines that they'll stand," he ordered.

The engineer shook his head dourly. "You're riskin' those patched-up boilers, Cap'n," he warned.

"That's no worse a risk than we're already runnin'," Yorke pointed out, and the engineer couldn't argue with him. They faced possible destruction either way.

It took some time to build up steam, but once the engines began adding their power to that of the sails, the little cutter was left behind. Allard watched it fall astern and thought bleakly that the few members of the crew still on it likely were doomed to capture now. They would probably spend the rest of their lives in a Yankee prison camp. If there had been time, Yorke could have taken the prize crew off the cutter and then scuttled it so that it would sink and be of no further use to the Yankees. That hadn't been an option, though, so the men on board the *Ross* had to take their chances.

The sun had begun to lower toward the horizon, and darkness would be the Confederates' ally too. The irregular shoreline was clearly visible now, and it looked like they would reach it before night fell. If they could just elude the Yankees for a while longer.

Allard could see the onrushing Federal cruiser quite clearly now with the naked eye. If the *Ghost* wasn't already within range of the cruiser's big guns, it soon would be.

Yorke realized the same thing. He said bitterly, "If they'll just hold their fire a mite longer, they'll be close enough we can give 'em a fight."

Unfortunately, that wasn't going to be the case. A few moments later, smoke jetted from one of the guns on the cruiser, and with an unnerving whistling sound, the shell passed over the *Ghost*'s deck to splash into the water on the port side.

"That wasn't a warning shot!" Allard exclaimed. "They're trying to sink us!"

"Aye," Yorke agreed, "they must know who we are. Word's got back to the Yankees about that frigate they lost when they tried to trap us. I reckon they've got blood in their eye now. They're out for revenge." He grabbed the speaking tube that connected the bridge with the engine room and bellowed into it, "All ahead full! Give me everything you've got!"

Allard could just imagine the chief engineer squawking about that, knowing how worried the man was about the boilers holding up under the strain.

What did it matter, though, whether the boilers blew up or the schooner was blasted to splinters by the guns on that Yankee cruiser? The ship and everyone on her were doomed either way.

"I'm sorry, Diana," Allard whispered. "I truly believed I would come home safely to you."

Another round came screaming across the water. This one slammed into the *Ghost*'s stern, blasting the 18-pound gun that was mounted there and killing the gun crew. The whole ship shuddered from the impact. Yorke shouted at the helmsman, who spun the wheel and sent the schooner angling to port. Their only hope now was to zigzag. That might throw off the aim of the gunners on the cruiser, at least for a while.

There was no point in returning the fire. The other 18-pounder was mounted on the bow, and the only hope of survival lay in reaching the coastline ahead of the cruiser and eluding pursuit there, not in turning around and trying to match the Yankee vessel shot for shot.

Allard gripped the railing around the bridge and watched the cruiser draw closer. The shore wasn't far away now, though. Maybe they would make it. The deck vibrated wildly under his feet as the engines labored to push the *Ghost* faster and faster.

Another round from the cruiser slammed into the water just off the starboard bow. The helmsman whipped the wheel around, turning in that direction in hopes that would cause the Yankees to overcorrect and miss them high with the next shot. But the federal gunners were canny, and the next shell crashed against the schooner's hull, shaking the ship so badly that Allard was tossed off his feet. He rolled over and scrambled up, lurching to keep his balance as the *Ghost* began to list to starboard.

"They've holed us, Cap'n!" he shouted to Yorke, who nodded grimly.

"Aye, we're takin' on water," Yorke agreed. "That means we're done for." He grasped the speaking tube and ordered, "Tie down the valves and abandon ship!"

Allard gasped. "Cap'n, that'll blow the boilers for sure!"

"It damned well better. It'll be a cold day in hell before I let those blasted Yankees get their hands on a fine ship like this! I don't want 'em findin' those rifles in the hold, either. The less they know, the better. Valencia might be able to get another shipment through on a different ship."

Allard understood, but he hated to think that the *Ghost* would soon be blown to kindling.

Yorke snatched up a megaphone and bellowed, "Abandon ship! Abandon ship!" Some of the crew began struggling to lower the single small boat from its davits, others just headed for the railings and leaped overboard. Sharks were known to be in these waters sometimes, but better to take a chance with them than to stay on board a ship that would soon explode.

Yorke took the helm himself, relieving the crewman who had been manning the wheel. Allard caught at his sleeve and shouted, "Come on, Cap'n."

The *Ghost* was almost deserted now, the crew—including the ones who had been below—having fled for their lives in a matter of scant moments.

"I'll be stayin' right here," Yorke said with a shake of his head. He turned to grin at Allard. "But you get on outta here, lad. It was an honor and a pleasure sailin' with you. Once you're married, give that pretty redheaded wife o' yours a kiss for me, will you?"

100

"You can kiss her yourself at the wedding," Allard said desperately. He knew there wouldn't *be* a wedding if he didn't soon get off this doomed ship. "Cap'n, you can't stay on board. That . . . that's suicide."

"Sort of like when your grandfather, ol' Black Nick hisself, blew up Phu Dan and that ship full o' Malay pirates in the China Sea?" Hand over hand, Yorke hauled the wheel around, and with a great shudder, the mortally wounded schooner began to turn. "I just hope that cruiser's close enough to feel it when those boilers blow."

Allard understood now. Yorke intended to ram the Yankee cruiser. But it wasn't going to work. The boilers would never hold for that long. Besides, when the Yankees saw that the schooner was on a collision course, they would just blast it out of the water, assuming the exploding boilers didn't do the job first.

"Sorry, Cap'n," Allard murmured. He had the Colt Navy tucked in the waistband of his trousers, where he had carried it nearly all the time he was at sea. Now he slipped it out, reversed it, and stepping close to Yorke, he slammed the gun butt against the back of the captain's head.

Allard had struck quickly, without hesitating, almost without thinking about what he was doing, and he had struck true. Yorke crumpled toward the deck, his fingers slipping off the wheel. Allard caught him and dragged him toward the edge of the bridge. Black smoke boiled from the stack amidships, and more smoke curled up through the open hatches. Fires were no doubt blazing belowdecks. Allard knew he had just minutes, perhaps only seconds.

He toppled Yorke's senseless form over the railing and then dove in after him, striking the surface awkwardly with a stunning force. For a long moment he was underwater and disoriented, but then he regained his wits, kicked himself up into the air, and looked around for Yorke. Spotting the captain a few yards away, Allard stroked strongly toward him. Yorke was beginning to sink, but he reached him in time to grab his coat and pull him up.

He managed to work off his own boots but couldn't do anything about Yorke's. Struggling against the pull of the water, he began kicking toward the distant shoreline, hauling his captain with him. Glancing behind him, he saw flames spurt up through one of the open hatches on the *Ghost*. And then the schooner came apart in a huge explosion that seemed like the end of the world. Flames and noise filled the air, and a horrible concussive force slammed into him and Yorke and drove them under the water. The blast sent a good-sized wave racing toward the shore.

Seconds ticked by, stretching out to more than a minute, and there was no sign of Allard or Yorke in the disturbed water. Then, with a great floundering splash, Allard broke the surface. He reached down and, with a grunt of effort, pulled Yorke up into the air as well. The captain was beginning to come around, but he was dazed and less than half conscious, with no idea of what was going on.

"Hang on, Cap'n," Allard said into his ear. "For God's sake, hang on! I'll get you to shore."

Holding Yorke up with one arm, he used the other to stroke toward the coastline, kicking wearily with his legs as he did so. Their progress was slow but steady. If Allard didn't tire and let them go under . . . if the Yankees didn't come along and pick them up as prisoners . . . if the sharks stayed away . . . they might have a chance. They might live.

Behind them, floating debris from the *Ghost* blazed on the surface of the water. The blast had broken the ship into two main sections. Those larger pieces went down, sliding through the Atlantic waters toward the bottom. That beautiful boat, the pride of the Tyler shipyard, the pride of Malachi Tyler himself, was gone.

But Allard wouldn't allow himself to think about that. All he thought of was staying afloat and reaching the shore. He thought of Diana, and somehow, despite everything, he kept going.

CHAPTER SEVEN

Homecoming

A UTUMN HAD COME TO Charleston, and with it came the realization that the man Diana loved had been gone far longer than she had expected. There had been no word from Allard, Barnaby Yorke, or anyone else connected with the *Ghost*. When Allard had left, he had said the ship would be out a couple of weeks, maybe a month. But more than two months had gone by since then.

During the days, Diana was able to cope fairly well. She told herself that Allard was fine, that the *Ghost* had simply found plenty of Yankee shipping upon which to prey, and that he was probably having the time of his life playing privateer. That was what he had wanted since he'd found out about his grandfather. He wanted to live up to the legacy of Black Nick Tyler.

But surely this voyage would get all that out of his system, Diana told herself, and when it was over, and he was home again, he would be able to settle down, to make a life together with her and the children they would have. And when the war was over, everything would be fine. Everything.

At night, though, it was a different story. At night Diana lay in the bed in her room in the Tyler mansion—because she still stubbornly refused her mother's pleas that she move to the Oaks—and horrible images crept unbidden into her mind. Images of Allard languishing behind bars in some Yankee prison, where he had been locked up after being caught. Worse still, sometimes she saw his lifeless body drifting under the sea, pale and drowned and dead, with fish plucking his eyes from his head and gnawing on his flesh. What if the *Ghost* had been sunk? There was a war on, after all, and men died during times of war. What if he was gone? What if she never saw him again?

Those were the thoughts that tortured her in the darkness. She wished she could sleep as well as Lucinda seemed to. The older girl was spending more and more of her time in a stupor these days, and Diana began to wonder if she was using some sort of drug to achieve that. Maybe she ought to ask Ellie, she thought. The housemaid always seemed to know everything that was going on in the mansion.

On a rainy day in late September, a gray, gloomy day that matched her mood perfectly, Diana sat in the parlor and tried to work up some interest in the things Katherine Tyler was saying. Katherine was talking about the wedding, a subject she brought up less and less often these days. Diana knew from the look in the woman's eyes that she was tormented by her own worries about Allard. That was understandable. He was her baby, after all. Her only son.

Diana waited until Katherine paused and then said, "You know, Allard should be here for all these plans. Maybe we should wait until he gets back before we decide everything about the wedding."

Katherine laughed, but the sound lacked its usual vibrancy. "Dear, men don't care about such things," she said. "When you get right down to it, weddings are for the women. The men are perfectly happy to just show up when they're supposed to, stand where you tell them to stand, and say what you tell them to say. And if they actually do all of that, you're incredibly lucky and the wedding is perfect!"

"Maybe so," Diana said. "I just thought Allard might like to have something to do with the planning."

"I promise you, dear, whatever he's doing now, he's too busy to even be thinking about such things. And if I know Barnaby Yorke, he's probably having too good a time, as well!"

"You know Captain Yorke pretty well, don't you?" Diana asked, thinking about the rather scandalous things her mother and grand-mother had hinted about during that dinner at the Oaks.

"Oh, of course. He was the first mate on most of the ships that Nick Tyler—that's Malachi's father—captained."

Diana smiled and murmured, "Black Nick."

"Allard's told you about his grandfather, has he?" Katherine frowned a little in disapproval, but the expression was short-lived. Her face became wistful instead as she went on, "Back in the days when Malachi and I were first married, when he was working so hard to get the shipyard started, Nick would sail into Charleston Harbor in one ship or another and stop to visit on his way to China or India or Africa, all those wild places where he went all the time. And of course, Barnaby would be with him, so I came to know him quite well. I mean, Malachi and I came to know him, of course. He became a good friend."

Katherine sighed, and as Diana looked at the expression on the older woman's face, saw the warmth in her eyes, and heard the long-ing in that sigh, she thought, *It's true. What Mother and Grandmother said was true.* Katherine Tyler had been in love with Barnaby Yorke back in the days when she was a young wife and not yet a mother.

Diana glanced at the ceiling, thinking about Lucinda lying in her bedroom, and wondered suddenly if it was possible . . . if there was even a chance . . . that Captain Yorke was really Lucinda's father.

She banished that thought. For one thing, it was none of her busi-ness, and for another, Katherine had been incredibly kind to her, and she had no right to be thinking such shameful things about her. What was past was past, and Diana knew she would never dare ask her fu-ture mother-in-law if she had had an affair with a dashingly handsome sailor more than twenty years ago.

The memory-laden silence in the room was threatening to become awkward. Diana was grateful when it was interrupted by the jangling of the bell from the front door.

"My, who would be out visiting on a miserable day like this?" Katherine wondered aloud. "Thomas, see who's there, please."

"Yes'm," the elderly servant answered from the foyer. "On my way, ma'am."

Katherine took a deep breath, smiled at Diana, and said, "Now, where were we, dear? We were talking about the music for the wedding, weren't we?"

"Yes, but I—"

Diana stopped her response short as she heard shuffling footsteps and a murmur of voices from the foyer. Then Thomas exclaimed, "Oh, my dear Lord!" and she knew something was terribly wrong. It was bad news on the doorstep. What else could it be on a day like today? And bad news meant Allard.

Without thinking, she bolted to her feet and lunged for the door of the parlor, ignoring Katherine as the older woman called out to her. Diana reached the door and caught hold of the jamb for support, thinking that she might collapse if someone had come to the Tyler mansion bearing the news that Allard was dead. Her fingers clutched tightly at the smooth wood as she saw the two raggedly dressed men standing there with Thomas, rainwater sluicing off their sodden clothing and forming puddles on the fine parquet floor. Their hair and beards were long and untrimmed. Soaked as they were, the men looked like half-drowned wharf rats.

But as Diana's heart began to slam madly against the wall of her chest, she recognized the more slender of the two disreputable-looking figures and knew that it was not bad news that had come to call today after all. Instead, it was the best news of all.

"Allard!" she screamed.

She flung herself toward him, going into his open arms with no thought of how soaked his clothes were. She didn't even notice her own clothes growing wet as he enfolded her in a tight embrace. All she felt was the way his heart beat against hers and how his gaunt frame was shaken by tremors that went all through him.

"Diana," he whispered hoarsely into her ear as he lifted one hand to her head and shakily stroked her long red hair. "Diana . . . I thought I'd never again hold you like this . . ."

"Good Lord!" Katherine exclaimed as she followed Diana into the parlor. "Allard, is it . . . is it really you? I'll swan, it is!" She stepped forward, laughing and crying at the same time, tears of joy and relief rolling down her face as she hugged both Allard and Diana, spreading her arms wide to take them both in.

The three of them stood there holding each other and crying, not knowing or caring how much time was passing. Finally, Katherine lifted her tear-streaked face and looked at the drenched figure in the foyer. "Barnaby . . . ?" she asked.

"Aye, Katie," he told her. "It's me, all right, big as life and twice as ugly." He grinned. "You know what they say about a bad penny always turnin' up."

She released Allard and Diana and stepped over to Yorke, tentatively lifting a hand and holding it out to him. She touched him lightly on the arm, as if to make sure that he was really there. Then she moved her hand up his arm until it rested on the back of his neck, and she pulled him down from his great height so that she could raise her face to his and press her lips against his in a long kiss.

Ellie had heard the commotion and come down from upstairs in time to join Thomas as the butler held back while the white folks had their joyous reunion. The two slaves exchanged a worried glance as Katherine kissed Barnaby Yorke with such obvious longing mixed with her relief. As happy as they were to see that Marse Allard was still alive, Captain Yorke's arrival might stir up the Tyler household, and neither of them wanted that.

Katherine finally broke the kiss and stepped back quickly, pressing her fingers to her mouth as if she couldn't believe what she had just done. Yorke smiled faintly and said, "I'm mighty glad to see you too, Katie, but maybe we'd best leave it at that." He inclined his head meaningfully toward Allard and Diana, who were still so wrapped up in each other that they didn't seem to be aware of anything going on around them.

"Yes," Katherine said, her voice trembling a little. "It . . . it's good to see you, Barnaby. We were starting to get worried about you and

Allard." She laughed. "I should have known you were all right, though. You're the luckiest man I've ever known. You always have been."

"Aye," Yorke said. "I'm lucky." But there was a certain touch of hollowness in his tone that belied the words.

Suddenly, a fit of coughing seized Allard, shaking him so badly that Diana was forced to step back. She held his shoulders and asked anxiously, "Are you all right?"

"The lad's got the grippe and maybe a touch o' fever," Yorke said as he put a hand on Allard's shoulder to steady the younger man. "We've been out in the weather a lot lately. He needs some dry clothes and a warm bed."

"Why, he certainly does!" Katherine said. "You both do."

"I'll take the dry clothes," Yorke said, "but I'd rather have a good stiff drink instead o' the bed."

"Thomas, take Allard and Captain Yorke upstairs and see to getting them dry," Katherine ordered briskly.

Diana clutched at Allard's arm. "I can help," she said.

Katherine took hold of her and steered her away. "No, let Thomas tend to this. In a little while, you can go upstairs and see Allard again."

Clearly, Diana didn't like it, but she stepped back and let Thomas take Allard's arm and help him upstairs. Yorke lingered for a moment at the bottom of the staircase, and Katherine said, "I don't see how the two of you got so wet and ragged-looking just coming here from the docks."

"We didn't come from the docks, Katie," Yorke explained.

She frowned. "Then where did you leave the ship?"

"The *Ghost* is gone." Bleak lines were etched in Yorke's weathered face now. "The Yankees sank her off the coast of Georgia."

Katherine pressed her hand to her mouth again. "Oh, my God." Malachi was going to be devastated when he found out that the schooner had been sunk. Surely, though, his relief at Allard's homecoming would more than offset the loss. Katherine wanted to think so, anyway.

Yorke started up the stairs, but Katherine stepped forward to stop him again. "Barnaby . . . thank you for bringing my son home."

Yorke smiled but shook his head sadly. "'Twas him who brought me home, Katie, not the other way around. You have Allard to thank for that. If it had been up to me . . . I would have gone down with the ship."

SOMEWHERE ALONG the way Allard passed out. Either that, or he simply went to sleep. He was never sure which, and of course it didn't really matter. What was important was that, when he woke up, he was clean and dry and comfortable for the first time in what seemed like ages. He let out a little moan as he shifted slightly and felt clean, smooth sheets against his skin.

"Allard? Allard, are you awake?"

The anxious voice belonged to Diana. Eagerness to see her pried open his heavy eyelids, and he looked up into her face, her beautiful face, as she hovered over him with a worried frown creasing her forehead. The expression didn't make her any less lovely, though.

"Diana," he whispered.

His arms lay outside the covers. She caught hold of his left hand in both of hers and said, "I'm here, Allard, I'm right here with you, and I'm not going anywhere."

With a sigh, he closed his eyes. "Diana," he said again, and her name was like a prayer, a prayer of thanksgiving.

He went away again for a while, but when he woke up for the second time, she was still there, just as she had promised she would be, and she still held his hand. More than just the warmth of the covers spread over him in the bed in which he lay. He was filled with an even greater warmth that flowed into him from her, the warmth of the love they felt for one another. Even before he opened his eyes, his lips curved into a smile, and Diana must have seen it, because she said, "He's waking up again."

Someone rested a hand on his forehead, and he heard his mother say, "He's burning up too. Thomas, send the carriage to fetch the doctor right away."

"Yes'm," Thomas answered. "And should I send word to Marse Malachi that Marse Allard has come home?"

"Yes, of course."

Allard heard the door open and close. A great weariness had him in its grip, but he forced his eyes open anyway and looked up to see both Diana and his mother looking down at him. "I think I've died . . . and gone to heaven," he rasped.

"Goodness, this isn't heaven," Katherine said, "but it's a gift from God that you've come back to us, Allard. Barnaby told us about how the ship was lost."

"I'm . . . sorry."

"Don't be. Your father can build more ships, but there's no way to replace *you*."

He felt an urge to sit up, and as he tried to, he said, "I'm all right—"

"No, you're not," Diana said as she put a firm hand on his shoulder and held him down. "You're sick, Allard, very sick. You have a fever."

He realized he was too weak to struggle, so he allowed his head to sag back against the pillow. "All right," he breathed. "I guess I'm . . . not going anywhere."

"You're most certainly *not* going anywhere," Katherine announced. "You're going to lay right there and let us take care of you until you're well again."

Allard didn't feel like arguing, especially because another coughing jag hit him just then. He had been suffering from similar spells for several days now, ever since it had started raining so much as he and Captain Yorke walked along the roads that led them toward Charleston. Occasionally they got a ride on a wagon from a passing farmer, but most of the time they had to travel by shank's mare. It had taken them over a week to get here from the isolated spot on the southern Georgia coastline where they had finally washed ashore in the darkness after the sinking of the *Ghost*.

Diana put an arm around his shoulders and supported him until the coughing fit passed, leaving him weaker and more shaken than ever before. He wondered suddenly if he were going to die from the illness that gripped him. Wouldn't that be the most terrible luck, to have survived the loss of the schooner and the long, grueling walk home, only to succumb when he finally got here? That couldn't happen, it just couldn't, not when he was finally back with Diana.

Someone lifted a cup of hot broth to his lips. He sipped from it eagerly, and it eased his throat. He drifted in and out of awareness for an unknowable time after that. His illness distorted everything. He didn't know if the things he saw and heard were real or just images generated by his fevered imagination.

He thought his father came in, patted him awkwardly on the shoulder, and told him he was glad that he was home. Captain Yorke was there part of the time too, and so was Lucinda, who looked rather sick herself. And a burly man with muttonchop whiskers lifted his eyelids and then pressed an ear to his chest while thumping on him. Allard heard murmuring, then angry words from his father that he couldn't make out, and then quiet crying from someone, probably his mother or Diana or both. The doctor had told them that he was going to die. Allard expected as much. He wanted to tell them all good-bye first, before he went into whatever lay beyond death. He especially wanted to talk to Diana, to tell her how much she meant to him and to urge her to go on with her life, to find whatever happiness she could without him. He couldn't bear the thought of her mourning him for the rest of her days. After all, it was his own fault that this was happening to him. If he hadn't insisted on going back to sea with Captain Yorke for one last voyage. But he fell asleep before he could say anything to anybody.

THE NEXT time he woke up, he thought for a second that he must still be trudging through the rain again, because he was soaking wet. He must have imagined reaching Charleston and making his way to his parents' house. Now he was right back where he had started, and that was so discouraging that he felt like giving up. He was never going to get home.

Only he *was* home. He had to be because he heard his mother's voice calling urgently, "The fever's broken! Praise the Lord, the fever's broken!"

A soft, dry cloth mopped the sweat away from his face. Warm lips pressed against his forehead. And he felt Diana's fingers clasp his. He knew that everything was going to be all right now. The worst of the ordeal was over.

By that evening, he was dressed in a clean, dry nightshirt again, and the sweat-soaked bedding had been changed. He sat propped up in bed with several pillows behind him, weak as a kitten but alert and aware of what was going on around him.

Diana sat in a chair beside the bed, close enough that she could hold his hand. His mother was on the other side of the bed, and his father and Captain Yorke were in armchairs near the foot.

Malachi said, "The doctor tells us you're going to be just fine, son. You just need a lot of rest to recover from being so sick."

"A lot of rest and people who love you to take care of you," Katherine added. She reached over and patted his leg through the covers.

Allard looked at his father and said, "I'm sorry about the *Ghost*."

Malachi's mouth tightened, but he said, "Don't worry about it, Allard. There are losses in war. I'm just glad you made it home safely."

"Along with Cap'n Yorke."

Malachi glanced toward Yorke and flatly said, "Yes, of course."

"How's the war going?"

"Oh, let's don't talk about that," Katherine said. "Can't we discuss something more pleasant? I'd like to hear about how you got back to Charleston, Allard."

"There wasn't anything pleasant about that," he said. "We swam ashore, and from there it was just a long, hard walk. I didn't have my boots, but I remember I managed to get some shoes somewhere."

"We bought 'em off a farmer," Yorke supplied. "I still had some coins in my pocket, so we were able to buy shoes for the lad and food to keep us goin' along the way."

Allard nodded. "Yes, we bought what food we could, but as you can tell by looking at us, we went hungry a lot of the time."

"Yes, you're skin and bones!" his mother said. "But we'll fatten you back up, just you wait and see."

"Go on with your story," his father urged.

"Well, that's really all there is to tell. It was worse after it started raining, of course. I guess I caught a touch of the grippe somewhere along the way—"

Malachi grunted. "More than a touch. Dr. Sanders told us you probably weren't going to make it."

Katherine glared at him and said, "Now, Malachi, don't exaggerate. I never gave up hope, and neither did Diana."

"That's just my point." Malachi leaned forward and clasped his hands together between his knees. "It's these two women right here who pulled you through, son. I never saw a more determined pair in all my life. They nursed you night and day until your fever broke. I hope you appreciate what they've done for you."

He squeezed Diana's hand, looked from her to his mother and back again. "I do," he said.

"Good," Malachi said with a curt nod. He sat back again and added, "Maybe now you'll have sense enough to stay home in the future instead of giving in to every little whim."

"Malachi!" Katherine exclaimed.

"I'm just telling the boy straight out what he needs to hear, Katherine," Malachi defended himself. "He's lucky to be alive, and he's old enough now to forget all that nonsense about glory and adventure. That never accomplishes anything. Why, he went sailing off before, and all it did was nearly get him killed. Not only that, but a lot of good men *did* get killed, and there's a fine ship in pieces on the bottom of the ocean. It wasn't any sort of grand adventure, it was just a waste!"

Allard looked at Yorke, expecting the captain to say something in his own defense, but Yorke just sat there, looking at the floor.

"Father, I've already given my word that I'm not sailing again, but you can't say that what the cap'n and I did was a waste. We were trying to help the cause. You *do* think the Confederacy needs to win this war, don't you?"

"Allard, please," Diana said. "Don't get all upset—"

"Wars are necessary sometimes," Malachi broke in, "but they should be fought by men who know what they're doing, not by boys who think it's going to be fun."

"I'd wager that a lot of the soldiers who enlisted were boys who thought it would be fun to fight the Yankees," Allard argued. "But after what happened at Manassas, they know now it's not. They haven't quit, though."

Katherine said, "I really don't think it's a good idea to get Allard all worked up, as weak as he is. He needs to get his strength back—"

"I just want to make sure he hasn't gotten some foolish notion in his head about going back to sea," Malachi insisted. "Yorke can if he wants to, but not my son."

Allard looked at Yorke and said, "Is it true, Cap'n? Are you going back out?"

Yorke finally looked up and met Allard's eyes. "What else can I do, lad?" he asked. "I'm a seagoin' man. Always have been, always will be. I can't have solid ground under my feet for too long at a time."

"What are you going to do for a ship?"

Malachi said, "We've already talked about that."

Allard's eyebrows rose in astonishment. The very idea that his father might be willing to provide another ship for Yorke came as a total surprise. He had supposed that Yorke would have to seek a berth on some other vessel, even though it would mean he wouldn't be the vessel's captain.

"All right, I'm going to have to put my foot down," Katherine said firmly. "There's been enough talk for now. You men, just shoo on out of here. Allard needs to rest."

"Fine with me," Malachi said. "I have work to do." He got to his feet but paused before leaving the room. He looked at Allard and said, "It really is good to have you back, son."

"Thanks," Allard said grudgingly. He knew it was difficult for his father to express any emotion—except for anger, frustration, or anything else that involved planting a good swift kick in someone's backside.

Malachi left the bedroom. So did Yorke, but not before saying quietly, "We'll talk later, lad."

"Aye, Cap'n," Allard told him, and that brought a fleeting smile to Yorke's weathered face.

"Now that those two are gone," Katherine said, "you can just lie back and rest."

"Mother . . . do you think I could have a moment alone with Diana?"

"Are you asking me to leave?" For a second, hurt appeared in Katherine's eyes, but it was quickly replaced by understanding. "Well, of course you are, and that's a good sign," she added her usual laugh. Then she turned to Diana, "But remember, he needs his rest. Nothing strenuous, you two."

Blushing prettily, Diana said, "There won't be, Mrs. Tyler. I can promise you that."

"All right, then. I'll just go downstairs." She left the room and eased the door shut behind her.

"She'll probably stay and listen at the door," Allard said with a grin.

"I will not!" Katherine called through the panel. They heard her footsteps receding down the hallway.

Allard patted the bed beside him. Diana hesitated, then perched on the edge of the mattress. "I know you're weak," she said. "This is probably as close as I should get."

"I just want to hold you for a minute," he said. She leaned against him, and he put his arms around her, holding her tenderly as she rested her head on his shoulder.

"Oh, Allard," Diana whispered. "I thought I had lost you."

"I thought I was lost," he told her. "I thought I'd never see you again, and that hurt worse than anything else. But now that we're together, nothing will ever part us."

She lifted her head a little so she could look into his face. "Do you mean that?"

"Of course I do."

"You don't feel . . . trapped? You don't really want to go back to sea with Captain Yorke?"

He smiled and shook his head. "I know what's really important now. I can help the cause by working here in Charleston, and I can be with you too. The way it all turned out, I don't regret sailing with the cap'n, but that was enough for me." He chuckled. "Just don't tell my father I said that. I don't want to give him the satisfaction of thinking that he's right any more than he already does."

Diana nuzzled against him again. "Now if the war were just over," she murmured, "everything would be perfect."

"Yes, it would," Allard said.

But he was afraid that that might be a long time in coming. Perfection always was.

HIS STRENGTH came back amazingly quickly. Good food and plenty of rest proved to be just what he needed, and after a week had passed, he was up and around and, truth be told, champing at the bit for something to do. A man could only lie in bed and be waited on hand and foot for so long.

So over his mother's objections and with Diana's worried frown following him, Allard dressed and took the carriage to the shipyard. The rainy weather had finally cleared, and it was a beautiful autumn day. From the docks, Fort Sumter was clearly visible out in the harbor, the Confederate flag fluttering gently above the fortress.

When the groom handling the team brought the carriage to a

stop, Allard climbed out and looked around the sprawling shipyard. Numerous vessels were in various stages of completion, and floating alongside the wharf were those that were almost finished. His back stiffened and his eyes widened as he thought that he recognized one of the ships moored there. He walked toward it.

Before he got there, he noticed the two men standing on the dock and recognized them as his father and Barnaby Yorke. They saw him coming and moved to meet him.

"What are you doing here, son?" Malachi asked with a frown. "Does your mother know you left the house?"

Allard answered. "She didn't particularly like it, but she knows."

Malachi grunted. "I'm surprised she let you get away."

"How are you feelin', lad?" Yorke asked.

"Much better," Allard replied. "Too good to stay cooped up inside any longer." He waved a hand toward the ship tied up at the dock. "Is that . . . ?"

"Aye." Yorke smiled. "The *Albert Ross*."

"I figured the Yankees got her."

"I thought they would have too, but when that cruiser came after us, she was able to slip away. The boys took her out to sea and circled 'way around to avoid the Yankees before they slipped past the blockade. It was a mighty fine bit o' sailin', and I couldn't be any prouder of them than I am."

"I'm just glad the trip wasn't a total loss," Malachi said.

Yorke grimaced briefly but didn't say anything in response.

Allard nodded toward the *Albert Ross*. "What are you going to do with her?"

"Well . . . Captain Yorke and I have been talking about outfitting her as a blockade-runner."

Allard was surprised again. "That's what you meant when you said you were going to help the cap'n go to sea again."

"I have a considerable investment to recoup," Malachi said dryly. "And running the blockade promises to be considerably more lucrative than privateering. I've already spoken to George Trenholm about it, and he agrees with me." Trenholm was probably the most important and influential businessman in Charleston, heading up as he did a consortium of importing and exporting firms with offices in Charleston as well as in New York and London. "I'm going to provide several ships for him," Malachi went on, "as well as retaining ownership of this one." He gestured toward the *Ross*.

"And you'll be in command?" Allard asked Yorke.

The older man nodded. "Aye. And it's grateful I am to your father for the opportunity, lad."

"Just don't let me down this time," Malachi growled.

Allard wanted to leap to the captain's defense, but Yorke caught his eye and gave him a minuscule shake of the head. He thought he understood what Yorke meant. The proof was in the doing. The best way to make Malachi eat his words was to be successful in running the blockade.

One of the shipyard workers called Malachi over to discuss some problem with him, and that left Allard and Yorke alone for a minute beside the captured cutter. Quietly, Yorke said, "I'll be needin' a good first mate when I ship out again, but I know better than to ask you if you want the job, Allard."

"I couldn't take it even if I wanted to. I made a promise, Cap'n . . . I intend to keep it."

"I'd think less of you if you didn't."

"I'll be thinking about you while you're at sea, though." Allard frowned in thought. "There's one thing you could do for me, Cap'n."

"Whatever you say, lad."

"I assume this ship will need a new name?"

"I don't know who Albert Ross was, but I'd be willin' to lay odds that he was a damned Yankee. So, yes, it surely will."

"You asked me once about calling your other ship the *Diana*. I'd be honored if you'd give that name to this one."

A grin split Yorke's face. "Done and done!" he said. "The *Diana* she'll be. And I'm glad to do it in honor of a good friend and his beautiful wife."

"She's not my wife yet," Allard pointed out with a smile.

"When *is* this weddin' I've heard so much about supposed to happen? I'd sort of like to see you two hitched before I head back out to sea."

"Soon," Allard said. "And to tell you the truth, Cap'n, it can't be soon enough for me. I'd just as soon skip all the fancy plans and just find a preacher to marry us."

"You can't do that! Katie would never get over it."

Allard grinned. "I know. She'd never forgive me, either."

"Well, maybe you can hurry things along a little. I know the sea will always be out there, but it's beginnin' to call to me again."

IN LATE November 1861, in the famous Circular Congregational Church, next to Institute Hall where the Ordinance of Secession had been signed eleven months earlier, Allard Kent Tyler and Diana Laura Pinckston were joined in holy matrimony in a beautiful service packed with friends and family from all over Charleston and the surrounding area. The bride wore a lovely white gown trimmed with yards of gossamer lace, and the groom was exceedingly handsome as he stood next to her. If it had been possible, of course, Allard would have had his longtime friend Robert Gilmore as his best man, but since Robert was serving with the Hampton Legion, his brother, Michael Campbell "Cam" Gilmore, took his place in the wedding party. Diana's maid of honor was her friend Jacqueline Lockhart, who came into the city along with her family from their plantation, Four Winds. Diana's father, Maj. Stafford Pinckston, was also unable to attend due to his military obligations, so the bride was given away by her maternal grandfather, retired Col. Francis Rutherford. The wedding went off without a hitch—so to speak—and everyone in Charleston agreed that it had been absolutely beautiful. Katherine Tyler, the groom's mother, cried for hours and had the time of her life.

Less than a week later, the former Federal revenue cutter *Albert*

Ross—now painted gray so as to blend in with the night and the sea, equipped with a small but powerful steam engine, and newly christened the *Diana*—slipped out of Charleston Harbor one foggy night, raced unmolested past the Yankee blockade, and set sail for Nassau with Capt. Barnaby Yorke in command. The ship had been largely gutted belowdecks to make a larger cargo hold, which was now filled with bales of cotton that would be unloaded at Nassau and put on a ship belonging to Fraser, Trenholm and Company of Liverpool, England. The *Diana* would return from Nassau with supplies for Charleston. The Yankee blockade was a good military tactic, but it was going to be beaten. Men like Barnaby Yorke would see to that. But he would have to do it without the help of Allard Tyler, who was enjoying a brief honeymoon with his new wife. Somebody else could deal with the damned Yankees for a while.

PART TWO

"What a cruel thing is war."

—*Gen. Robert E. Lee, in a*
letter to his wife

CHAPTER EIGHT

Sins of the Past

ALTHOUGH ON OCCASION HE still thought of himself as a farm boy, Cam Gilmore had spent quite a bit of time in Charleston. Thus the city hadn't overwhelmed him with its size and cosmopolitan air when he reported to the Citadel in September 1861. And his year of instruction at the Arsenal, the junior branch of the South Carolina Military Academy situated upstate in Columbia, had prepared him reasonably well for his courses at the Citadel—even though he had spent more time at the Arsenal gambling and dallying with many agreeable, attractive ladies than he had on his studies.

And of course there was no shortage of young women in Charleston who were more than happy to spend time with a tall, handsome, brown-haired lad in the natty gray uniform of a Citadel cadet. Considering that the cadets were officially a part of the Confederate army now and were counted upon to defend the city if the Yankees came calling, it was almost patriotic for the young women of Charleston to lavish their affections on the boys from the Citadel.

Given all that, and despite the fact that there was a war on, Cam was, as the country folks sometimes called it, as happy as a pig in a mud wallow.

It was a good life. Due to his natural intelligence, he was able to handle his studies without devoting a lot of time or effort to them, which left him free to seek out more enjoyable activities. Sometimes, though, he felt a twinge of regret when he thought about Lucinda Tyler. The sister of his brother's friend, Lucinda was several years older than Cam, but that hadn't stopped her from spending a great deal of time with him the previous winter. He couldn't exactly say that Lucinda had introduced him to the pleasures of the flesh—but she had certainly pointed out some interesting variations to him and had performed them enthusiastically, even eagerly. They had been together as often as possible over the long holiday vacation at Christmastime.

But then he'd had to return to Columbia and the Arsenal, and he hadn't seen Lucinda again. Since coming to the Citadel he had visited the Tyler house on a couple of occasions, but each time, Lucinda had been feeling poorly, according to her mother, and Cam hadn't been able to see her. He hoped that she was all right—whenever he devoted that much thought to the matter.

In early November, the Yankees attacked Fort Walker and Fort Beauregard, which were situated on points of land guarding the entrance to Port Royal Sound, a fine harbor about seventy-five miles south of Charleston. Pounded by a terrible barrage from a fleet of Federal warships, the defenders inside the forts held out for a while but were finally forced to flee. The Yankees steamed into the harbor and took control of it. The idea of the hated Northerners being in control of any part of the Palmetto State enraged South Carolinians everywhere, but the outcome of the battle was especially worrisome to the citizens of Charleston. It seemed quite likely to them that the Federals would use Port Royal Sound as a base of operations from which to launch an invasion of the city. Confederate defenders scrambled to get into position to defend Charleston from such an invasion.

The Citadel cadets formed one of the front lines of that defense. They were sent to Wappoo Cut on James Island, just south of the city, where for several days Cam crouched in a hastily dug trench with his rifle in hand, waiting for the Northern barbarians.

It was then that the realization began to soak in : if the Yankees came, they would do their best to *kill* him. The only way he could stop them would be by trying to kill them. He scratched at the sand that got into everything and swatted at the bugs that swarmed even in the winter and told himself that he might actually *die* here.

It was a sobering moment for a young man who had always considered himself indestructible. He didn't want to die, especially not without having experienced even more of life than he already had. He vowed to himself, then and there, that he was going to see Lucinda Tyler again.

The Union invasion of Charleston from Port Royal Sound never materialized, and after several days the cadets were sent back to the Citadel. Not long after that, Allard came to see Cam and asked him to be the best man at his wedding to Diana Pinckston, since Robert was somewhere in Virginia with the Hampton Legion. Cam agreed without hesitation. After all, Lucinda was Allard's sister, which meant she was bound to be at the wedding.

That was how Cam came to find himself standing stiffly in his dress uniform in the Circular Congregational Church while a black-robed minister droned on about the sacred institution of holy matrimony. He didn't have any real interest in the ceremony, so he looked across at Lucinda instead as she stood beside Jacqueline Lockhart, Diana's maid of honor.

Cam had attempted to court both Diana and Jacqueline in the past, but somehow both girls had managed to withstand his charms. Diana had only been interested in Allard, and Jacqueline was in love with Robert. Lucinda had been a challenge at first. She seemed to enjoy insulting Cam and pretending that she didn't like him, but eventually she had come around. She had actually been quite aggressive, so he hadn't had to pursue her very hard.

Now, after not having seen her in months, Cam was surprised at the way she looked. She was still beautiful, but she had lost weight and her face was rather thin and delicate-looking. Cosmetics gave her skin some color and to a certain extent hid the dark circles under her eyes, but Cam had made a long, intensive study of women and could tell that something was wrong. He had no idea what it was, but he intended to find out.

When the wedding ceremony was over, there was a ball next door in Institute Hall. Cam found a cup of punch first and then sought out Lucinda, finding her at the edge of the area that had been cleared for dancing. Allard and Diana were taking the traditional first dance alone in the middle of the floor when he came up to Lucinda. "Would you like some punch?" he asked and held the cup toward her.

She flinched a little, as if surprised that he had spoken to her. "No, thank you," she said quietly.

"Are you sure?" He took a sip. "It's good."

Lucinda smiled thinly and shook her head. "No, that's all right."

"How are you, Lucinda? It's been a long time."

"It certainly has." Her voice had a husky edge to it that sounded a bit strange coming from her frail figure. She looked like someone who had been sick for a long time. He wasn't the sort to worry a great deal about other people's health, but he felt some concern for Lucinda, for old time's sake if for no other reason. But there was more to it than that, of course, because he wanted to get together with her again. His experience at Wappoo Cut had made him determined to embrace life as fully as possible. And he couldn't think of any better way to do that than by embracing Lucinda Tyler.

"Well, how are you?" he asked again. "You're looking lovely." That wasn't a lie. Despite everything, she was still one of the most attractive girls in the city.

"Thank you," she murmured. "And you're very handsome in your uniform."

"You think so?" he asked with a grin.

"Of course."

He set the half-empty cup aside on a small table. "Why don't we dance?" he asked. By now others had joined the happy couple on the dance floor, and Cam saw no reason why he and Lucinda shouldn't be out there as well.

She shook her head. "I don't think so."

"Why not? Don't you like me anymore?"

For a second, something blazed in her eyes, and he thought she was going to slap him. If she did, it would hardly be the first time a girl had slapped him. That was part of the price a fellow sometimes paid to get what he wanted.

But rather than striking him, Lucinda controlled herself and said in quiet, icy tones, "I don't want to dance with you, Cam. In fact, I think it would be a good idea for you to go away and leave me alone. I'd rather you didn't speak to me again."

That took him by such surprise it was all he could do not to stare at her. "Not speak to you?" he repeated. "Why in the world wouldn't I want to speak to you? I want to do more than that. I want to dance with you, and I want to—"

She stepped closer to him, obviously forcing a smile onto her face, and spoke in a voice so low that only he could hear it over the sound of the music playing in the hall. "I know what you want to do, you bastard. It was all you ever wanted to do last winter. But it will never happen again, do you understand me? Never again!"

She was mad at him, and he felt a surge of his own anger at the patent unfairness of it. "Look, Lucinda, if you're upset because I left, that wasn't my fault. I had to go back to the Arsenal, and then, when the term there was over, I had to go home. But since I've been in Charleston this fall, I've been to your house several times, and your mother wouldn't let me see you. She said you were feeling poorly."

"That's what I *told* her to say," Lucinda hissed, "so I wouldn't have to see you."

Cam blinked rapidly. "I don't understand. I thought we got along just fine. Better than fine. When we—"

"Don't say it," she warned. "Don't you dare say it."

He lowered his voice and forged ahead stubbornly. "When we were together, you were just as eager as I was. Hell, most of the time it was your idea! You couldn't keep your hands off me!"

Again she looked like she wanted to slap him or choke him or claw his eyes out. Instead, she said, "If you don't go away and leave me alone, I'm going to ask my father to make you leave the hall. He'll do it too. You know he will."

Cam frowned. He knew Malachi Tyler didn't like many people to start with, but he was one of the man's least favorite people. Malachi probably wouldn't hesitate to escort him out of the ball, probably hurrying him along at the door with a swift kick in the pants.

He didn't want that, but it bothered him that Lucinda didn't like him anymore. Worse than that, really, because she seemed to actually hate him now. And he couldn't think of a thing he had done to make her feel that way. Still, you couldn't argue with a force of nature, and that was just about what an angry woman amounted to.

He said, "All right, I won't bother you, if that's the way you want it. But do I have to leave the ball?"

She relented a little. "No, you can stay. Just get as far away from me as you can and stay there. Do you understand?"

"No," he said sullenly, "but I'll do it anyway. I have to tell you, though, Lucinda, I think you're making a big mistake."

She laughed, but there was no real humor in the sound. "I'm making a big mistake, am I? How do you figure that, Cam?"

"Well, I live here in Charleston now, at the Citadel. You and I could see each other all the time. It wouldn't be quite like last winter, when I was staying with your family, but we could still be together and have a fine time."

She shook her head. "No. Just get that idea out of your head, Cam Gilmore. That will never happen again."

He shrugged. "As you wish, Lucinda." He started to turn away but paused to look back at her. "I can tell, though, that you still want me. I can see it in your eyes. You can deny it all you want, but it's the truth."

"*Go away,*" she said through clenched teeth.

With a smug smile on his face, he left her there and went to find some other young woman with whom to dance. He couldn't help noticing that, despite all her insistence that they could never be together again, she hadn't actually denied the last charge he had leveled at her. She hadn't denied that she still wanted him.

THE WORST of it was, Lucinda thought, the self-centered bastard was right. She was already suffering the torments of the damned because she'd had to taper off on the raw opium that she forced Ellie to bring to her from the waterfront apothecary. But this was her brother's wedding day, and she knew her father would be furious and her mother would be humiliated if she was drugged into an insensate state, as she had spent so much of the past few months.

She couldn't help it. The drug was the only thing that allowed her to sleep undisturbed by dreams, and that dreamless sleep was the only haven from the guilt that haunted her.

Lucinda's fingers started to tremble, so she clasped her hands together in the hope that the shaking wouldn't be as noticeable that way. She saw her father making his way toward her across the crowded ballroom and forced a smile onto her face.

"Hello, Father," she said. "It was a lovely wedding, wasn't it?"

"Yes, it was," he agreed. "And Diana certainly made a beautiful bride." He grunted. "Better than that brother of yours deserves, I'm afraid."

"I'm sure she and Allard will be very happy together."

"Only if he actually grows up, as he's promised." Malachi took Lucinda's hand. "Dance with me."

Getting out there and twirling around on the polished hardwood floor was one of the last things in the world Lucinda wanted to do right now, but she couldn't refuse her father's request. For that matter, it hadn't really been a request so much as a command, but that was common with Malachi Tyler. If he could have, he would have ordered the sun to rise in the west and set in the east, just to impose his will on the cosmos.

Lucinda had to grit her teeth against the sickness that churned inside her as she and her father began dancing. Only the fact that she didn't want to disappoint him kept her from bolting from the room.

Unlike most people, she didn't really fear him. Ever since she was a little girl, she had been able to get her way with him. It was like the only soft spot left in his heart was reserved for her. Lord knew she had never done anything to deserve such affection and devotion from him, but she wasn't going to do anything to unnecessarily jeopardize it, either. At least, nothing that he would ever find out about.

"Lucinda, what's wrong? You're, ah, glowing rather, ah, strongly."

What she was doing, she thought, was sweating like a pig, despite the fact that the room wasn't overly warm. She felt the beads of moisture pop out on her forehead and roll down her face.

"I . . . I'm sorry, Father," she managed to say. "I'm suddenly feeling a little faint. Perhaps you should dance with Mother instead."

"I'm not going to dance at all," he said as he came to a stop, "and neither are you." He grasped her arm. "Come along. You need to sit down and rest for a moment."

What she needed was a draft of opium, but of course she couldn't tell him that. She allowed him to lead her to some chairs against the wall, where she sat down and dabbed at her face with a lacy linen handkerchief.

"Should I get you something to drink?" Malachi asked.

Some whiskey laced with the flower of the poppy . . . that would take care of what ailed her. But since she couldn't have that, she just shook her head and said, "No, thank you, I'm fine."

Malachi frowned down at her. "You don't *look* fine. In fact, you look ill. I'm going to find a doctor—"

She reached up and grasped his sleeve. "No, please don't. This . . . this is Allard and Diana's special day. I don't want to ruin it for them. I'll just sit here and rest. I'm sure I'll be all right in a few minutes."

Malachi didn't look convinced, but after a moment he nodded reluctantly. "Very well. But if there's anything I can do to help . . ."

"There's not," Lucinda assured him. "Now, go dance with Mother. I'm sure that would make her very happy."

"I doubt that," he growled. "The last time I looked, she was dancing with that Barnaby Yorke. I'll be glad when he goes to sea again."

Malachi wandered off into the crowd, and Lucinda was glad to see him go. It was difficult keeping up even as flimsy a facade as the one she had erected tonight. She closed her eyes and forced herself to breathe deeply and regularly, telling herself at the same time that she would get through this—somehow.

She had been sitting there about a quarter of an hour and wasn't feeling any better—worse, in fact—when her mother came over with a worried look on her face. She sat down beside her, took hold of one of her hands, and said caringly, "Your father tells me you're not feeling well."

"It's nothing, Mother," Lucinda said, mentally cursing her father for involving her mother in this.

"You don't need to lie to me, dear. I can see with my own eyes that you're sick. The carriage is right outside. Why don't I have you driven home?"

Lucinda was about to argue when she thought about how good it would feel to stretch out in her bed. Not only that, but the wedding was over now. She could have Ellie fetch her what she really needed, and no one would be the wiser.

"All right, Mother," she said, her voice weak. "If you're sure Allard won't be upset that I didn't stay for the whole evening."

"Oh, goodness, Allard won't care. He just got married, so all he's thinking about is his new wife. I'll convey your congratulations on the marriage to him and Diana later, along with your regrets that you couldn't stay."

"Thank you." Lucinda started to get to her feet, but a wave of dizziness hit her, and her mother had to take hold of her arm to steady her.

"I'll swan, you *are* sick, you poor dear."

"Did you think that I didn't want to be here?" Lucinda asked.

"Well, dear, you and your brother have never been all that close. . . . No, no, never mind about that. Let's just get you home, so that you can feel better."

Yes, Lucinda thought, let's get me home so I can talk to Ellie. Then I'll feel better.

Later she remembered little about the carriage ride back to the Tyler mansion, and her memories of being helped inside and up to her room were blurry as well. Somehow Ellie helped her to undress and get into her nightclothes and onto the bed. But Lucinda recalled vividly the frightened look on Ellie's face when she rasped at the housemaid, "Bring it to me."

"Miss Lucinda, I ain't got—" Ellie began.

"Don't lie to me!" Lucinda snapped as she lay back against the pillows piled up behind her. "I know you still have some for emergencies. You'd damned well better not have been nipping at it yourself!"

Ellie made a face. "No ma'am. I ain't touched the stuff. Are you sure—"

"Get it."

Ellie nodded curtly and left the room. Lucinda lay there in agony, both physical and mental, until she came back.

When Ellie returned with the small brown bottle in her hand, Lucinda almost wept in relief and joy. Her own hand shook badly as she held it out. "Let me have it," she said.

Ellie uncorked the bottle and pressed it into Lucinda's hands. She was shaking so badly that Ellie kept her hands wrapped around Lucinda's hands as she lifted the bottle to her lips and took a long swallow.

And then it was gone, and she felt horror course through her because she knew what she had just swallowed wasn't enough. It wouldn't put her to sleep, at least not deeply enough to escape the nightmares.

"Get another bottle!" she gasped.

"There ain't no other bottle, Miss Lucinda. That's all."

"Then go get some more!"

"Can't. Not until tomorrow mornin'. There wouldn't be nobody at that apothecary shop at this time o' night."

Lucinda caught hold of her wrist. "Go pound on the door! Wake the bastard up!"

"I don't know if'n he lives there. I don't 'spect he does."

"He must live around there somewhere," Lucinda said desperately. *"Find him!"*

Ellie shook her head, wide-eyed with fear. "Miss Lucinda, if'n I sneak out o' the house at this time o' night, Thomas gonna find out fo' sure, an' then he'll tell Marse Malachi, and if Marse Malachi ever finds out what I been doin' fo' you, he'll sell me! I can't take the chance."

"I'm . . . I'm ordering you . . ." Lucinda had swallowed enough of the drug so that it was taking effect now, easing her shaking and causing an undeniable lassitude to steal over her. It felt good. It felt wonderful. But Lucinda knew it wouldn't be enough, it wouldn't take her out of reach of the demons that pursued her.

"Miss Lucinda, if'n Marse Malachi was to sell me off, I couldn't he'p you at all. Tomorrow I'll go an' get you some more. I swear it!"

"'S'all right, Ellie," Lucinda slurred. "'S'all right. You jus' . . . run 'long now. Lemme sleep."

"Yes'm," Ellie said with obvious relief. "And I sure hope you gets to feelin' better." She went to the door of the bedroom and slipped out, closing it softly behind her.

Why had that damned Cam Gilmore had to come over and bother her after the wedding? Lucinda asked herself as she sank deeper into the pillows. It was bad enough that she'd had to stand up there at the front of the church with him only a few feet away. She had seen him smirking at her during the ceremony, and she'd wanted to lunge at him and make him pay for what he'd done to her. All the hell she had gone through in the past several months was *his* fault—and he didn't even know it. He didn't care enough to find out what he had done.

Of course, with all those people watching, she hadn't been able to do anything except stand there with a false smile plastered on her face and pray that she would make it through the day.

Thankfully, she had been able to last until after the wedding itself, before the sickness caught up to her. But she was convinced that she would have been able to control it even longer if Cam hadn't come swaggering up, as arrogant as ever, convinced, just as he always had been, that he was irresistible to every woman in the room. The mere sight of him was enough to make her start trembling inside, and once he was that close to her, leaning in to talk to her, so that she had a good view of his soft brown eyes and could smell the bay rum on his freshly shaven cheeks as the tang of it blended with his uniquely masculine scent . . .

My God, she thought as her heart began to pound more heavily. He was right. Even after everything that had happened, despite all the pain he had put her through, a part of her still wanted him. Still remembered what it was like to be with him. She had never loved him, but he had filled something empty and aching inside her. Sort of like the drug did now.

But there was an ache that neither of them could ever touch, a feeling of loss that would never go away. Ever since that horrible night when she had sent Ellie to fetch Aunt Susie . . . the night that her baby was taken from her forever.

It had been Cam Gilmore's baby too, and that was why she could never have it. Forget the shame that would have descended on her and her family alike if it had been known that she was unmarried and in the family way. Forget the fact that her father, in his inevitable rage, probably would have disowned her and cast her out, because not even his tolerance for her excesses would extend that far. Forget the gossip and the sickness and the sheer sordidness of it. She couldn't have the baby because it was Cam's, and she hated him.

Hated him because he wasn't his brother, Robert.

She lay there, shaking with grief now as sobs wracked her, crying even though she was halfway between waking and sleeping. As the moments passed, the images, half nightmare and half dreams of what might have been, stole into her head just as she had feared they would. She heard the crying, the thin wailing that called out to her like a siren's song, and she rose like a phantom soul leaving its body and crossed to the crib that wasn't there, reaching down to lift the soft bundle of warmth and cradling it to her bosom. And then the tiny lips fastened onto her and life began to flow from it, life that would never be, life that had been cruelly ended before it had a chance to begin, and suddenly she was no longer in her room but on a road some-where, a road that led through dark woods, where a cold night wind whipped the branches of the trees back and forth, where evil creatures howled and chuckled in the stygian gloom, where a voice cried for her, a lost and lonely voice. And as the voice receded, she ran after it. But no matter how fast she ran, she could never catch it. But the cry-ing was there always there, and she couldn't stop it, couldn't find the one who was forever lost, lost, lost.

IN THE hallway outside Lucinda's room, Ellie pressed her back against the wall, hugged herself, and shivered as she heard the faint whimper-ing cries from within. She knew that Lucinda was making those noises in her sleep. The drug had helped her, but not enough. She couldn't es-cape her own guilt.

Nor should she be able to, Ellie thought as cold hatred mixed with the sympathy she couldn't help but feel, even though she didn't want to. Miss Lucinda never would have been in this fix if she hadn't got her-self with child by Marse Cam and then had Aunt Susie get rid of the sucker. And that never would have happened if she hadn't carried on so shamelessly with Marse Cam like some sort of waterfront tramp. What in the name o' heaven had she been thinkin', that her and Marse Cam could rut like animals every time they could steal a few minutes alone and there wouldn't ever be any consequences? Miss Lucinda was stu-pid, bone-deep stupid, but even she should've known better than that.

And Ellie suspected that she had. She'd carried on like that with Marse Cam because she couldn't have the man she really wanted, and Marse Cam was the next best thing. Only when it came right down to it, he wasn't the next best thing after all, and Miss Lucinda couldn't bear the thought of havin' his baby. Ellie was a smart girl. She'd seen and heard enough to know how things were. Black folks always saw and heard and understood a whole heap more than white folks thought they did.

Ellie asked herself sometimes why she helped Miss Lucinda the way she did. Was it because her mistress ordered her to, because she felt sorry for her, or because she saw Miss Lucinda spiraling down farther and farther into damnation and took some pleasure from that? That blonde bitch had it comin'. Lord knows she had it comin'. She'd never had any right to fall in love with Marse Robert. No right at all.

And of course, Ellie reminded herself, *she* had no right to love Robert Gilmore, either. But she did, and there wasn't a blessed thing she could do about it.

CHAPTER NINE

Virginia Standoff

A COLD RAIN SPATTERED against the tent, but Robert Gilmore was warm enough inside with a blanket wrapped around his shoulders as he sat on his cot and read the letter by the smoky light of a small lamp. It had taken weeks for the epistle to reach him from South Carolina. Allard and Diana had been married in November, and now Christmas and New Year's had come and gone and 1862 had begun. The letter must have gone astray somewhere, Robert thought. Normal mail delivery wasn't overly fast, but it was faster than *that*.

He had been greatly relieved to hear from his old friend. The last letter he'd had from Allard had been written before the second voyage of the *Ghost*. In the long months since then, Robert hadn't known whether Allard survived that trip to sea or not. Now, from what he read in the letter, it appeared that Allard had come perilously close to *not* surviving.

But he had lived through the adventure and recovered from the sickness that had gripped him afterward, and he and his beloved Diana were now husband and wife. They were living in the Tyler mansion for the time being, and Allard had already started working with his father at the shipyard. Robert smiled to himself as he read those lines again. Allard didn't say much about it, but Robert would have been willing to bet there was considerable tension between him and Malachi. Those two were just too much alike, although both of them would have been appalled to hear someone else say that. Each wanted his own way and was reluctant to compromise. Putting the two of them together might lead to disaster, Robert mused—but if they could put aside their differences, their combined intelligence and ambition might also accomplish great things.

Allard's letter described the wedding, although not in great detail. Robert felt a pang in his heart when he read that Jacqueline had been Diana's maid of honor. She must have been beautiful. She always was. But never more beautiful than she had been on that summer day in the gazebo by the pond at Four Winds, the Lockhart plantation. The day Jacqueline had given herself to him. As a Southern gentleman, Robert had felt moments of intense guilt over what had happened that day. He had compromised the young lady he loved. Both of them should have had more self-control. But the passion between them was a juggernaut, an irresistible force. And their restraint had proven to be hardly an immovable object.

He knew from the letters he had received from Jacqueline that she was fine. He had worried that she might be with child, but that had proven not to be the case. That was a relief, of course, and yet . . . and yet a small part of Robert felt a twinge of disappointment. Given his current situation, that one afternoon might be the only time he and Jacqueline would be together that way, their only chance to create a new life uniquely formed from the essence of both of them.

"His current situation," he thought with a wry smile. That was one way to refer to the fact that less than half a mile away were tens of thousands of Yankees who wanted to kill him.

After the battle of Manassas, the Confederate army had set up a defensive line just north of the battlefield, in case the Yanks got over the whipping they had received and tried to attack again. The troops dug rifle pits and waited, their guns pointed toward the enemy.

The Yankees didn't attack, though. They just sat there, so close their campfires could be seen at night and the music of their fiddles and fifes drifted through the air to the Confederate line. Every so often a balloon ascended somewhere behind the Federal lines, and an observer studied the Southerners' position. Some of the men under Robert's command in Company E of the Hampton Legion wasted powder and shot firing at the observation balloon before Robert ordered them to stop. They were just squandering their time, not to mention the ammunition. The balloon was out of range.

Occasionally shots would be exchanged between outlying pickets on both sides, but that was the extent of the excitement during the rest of the summer and the fall of 1861. By far the greatest number of casualties came from typhoid fever after an outbreak of the disease swept through the camps before it finally petered out.

As winter arrived and '61 turned to '62, the standoff continued. At the beginning, after the Union's defeat along the meandering creek known as Bull Run, there had been considerable speculation that the North would negotiate a peaceful settlement to the conflict. That didn't happen. In the few newspapers that made their way to the front, Robert read that Yankee president Abraham Lincoln was standing firm and asking for more troops rather than trying to find a way to bring the war to an end. The man was insane, Robert thought. No country could maintain by force a union that was no longer wanted by part of its citizens. It was simply wrong to even attempt such a thing.

Robert had no idea what was going to happen, but it seemed likely that the North wasn't going to be giving up any time soon. Eventually the Federals would launch another attack at Richmond, the Confederate capital. And likely the Hampton Legion would be part of the army blocking that thrust.

But in the meantime, the night was quiet, except for the continued patter of rain, and Robert was able to sit in peace and reread for the fourth or fifth time the letter from his old friend. He felt happiness for Allard and Diana and longing for Jacqueline, and he even wondered how his brother, Cam, was doing in Charleston at the Citadel. When he wrote back to Allard, he decided, he would ask about Cam.

THE RAIN never let up for very long. The spring of 1862 promised to be a wet one. But despite that, the Confederate army was on the move again at last. Orders came in early March for a withdrawal to positions along the Rapidan and Rappahannock rivers. Gen. Irvin McDowell, who had been in command of the Union army during its disastrous foray to Manassas, had been replaced by Gen. George B. McClellan, and it was thought that McClellan might set his sights on Richmond from a different direction.

This proved to be good thinking. Bringing an army of a hundred thousand men with him on ships that departed from Alexandria, Virginia, McClellan landed at Fort Monroe, at the very tip of the peninsula formed by the York and the James rivers. Like a turnpike, this peninsula led due northwest.

Straight toward Richmond.

But McClellan would not reach his goal unopposed. Twenty miles up the peninsula, the Confederate army that had slogged down from northern Virginia during the past few weeks laid down a defensive line stretching from Yorktown on the York River southward along the Warwick River, a smaller stream that cut across the peninsula.

The rain continued and slowed everything down, but inevitably, the two behemoths that were the Union and Confederate armies kept lumbering toward a confrontation.

ROBERT HAD tramped through the mud every step of the way with his men. He had learned to hate the gumbolike soil of the peninsula as the Hampton Legion, along with the rest of Gen. Joseph E. Johnston's army, moved into Yorktown and established their positions.

Eighty-some years earlier, during the Revolutionary War, the British had occupied Yorktown and had erected sturdy earthworks around the city to defend it from the rebellious American patriots. Those earthworks still stood, and the Confederates immediately set to work strengthening them. In the area just to the rear of the defensive line was a network of underground shelters and tunnels that were supposed to be strong enough to withstand the bursting of enemy artillery shells. These bombproofs, as they were optimistically called, would serve as the home of the defenders as long as they stayed at Yorktown.

The only thing more miserable than being outside in the rain all the time, Robert discovered, was having to live underground while it was raining. There were always puddles underfoot as water seeped through the walls of the bombproofs, even though they were fortified with planks. Water dripped from the ceilings, and the air was thick and cloying with the smell of soggy earth. A few hours down there and a soldier started to feel more like a mole than a man. It was a relief to go outside, even when the rain was falling in torrents.

Scouts reported that the Union army's progress up the peninsula was grindingly slow. McClellan had started out on one of the rare sunny days and had expected to make good time as he sent two long columns up the Virginia peninsula, one heading straight toward Yorktown, the other moving parallel and several miles west of the first column. But as soon as the rain returned, the roads became muddy again, and McClellan's wagons sank to their hubs. After that the columns moved at a snail's pace.

Water dripped from the bill of Robert's campaign cap as he stood on a wooden parapet behind one of the earthworks just outside Yorktown. It was early morning. The sun was up, but it was difficult to tell that through the thick gray clouds that hung over the peninsula. Robert could barely see across the river to Gloucester Point, where Confederate gunners were waiting at their batteries if the Yankees tried to slip any gunboats past the town. But at least it wasn't raining at the moment, although the air was still heavily laden with moisture.

"You think the Yanks will show up today, Lieutenant?"

The question came from one of Robert's men who leaned against the muddy earthworks with rifle in hand, a rag draped over the breech to keep it dry. Sgt. Ed Flanagan was raw-boned and rusty-haired, a good shot and a fearless fighter who had been handpicked by Robert to be his company sergeant.

"I don't know, Sergeant," Robert replied. "But they're out there somewhere, and they're coming, you can count on that."

Flanagan spat on top of the earthworks. "I sort of wish they'd hurry up and get here. I don't like just sittin' around and waitin' for a fight. Manassas was pretty bad, but I ain't sure it was any worse than this."

Robert didn't think he would go so far as to say that. Manassas was the only real battle he had taken part in, and he remembered vividly what a frightening, chaotic experience it had been. He had seen men killed right in front of his eyes, including his former company commander, Capt. Jeremiah Connelly, and he had come awfully close to dying himself on several occasions. He wasn't really looking forward to going through something like that again.

Of course, when the time came, he would take part without hesitation in whatever conflict erupted. He was a soldier, and a soldier did his duty. And Flanagan had a point—the waiting was hard.

The rain held off during the morning, but the overcast remained. Robert walked up and down the part of the line where his company was posted. Toward the middle of the day, he saw scouts riding in hurriedly from the southeast. He knew that McClellan was somewhere in that direction. So it didn't really come as a surprise when Lieutenant Forsythe, Colonel Hampton's aide, came along a short time later and announced, "The Union forces are within a mile now, Lieutenant. We're going to try to stop them with artillery, but be prepared for a fight if they get this far."

"Yes sir," Robert replied. Although he and Forsythe were both lieutenants, Forsythe had held the rank longer, and he was the colonel's aide, to boot.

Hampton, though technically a colonel, had been an acting brigadier general after Johnston had given him command of three infantry regiments—the Fourteenth and Nineteenth Georgia and the Sixteenth North Carolina—in addition to the Hampton Legion. His promotion was supposed to come through at any moment, but Robert still thought of him as Colonel Hampton.

Forsythe continued his rounds, alerting the company commanders along the line of the possibility of impending action. Robert lifted his field glasses to his eyes, but he couldn't see much of anything except a gray mist cloaking the flat, soggy landscape.

He heard something a short time later, though. With a thunderous roar, Confederate guns opened fire, flinging shells over the earthworks and the deep trenches just outside them. Robert heard the reports from the big guns, heard the shells whistling through the heavy air overhead, heard the blasts as they detonated in the distance. The barrage was tremendous, and he didn't see how any army could continue to advance in the face of it.

"Boy, we're pourin' it to 'em!" Flanagan said excitedly during a brief lull in the artillery fire. "I'll bet McClellan's gettin' a hotter welcome than he expected."

"Maybe he'll turn around and go back where he came from," another soldier suggested.

That would be nice if it happened, Robert thought. Unfortunately, the odds were against it.

The gunners kept up the bombardment for a long time. Robert wasn't sure what they were aiming at; he still couldn't see the Yankees. Obviously, though, there had to be scouts and spotters directing that fire.

Around midafternoon, Robert lifted his head suddenly as he listened to the scream of an artillery shell burning its way through the air. There was something different about that sound, and after a second he realized what it was. The whistling was getting louder rather than fading. That shell wasn't going away from them; it was coming *toward* the earthworks.

"Everybody down!" he yelled and pitched himself forward on the parapet, below the top of the earthworks. The soldiers lining the thick earthen wall followed his lead, and it was a good thing they did, because a heartbeat later a violent explosion erupted nearby, shaking the parapets and making the very earth itself jump. Clumps of mud rose high in the air, thrown up by the blast, and then pelted down on the crouching men.

"Yeee gads!" Flanagan exclaimed in the silence that echoed after the blast. "That was close!"

The explosion had been so close, in fact, that Robert was half deafened by it. He could hear the sergeant's excited words, but they sounded muffled, as if he had his hands over his ears. He scrambled to his feet and looked over the earthworks. Twenty yards to his left, a depression had been gouged out of the front of the barrier by the Yankee shell. The damage was surprisingly small, though, considering how loud the blast had been. The Redcoats had built these earthworks to last, all those years ago, and the work the Confederates had done had only strengthened them.

The earthworks wouldn't help, though, if a shell caught men standing outside. Robert knew that if a Yankee shell had landed here, another could at any time. Now that they had their big guns up, they would probably sit back in the mist and trade long-range fire with the defenders for God only knew how long.

"Into the bombproofs!" Robert shouted to his men. "Fall back and get below!"

"Lieutenant, ain't we supposed to watch for the Yankees?" Flanagan asked.

"I'll do that," Robert said. "The rest of you get down there where it's safer. When the Yankees come, you can't fight them if you've been blown to bits."

"You best let me stay up here and stand watch," Flanagan said stubbornly. "I'm just a sergeant. You're our commandin' officer. We won't be able to fight without you."

He was right, and Robert knew it. One of the things he had learned at the Citadel—which now seemed so far away in both time and distance—was that command carried certain responsibilities. Decisions always had to be made in battle, and officers had to make those decisions. Which meant that officers had to protect their own lives to a certain extent. Distasteful as it was for Robert to contemplate, in military terms Ed Flanagan was more expendable than he was.

"All right, Sergeant," he said reluctantly. "Pick a couple of men to stand watch with you at hundred-yard intervals. The rest of the company will withdraw to the bombproofs."

Flanagan grinned. Robert had a pretty good idea what the sergeant was thinking—if the Yankees *did* launch an attack, he would get first shot at them.

"Oswald! Siler!" Flanagan called. "Take positions a hundred yards either way along this wall o' dirt! I'll maintain position here." He flashed Robert another grin. "Better get movin', Lieutenant, 'fore the Yanks drop a round down your shirt collar."

Robert nodded and gave the sergeant a grim grin as he climbed down the ladder from the parapet. The other men were already moving into the tunnel-like entrances to the bombproofs.

Feeling a little like a worm crawling into a hole in the ground, Robert joined them in the bombproofs. The tunnels and shelters were dimly lit by lanterns. His skin crawled as the dank, musty odor assailed his nostrils. It was like voluntarily going into the grave, even though the purpose was to save them from death.

The tunnel Robert followed opened into a large, cavernlike area with a low ceiling. Men sprawled around because it was hard to stand comfortably without bumping their heads. Several of them started to get up when Robert entered, but he waved them back down. Under these circumstances, he wasn't worried about military protocol. "At ease, men," he told them, noticing as he listened to his voice echo that his hearing seemed to be normal now.

No sooner were the words out of his mouth than another blast went off. The roar wasn't as loud down here, but the shaking of the earth was pronounced. Robert glanced at the thick timbers propping up the ceiling of the bombproof. He hoped those timbers held. If they didn't, he and his men would be crushed under tons of earth.

Again and again the line was pounded by the Federal barrage. Robert found a small three-legged stool to sit on while the bombproof was rocked by explosion after explosion. The shelling went on all afternoon, although down in this hole in the ground it was difficult to judge the passage of time. Robert fought the impulse to check his watch in the smoky lantern light. He didn't want the men to see that he was as nervous as they were.

Some of the men played cards, some talked when it was possible to be heard during lulls in the bombardment, and others just sat in the mud and stared, waiting for the waiting to be over. Miraculously, a few dozed, although Robert didn't see how anyone could sleep through this. To keep his mind occupied, he thought of Jacqueline, recreating her face in his mind's eye, remembering the warmth of her touch and the sweet scent of her hair. When this war was over, he told himself, they would be married. He knew that her mother opposed that—it probably would not be going too far to say that Priscilla Lockhart hated him—but her father seemed to like him. Somehow they would overcome Priscilla's objections, and they would be joined together and nothing, short of death, could ever part them. They would build a life together, a life of love and happiness and children . . .

"Lieutenant," one of the men said, breaking into his thoughts. "I think it's stopped. There ain't been any blasts up there for at least five minutes."

Robert finally pulled his watch out. The hour was past six o'clock now. Given the overcast, it was probably dark outside. The Yankees had called off the bombardment for the night.

"Calloway, Higgins, come with me," he said as he stood, hunched over slightly because of the low ceiling. "The rest of you stay here until we're sure it's clear."

As he led the way along the tunnel with the two troopers following him, he wondered what he would find. Had Flanagan, Oswald, and Siler survived, or had they been blown to bloody bits by the barrage?

A light rain was falling when Robert stepped into the open air. As he had thought, twilight had settled thickly over the landscape, but his eyes were able to penetrate it well enough for him to see that the earthworks still stood. Despite all the pounding they had endured from the Yankee guns during the long afternoon, the fortifications were intact.

From the edge of the parapet, his legs dangling, Ed Flanagan saluted and called out, "Howdy, Lieutenant! We're a mite deaf right now from the world blowin' up around us all afternoon, but other'n that we're fine as frog hair!"

IF IT was possible to grow bored while being under attack, the defenders of Yorktown did so as the weeks of soggy April 1862 rolled on. Federal guns continued to bombard the earthworks around the city nearly every day, but the field artillery being used by the Yankees simply wasn't powerful enough to make a dent in the fortifications. Rumor had it that the Yankees had bigger guns, so-called siege guns that could fire 200-pound shells, but those weapons were so heavy and ponderous that they were extremely difficult to move, especially in muddy conditions.

Reports indicated that the other Federal column was bogged down on the southern bank of the Warwick River, held back by the rain-swollen stream as well as the accurate fire of Confederate riflemen and artillerymen. McClellan was a cautious man, the sort of commander who preferred to make slow, steady progress and not risk the lives of his men unless he had to. He was made for siege warfare, and that was what developed on the Virginia peninsula.

The soldiers manning the Yorktown earthworks grew so accustomed to the artillery barrages that they stayed outside the bombproofs much of the time, and when the shells began to fall too closely for comfort, the men meandered rather than ran into the tunnels.

They were more cautious when it came to dealing with the Union sharpshooters who crouched in the cover of some trees nearly half a mile distant. More than one careless Southerner had peered over the top of the earthworks and received a Yankee bullet for his trouble. The lucky ones were just wounded; the less fortunate had their brains blown out. The soldiers learned to stay low or risk being shot at long range.

Hampton's promotion was now official: Brig. Gen. Wade Hampton. Robert thought it was about time. Hampton was one of the ablest commanders in the army as far as Robert could see. Of course, no one asked his opinion about such matters. His responsibility was to guard the earthworks, and that was all.

When May rolled around, it had become obvious that such duty was a waste of time. Union infantry was not going to attack. The wide, deep ditches in front of the earthworks and the open ground beyond them ensured that, if the Yankees tried such an assault, the defenders would mow them down ruthlessly. So this battle continued to be fought primarily with artillery on both sides. Which meant it was only a matter of time until the Yankees were able to bring up their bigger guns. Those ten-ton monsters would put an end to the siege.

Reports from the scouts on May 3 indicated that the big guns were finally in place. That afternoon, orders were issued. While the Confederate artillery threw up a tremendous barrage as a distraction to keep the Yankees occupied, the Southern infantry began a withdrawal from Yorktown. As night fell, Robert found himself marching his men on the muddy turnpike that led northwest toward Williamsburg, which in colonial days had been the state capital. Ed Flanagan was on the far side of the company, keeping them in line.

For almost a month, the Confederate army had hunkered down in Yorktown and across the peninsula, delaying the always-cautious McClellan. But now the time had come to seek a new defensible position, and at Williamsburg the Southerners would make their stand.

The battles to come had merely been postponed, not averted. Before this campaign was over, there would be plenty of blood spilled. Robert didn't doubt that for a second.

CHAPTER TEN

Reconciliation

WHEN CAM GILMORE RETURNED to Charleston in January 1862, following the holidays he had spent at his family's farm, he had made up his mind. He was going to see Lucinda Tyler again, and she was going to tell him what was wrong and why she was avoiding him. He couldn't get thoughts of her out of his head. Whatever the problem was, it had to be settled.

For one thing, his holiday vacation from the Citadel had been frustrating. He hadn't even been able to get together with Melody Harper, who lived on the farm next to the Gilmore place, because her father was still keeping an eagle eye on her. The previous summer, Granville Harper had caught his daughter trying to sneak out of the farmhouse at night, and he had guessed correctly that she was on her way to meet a boy, in this case Cam. Melody was a lusty, good-natured gal, the sort who was bound to wind up with her belly swollen with child long before she was within shouting distance of marriage, and she and Cam were especially good friends. But not good enough that Cam wanted to risk dodging buckshot from her daddy's old scattergun.

All the other eligible girls around that part of the country—like Susannah Milligan, who lived on the farm in the other direction and who had been Cam's first lover, and Judith Culhane, the minister's daughter who had a fondness for sinning—were wise to him and knew what sort of scoundrel he was, so they kept their distance now. As a result, he was desperate for female companionship when he returned to Charleston. Lucinda would just have to be reasonable.

But whenever he could get away from the Citadel long enough to visit to the Tyler mansion, Lucinda stubbornly refused to see him, just as she had the previous autumn. Frustrated and angry after one such refusal, Cam demanded of Allard, who had carried Lucinda's response downstairs, "What's wrong with that sister of yours, anyway?"

"Lucinda has always been the sort to know what she wants . . . and what she doesn't want," Allard said. "Sorry, Cam. It appears that she doesn't want to see you."

"Well, she's making a mistake!"

Allard put a hand on Cam's arm. "Maybe you'd better just go back to the Citadel," he suggested.

Cam shook off the hand and snapped, "You're not an upperclassman anymore, Allard. You can't tell me what to do."

Allard didn't even look like a soldier anymore, Cam thought. He had put on a little weight, his face filling out some under the close-cropped beard. And the dark, sober suits he wore made him look like a businessman—or a preacher. Cam couldn't imagine spending his days cooped up in an office. Being in a classroom so much was bad enough, but at least as a cadet he was on the parade ground quite a bit, marching and drilling. And there was no way of knowing when the cadets might be called upon again to defend the city.

"Look," Allard said with obviously forced tolerance, "because you're Robert's brother and because you've spent time in this house as a guest, I'm not going to call the servants and have you thrown out. But you need to forget about courting my sister. She's not interested, and you're not a suitable match for her anyway. You're too young."

Cam's chin lifted defiantly. "I'm old enough to—"

Allard held up both hands to stop him. "Whatever you're about to say, Cam, I'd prefer not to hear it. I don't want to have to give you a thrashing or challenge you to a duel. Now, I'll bid you good evening."

"Damn it, Allard!" Cam burst out. "I just want to talk to her."

That wasn't true, of course. He wanted to do a lot more than just talk. But right now, he would settle for that.

Allard just shook his head and held out a hand, as if to usher Cam to the front door and out of the house.

Cam sighed. "All right, I'm going," he said. "But tell Lucinda that I'm not giving up. She's going to have to see me sooner or later, and when she does, she's going to tell me why she hates me so much."

He turned on his heel and stalked out of the mansion without looking back, but he paused on the walk outside to glance up at the majestic house looming over him in the dusk. Lucinda was up there somewhere, and he felt a surprisingly powerful longing for her. He wasn't sure he had ever felt anything like this before. It was almost like he felt real emotion toward her. But that was impossible, of course.

LUCINDA MOVED the curtain aside just enough to see Cam standing there for a moment and then walking away. A heavy sigh came from her. She wished he would stop coming here. It was getting more and more difficult to refuse to see him. Even though he wasn't the Gilmore brother she really wanted, at least he was a man. At least he wanted to touch her, to make her feel like a woman again.

She heard footsteps in the hallway then a soft knock on her door. She turned toward it as her brother called, "Lucinda? It's Allard."

She tightened the knot on the belt of her dressing gown. She didn't want to talk to him, but he could be as stubborn as Cam Gilmore. And she could tell that he wasn't going to go away, at least not easily.

"Come in," she said.

The door opened and she saw his silhouette against the hall light. He wasn't as gaunt now as he had been when he returned from the sea. When he had come up to tell her that Cam was there to see her, she hadn't let him into the room but had told him through the door that she wasn't receiving any callers, especially Cam Gilmore. Now as Allard stepped into the room, he asked, "Why is it so dark in here?"

"That's the way I like it," she said. As he moved toward the dressing table, she added sharply, "Don't light that lamp."

"All right." He stopped, stood there awkwardly for a moment, and then crammed his hands into his pockets. "Lucinda, you and I have never been close, but even I can tell that you're not happy these days. Does it have something to do with Cam? Is that why you won't see him? Did he do something to upset you?"

"You're just full of questions, aren't you, little brother?" Ask your wife what Cam did to me, she wanted to say. Ask her why I don't ever want to see the bastard again. But of course she couldn't say that. Diana had never said anything, and Lucinda wanted it to stay that way.

"You can't take anything Cam says or does too much to heart," Allard was saying. "I don't think he's ever had a serious moment in his life. Robert hoped that attending the Arsenal and then the Citadel might help him grow up, but I haven't seen any evidence of that so far."

Cam was grown up in his own way, Lucinda thought. Grown up enough to get a woman with child, anyway.

"Just stay out of it, Allard," she said. "It's none of your business."

"True enough. But Father and Mother are worried about you, and I don't like to see them upset. Well, I don't like to see *Mother* upset. It's pretty much a way of life for Father."

Lucinda ignored that. Instead, she said, "I'm not feeling well. So I'll thank you to go on now and let me get some rest."

"Fine," he said curtly. "I just thought maybe I could help."

"Well, you can't."

He shrugged and left the room. Lucinda stood there stiffly until he was gone, then she slumped into the chair in front of the dressing table. She was trying again to wean herself off the opium, and as a result she felt terrible most of the time and wasn't sleeping much. She didn't need Allard to take an uncharacteristic interest in her problems, complicating her life that much more.

And the possibility suddenly occurred to her that he *might* talk to Diana about her, even though she hadn't mentioned that, only thought it. Her brother might be one of those men who actually talked to their wives when they were worried about something. She didn't really know him well enough to say. And Diana might be the sort of wife who didn't like to keep secrets from her husband, in which case she could break down and tell Allard everything that had happened. And if he knew the truth, he would probably run straight to their parents with it.

Lucinda let out a groan of despair and lowered her head, resting it on her arms as they lay crossed on the dressing table. She had to do something about these problems, even though taking action about anything was just about the last thing she wanted to do. She would have much preferred simply lying in the darkened room and letting the world fade away around her. That wasn't going to happen, though.

Maybe she *did* need to talk to Cam. Maybe if she told him again, in no uncertain terms, that she didn't want anything to do with him, he would stop coming around and stirring everything up. But how could she do that, though, without letting anyone know about it?

Lucinda lifted her head. Ellie would help her. The housemaid had done plenty for her in the past, and she could help Lucinda solve this problem, too, whether she wanted to or not. If the little black ninny knew what was good for her, she would do as she was told.

GAMBLING HAD gotten Cam into trouble at the Arsenal. An accusation of cheating at cards had led to a brawl and almost caused the school to take disciplinary action against him, on top of the damage done by several angry cadets. The whole experience had taught him a valuable lesson: if he was going to cheat, he had to get better at it.

Since then he had put in even more hours with the pasteboards. He could mark a deck with his thumbnail so that no one but him would ever see the markings. He could deal from the bottom with no one being the wiser and slip a card up his sleeve, or out of his sleeve, with such speed and dexterity that the action was all but undetectable. If he cut the cards, he knew which cards in the deck fell above the cut and which below. He had heard about the gamblers who plied their trade on the riverboats that cruised the mighty Mississippi. If it hadn't been for this blasted war, he might have been tempted to leave South Carolina and try his luck on one of those gaudy paddle wheelers. So he satisfied his urges—his *gambling* urges, anyway—in the illicit games that went on in the barracks at the Citadel.

Oddly enough, he found that the more he practiced cheating, the less he had to use the techniques he perfected. He was capable of winning honestly most of the time. Poker was a game of both chance and skill, and he had the skill to overcome the chance.

He had just raked in a pot that he had taken fair and square with three queens when a surreptitious knock sounded on the door of the storage room where the game was being played. Cam glanced at the other five players. As far as he was aware, the six of them were the only ones who knew about tonight's game.

"Did any of y'all say anything to anybody?" he asked in a whisper.

Four shook their heads, but the fifth one, Sam Larson—a short, curly-haired young man—looked embarrassed and said, "I might've mentioned where I'd be to my friend Wilbur. Just in case somebody came looking for me, you know? I didn't want to get in trouble."

Cam glared at him. "Well, we may all be in trouble now." He made a slashing motion with his hand. "Nobody say anything! Maybe whoever it is will go away."

The knock sounded again, and a young man's voice called quietly, "Damn it, I know you're in there! Open up!"

"Everybody pick up your money," Cam told the other players. "Put the cards and the blanket away. We'll bluff our way through this. Nobody has to know we were playing cards in here."

"What are you going to tell them we were doing?" one of the other cadets asked dryly.

Cam frowned. He didn't have an answer for that. But he knew from experience that sometimes it was best to just bull ahead, whether you knew what you were doing or not. Inaction was often the most dangerous course of action of all.

With his jaw set tightly, he got to his feet and went to the door. A quick glance told him that no evidence of the game remained in sight. He opened the door a couple of inches. "What is it?"

The young man in the corridor was Wilbur Halliburton, Sam Larson's friend. He said, "Sam told me you had a game going on in here, Gilmore. Someone asked me to give you this."

He surprised Cam by holding out a folded piece of paper.

Frowning, Cam took the paper and asked, "Who gave it to you?"

The answer was even more surprising. "Some darky wench. I was walking back here from paying a visit to, ah, a young lady in town, and just as I was about to enter the grounds, this woman stopped me and asked if I knew you. When I said that I did, she asked if I could give you that note. She said it came from her mistress and she'd be whipped if she didn't get it to you."

Cam's fingers clenched involuntarily on the paper, making it crinkle in his hand. *Lucinda,* he thought. The note had to be from her. The slave who had delivered it was probably that housemaid . . . what was her name? . . . Ellie. Lucinda always had Ellie running errands for her, Cam remembered from those better days when they had been together. And he couldn't think of any other woman in Charleston who would be sending him a note.

"Thanks, Wilbur," he said.

"No thanks necessary," the other cadet replied curtly. "If anybody asks, I don't know anything about this. I don't want any part of your intrigues, Gilmore."

"Whatever it is, you won't be brought into it," Cam promised.

Halliburton peered over his shoulder into the storage room, where the other five young men were standing around sheepishly. "The game is over, I take it?"

Cam rubbed his fingertips over the piece of paper in his hand. A faint scent of familiar perfume rose from it. "This game is over," he said. But he had yet to see what other game might be played tonight.

HE WAITED until the others were gone before reading the note. He recognized the delicate handwriting right away, although it was more of a scrawl now than it had been in the past. *Will you meet me?* it read. *Ellie will show you the way.* The note was signed with the initial *L.*

She wanted to see him after all, although she had picked a strange way to go about it. Cam didn't really care about that. He just wanted to see her again and take her in his arms and kiss her and . . .

Think about that later, he told himself as he shrugged into his coat and slipped out of the building.

Halliburton had likely used the main entrance to Marion Square. Cam strode quickly across the parade ground known as the Citadel Green and stepped onto the sidewalk that ran between King and Meeting streets. He looked around.

"Marse Cam?"

Even though he was expecting Ellie to be waiting for him, her voice surprised him and made him jump a little. He turned as a shape emerged from the shadows and came toward him, seemingly floating like a phantom. But that was just because the housemaid was wrapped in a long dark cloak and he couldn't see her legs, he told himself.

"Ellie?" he said. "Is that you?"

"Yes suh, Marse Cam. You got Miss Lucinda's note?"

"Yes." Cam's nerves were settling down now, and his voice was steadier as he went on, "Where is she?"

"Come with me. I'll take you to her."

Cam walked alongside the slave for a couple of blocks. Some Southerners would have made Ellie walk behind them, even if they didn't know where they were going, but Cam had been raised on a farm where there were no slaves and was not in the habit of caring about such so-called improprieties. Ellie's walking beside him didn't have anything to do with equality or the lack of same as far as he was concerned; it was just a matter of common sense.

Ellie stopped beside a carriage parked across the street from a tavern. Cam thought the vehicle wasn't one of the carriages owned by the Tylers. It looked more like the sort that was for hire.

"The driver's over yonder havin' a drink," Ellie said as she nodded toward the tavern. "I'll be waitin' in that doorway." She pointed toward a nearby building. The business that occupied it was closed for the night, and the alcove in which the front door was set was dark.

As Ellie retreated, Cam stepped to the open door of the carriage and said tentatively, "Lucinda?"

"I have to talk to you, Cam." Her voice revealed the strain she was under, but Cam recognized it and felt a leap of excitement. He hadn't realized until now just how badly he really wanted to talk to her.

Quickly, he climbed into the carriage and sat down in the rearward-facing seat. It was awfully dark in there, with only a little light filtering in from the nearby buildings where lamps were still lit, such as the tavern. But he could see well enough to make out the pale sheen of her face and hair. He leaned toward her and said, "Lucinda, you don't know how much I've missed—"

"Stop it," she said, cutting into his declaration. "Cam, listen to me. You have to stop coming to my house. You have to stop acting like . . . like you're my beau and you want to court me."

"But I *do* want to court you, if that's what you want. Just so we can be together again."

"So you can make love to me again, you mean?"

"If that's what *you* want . . ."

The words came easily. He had always had the ability to make the women in his life think it was entirely their idea to go to bed with him. In most cases, it was. Why wouldn't they? He was handsome and a very skilled lover, especially for someone his age.

"Cam, it's going to cause trouble for both of us if you persist in this. Nothing is going to happen between us ever again. You have to understand that and accept it." Her voice hardened. "Otherwise, sooner or later my father or my brother will have to shoot you."

"Allard wouldn't shoot me! Robert would never forgive him."

"My father would."

Cam didn't have to think about that. Malachi Tyler would probably take great pleasure in peppering his backside with buckshot.

With a frown he said sullenly, "I don't know why people keep getting angry with me. It's not like I'm really hurting anybody."

"Oh, no?"

"Of course not. You're fine, and we were together a lot."

A match suddenly rasped, and Lucinda lifted the flame so that its harsh glare fell over her face. "Look at me," she said, "and tell me I'm fine."

Cam fell back against the seat behind him, half blinded by the unexpected glare of the match but equally affected by what his eyes were still able to see. Lucinda had been thinner and paler than usual at her brother's wedding, but now her face held a gauntness that reminded Cam of a cadaver. Her skin was so devoid of color that he could see the blue tracery of veins beneath it. Her eyes were huge and dark and haunted by demons that he could only guess at.

"My God, Lucinda, what happened to you?"

She opened her mouth, and for a second he thought she was going to tell him. But then she turned her head and wouldn't look at him, and the match burned down. She shook it out and dropped it from the window of the carriage onto the street.

Cam hesitated, but only for a second. Sympathy welled up inside him, and again it was unfamiliar because it was so genuine. Before she could stop him, he moved onto the seat beside her.

"No," she said, putting her hands against his chest. "Get away from me."

"Lucinda, I'm sorry," he murmured. "I'm so sorry." She was too weak to stop him as he put his arms around her and drew her against him. She was so thin and felt so fragile in his embrace. She balled a hand into a fist and struck it against him to no avail. He didn't let go of her.

But he didn't do anything other than hold her. A long, tense minute went by, and then her resolve crumpled. She sagged against him, and he felt her shake as she began to sob. He couldn't feel her tears because they fell on his coat. But as he lifted a hand to her face and stroked his thumb across her cheek, he felt the dampness.

"It's all right, Lucinda," he said softly. "Whatever happened, it's all right now."

She shook her head and whispered, "No . . . no . . . I don't want this . . . it's not supposed to be this way."

"How do we know how things are supposed to be? Sometimes we just have to accept the way they are."

"Oh, God, Cam . . ."

Then he felt her lift her head, and instinct guided him as he brought his mouth down on hers. Her lips were cold and a little stiff at first, but they soon warmed and became pliant, even urgent as they moved against his lips. Her hands clutched at his chest. He could feel the wanting surge within her, just as it was blossoming within him. She might not look like herself now, but he remembered how she used to be and sensed that the same beauty was still there inside her.

She broke the kiss and whispered, "How can you do this, you bastard? How can you make me feel this way all over again when I swore . . . I swore I would never . . . This isn't what I wanted!"

"Maybe it was," he said. "Maybe you just didn't know it."

"You son of a bitch! I hate you!" Her mouth found his again in the darkness. She whispered against his lips, "I hate you . . ."

But it was as clear as could be to him that she didn't mean it.

ELLIE SAW Cam Gilmore climb down out of the carriage a while later. She had kept her eyes averted after the vehicle had begun to rock slightly on its leather thoroughbraces. She could barely believe what was happening. Miss Lucinda had forced her to help her slip out of the mansion and find a carriage, then ordered her to get a note to Marse Cam some way. Even though Ellie hadn't asked any questions, Miss Lucinda must have felt compelled to explain, because she had said that she wanted to see Marse Cam one more time, to end it with him forever so that he would stop coming to the house and embarrassing her.

Well, *that* sure hadn't worked out the way Miss Lucinda had intended. What had that crazy white woman been thinkin'?

Ellie stepped out of the shadows and said quietly, "Marse Cam?"

He turned toward her, moving easily, languidly, like a big cat. A big, satisfied cat. "I'll go over to that tavern and fetch the driver, Ellie," he said. "I don't expect that you should go in there."

"No suh, they wouldn't let the likes o' me in a place where white folks drink."

"Thank you for helping Miss Lucinda."

"Yes suh, I was happy to," she lied. She hadn't liked anything about this, and after what had just happened, she liked it even less. Gathering up her courage, she ventured, "Marse Cam . . . does this mean you're gonna be comin' back to the house more?"

He laughed softly. "Oh, I expect it does, Ellie. I surely do expect it does."

Well, damn, she thought. She sure hadn't figured on this.

"Good night, Ellie," Cam said and then strolled across the street toward the tavern.

Ellie hesitated but knew she couldn't postpone the inevitable. She went to the carriage door, opened it, and asked worriedly, "Miss Lucinda, are you all right in there?"

"I'm fine, Ellie," she said. "Better than I've been in a long time."

Leave it alone, Ellie told herself, but her curiosity wouldn't let her. "I thought you was gonna get rid o' Marse Cam once and for all."

"So did I. But things don't always turn out the way we plan."

No, they didn't, especially where men and women were concerned, and Ellie had never seen a better example of that than tonight. She sure hoped nobody caught them while they were sneakin' back into the mansion. Her nerves were already worn to a frazzle.

CHAPTER ELEVEN

Fair Oaks, Seven Days

I T SEEMED THAT THE rain was never going to end. And neither was the fighting. Johnston's army had completed its slow, steady withdrawal to Williamsburg, and McClellan's army had continued its slow, steady pursuit. Two miles east of the town, Johnston positioned some men at Fort Magruder, a line of earthworks named after the commander of the soldiers who had constructed them. On May 5, 1862, advance units of McClellan's column approached the Confederate position in a driving rainstorm. The storm didn't stop gunfire from breaking out, and soon both sides were engaged in a battle that neither had expected.

The Hampton Legion was on the field that day, but other than the cavalry units, the legion played little part in the fighting. To Robert, who waited in the rear with his company, the battle seemed odd and somehow insubstantial. The rain muffled the roar of cannon and the crackle of rifle fire and also prevented him from seeing the clouds of powder smoke that had to be floating above the battlefield. He was sure, though, that the combat was real enough to the men who were involved in it. And it was all too real to the men who were bleeding and dying in the mud of the redoubts.

After a day of attacks and counterattacks, the Confederates withdrew. The fighting had been a stalemate, but since Johnston's army was retreating, Robert couldn't help but consider the outcome a defeat. They had to stop the Yankees somewhere, or else McClellan would grind his way all the way up the peninsula and on to Richmond.

A couple of days after the battle near Williamsburg, Federal troops tried a flanking maneuver, steaming up the York River to Eltham's Landing and disembarking there to threaten the right side of the Confederate column. Getting wind of this, Johnston immediately dispatched troops to block the Yankees, including the Hampton Legion. This time Robert was in the thick of the fighting, leading his men through some woods toward the river as bullets rattled through the leaves and thudded into trees all around him. The battle was brief but intense, and Robert found that he was too busy to be overly frightened. In a bizarre way, action was a blessing, because it was during the slow, boring times that fear gnawed most viciously on a man's guts.

The flank attack by the Yankees was swiftly turned back, and their retreat toward the York was a rout in which the pursuing Confederates captured quite a few of them. Robert's company grabbed a couple of prisoners, including a Yankee captain who somehow wound up alone among the South Carolinians. The officer tried at first to pretend he was one of them, since some of the Confederates had replaced their ragged gray or butternut uniforms with blue garments taken from the Yankees. After that trick failed, the captain then played possum when his horse was shot out from under him as he attempted to flee. That ruse hadn't worked, either, so he had good-naturedly surrendered to Robert, only to dash away on foot a few minutes later when some artillery shells exploded nearby, providing a distraction. Sergeant Flanagan and some men wanted to go after him, but Robert called them back. One Yankee captain wasn't worth the effort.

Not one man in Robert's company was even wounded in the engagement. He was proud of that but knew it was unreasonable to expect such a record would be repeated.

The retreat and the rain continued the entire month of May. Streams all across the peninsula were swollen out of their banks. Even normally placid creeks became raging torrents that slowed the progress of both armies. Skirmishes between Johnston's rear guard and McClellan's advance units were common. On the next to last day of May, another downpour turned the Chickahominy River, not far outside of Richmond, into a shallow, mile-wide lake that split McClellan's forces almost in half, with three divisions on one side of the river and two divisions on the other.

At long last, Johnston sensed that the moment had come to stop running, to turn and fight instead. And it was about time, since Richmond was only six miles away and the steeples of the capital city's churches probably would have been visible if it hadn't been raining so hard.

"I HEAR tell the folks in Richmond are in a right smart panic," Ed Flanagan said as he and Robert sat on a log in the midst of a wooded, swampy stretch of ground north of the little settlement of Fair Oaks, a depot on the Richmond and York River Railroad. The rest of the company was scattered around them, waiting for orders.

Robert grunted, "Anybody still in Richmond has good reason to be worried. If we don't stop the Yankees, they'll be marching into the city in another couple of days. Then the war will be over."

He felt hollow inside as he said that. After all the outrage at the Yankees' brazen invasion of Virginia, after the heady triumph of the battle near Manassas, it was hard to believe that it was all going to come to nothing. The arrogant Northerners were going to impose their will on the South by force after all. It just wasn't right. The American nation had begun because the English had tried to force the colonies to submit and remain subservient. As far as Robert could see, this was the same situation. If the colonies had had the right, even the moral obligation, to break away from England, why didn't the Southern states have that same right to separate themselves from the Union? Why couldn't the Yankees see that it was the same thing?

He had no answers to those questions, other than to acknowledge that in their blind self-righteousness, the Yankees couldn't see anything, even though the facts were as plain as the noses on their faces.

"We'll stop 'em, all right," Flanagan said confidently as rain dripped around them. "A Yankee's like a hunter chasin' a boar through the woods. He don't realize that sooner or later that ol' boar's gonna turn around and come at *him* with some mighty sharp tusks."

"You're saying that we're boars, Sergeant?" Robert asked with a chuckle.

"Naw suh . . . but we may be fightin' like 'em before the day's over. Root hog or die!" Flanagan rasped his fingers over the rusty stubble bristling on his jaw. "Anyway, even if Richmond was to fall, it don't mean the war would be over. The Confederacy'll just move the capital somewheres else. Raleigh, maybe, or even Charleston. And we'll just keep on afightin' the bastards."

"Maybe it won't come to that," Robert said.

Hoofbeats penetrated the sound of the rain. Robert and Flanagan stood up to see who was coming. Several riders loomed out of the mist, and Robert recognized one of them as the tall, handsome, distinguished figure of Wade Hampton.

The general reined his horse to a stop, and of course his staff officers followed suit. Water dripped from the brim of his hat as a smile spread across his fiercely mustachioed face. "Lieutenant Gilmore," he said as Robert came to attention and saluted, along with the other soldiers gathered in the swampy woods. Hampton added, "At ease, Lieutenant."

Robert's father and Hampton were old friends from college days, so Robert was well acquainted with his commanding officer. He suspected that was one reason Lieutenant Forsythe, Hampton's aide, didn't like him. Forsythe probably thought there was a chance Robert might replace him one day. Robert didn't really want Forsythe's job, even though he probably would have enjoyed working more closely with the general. He preferred to be in the field with Flanagan and Company E, the men he had come to admire as staunch, courageous fighters.

"We'll be moving up shortly, Lieutenant," Hampton said. "Down south of here a ways, our forces are engaging the Yankees at a cross-roads called Seven Pines, but our scouts report that some of the Federals are moving around to threaten our left flank. The responsibility to stop them falls to us."

"Yes sir," Robert said with a nod. He appreciated the general filling him in on the details; Hampton certainly didn't have to do that. It was enough for him to issue orders. Robert added, "We'll stop them, sir."

"I do believe you're right, Lieutenant." Hampton turned his horse to ride on along the line, instructing over his shoulder, "Advance through these woods, but wait until they're close before you engage them. Don't fire a shot until you can feel the enemy on your bayonets."

Robert nodded in understanding. The Yankees didn't know they were waiting in these gloomy woods. Hampton wanted to take them by surprise.

Quickly, Robert and Flanagan got the company stretched out in a skirmish line and began moving through the trees, splashing through the puddles on the ground. Robert was at one end of the line, the sergeant at the other. Robert could no longer see Flanagan, but he felt better knowing the sergeant was there in the mist.

Suddenly he heard a clatter and clank and then the tramp of marching feet. The sounds came from up ahead and were unmistakably those of soldiers on the move. Robert drew his saber, transferred the weapon from his right hand to his left, then unsnapped the flap on his holster and drew his revolver. He stepped around a tree and saw a handful of Yankees no more than thirty yards away. They didn't seem to notice him at first as he strode decisively toward them. Then, abruptly, one of the men jerked his head up and let out a yell.

Robert lifted his revolver and shot him. The bullet drove the blue-clad figure off his feet.

"At 'em, boys!" Robert shouted, and then as he charged forward, he howled out the distinctive Rebel Yell that was said to strike fear in the hearts of the enemy.

A volley exploded from the rifles of his men and ripped through the Yankees, cutting down several of them before they'd had time to know what was hitting them. The ones who survived put up a fight, though, and bullets sizzled through the damp air around Robert. He went to one knee and emptied his pistol at the enemy. Two more Union soldiers went spinning off their feet as they scurried for cover. Robert lunged up and ducked behind a tree to reload.

"Take cover and keep fighting!" he bellowed at his men. "Take cover and keep fighting!"

The soldiers of Company E obeyed, darting behind trees, throwing themselves behind deadfalls, hunkering in water-filled depressions. And all the while, as quickly as they could reload, the rifles in their hands continued to spout death.

The Yankees had gone to ground, too, so for the next little while the woods were filled with the clamor of shots as the two sides fiercely traded fire. Robert sheathed his saber. Though the quarters were close in this battle, they weren't close enough for the blade to be of any use—yet. Who knew what would happen before the day was over? One side or the other might charge, and the fighting could quickly turn into a hand-to-hand fray.

Gradually the shooting began to slow down as the soldiers realized that firing blind was a waste of powder and shot. They began picking their targets more carefully. Then, somewhere nearby, a cannon roared as Federal light artillery was brought up and put to use. A shell burst to Robert's left, where another company of the Hampton Legion was deployed. More rounds poured in, filling the woods with a hellish racket, toppling trees, and blowing unlucky men into bloody pieces.

Robert gritted his teeth as horror filled his mouth with a bitter taste. He knew it was just the luck of the draw that had spared his men from that awful barrage. It could just as easily have been them being slaughtered right now. He heard yelling as the Yankees charged at the part of the Confederate line that had been softened up by the artillery. A part of him wanted to rush over and help those poor boys, but he knew he couldn't do that. If he did, the enemy would rush through the gap left in this part of the line. He had to hold his ground, no matter what went on around them.

And he couldn't let himself think that they might be next in line for a bloody battering from those cannon. Fight the battle at hand, he told himself, not the one waiting for you.

His men were good shots. Most of the time, whenever one of the Yankees was foolish enough to expose even a little of his body, he was ventilated for his carelessness. But no matter how many of the blue-clad troopers fell, more took their place. How many of the bastards were there? Robert wondered. Was there no end to them?

He heard hoofbeats again and turned his head to see General Hampton riding perilously close to the front. The general rode tall in the saddle as he shouted orders and encouragement, rallying his men in the face of the enemy.

Robert saw Hampton's leg jerk suddenly, and the general lurched to one side but managed to stay in the saddle. Hampton's horse tried to rear in alarm, but Robert leaped toward the animal and grabbed its bridle, holding the horse down and bringing it under control.

"General, you're hit!" he said as he saw a steady stream of blood welling from a hole in Hampton's right boot. He turned his head and called toward the rear, "Surgeon! We need a surgeon up here! General Hampton's hit!"

"You're making too big a fuss over a little scratch, Lieutenant," Hampton said, but the strain in his voice told Robert otherwise.

Bullets continued to whistle through the woods around them. A Confederate officer charged toward them on horseback, and as the man drew closer Robert recognized him as Dr. Gaillard, one of the legion's surgeons. Just as Gaillard reached them, his horse threw its head up, blood spurting from a wound it had just received. The horse collapsed, sending the medical officer tumbling from the saddle.

Robert would have gone to Gaillard's aid, but he was afraid to release Hampton's horse. Gaillard proved to be all right, though, because he scrambled to his feet a moment later and calmly took his medical bag from the saddle of his dead mount. "You'd better get down off there, General," he said as he turned to Hampton and Robert.

"Can't do it, Doctor," the general gritted. "I might not be able to get back on my horse later. Deal with the wound the best you can."

Gaillard grimaced but shrugged in agreement. While Robert held the general's horse, Gaillard worked the bloody boot off the injured foot.

"Looks like the ball's still in there," the doctor said. "It'll have to come out. You ready for this, General?"

"Do your worst, Doctor," Hampton said with a grin.

With bullets still flying around, Gaillard stood close beside the horse and worked on the wounded foot with a clasp knife and a long, thin probe. Robert heard a groan of pain as he held the horse. After a few minutes that seemed more like an hour under these tense conditions, Gaillard announced, "I've got it." He held up a misshapen piece of lead. "Would you like to have it, General?"

Hampton shook his head without saying anything. His lips were clamped together against the pain.

Gaillard tossed the spent ball aside and quickly wrapped a dressing around the foot. Hampton tightened his grip on the reins and said, "Get my boot, Lieutenant."

Robert picked up the bloody boot, and he and Gaillard drew it over the bandaged foot. It was a tight fit, but Gaillard said that was good. "It should help stop the bleeding," he said.

"Thank you, Doctor," Hampton said. He was pale but composed. "Sorry about your horse."

Gaillard shrugged. "I'll find another. There should be plenty of mounts around here."

That bit of grim prediction was certainly true, Robert thought. Casualties had been high. Just from where he was, he had seen several of the men from his company fall during the battle.

Hampton rode on, and the line held, despite repeated attacks by the enemy. The thick overcast and the dense woods meant that darkness settled early over this part of the soggy Virginia countryside. As the shadows gathered, the firing dwindled. During the past month of skirmishing, Robert had learned that battles often didn't reach a conclusive end. They simply stopped, for one reason or another, and both sides slunk away to lick their wounds.

That was what happened at Fair Oaks. Robert moved along his section of the line and detailed some men to stay in place and serve as pickets. The others were allowed to pull back a short distance to tend to their injuries and try to find a place dry enough to build a fire—if they could find any dry wood.

As he neared the place where Ed Flanagan should have been, he asked one of the men about the sergeant. "Over there, Lieutenant," the soldier replied and jerked a thumb toward a deadfall. Robert felt a chill go through him.

Walking closer, he saw Flanagan sitting with his back propped against the trunk of the fallen tree. His head leaned forward on his chest. At first he thought he was asleep. Then he knelt next to Flanagan and lifted his head. In the last of the fading gray light he saw the dark hole in the sergeant's forehead above his sightlessly staring eyes.

Gently, Robert lowered Flanagan's head. He felt the hot sting of tears. He had known the sergeant for only a few months, but during that time Flanagan had come to be his friend as well as a dependable subordinate. "Damn it, Ed," Robert said softly.

There was nothing to be done other than to close Flanagan's eyes for him. Then he stood, swallowed hard, and turned to finish giving his orders to the men. The time for mourning not only Flanagan but also all the other dead would come later, after this battle was truly over.

"Get something to eat and try to get some rest," Robert told the men. "Morning will be here before you know it."

Morning came soon, and with it came more fighting. The clashes were more desultory on this day, not as fierce as they had been the day before. The result was a continuing stalemate.

Morning also brought news that General Johnston had been wounded the previous evening, taking a bullet in the shoulder. President Jefferson Davis, who had come out from Richmond in a carriage to see for himself how the battle was going, happened to be nearby when Johnston was hit. With the president was his military adviser, Gen. Robert E. Lee. Seeing that Johnston was unable to continue in command, Davis appointed Gen. Gustavus W. Smith to replace him.

Robert learned later that the fighting was the heaviest around Seven Pines on May 31, south of the woods where the Hampton Legion's infantry held off the Yankees. Although the Confederates got the better of the clashes around Seven Pines, through a series of blunders and inaction on Smith's part, the Federals escaped from what might have been utter destruction. As often happened in battle, the pendulum swung one way and then the other, and neither side was prepared to seize the advantage and put a decisive end to things. The second day of fighting ended in a stalemate as well, with neither side anxious to continue for the moment.

The most significant developments to come out of the clash were Smith's failure to properly lead his troops and the rumored nervous breakdown that afflicted him. President Davis had no choice but to find another commander for the army. The man he chose was a veteran of the Mexican War, like so many other leading officers on both sides of the conflict. His name was Robert E. Lee.

Though he shared a given name with the new commander, Robert Gilmore knew little about Lee and didn't really care. He was more concerned with finding a new company sergeant to take Ed Flanagan's place. He promoted a corporal named Norman Doolittle, whose energetic nature belied his name.

The legion also found itself without its leader. The day after his injury, Hampton's wounded foot was so infected and swollen that his boot had to be cut off of it. Over the general's protests, Dr. Gaillard declared him unfit for duty and sent him home to recuperate.

With McClellan and the Yankee army sitting in the distance, still menacing Richmond but showing no sign of movement for the time being, Lee's first orders had his new command digging rifle pits and erecting earthworks. Robert's Company E did as they were told, of course, but Robert doubted the wisdom of this action. They had been fighting defensive battles for more than two months now, and the end result was that the Yankees were almost within spitting distance of the capital and the defenders had been whittled down to fewer than ever before.

Help was on the way, though. During June 1862, Gen. Thomas J. "Stonewall" Jackson and his men had been summoned from the Shenandoah Valley, where they had been making life miserable for the Yankees up there with a string of decisive victories that threatened Washington DC and worried the hell out of President Lincoln. Once Jackson arrived, Robert thought, they might finally *do* something and carry the fight to the Yankees.

By late June, Jackson had reached the area where the Confederates had dug in, and Lee was ready to move. The rains that had bedeviled the armies all spring and into the summer had finally moved on, and the roads were beginning to dry out. Cavalry under the dashing Gen. James Ewell Brown "Jeb" Stuart made an incredibly daring reconnaissance completely around the Union army and brought back valuable intelligence.

By this time, Hampton had recuperated enough from his wound to return to the field and take command of the legion again. Robert was glad of that when he heard rumors that the army would soon be on the move. The general's absence hadn't hurt anything during the weeks of relative inactivity, but if they were going into battle again, Robert felt better knowing that Hampton would be in command.

The legion infantry was attached to the third brigade of Jackson's division. Robert had heard stories about Jackson's audacious campaign in the Shenandoah, and he had no doubt that his company would soon be in the thick of things again.

On June 25 a reconnaissance in force by some of McClellan's troops resulted in a brief battle at Oak Grove when the Yankees ran into the Southern defenders. The next day, June 26, Lee launched his offensive, sending three divisions across the Chickahominy to engage the Federals east of the settlement of Mechanicsville. Jackson was supposed to take part in this advance, but for some reason held back. Even without Jackson's troops, the Confederate attack was successful enough to rattle McClellan, who had already begun to have doubts about his strategy after the brutal fighting around Fair Oaks and Seven Pines. The Union commander began shifting his troops to the south and west, away from the York River and toward the James. McClellan wasn't exactly retreating—yet—but his interminable advance toward Richmond had been blunted.

There was more maneuvering on June 28–29. So far the legion had not taken part in any of the fighting, a situation that had to be eating at Hampton. Robert knew the general was no warmonger—indeed, no one had worked harder before the war to head off the conflict—nor was he the sort of man who was content to stand on the sidelines when something was going on.

On June 30 Hampton and the legion finally had their chance. Along with the rest of Jackson's division, they advanced to White Oak Swamp. All they had to do was cross the swamp to be in position to fall on the rear of the Union forces. There were Yankees in the swamp, though, and they put up a fight.

As the infantry made its way through the thick woods surrounding the marshy area, Robert again found himself in a hornet's nest of bullets and minié balls. The tangled undergrowth was so thick, it was impossible to maintain any sort of line as the company advanced. Within a short time, the fighting had deteriorated into a hellish melee of single combats as the Confederates tried to drive the Yankees back.

Robert lost track of time. He emptied his pistol again and again, and when he had no more ammunition, he used his saber, hacking at the Federals who rushed at him out of the brush. A bayonet cut his left arm, but not too deeply. A second later, the blade of Robert's saber sheared cleanly into the side of his enemy's neck. Blood spurted as Robert yanked the blade free. The Yankee toppled, dead before he hit the ground. Robert gulped down a breath, feeling an instant of nausea as he inhaled the coppery scent of the fresh blood. He was able to suppress the sickness and press on.

The Confederate advance faltered when the Yankees retreated across a bridge that spanned the stream winding through the swamp and then burned the bridge behind them. Hampton himself scouted out a place where a new bridge could be constructed quickly. His men fell to work, putting down their guns and taking up axes. Robert wielded an ax himself, chopping down trees until his arms felt like lead and his uniform was soaked with sweat. But the bridge was soon finished, and the Confederates were ready to cross over, strike the Federal right with smashing force, and possibly even defeat McClellan's entire army.

Jackson, the daring wizard of the Shenandoah, did nothing, however. All of Hampton's work went for naught as the order to attack never came, and that night and the next day McClellan continued his withdrawal from the vicinity of Frayser's Farm, near White Oak Swamp.

If Hampton was seething with frustration at Jackson's failure to act, so were his men. "We could've had 'em, Lieutenant," Norm Doolittle said in camp on the night of June 30. "We could've kicked Little Mac's tail from here to yonder."

"I can't disagree with you, Sergeant," Robert replied. The instinct to trust his commanding officers made him add, "But I'm sure General Jackson knows what he's doing."

Deep down, however, Robert wasn't sure at all. He was afraid they had missed a wonderful chance, perhaps the best chance so far of forcing the North to agree to a negotiated peace and independence for the South.

When the sun rose on July 1, McClellan was still retreating toward the James River, and Lee was still pursuing. This campaign was ending exactly opposite of the way it had begun, with the Confederates now chasing the Federals. The pace was a bit more brisk than it had been during the spring, though, during McClellan's advance. Clearly, the Yankees had abandoned any hope of reaching Richmond and now just wanted to get away. If they could make it to the James, steamboats could pick them up and carry them to safety. But Lee didn't want them to escape.

So Lee sent Jackson chasing after the Yankees again, who by now were ensconced atop a height known as Malvern Hill. Their artillery commanded the field. Before the Confederate attack could get under way, the big guns began to roar, sending bloody destruction thundering into the ranks of gray and butternut.

To Robert, trying to lead his company up the hill into the teeth of the Federal bombardment, it seemed as if the heavens had opened up a rain of fire and steel and lead. He was waving his saber over his head, firing his pistol toward the Yankee line, and shouting to his men to keep moving when the earth suddenly erupted in a huge blast right in front of him, flinging him up and back. An image of his beloved Jacqueline's face flashed through his mind, then blackness engulfed him.

The Yankees on top of Malvern Hill repulsed every Confederate attack during that long day. And while they were doing that, the rest of McClellan's army was making its getaway. This was the last engagement of what came to be known as the Seven Days' battles, and although Richmond had been saved, the Southerners had lost their first—and perhaps last—best chance to destroy their enemy.

But Lt. Robert Gilmore knew none of that, because while the Yankees slipped away, he lay senseless on the bloody, artillery-torn, corpse-littered field in front of Malvern Hill.

CHAPTER TWELVE

Showdown on James Island

THE SPRING OF 1862 was a good one for Cam Gilmore. Not only was he getting rich from the poker games in his barracks, but he was also seeing Lucinda Tyler again on a regular basis. Since that nighttime rendezvous in the carriage, Lucinda had begun to flourish, putting on some weight, regaining her color, and emerging from the deep melancholy that had gripped her. Cam wasn't surprised by Lucinda's dramatic improvement. Making love with him was good for whatever ailed a woman.

Neither Allard nor Malachi cared much for his being around the Tyler mansion more often, but they didn't try to run him off. Maybe they saw that Lucinda was doing better with him back in her life. Besides, the Tyler men had other things on their minds. Cam had heard them arguing heatedly on several occasions about the work at the shipyard. Obviously Allard had strong opinions and didn't mind expressing them, and that naturally rubbed Malachi the wrong way. Malachi still regarded his son as a stubborn, ignorant boy, but in reality, Allard had become a man.

Cam wouldn't have put up with being treated that way. He would have taken Diana and moved out of the mansion, that is, if he were married to her. But he suspected Katherine Tyler played a large part in keeping Allard at home. She, too, thought of him as a boy, and she didn't want to lose him.

Cam didn't devote a lot of time or energy to worrying about such things, though. He was more concerned with snatching every opportunity he could to be with Lucinda, who was proving to be as eager and inventive a lover as she had been during their first dalliances. He had his classes at the Citadel to keep up with, too, and the almost nightly poker games. It was a full, happy life—so full, indeed, that he barely thought about the war and the damned Yankees.

And then they had to go and try to invade Charleston again.

THE SEMIANNUAL examinations and the end of the Citadel's term came in late May. Instead of being given the usual holiday, the cadets were ordered to remain in Charleston since they were considered part of the city's defensive forces. Cam didn't mind. He liked his family well enough and usually enjoyed the time he spent on the farm, but given the intensity of his relationship with Lucinda, he was just as happy to stay close to her.

They were walking in the garden behind the Tyler mansion on an evening in early June when Cam heard a commotion of sorts coming from downtown. Bells began to ring, and he even heard shouts carried through the warm, flower-scented air.

"What the devil?" he muttered as he turned to frown toward the source of the distant uproar.

"Don't pay any attention to it," Lucinda said as she clutched his arm. She turned him to face her. "Kiss me instead."

Cam's frown became a grin. He could always find out what the ruckus was all about later. He put his arms around Lucinda and drew her close to him. She felt solid in his embrace now, not fragile and brittle as she had been before, when he had feared she would break somehow if he held her too tightly.

His mouth found hers. Their lips clung together with a heated urgency. Cam felt desire welling up within him and wondered if they dared do anything adventurous in the garden, where they could be discovered easily. He wouldn't mind trying, he decided. A hint of danger always added spice to their liaisons, and he knew Lucinda felt the same way.

Brazenly, her lips parted and her tongue probed his mouth. Cam responded strongly, as Lucinda must have felt, because her belly was pressed firmly against his groin.

Before things could go any further, though, the slamming of a door from the house made them release each other and practically leap apart. Footsteps crunched on the gravel path that led through the garden. They turned toward the approaching interloper. Cam reached down and took Lucinda's hand to make it look like they were simply out for an innocent walk—although he suspected that that wouldn't fool most of the occupants of the mansion. Still, as long as they could maintain the appearance of propriety, the others would turn a deliberately blind eye to the carrying on. That was easier than causing a big scene that would inevitably result in a brawl or a challenge to a duel.

Allard appeared on the path as he rounded some shrubs. "There you are!" he said. "Cam, you need to get back to the Citadel." Allard seemed to be upset by something more than just finding his sister in the garden with Cam.

"What's wrong?" Cam asked. "Something has happened, hasn't it? Is it the Yankees again?"

"One of Mr. Trenholm's servants has just brought word that there are Federal gunboats on the Stono River," Allard replied grimly, "and rumors that troops are going to land on James Island, around Secessionville."

The area south and west of Charleston was a veritable maze of islands, some large, some small. The largest, James Island, bordered the harbor and part of the city. The Stono River divided James Island from John's Island to the west, and it ran to within a very short distance of the city itself. There had been a great deal of talk in Charleston about the possibility that Yankee gunboats might steam up the Stono and then reach the inner harbor by way of Wappoo Cut, a distance of less than a mile. The Citadel cadets had been dispatched to guard the cut the previous November. Should Federal troops occupy James Island itself, they could set up batteries that would have no trouble firing on the city and pounding it to ruins. It was a possibility that filled most of Charleston's residents with cold horror. If the Yankees were about to launch such a campaign, they had to be stopped.

Lucinda's fingers tightened on Cam's hand. "Do you have to go?" she asked in a small voice.

He nodded. "I reckon so. If the city is in danger, we'll be called out to help defend it, for sure."

"Be careful, Cam."

"Oh, I intend to be," he said, meaning it with all his being. If there was a fight, he would keep his head as low as possible. Life was too sweet for him to even think about getting himself killed.

Allard urged him on, saying, "You'd better go now. They may be looking for you."

"I had permission to leave," Cam said. "And there's been no official recall orders."

"You don't know that," Allard pointed out.

Cam shrugged. "I'm going." He turned to Lucinda. "I'll be back to see you as soon as I can, but it may be a few days."

"Just don't let anything happen to you," she said as she looked into his eyes in the rapidly fading light.

"No chance of that," he said with his usual cocky grin.

Allard finally perceived the hint and turned to walk back toward the mansion. Cam cupped a hand under Lucinda's chin and bent his face to hers again, brushing his lips across hers in a kiss that was tender and gentle rather than hot and wanton with passion. She moved her hands to his arms, and her fingers dug in briefly from the depth of the emotion she obviously felt.

What had happened between them? Cam wondered dazedly. Had she actually fallen in love with him? That didn't seem possible. Neither of them were the sort to be swept away by foolish romantic notions. They just took their pleasure where they found it and never worried about such things as love and commitment. Maybe the war really did change all that. But he would have to ponder those possibilities later. Right now, he had to return to the academy. Allard was right. If they looked for him and couldn't find him, he might get into trouble.

Giving Lucinda one last smile, he turned and hurried after Allard, catching up with him before they reached the mansion. "Do you think there'll be a battle?" he asked in a quiet voice.

"If the Yankees land on James Island, there will be. We can't afford to let them occupy it. Charleston would fall in a week if they do."

"You sound like you wish you could be in on the fighting."

Allard nodded. "This is my home too. I want to defend it. But that job will fall to the army . . . and the cadets."

Cam swallowed hard. "Yes, I suppose it will. It's up to us to stop the Yankees." And suddenly, that responsibility seemed almost overwhelming.

BY THE next day, Charleston was in a state of near panic. Convinced that the city would soon be in the hands of the Yankees, some residents loaded up carts and wagons with their furniture and possessions and abandoned their homes, heading out for some place they considered safer. From the Citadel Green, where the cadets were assembled, Cam saw quite a few of the heavily laden vehicles rolling past. Men on horseback, some on mules, also thronged the streets. But the cadets couldn't leave. As Cam had suspected would happen, they had orders concerning the part they were to play in the city's defense.

For the past few months there had been considerable debate about the proper role for the academy's students. Some thought they should be released from their commitment to the Citadel and allowed to join whatever army units they chose. There was considerable sentiment for this course of action among the cadets themselves. Many of them wanted to serve with the regiments that had been raised in their home counties. Others believed it would be better to keep the cadets where they were, since they already formed a cohesive, well-trained force that could be employed in Charleston's defense. The stalemate had yet to be resolved, and now it looked as if events beyond the control of the Confederates were going to decide the issue.

Maj. J. B. White, superintendent of the Citadel, addressed the cadets assembled on the parade ground: "Gentlemen, the rumors you have no doubt heard by now are true. Federal infantry, supported by gunboats on the Stono River, landed yesterday on James Island, below Secessionville. The Twenty-fourth South Carolina under the command of Lieutenant Colonel Capers engaged them, but our forces were forced to withdraw by the heavy fire from the Yankee gunboats. I regret to inform you that the Federals now occupy the southwestern part of James Island as well as Folly Island and part of John's Island."

That was bad news, all right, Cam thought, almost as bad as what everybody feared. But there was still hope. The Yankees were still on the side of James Island farthest from the city, and from the sound of what Major White had said, they controlled only a small portion of the island. They could still be stopped.

"Accordingly," White continued, "General Pemberton, the commanding officer of the Department of South Carolina, Georgia, and Florida, has issued the following order." He read from the piece of paper in his hand: "The City of Charleston being at this time threatened, Major J. B. White, Superintendent of the State Military Academy, will proceed with as little delay as possible with the Corps of Cadets and the eight pieces at the Citadel belonging to the State of South Carolina to James Island and report to Brigadier General S. R. Gist, Provisional Army of the Confederate States, to occupy the west side of the line of entrenchments at Newton's Cut. Signed, J. C. Pemberton, Major General, Commanding."

White lowered the paper. "Gentlemen, I don't have to tell you that before this is over, the outcome may depend on those eight artillery pieces and our gallantry in manning them. I know that, come what may, none of you will let me down, and none of you will dishonor the Citadel or our beloved Palmetto State."

With that, the major saluted, and all the cadets returned his salute. He turned and walked briskly toward the building while his subordinates took charge of the cadets, directing them in the task with which they had been charged.

Loading the heavy guns on their carriages and transporting them was backbreaking work, but the cadets threw themselves into the job with the enthusiasm they always mustered. There was an added urgency to their actions now, because they all knew that the survival of Charleston might hinge on what they did.

Luckily, for the moment, the Yankees seemed content to sit where they were on the Grimball plantation southwest of the hamlet of Secessionville, named for a dispute that had occurred within a group of plantation owners and had nothing to do with the war or secession from the Union. It was an apt name, though, considering the confrontation that might soon occur near here.

Two weeks passed, during which time the cadets, along with Major White and the other officers and professors who supervised them, transported the Citadel's big guns to James Island and assisted in mounting them in a line stretching south from the Wappoo Cut to an earthen fort known as the Tower Battery. The nine-foot-tall earthworks that shielded the Tower Battery were formed roughly in the shape of a M, with the points aimed at Secessionville. Behind the earthen walls were nine cannon, including a massive 24-inch Columbiad, with soldiers from the South Carolina Artillery manning them, Col. Thomas G. Lamar commanding. There were also approximately seven hundred infantrymen stationed at the fort, with two thousand more in reserve not far away at Fort Johnson, on the harbor side of the island.

There were more cadets on James Island than were needed to man the guns they had brought with them, so they were spread out along the line and temporarily attached to other units. Cam found himself assigned to the Tower Battery, and it didn't escape his notice that this post was the closest to the Yankees and more than likely the first place they would strike when they began their inevitable advance across the island. But there was nothing he could do about it other than wait and hope that the Yankees would change their minds and go away. There was only a slim chance of that happening, but he wasn't going to give up on the possibility.

In the two weeks since leaving Charleston, he hadn't seen Lucinda, of course, or even heard from her, although some of the cadets had received notes from loved ones brought out from the city. He missed her fiercely, even more than he had thought he would, and he wondered what she was doing. He hoped that she longed for him as much as he longed for her. When this threat from the Yankees was over, they would have quite a reunion. Yes sir, quite a reunion.

That is, if she was still in Charleston. For all Cam knew, Malachi Tyler had packed up his family and left the city like so many others. But that didn't seem like something Malachi would do. He was so stubborn and defiant, he was more likely to stay where he was and spit in the eye of any Yankee bold enough to march up to him.

Cam was standing guard on the parapet behind the earthworks of the Tower Battery early on the morning of June 14. The sky was still dark, but there was a line of light on the eastern horizon heralding the approach of dawn. He yawned prodigiously. He hated predawn guard duty; it was almost impossible for him to stay awake at this time of day. Anyone civilized would still be curled up in a nice, soft bed rather than leaning on some earthworks in the middle of a marshy, palmetto-dotted island plain. He yawned again and then coughed because he had almost swallowed a mosquito. He hated the damned flying, biting pests almost as much as he hated the fleas that infested the sand of the island and the Yankees for causing him to be out here in these miserable conditions.

He remembered listening to Robert and Allard talking about their adventures with the cadets when their battery had turned back the *Star of the West* as it tried to reach Fort Sumter. Now, something like that would be exciting . . . the roar of the cannon, the fiery trails of the shells arching through the sky, the brilliance of the explosions as they burst above the enemy and sent him scurrying away ignominiously. Cam wouldn't mind if he could take part in something like that instead of just standing here in the muggy predawn darkness.

He heard something in the blackness beyond the earthworks. A jingle and a rattle, a shuffle and a rustle, the hiss of a voice issuing commands. As the significance of those tiny, almost inaudible sounds penetrated his weary brain, he stood up straight, his back stiffening and his eyes widening in alarm.

"Sergeant of the Guard!" he yelled, forgetting at this moment the proper way for a sentry to report. "Sergeant of the Guard, somebody's out there! Must be the damned Yankees!"

The next instant, a burst of flame gouted in the darkness as a rifle blasted, and Cam heard something he recognized instantly, even though he had never experienced it before: the sound of a bullet whistling past his ear.

He threw himself flat on the parapet and uttered a heartfelt expletive. They were shooting at him!

More rifle fire began to rattle, from both the earthworks and the marshes around the fort, as the attacking Union force and the Confederate defenders opened up on each other. Cam knew he couldn't just lie there on the parapet, out of the line of fire, no matter how much he wanted to. He was a soldier. He had to fight. Sick fear roiled his stomach as he tried to push himself upright.

Not far away, Colonel Lamar had taken command of the giant Columbiad. The gunnery crew prepared the cannon for firing, then Lamar issued the order. With an ear-pounding roar, the big gun blasted a devastating charge of grapeshot, chain, and nails into the center of the advancing Federal line. Cam finally succeeded in sticking his head above the earthworks just as the deadly storm of lead and steel scythed through the Yankees. Even half deafened from the roar of the cannon and the constant rattle of rifle fire, Cam heard men screaming as they were cut down.

Shakily, he thrust the barrel of his rifle over the top of the earthen wall and aimed at the flickering muzzle flashes of the enemy. He pulled the trigger and felt the butt kick against his shoulder, well aware that under the circumstances he would never know if his shot hit anything or not. That wasn't entirely a bad thing. He crouched down and began to reload, his movements fumbling at first but becoming smoother as all the training and drilling began to come back to him.

As Lamar shouted orders, the other guns in the battery joined in the battle. Manning them was dangerous work, because the Yankees had worked their way along three sides of the fortress in the darkness, and deadly fire from the trees a couple of hundred yards away swept the parapets. Several gunners fell.

Cam fired and reloaded several times, and then as he rose from his crouch to fire, he heard yelling close by. At first he thought it came from inside the fort, but then he realized with a sickening feeling that the shouts came from outside. The Yankees were right there, only a few feet away, trying to scale the earthen walls.

"Damn it! Damn it! Damn it!" Cam muttered to himself. The battle was only a few minutes old, and already they were in danger of being overrun. He poked his rifle over the wall and angled the barrel down as much as he could before he fired. As flame geysered from the muzzle, the glare lit up the faces of the Yankees who were trying to scramble up the muddy earthworks. Cam saw one of them thrown backward and knew that he had just shot the man.

He ducked back as bullets swarmed around his head like bees. More soldiers crowded around him as his just-slumbering comrades from the camp behind the fort rushed forward to reinforce the men on the walls.

Cam slipped down until he was sitting on the parapet. He scooted over to the edge and dropped off so that he landed on the ground. This was insane, he thought. If he stayed up there, he would get himself killed, and he had promised Lucinda he wouldn't do that.

An officer hurrying past him grabbed his arm and practically flung him toward the north wall. "Over there!" the man shouted. "They're trying to flank us! Get up there and hold them off!"

"By myself?" Cam yelped, but it was too late. The officer was gone, running on to grab more men and order them to the north wall.

Cam's heart slammed against his chest. He had never been so scared in his life. The part of his brain that was still calm, though, reminded him that he had been given a direct order. He had already pretty much deserted his post under fire, although in all the confusion he doubted anyone had noticed him leaving the parapet. Could he refuse to obey an order that would put him back in the line of fire? Was he that big a coward?

The press of men around him carried him toward the wall. He didn't fight against it. That was as close as he came to making an actual decision. Like a bit of human flotsam in the tide of war, he was carried back into the battle.

He scrambled onto the parapet and paused to reload before straightening and firing. A few yards away, one of the Yankees succeeded in leaping on top of the wall, but he lost his balance and fell with a scream onto the waiting bayonets of the Confederate troops inside the fort. Cam looked away, feeling sick again. The memory of spurting bright red blood was imprinted on his brain anyway, and as he thought about that, he realized it had grown light enough for him to be able to see that crimson horror.

He didn't have time to reload because more Yankees had reached the top of the wall and were trying to get over it. A Union officer fired a pistol down into the body of the man right next to Cam. The unfortunate soldier grunted in pain and folded up. Without thinking, Cam drove his bayonet at the Yankee and felt the sharp blade punch through the man's uniform jacket and penetrate his belly. The dying Yankee screamed and tried to swing his pistol toward Cam, but Cam shoved with the rifle and sent the man flying backward off the wall. Blood flew in the air as the bayonet ripped its way free of muscle and sinew.

Another Yankee appeared and hacked down at Cam with a saber. Cam twisted his rifle sideways and blocked the blow, then drove the rifle butt into the attacker's midsection. The man toppled backward off the wall, too, but he would live to keep fighting.

More troops crowded onto the parapet. Cam was forced forward until he was pinned between the weight of the soldiers and the earthen wall itself. He was vaguely aware that he was screaming curses as he jabbed with his bayonet again and again at the Yankees trying to overrun the fort. For a while he thought it must have begun to rain, because he felt fat wet drops falling on his face. Then he realized that it wasn't rain but blood showering down, coating his face, his hands, his body with gore. Tears welled from his eyes and rolled down his cheeks, leaving trails in the red smear. The fight went on and on . . . and on . . .

By nine o'clock, the sun was well up and the guns had fallen silent. Wave after wave of Yankees had rolled up against the earthen walls of the Tower Battery, but each time the attacks had been repulsed. Confederate reinforcements had arrived from Fort Johnson, and their deadly fire had swept the trees clear of the enemy. The Yankees had been forced to fall back and were now in full retreat, heading for their camp on the Grimball plantation half a mile away.

As clouds of smoke that had hung low over the battle began to disperse in the morning breeze, Cam sat on the parapet and leaned his back against the wall, surrounded by other weary men. He had a powder burn on his right cheek where a Yankee rifle had gone off almost in his face and nearly blown his brains out. A bruise and a gash on his forehead showed where he had taken a glancing blow from the barrel of an empty pistol wielded as a club by a Yankee officer. An instant after that blow had landed, Cam had gutted the man with his bayonet. Other than that, he was uninjured. Providence had been with him. More than fifty defenders had been killed in the battle, and hundreds more were seriously wounded.

His rifle lay across his lap. He lifted his hands and idly studied them. A sticky layer of blood had begun to dry on them. The blood was all over him, and he wondered if it would all wash off. Would he ever be able to get all of it off?

A cheer shattered his thoughts, and Cam lifted his eyes to look dully across the fort. They were cheering Colonel Lamar, who had led the defense and never given up. One of the men sitting beside Cam said, "They oughta change the name o' this place to Fort Lamar."

Whatever they called it was fine with Cam; he didn't give a damn either way. But if they wanted to give this place a new name, he knew what it should be. They ought to dub it Hell on Earth, because for several hours this June morning, that's exactly what it had been.

IN CHARLESTON that morning, Lucinda Tyler rose from her bed, went to the window of her room, and swept the curtains back. From here she could look southwest, toward James Island where Cam was. And as she peered in that direction she heard the distant rumble of artillery.

The Yankees were coming, and it would be up to Cam and the other cadets and the men with them to hold them back, to save Charleston from the pillaging hordes of Northern barbarians. Lucinda hoped the other soldiers would be brave. She had no confidence in Cam's bravery. He was a coward and a fool, and she had no illusions about that. But he had done what she wanted him to do. She put her hand on her belly and rubbed it through the thin nightdress. This morning it was still flat, but soon enough it would begin to swell as the life within her grew and flourished.

A second chance, that was what she had now, but the new life inside her represented more than that, far more. She hoped that Cam survived the battle, but she supposed it didn't really matter.

Her lips curved in a smile as the cannon roared. Whether Cam Gilmore was alive or dead, her plans were working out just fine either way.

CHAPTER THIRTEEN

A Visitor at Four Winds

J ACQUELINE LOCKHART WAS A petite, dark-haired girl who was possessed of a soulful beauty that could turn tempestuous when she was crossed. Her father had learned this early on and generally went out of his way to give his daughter whatever she wanted, that is, if it was within his power to do so.

Likewise the house servants at Four Winds, the Lockhart plantation northwest of Charleston, near the village of Mount Holly, tended to pamper Miss Jacqueline, partially because she was so small and pretty and could be very sweet when she wanted to be . . . but partially because they were afraid of her too. As a child, her tantrums had been epic, the stuff of legend in the Lockhart household. Everyone loved Miss Jacqueline, but no one wanted to cross her.

The only person at Four Winds who seemed to be totally unafraid of Jacqueline and unaffected by her occasionally bad behavior was her mother, Priscilla. She never hesitated to stand up to Jacqueline. Her husband, Everett, had thought more than once that was because the two of them were so similar—self-centered, opinionated, and utterly convinced that they were always right. He was, of course, much too wise a man to have ever expressed that thought to either of them.

On this beautiful August day in 1862, Everett Lockhart was in his study, going over accounts with one of his overseers. Priscilla was in the kitchen, instructing the cooks on the preparations she wanted made for dinner. Jacqueline was outside, riding along the lane between the house and the main road on a mare she had named Domino. Her skirts were pulled up, and she rode astride, like a man, with only a blanket on Domino's back. She had pulled the sidesaddle off the mare and dropped it at the side of the lane with an unladylike expletive a few minutes earlier. She couldn't gallop properly on the damned thing, and today she wanted the sun on her face and the wind streaming through her long black hair. She leaned forward, tightened her knees on Domino's flanks, and heeled the mare into a run.

The fields flashed by on both sides of her. At this speed, with her attention focused on the horse and the road ahead of her, she barely saw the slaves working in the fields.

They saw her, though, and some of them paused in their labor long enough to shake their heads in dismay at Miss Jacqueline's wild behavior. She'd be lucky if she didn't fall and break her neck, racing that horse that way. It would have been a stretch to say that any of them felt any real affection for the Lockhart family, even though their master wasn't cruel like so many plantation owners, but they didn't want to see the Little Miss get hurt, either.

The lane curved up ahead, and some trees and shrubs partially blocked the view around the turn. Jacqueline pulled on the reins and sent Domino pounding around the curve without slackening her speed. Then she saw the buggy right in her path and hauled back sharply on the reins, trying to bring the horse to a stop before there was a collision.

Domino's head came up and her legs flailed, almost out of control. She twisted and reared, and with a cry of alarm, Jacqueline felt her grip on the horse slipping. Suddenly there was nothing beneath her but air. That dizzying feeling of emptiness lasted only a split second. Then with an impact that knocked every bit of breath from her body, she hit the ground.

Jacqueline rolled through the dust of the lane, unable to stop herself, her arms and legs flopping loosely. She came to a stop lying on her stomach, too stunned to really know what had happened. All she was aware of was the terrible need for air. She tried to push herself up so that she could gasp for breath, but her muscles refused to work.

The thought shot through her mind that she was going to die of suffocation, lying on the ground like an animal. But not even that fear was enough to overcome the shock of falling and landing so hard.

Then strong hands grasped her and lifted her, and her lungs inflated again as she drew in a deep, shuddery breath. As she sprawled there, half lying and half sitting in the road, supported by whoever had helped her, she gasped several more times until the dizziness that gripped her began to ease and the terror of death subsided. Panting now, she turned her head and stared through the hair that had fallen over her eyes at a broad, dark, familiar face.

"T-Tobias!" she choked out.

He nodded. A former slave on Four Winds, he was now a freedman and, in partnership with Jacqueline's father, owned a blacksmith shop and livery stable in Mount Holly. Everett Lockhart had manumitted him several years earlier after Tobias had saved Jacqueline from being killed by a wild horse.

"Yes'm, Miss Jacqueline, it's me," he said. "Are you all right?"

"I . . . I think so." She moved her arms and legs. Everything seemed to be working like it was supposed to. She drew in another deep breath and didn't feel any stabbing pains. That meant she probably didn't have any broken ribs. She was willing to bet that she would be awfully bruised and sore from the fall come the next day, though.

Her mind was still a little stunned. Now she thought back on what had happened, she remembered that a black man had been driving the buggy she'd almost run into. That was probably Tobias. But there had been another man on the seat with him, a white man, and as Jacqueline lay there and gave a shake of her head, she realized that there had been something familiar about the other man.

"Jacqueline! Jacqueline, my God! Are you all right?"

The voice was familiar, too, and as Jacqueline recognized it, she stiffened in surprise and jerked her head toward the buggy. The man had climbed down from the vehicle and was now moving awkwardly toward her, limping heavily and supporting himself with a cane. His face was pale with strain and worry, and there were dark hollows under his eyes.

But Jacqueline had never seen a more handsome man in her life. "Robert!" she screamed and scrambled to her feet, the fall from the horse and the resulting aches and pains forgotten in that instant of recognition.

She threw herself into his arms and almost knocked him down. He caught himself with the cane and balanced on it as she wrapped her arms around his neck and hugged him tightly. He held her and murmured her name.

She held on to him with a desperate strength that was surprising for such a petite young woman. Her body shook a little as she began to cry. Robert continued to hold her while Tobias retrieved Domino and watched them with a grin on his face.

After a while, Jacqueline finally sniffled a few times, lifted her head, and took one arm from around Robert's neck so that she could wipe her eyes and face. "Robert," she whispered. "What are you doing here? You . . . you look like you've been hurt." She stepped back a pace. "Let me take a look at you."

He wore a clean gray uniform and hat with a captain's shoulder boards. Despite the military outfit, he wasn't carrying a pistol or a saber, only the cane. And he had lost weight. His normally rounded face was now more sharp planes and angles, and there were a few touches of gray in the brown hair under his hat, even though he wasn't quite yet twenty years old.

"What happened to you?" she asked in a worried voice.

"The war happened to me," he said with a faint smile. Then added, "Actually, I was wounded at a place called Malvern Hill. We were trying to chase down the Yankee army before it could get away. We couldn't stop it, though."

Jacqueline put a hand to her mouth. "Oh, my God," she said. "I don't care about the war right now, Robert. What happened to *you*?"

"A shell burst right in front of me. If I'd been a little quicker going up the hill, I wouldn't be here now." He shrugged. "As it was, it was a pretty near thing. I was blown backward and knocked out. Shrapnel from the bursting shell wounded me in several places, the worst in this leg." He patted his right thigh lightly. "I probably would have laid there and bled to death if the order hadn't come just a few minutes later for us to pull back. My company sergeant found me and hauled me to the rear. I owe Norman Doolittle my life. After that the field surgeons patched me up as best they could and sent me into Richmond, where I was in the hospital for a couple of weeks."

Jacqueline moved closer to him and rested her forehead against the his uniform jacket. "Thank God you lived," she murmured. "Thank God. I can't imagine a world without you."

Robert put his free arm around her again. "You can give yourself some credit for that," he told her. "It was thinking about you, about your beautiful face and how much I wanted to hold you again, that kept me from giving up when things got really bad."

"Was . . . was the pain awful?"

"Not as bad as the thought that if I didn't recover, I'd never see you again."

She nuzzled wordlessly against him.

After another while had passed, Tobias cleared his throat and said, "I hate to say anything, but you two gon' get sun stroke if'n you don't get in some shade. C'mon up here in the buggy. I'll tie your horse to the back, Miss Jacqueline, an' we can go on to Four Winds."

Jacqueline looked up at Robert and nodded. "That's a good idea. You need to get off your feet. And I'm sure Mother and Father will be so happy to see you."

"Your father, maybe," Robert said. "I'm not so sure about your mother."

Her blue eyes narrowed into a stormy look. "She won't be rude to you. I won't have it."

"Let's don't borrow trouble ahead of time," Robert said as he rested a hand on her shoulder. "Come along."

They walked over to the buggy, where Jacqueline helped Robert climb to the seat and then stepped up and settled herself beside him. Tobias tied Domino to the back of the vehicle and then walked up to take hold of the buggy horse's harness.

"I'll just walk and lead this critter," he said, "'stead of crowdin' you folks."

"We can make room for you, Tobias," Jacqueline offered. Most well-bred Southern girls would have blanched at the idea of sharing a seat with a black man, even a freedman, but Jacqueline didn't care about such things.

"Don't you worry 'bout it," Tobias said with a grin and a wave of a big hand. "'Tain't far to the house. I can walk it easy."

He set off along the lane, leading the horse. As the buggy lurched into motion, Robert's breath hissed between his teeth for a second, and Jacqueline knew that he was still in some pain from his wounds. She took his hand and asked, "Will you be all right?"

"Sooner or later," he said. "It'll take some time. But I'm already a lot better than I was. The doctors let me out of the hospital and said it would be all right for me to go home and recover. I spent a week on the farm with my family, and then I knew that I had to see you."

"You shouldn't have made the trip if you weren't up to it."

"I'm fine. Anyway, I'd have been a lot worse if I'd had to go back without seeing you."

She held his hand and leaned her head on his shoulder, and they rode together in companionable silence for a few moments.

Robert chuckled and asked, "What were you doing racing the horse along like you were some sort of wild Indian? And did I see that you were riding astride? I only caught a glimpse before you were thrown off."

She lifted her head and gave it a defiant toss. "I like to ride fast, and you can't do that on a stupid sidesaddle. Not fast enough, anyway."

He laughed this time. "You really haven't changed much, have you?"

"Would you want me to?"

"No," he said without hesitation. "No, not really."

When they came to the spot where Jacqueline had thrown down the sidesaddle and also discarded the wide-brimmed straw hat she had been wearing, Tobias picked up the saddle and placed it in the buggy, then handed her the hat. She settled it on her head, and he said, "Pretty as ever, Miss Jacqueline."

"Thank you, Tobias." She turned to look at Robert. "I don't believe *you've* told me how pretty I am today, Mr. Gilmore."

"I assumed that went without saying," he grinned.

"It *never* goes without saying."

"In that case, you look absolutely lovely, Miss Lockhart. Ravishing, even."

"Don't get carried away. You're still weak from your injuries, you know."

As Tobias led the buggy along the lane, he waved and called out to some of the field hands he remembered from his years on the plantation. They responded, but Jacqueline noticed that they didn't seem that happy to see their old friend. The fact that Tobias was free made everything different. Now there was a barrier between him and the slaves, just as there was between black and white. Tobias's expression became a little glum, and Jacqueline felt sorry for him. She supposed he was a man with no place to really call his own. If the Yankees could see that, she mused, they might not be so quick to want to free all the other slaves. They might have thought twice about tearing the country apart with an unnecessary war. A war that put the man she loved with all her heart at the risk of losing his life.

"Robert," she said, "will you have to go back? Or are you finished with the army?"

Before he could answer, the buggy reached the drive that circled in front of the magnificent house with its wide gallery and impressive columns. As they started toward the house, Robert said, "We'll talk about that later."

Jacqueline didn't like the sound of that answer. She didn't like it at all.

Everett Lockhart was indeed glad to see Robert. He grabbed the young man's hand and enthusiastically welcomed him to Four Winds. "We'll have to have a long talk while you're here, son," he said warmly. "I want you to tell me everything you can about the war."

"I'm not sure I know that much, sir," Robert said.

"Nonsense. You're an officer, a captain now. Last I heard you were a lieutenant. You've been promoted."

"A battlefield promotion," Robert explained. "General Hampton thought I deserved it for my action during the Seven Days."

In fact, Hampton had visited his wounded lieutenant in the hospital ward in Richmond to inform him of the promotion. Robert wasn't sure why he was being promoted, but he wondered if it was because he had survived when so many other officers had not. The other way to look at it was to figure that he'd been promoted for nearly getting himself blown to bits.

But whatever the reason, he was a captain and still in command of Company E, although Norman Doolittle was the company's acting commander until Robert returned. That thought cast a pall over him. He wasn't looking forward to the conversation with Jacqueline when he had to explain that.

Nor was he looking forward to seeing Jacqueline's mother again, but that couldn't be avoided, either. Priscilla Lockhart greeted him politely in the parlor, giving him her hand while Jacqueline stood by, clutching Robert's arm, ready to spring to his defense if her mother dared to say or do anything uncivil.

Priscilla smiled, though, and said, "Welcome to our home, Captain Gilmore. Please, won't you sit down? Jacqueline tells me that you were wounded in defense of our gallant cause. It's fine, just fine, to have a hero in our home."

Robert managed to say thank you, wondering if his military service had improved her opinion of him. He wasn't going to count on that, but he supposed it was a possibility. "I wouldn't mind getting off my feet for a while."

He sat on a comfortable divan while Jacqueline perched close beside him. Her parents took wing chairs across from them. Everett took out a cigar, offered it to his guest, then took it himself when Robert declined it.

"We're honored that you came to see us," Everett said. "Did you take the train from Richmond?"

"Yes sir. When I got off at Mount Holly, I walked to Tobias's shop to see about renting a horse from him, the way I did when I visited before."

Immediately, he regretted mentioning that, because it made him think of the way he and Jacqueline had made love in the shed that day, the first and only time either of them had experienced the act. He was afraid that the guilt he felt would show on his face and that her parents would know what he had done. Their expressions didn't change, though, so he continued.

"Tobias remembered me, and once he saw I'd been wounded, he wouldn't hear of renting me a horse. He insisted on bringing me here himself in a buggy. And to tell the truth, I was very grateful that he did. I would have ridden if I'd had to, but it was a lot easier not to."

"You don't need to be riding a horse," Jacqueline said. "You don't need to be doing anything except resting and getting well."

"Well, that's pretty much the idea," he said with a smile. "I plan to go on to Charleston to see Allard. I hear he and Diana are married now."

"For quite some time, actually," Priscilla said. "It was a lovely ceremony. Jacqueline was maid of honor, you know."

"Yes. And my brother, Cam, was best man. I wish I could have been there to stand up for Allard."

Everett said, "War requires sacrifices of us all. Did you know that Allard almost died when the Yankees sank the ship he was on?"

"Yes, he sent a letter telling me about that and about the wedding and working for his father at the shipyard. It's all been quite a change for him."

Everett looked over at his wife. "Why don't we go to Charleston with Robert? I wouldn't mind visiting friends."

Priscilla thought about it, but only for a moment before she nodded. "I think I'd like that."

Jacqueline squeezed Robert's arm. "That's a wonderful idea. We can spend even more time together that way."

Robert was happy to go along with it. That way he wouldn't have to leave Jacqueline in order to see Allard and also Cam. While he was in the Richmond hospital, he had read that the Yankees had attempted an invasion across James Island directed at Charleston, but they had been repulsed by forces that included the Citadel cadets. Robert was curious to know if Cam had seen any action during that engagement. He was glad he hadn't known the battle was imminent before it happened; he would have worried about Cam. Sometimes ignorance was a good thing, he supposed.

A servant announced that dinner was ready. Smiling, Priscilla stood and said, "Gentlemen, shall we?"

She continued to be polite, even friendly, through dinner. Afterward, Everett insisted on brandy and cigars with Robert in his study. Robert didn't feel he could refuse. Not surprisingly, Everett wanted to talk about the war.

"Everyone was afraid that losing General Johnston was going to hurt the cause quite badly," Robert said as he sat in an armchair and held a snifter of brandy. "But General Lee acquitted himself very well in the defense of Richmond. It's little short of a miracle that the Yankees had that many men that close to the city and came away with nothing to show for it."

Everett said, "I don't know Bob Lee, but he has a good reputation from the Mexican War and his service out west. Doesn't seem to have done much so far in this war, though. He didn't want the war, you know. Thought it was a bad idea. But he's a Virginian, God bless him, and he had to come back to the Old Dominion when it needed him."

"We'll see what happens," Robert said. "I thought it was a little rash, throwing our forces against the Yankees on Malvern Hill the way he did, but he was eager to stop McClellan from getting away."

He wouldn't have made such comments, with the implied criticism of a superior officer, to another soldier, but Everett Lockhart was a civilian. And truthfully, Lee had shown some admirable daring during his time of command. If Jackson could break out of the unaccountable funk that had gripped him at White Oak Swamp, the two of them would make a formidable duo. The Yankees would have their hands full for sure.

"Robert," the older man said, leaning forward in his chair, "what are your plans?"

So far, Robert had managed to avoid answering that question from Jacqueline, but he could tell from the determined expression on Everett Lockhart's face that he couldn't dodge it here. "I'm on medical leave," he said. "When I've recovered sufficiently, I'll be returning to the Hampton Legion."

"These wounds of yours . . . they weren't bad enough for you to leave the army?" Everett held up a hand and added quickly, "You've served your country honorably, Robert. There would be no disgrace in hanging up your sword, so to speak."

"I know that," Robert said thickly, "but I don't think I can do that. This war is a long way from over, sir, and my men are counting on me to lead them."

"There are other officers, other men who can lead."

"Yes sir. But I feel my duty is still there."

Everett sat back and sighed. "Does my daughter know this?"

"We . . . haven't discussed the matter yet."

"She's not going to be happy about it, you know."

"Yes sir, I know."

"You'll do something for me?"

"Anything within my power, Mr. Lockhart."

"Be as gentle with her as you can when you tell her," Everett said. "It'll still hurt, but maybe you can cushion the blow."

"I'll try, sir," Robert promised, even though he didn't see any way he could make things easier on Jacqueline. However he told her that he was going to return to the army, she would be disappointed, scared, and probably angry.

Everett puffed on his cigar in silence for a moment. "You know, son, my daughter loves you."

"And I love her, sir." He felt a bit odd declaring it so bluntly, and to her father at that. But there was no point in beating around the bush.

"She hopes to marry you someday. I wouldn't mind it myself if that happened. I think you're a fine young man." Everett wiggled a hand. "My wife, now . . . Priscilla isn't as fond of the idea. But she's not as fond of you as Jacqueline is. She'll come around, given enough time." Everett's voice hardened. "See to it that you give her that time. Do you understand what I'm saying, Robert? I don't want to have to watch my daughter mourn you."

"I'll be as careful as I can, sir. I'd like to come back and marry Jacqueline."

"Are you asking me for her hand?" Everett asked sharply.

Robert took a deep breath. "No sir," he said. "I can't do that in good conscience when I can't guarantee what the future will bring. But the day will come when that's exactly what I'll be asking you."

"And I'll be looking forward to giving you my blessing." A grin spread over the old man's face. "Now I suppose we'd better get back to the ladies. Jacqueline will raise holy Ned with me if I monopolize your time while you're here."

They left the study and found Jacqueline and Priscilla in the parlor. Jacqueline hurriedly set aside her needlework and got to her feet to take Robert's arm. "I thought we'd take a walk down to the gazebo," she said. "There's a beautiful moon tonight, so there'll be plenty of light."

"I'm sure Captain Gilmore is much too tired for that, dear," Priscilla said before Robert could reply. "He was wounded, after all, and he probably has only a fraction of his strength."

Everett said, "Then some night air and a moonlight walk with a pretty girl might be just the thing he needs to invigorate him . . . eh, Captain?" He ignored his wife's quick glare. "Besides, young people are amazingly resilient."

"Some fresh air *might* do me good," Robert said.

"You see?" Everett waved a hand toward the door. "You two go right ahead."

"Remember, though," Priscilla said tightly, "Aunt Louella will be out there to chaperone."

"Mother . . ." Jacqueline began.

Priscilla's mouth firmed and her chin came up. Jacqueline sighed and said, "Oh, all right."

On their way out of the house, Robert leaned over to her and asked quietly, "Who's Aunt Louella?"

"My mother's personal maid. She has eyes like a hawk. We'll have to behave quite properly."

"I don't believe I'm up to any impropriety, anyway," he whispered. "I'm a wounded man, you know."

"I know." Jacqueline's voice was serious now. "And you and I have to talk about that, Robert Gilmore."

He closed his eyes for a second. First, Everett had pinned him down about his plans, and now Jacqueline was going to do the same thing.

Even though it was a lovely night, with the warm air scented with the fragrance of magnolia blossoms and soft silver light washing down from the big moon floating overhead and this most beautiful girl on his arm, Robert couldn't help but wish that he was facing Yankees again. At least in those battles, his side had a chance of winning.

CHAPTER FOURTEEN

Hard Times in Charleston

I N THE MONTHS THAT Robert had been away from the city, things had changed a great deal. Even though he had been born and raised on the family farm inland, he had come to know the city fairly well during the time he had spent at the Citadel. Because it was a busy port, with ships from all over the world docking there, Charleston had always possessed a certain cosmopolitan hustle and bustle. But at the same time, there was an undeniable graciousness to the place, a leisurely paced gentility and decorum that made it perhaps the most Southern of all Southern cities.

That sense of leisure and grace had been diminished by the tension everyone now felt because of the war. The Charlestonians knew all too well that the Yankees still occupied nearby Port Royal; indeed, the Federals still occupied parts of the marshy islands that lay along the shoreline just south of the city, and Yankee gunboats were spotted with increasing frequency as they cruised the Stono River with a sense of impunity.

To prepare for the full-scale invasion that seemed certain to come sooner or later, the areas around the harbor had been heavily fortified. Sandbags had been piled high to form earthworks, and behind them bristled the barrels of countless artillery. In some places along the shore, people's homes had been commandeered to quarter troops.

Other houses had been torn down to make way for gun emplacements. The citizens of Charleston and the surrounding area had been asked to make plenty of sacrifices, but most of them were made willingly, because the alternative was to be conquered by those ill-bred Northern barbarians.

Many of the big guns that were being set up to repel the Yankees had been brought from England by the ships that were regularly running the Union blockade, including Capt. Barnaby Yorke's *Diana*. The blockade-runners also brought in food and other supplies that the city desperately needed. But even their best efforts couldn't prevent shortages of some goods. The people bore up as well as they could under those hardships, too, still smiling, still determined to keep their beloved city from falling into the hands of the damned Yankees.

No one was more vehement about that than Malachi Tyler, who during dinner at the Tyler mansion with the Lockharts and Robert as guests, declared loudly, "Those scoundrels will never set foot in this city as long as one man in Charleston still has blood in his veins!" He banged his fist on the table for emphasis.

"Now, dear," his wife, Katherine, said with a nervous laugh, "there's no need to get so worked up about it. None of us like the Yankees, but you don't see us giving ourselves apoplexy over it!"

"You're right, Malachi," Everett Lockhart said from the other end of the table. "They can try, but they'll never succeed in wearing us down. Their blockade be damned!" He added, "My apologies, ladies."

Allard said, "You know, if it weren't for men like Cap'n Yorke, they'd be starving us out by now. We can still bring in supplies by rail, but not enough for the entire city."

"Yorke's performing a service, all right," Malachi admitted grudgingly. "He's made four trips to Nassau and back with the *Diana*, and each time he's returned with a hold full of supplies."

Everett smiled and asked, "That's a lucrative trade, isn't it, Malachi?"

"The money has nothing to do with it," Malachi insisted. "What's most important is the lifeline to the outside world that the blockade-runners give the Confederacy. Mark my words, England's going to officially recognize us and come into the fight on our side sooner or later. They need our cotton too badly to let the Yankees win."

"'Cotton is king,' so the saying goes."

"It's not just a saying," Malachi declared, "it's the truth. And that's what's going to win this war for us in the end."

Robert thought about that and knew that Malachi might be right. At the same time, the notion was a bit disheartening, because it was practically the same thing as saying that the Confederacy couldn't win the war on its own. They needed help from outside, probably the British, maybe the French. Whatever it took, though, was all right. The only thing that mattered was independence and peace with honor.

He looked around the table, feeling good that he was here despite the fact that his leg still ached from the now weeks-old wound. After everything he had gone through, it was nice to be surrounded by friends, if not family. Cam couldn't be here because he had responsibilities at the Citadel. Robert hadn't seen his brother since arriving in the city earlier that day with the Lockharts, but he had sent word to him, letting Cam know that he was in Charleston and would be for the next week or so.

Allard sat across from him. It was wonderful to see his old friend, even though Allard had changed somewhat from their days as cadets together. Married life had a way of changing a man, Robert reflected. And he supposed that having a ship blown out from under you did too.

The younger, more carefree Allard was gone, probably for good. With his beard and in his sober suit, he looked like the businessman he was these days. Beside him, Diana was as pretty as ever, although her thick red hair was pulled back into a bun now instead of flowing freely around her shoulders and down her back as it used to. Robert had halfway expected to see her belly swollen with child, but she was as slim as ever. If he got a moment alone with his old friend, Robert decided, he would have to chide Allard for not trying hard enough to become a father.

Lucinda sat on Allard's other side. She looked well, which came as something of a surprise. He had been under the impression from things Allard had written in his letters and comments Jacqueline had made that Lucinda had been ill for months. If that had been the case, she must have gotten over whatever plagued her, because she looked healthy enough now. She was glowing, in fact, and more beautiful than ever with her creamy complexion and waves of thick blonde hair.

Also surprising was Lucinda's attitude. She had been a royal bitch all the other times he was around her, enough so that he avoided her as much as possible. Today, she had greeted him warmly, smiling and hugging him and planting a sisterly kiss on his cheek. Maybe her ordeal with her health had changed her, made her more forgiving of herself and others.

He thought about the last time he had seen her, the day he left Charleston to join the Hampton Legion. She had kissed him then, too, but it hadn't been a sisterly buss. In fact, she had kissed him like a hot, passionate woman, then damned him to hell. Lucinda had been nothing if not contradictory in her nature.

That had been a disturbing day all around, because not only had Lucinda kissed him, but so had Ellie, the housemaid. Until that moment, Robert had never had any inkling that the girl felt any affection for him.

Of course, nothing could come from either of those encounters. Ellie was a slave—not *his* slave, but still a slave—and although Robert knew that some men bedded their slaves, that kind of relationship had never appealed to him. And Lucinda was . . . well, Lucinda. Robert didn't like her to start with, and he liked even less the way she had carried on with his brother whenever Cam was in Charleston. Despite the fact that he was taller and heavier than either Robert or Allard, Cam was just a boy, several years younger than Lucinda. To Robert's way of thinking, she had taken advantage of him, trifling with him the way an older and more experienced man might trifle with an innocent girl. Of course, Robert knew that Cam wasn't exactly *innocent*—but he still didn't like what Lucinda had done.

All that was in the past now. If Lucinda wanted to be friendly toward him, Robert would be polite to her. But if she had any idea of turning it into something else, she would just have to get those thoughts out of her head. He already had the most beautiful woman in all of South Carolina, maybe in all of the Confederacy, there at his side.

Jacqueline.

He felt a little uneasy as he glanced over at her. She smiled sweetly at him. He had spent the previous night at Four Winds before riding into Charleston on the train with the Lockharts. And somehow he had managed to avoid discussing his future plans with her. Today had been too busy, what with packing and train schedules and everything, for the matter to have come up. Sooner or later she would catch a moment alone with him, though, and then it was inevitable that she would want to know what he was going to do after his wounds had healed. He felt it looming over him like a thunderstorm about to break. Until it did, though, he was going to enjoy being here.

Malachi broke into his thoughts. "Allard tells me you've been involved in several battles, Robert. Why don't you tell us about them?"

Katherine objected before Robert could say anything. "Oh, I don't think battles are an appropriate subject for dinner conversation. Do you, Priscilla?"

From where she sat beside her husband, Priscilla Lockhart said, "I don't suppose we can blame the men for being interested in such things, Katherine. After all, they're the ones who start the wars in the first place."

"*We* didn't start this war," her husband said. "The Yankees did."

"But President Lincoln is a man," Priscilla pointed out. "So are all the other Yankee politicians and generals."

Katherine leaned forward and said with a smile, "They should let us women run things for a while, shouldn't they, Priscilla? We'd straighten out this old world!" She laughed merrily.

"Women running the world?" Malachi asked with a frown. "Lord help us! But you can wait about telling us about those battles, Robert," he added hastily as his wife's smile disappeared and she swung a frown in his direction. "We'll discuss the war later, over brandy and cigars in the study."

"Of course, sir," Robert said, wondering idly what men like Malachi and Everett would do if the blockade ever dried up the brandy and cigars.

As they went on with dinner, Katherine asked, "You're going to stay here with us while you're in Charleston, aren't you, Robert?"

He hadn't really thought about that. The Lockharts, including Jacqueline, would be staying in a hotel downtown. The previous December a terrible fire had destroyed a great many downtown buildings, including Institute Hall, where the Ordinance of Secession had been signed, and the Circular Congregational Church, where Allard and Diana had been married a month before the conflagration. But despite that destruction, several excellent hostelries were still available. Robert had assumed he would stay in the same establishment the Lockharts would be staying, but there was the problem of funds. He supposed that Everett Lockhart would have loaned him the money, but he didn't like the idea of accepting charity.

"Thank you, Mrs. Tyler," he said now, smiling at her. "I accept your hospitality."

When he glanced at Jacqueline, however, and saw the look of disapproval that flickered over her lovely face, he realized he might have made a mistake. He hadn't thought deeply enough about the matter. If he stayed at the Tyler mansion, that meant he wouldn't be able to spend as much time with her.

In the long run that might be a good thing. With the depth of the passion he felt for her, he might not be able to keep his hands off of her if they were ever alone and unchaperoned for too long a time. And he had already decided it would be better for them to control their appetites until after the war was over and they could be married. After his previous visit to Four Winds, he had spent a considerable amount of time worrying that Jacqueline might be with child. Neither of them needed that concern again right now.

He would talk to Jacqueline later, he told himself, and try to make her understand that it would be better this way. He probably wouldn't win the argument, but at least he could make the attempt.

Dinner continued pleasantly, and when it was over, the women went to the parlor while the men repaired to Malachi's study. For the next hour, Robert told them as much as he could remember about his battles. He didn't particularly enjoy reliving some of the experiences, but Malachi and Everett listened intently and asked question after question about strategy and the plans the Confederate command had for carrying out the war.

"General Lee was in charge of the defenses here in Charleston for a time, you know," Malachi commented. "I met him on several occasions. He struck me as a competent man. Rather old and . . . fussy . . . to be in charge of an entire army, though."

"We'll have to wait and see what happens, I suppose," Robert said. "It wouldn't surprise me if General Jackson wound up in command before it's all over."

"Stonewall Jackson," Everett said as he lifted his brandy snifter. "Now there's a fighting man."

Robert didn't say anything. He couldn't help but think about the way Jackson had let the Yankees slip away at White Oak Swamp despite the best efforts of General Hampton. Such hesitancy was uncharacteristic of Jackson, however; his brilliant campaign in the Shenandoah Valley had been proof enough of that. He would shake off whatever had afflicted him during the Seven Days.

When the older men finally tired of talking about the war, Robert and Allard were able to say good-night and leave the study. They wandered back into the dining room, and Allard nodded toward the french doors. "The shed is still back there, on the other side of the garden," he said with a conspiratorial smile.

Robert chuckled. "Yes, but we're grown men now, veterans of combat. We don't have to smuggle your father's cigars and brandy out there. Besides, I think I've had enough of both tonight."

Allard's smile widened into a grin. "Then how about some of the smoothest corn squeezin's you'll ever find?"

That piqued Robert's interest. "I'd expect a question like that from a country boy like me. How'd you come up with a jug?"

"I have my sources," Allard said mysteriously. "Could I interest you in a nip or two?"

Robert glanced around. He could faintly hear the voices of the women in the parlor, but he couldn't see anyone. He didn't think the Lockharts would leave for their hotel without saying good-bye to him. He hoped not, because he wanted a chance to bid Jacqueline good night. But he thought he could risk a few minutes with his old friend in the shed that had been their hideout from the rest of the world. Along with Cam, they had spent many happy hours in that hideaway, smoking and drinking and telling bawdy stories.

"All right," he said with a nod. "Let's go."

DESPITE ROBERT'S comment that he had already smoked enough, he couldn't resist a fine Cuban cigar, and Allard had two in his vest pocket. They fired up the fat, rich tobacco cylinders and passed the jug of fiery liquor back and forth as they sat in the shed at the rickety old table where they had played cards in an earlier, more innocent time. The air soon filled with smoke and laughter.

"Your father and Mr. Lockhart mean well," Robert said, finally growing more serious, "but neither of them have ever been in combat. They don't know what it's like. They still have the idea that there's something glorious about it."

"I know," Allard said with a nod. "They don't realize that during a battle, you're too scared to be thinking about glory or anything else other than somehow staying alive."

Robert puffed on his cigar and blew out a cloud of smoke. "Killing the other guy before he can kill you," he said grimly.

"Yes. That's it exactly." Allard was silent for a moment, then he asked, "Can we win this war?"

"Of course we can," Robert said without hesitation. "It's going to take boldness, though. And the Yankees have so blasted many men . . ." He shook his head. "It seems like whenever you shoot one of them, ten more pop up to take his place. How can we fight that?"

"I don't know," Allard said. "I guess we just have to be more stubborn than they are."

Robert clenched his cigar so that it jutted up at a jaunty angle. Around it, he said, "Stubbornness is something that isn't in short supply on either side in this war."

They pondered silently on that for a while, then Robert added, "I thought that you and Diana would be expectant parents by now."

Allard smiled. "These things take time, I guess."

"Do you enjoy being married?"

"It's . . . I can't tell you how good it is, Robert. To go to sleep next to her at night and wake up with her there in the morning . . . to kiss her good-bye when I leave for the shipyard and have her waiting for me when I get home . . . just to have someone to talk to who loves and understands me . . . it's the best thing in the world. I hope the time comes when you and Jacqueline . . ." Allard let his voice trail off meaningfully.

Robert puffed on his cigar. "We'll see," he said. "I certainly have hopes too." He paused. "You mentioned the shipyard. How has it been, working with your father?"

Allard took a long swig from the jug and set it down on the table with an emphatic thump. "Malachi Tyler is an obstinate cuss," he declared. "He has his own way of doing things and refuses to even listen to anyone else's ideas."

"Now that's the sort of response I expected from you," Robert said with a grin.

"I mean it. He thinks the only way to get anyone to do anything is to threaten them, so he runs the shipyard with an iron fist. I've told him that if he were to make things better for the workers, they might be willing to work even harder for him."

"But he doesn't see things that way?"

"He tells me I'm insane. A boot up the backside is the only thing people really understand, he says. He's been threatening me with that all these years, and it hasn't accomplished a damned thing. You'd think he could see that."

"People generally see what they want to see," Robert said.

"I suppose so. But I'm getting awfully tired of it. If it weren't for the promises I've made . . ."

"Promises to Diana?"

"Mostly."

"If it wasn't for that, you'd be on the sea, running the blockade with Cap'n Yorke, eh?" Robert guessed.

"I do miss it," his friend said with a touch of wistfulness in his voice. "There's nothing like being at sea, feeling the spray on your face, the wind in your hair."

"Better you than me," Robert said. "To tell you the truth, that doesn't sound all that appealing to me."

Allard smiled. "Well, we always knew the day would come when we'd go our separate ways."

"Yeah, I'm afraid I'll always be a landlubber at heart. But at least we can get together like this and visit from time to time."

"And we always will," Allard said as he held out a hand across the table. Robert gripped it firmly. The bonds of friendship were strong between these two.

They went back in the house a short time later and found the others sitting in the parlor.

"There you are!" Jacqueline said as they came into the room. "Where did you disappear to, Robert?"

"Oh, Allard and I were just taking a walk around the place," Robert replied. "You know, talking about the war and things like that." Actually, they hadn't discussed the war all that much, but Jacqueline didn't have to know that.

"I was afraid we'd have to leave before I could tell you good night. Are you sure you don't want to stay in the hotel with us?"

Robert had been hoping she wouldn't ask that question. He answered, "I couldn't insult Mrs. Tyler by refusing her hospitality."

"And we'd love to have you stay here, Robert," Katherine said from the divan where she sat with her husband.

"I think that's the best idea," Priscilla put in.

"You would," Jacqueline said with a quick frown at her mother.

Robert saw Priscilla's mouth tighten in anger, and he spoke quickly in hopes of heading off any disagreement. "I'll be here in Charleston for a while. We'll get to visit quite a bit, Jacqueline."

"Oh, all right," she said with a slight pout. "I suppose that's fine."

A short time later the Lockharts prepared to leave. Priscilla turned to her daughter, "Come along, dear."

"I'll be there in a minute," she said, looking pointedly at Robert.

Her father took the cue. He grasped Priscilla's arm and said, "Let's go ahead, my dear."

Priscilla went grudgingly, and Katherine accompanied them toward the door. "We'll see you out, you two. Come along, Malachi."

Allard yawned as his parents left the parlor, following the Lockharts. "I think I'm about ready to turn in," adding to Diana, "How about you?"

She blushed prettily. "That's a little indelicate."

"What's indelicate about wanting to go to sleep?"

"Nothing, I suppose . . . if that's all you want."

He grinned innocently. "That's all I *said*."

Diana smiled as she took his arm. "You're incorrigible."

"I hope so."

When they were gone, Robert and Jacqueline stood alone in the parlor. She said, "I can't stay but a moment . . . My parents are ready to go . . ."

"They won't leave without you," he told her.

He took her in his arms. She closed her eyes and pressed herself against him as she tilted her head back. There was no hesitation at the unspoken invitation. He kissed her. Instantly, the feel and taste of her lips filled him with passion and longing and excitement. He could have held her and feasted on her mouth all night, and that would be about as close to heaven as he had ever been, he reflected.

But as she had said, her parents were waiting for her, and neither of them could forget that fact. Eventually they had to break the kiss. Jacqueline was a little flushed and breathless when they did. Robert felt the same way.

"I wish we could be together," she whispered. "I wish we could—"

"I know," he broke in, not sure he could stand it if he heard her speak the words. "But we can't, so it's best not to torture ourselves too much. That's why I decided to stay here."

She nodded reluctantly. "You're right, of course. I can see that. But that doesn't mean I don't wish things were different. I wish we could be together all the time."

"Someday," Robert promised. "Someday."

He kissed her again, but only briefly this time. Then, steeling himself for what had to be done, he took her by the hand and led her to the gallery along the front of the mansion where her parents were waiting with the Tylers.

"Good night, dear," Katherine said to Jacqueline as she hugged her. "Please, come back any time. You're always welcome."

"Thank you, Mrs. Tyler." Jacqueline looked at Robert. "I'll be back. I think you can count on that."

"Well, I should hope so," Katherine said with a happy laugh.

Robert recalled a line from a play about parting being sweet sorrow, or some such. The truth of that sentiment had never been more apparent to him than now, he realized. He watched from the gallery as Jacqueline climbed into the carriage with her parents, and then the vehicle rolled away into the night. When it was gone, he turned and saw that Katherine and Malachi had disappeared into the house. He went in, too, and gently closed the door behind him.

Thomas came up and said, "You'll be stayin' in the same room as when you visited before, Marse Robert. You want me to show you?"

"No thanks," Robert answered. "Have my things been taken up?"

"Yes suh," the elderly butler said. "Saw to it myself."

"Thank you, Thomas." Robert started up the staircase with one hand on the banister and the other on his cane.

"Marse Robert?"

He stopped and turned to look back at Thomas. "Yes?"

"I sure am glad you came through all that fightin', suh. You a fine young man, and I'd purely hate to see anythin' bad happen to you."

Robert returned the butler's smile. "Thank you, Thomas. I appreciate that. Good night."

"Good night, suh."

Robert climbed slowly to the second floor and then limped along the hallway to the guest room that had always been his when he stayed at the Tyler home. The door was unlocked, of course. He turned the knob and stepped inside. Whoever had brought up his bags had also lit the lamp on the bedside table, trimming the wick low so that only a soft yellow glow filled part of the room, leaving the corners in shadow.

But that dim light was enough to show him that he had a visitor. Robert caught his breath and stiffened in surprise as he saw Lucinda smile up at him from an armchair.

"Come in, Robert," she said quietly. "Close the door behind you. We have a great deal to talk about."

"I'm sure I don't know what that would be," he said, but he eased the door closed as she had told him. Lucinda was none too stable, and sometimes the best thing to do with crazy people was to humor them.

"Don't worry, I'll explain everything," Lucinda went on. "I'm here to talk about the marriage."

"Marriage?" Robert repeated in confusion. "What marriage?" Maybe she was referring to the possibility that he and Jacqueline might get married. That wasn't going to happen until the war was over, though.

But that wasn't what Lucinda had in mind. Not even close, Robert discovered a second later as she said, "*Our* marriage. You and I will soon be wed, Robert."

He couldn't contain his amazement. "Why would we do that?" he burst out.

She smiled at him and said, "Because I'm carrying your baby, of course."

CHAPTER FIFTEEN

Sacrifices

ROBERT WOULD HAVE THOUGHT that the mere idea of him and Lucinda ever getting married would be the most flabbergasting thing he had ever heard. But now, as he stared at her in shocked disbelief, he realized what she had just said was even more astounding and insane.

"That . . . that's not possible!" he finally sputtered. "We've never . . . I mean, you and I, we haven't . . . it can't be . . ."

"Oh, it's not *actually* your child," she said with a casual wave of a slender hand. "But that's what we're going to tell everyone."

"You've lost your mind!"

"Not at all, Robert. In fact, I believe I'm thinking clearly for the first time in ages."

He half turned and reached for the doorknob. "You should get out of here right now, before I forget that I'm a guest in this house."

"Don't do that!" she snapped, and her voice projected such menace that he half expected to see that she had a gun pointing at him.

Instead she merely sat up straight in the chair, her languorous pose forgotten. She watched him with an intentness that made him feel uncomfortably like one of those Yankee sharpshooters back at Yorktown was drawing a bead on him.

"Why not?" he asked. "Other than consideration for my best friend and his parents, why shouldn't I just throw you out of here?"

"Because if you did that, you'd be ruining your brother's life," she said flatly.

He stared at her, wondering what Cam had to do with this, and then the answer hit him with a force almost as stunning as a shell burst on Malvern Hill had been.

"You really are with child," he choked out, "and the baby is Cam's!"

The sly smile reappeared on Lucinda's face. "Now you're beginning to understand . . . Robert, dear."

He suddenly felt dizzy, as if the room—no, the entire *house!*—had begun spinning crazily around him. He had to lean heavily on his cane to keep from falling. "What . . . what have you done?" he gasped.

"I'd say it's more a case of what your brother has done. He's soiled me, Robert. Taken my virtue and ruined my reputation and doomed me to a life of shame."

"He never did anything on his own! It was all your idea!"

"Who's going to believe that? Not my father. He'll believe anything I tell him. And he'll want to avenge my honor by killing Cam. You know he will."

Robert's pulse pounded maddeningly inside his skull. He knew what Lucinda said was true, all right. If she went to Malachi Tyler and told him that Cam had taken advantage of her and gotten her with child, Malachi would be insane with rage. Not even Katherine would be able to make him listen to reason. He would take a shotgun and go looking for Cam, and the odds were about even whether he would force Cam to marry Lucinda or just blast a hole in him. Either way, Cam would be doomed.

As that realization soaked in, Robert leaned on his cane with one hand and brought the other to his head, clenching it into a fist and grinding it against his temple as if he could rub out the terrible pain clawing at his brain. He closed his eyes and stood there for a long moment, shuddering, unable to speak or even think clearly.

Finally, when the spell passed, he asked in a dull voice, "What is it you want from me?"

"I already told you. We're going to be married. You'll be my husband, the father of my child. No one will ever know any different."

"You and I will."

She waved a dismissive hand. "That doesn't matter."

Robert looked around, found a chair, and sagged into it. "You did this," he rasped as he stared at the floor in disbelief that his life could be turned upside-down in a matter of seconds. "You did this on purpose."

"I did not!" Lucinda actually sounded offended by the accusation. He wasn't sure why she would bother. "When Cam came to Charleston and the Citadel, I stayed away from him for months. I wouldn't let him near me. Just ask Diana. She can tell you. Or ask your precious darky wench Ellie!"

The hatred in her voice made Robert look up again. "What do you mean by that?"

"Don't try to deny it, Robert. I saw you kiss her that day you left here. You bastard. You wouldn't pay the least bit of attention to me because you were too busy mooning over that little simp, Jacqueline Lockhart. But while you were doing that, you probably had Ellie crawling into your bed every night you were here." Lucinda's upper lip curled in a sneer. "Needed a little slave wench to keep your feet warm, did you?"

"That *never* happened," Robert insisted. "When she kissed me . . . well, it surprised me as much as when *you* kissed me." He chuckled, but there was no humor in the sound. It was as cold and hard as ice. "Your eyes are a little green now, Lucinda, instead of blue."

She shot up out of the chair and lunged at him, her hands reaching out to claw at his eyes. He dropped his cane and caught hold of her wrists before her hooked fingers could reach him. She fell against him, writhing in his lap as she hissed curses at him. Robert gave her a shove that sent her sliding off to sit down hard on the floor.

Lucinda gasped and rolled onto her side, and Robert felt a surge of fear as he remembered that she was carrying a child. He shouldn't have pushed her down, no matter how crazy she was acting. There was no excuse for what he had just done.

But then she rolled over again, looked up at him, and laughed. "Scared you, didn't it?" she said. "You thought you'd done something to your brother's child. I'm going to have to get used to calling it *your* child, though."

"Are you all right?"

"I'm fine. The baby's fine. What do you care?"

He wiped away the beads of cold sweat that had sprung out on his face. "I don't want anything to happen to you . . . to either of you."

"How sweet," she said with another sneer.

"Look, Lucinda, we . . . we have to talk about this."

She stood up and brushed herself off, straightened her dress. "There's nothing to talk about. Like I keep telling you, you're going to marry me."

"Why? Why do you even want to be married to me? I don't love you!"

"Oh, I'm well aware of that. But in another six months or so, I'm going to have a baby, so I have to have a husband. And I don't want it to be a foolish boy like your brother."

"So he was good enough to get you in your condition but not good enough to marry you?"

She shrugged. "You can look at it that way if you prefer. But I'd say that I've always known which of the Gilmore brothers is smarter and more likely to make something of himself. Cam will never amount to anything, and we both know it."

"So you're not claiming that you've always been in love with me from afar, or any foolish notion like that?"

Lucinda flushed. "I don't believe in romantic twaddle like that. If your brother hadn't been so damned persistent . . . if I hadn't found myself in the family way . . . we wouldn't be having this conversation. Believe what you want, Robert, but I didn't set out to trap you into marriage or anything like that."

Robert wasn't sure he believed her, but at this point it didn't really matter. What was done was done, and all that remained was deciding how best to deal with it.

"I can't marry you," he said.

"You have no choice."

"I'm in love with Jacqueline. When the war is over, we'll be married."

"Love has nothing to do with it. And you and I will be married *before* the war is over. We'll be married before you go back to the army, in fact. I'd like to have the ceremony as soon as possible, so that when the baby is born it won't look like he came too terribly early."

"No one is going to believe that the baby is *early*."

She laughed. "No one is going to care what the truth is, as long as appearances are kept up. The old biddies may whisper behind their hands, and the men may wink and nudge each other when they're not too busy talking about the damned Yankees, but they'll all put on a show just like we will. I know how these things go."

So did Robert, and he knew she was right. There might be a hint of scandal, but Malachi Tyler was an important man in Charleston and did business with a lot of other important men. He was on friendly terms with politicians who were high up in the leadership of the Confederacy. Everyone wanted to stay on his good side, so they would pretend that his first grandchild was simply born prematurely. In time, people would forget or no longer care about what had really happened, and the lie would become the truth. That was the way things worked.

"If I marry you . . . Cam's name stays out of it?"

"Except as the baby's uncle."

"But if I refuse . . . ?"

"Then I'll have no choice but to force *him* to marry me . . . that is, of course, if my father doesn't kill him first."

That would mean the end of Cam's career at the Citadel. And it would be the ruination of his life too. Lucinda was too smart for him. She would make him miserable. Any chance Cam might have for a normal life would be gone. It would be his own fault, of course, for having succumbed to Lucinda's lures in the first place . . . but that knowledge would be cold comfort to Robert if he had to watch his brother's life turned into a shambles.

It would be better for him to go along with what Lucinda wanted, he realized. He was smarter than Cam, better able to handle what would be required of him as Lucinda's husband. And his heart was harder, too, so he would be able to withstand the pain better.

As long as he didn't allow himself to think about Jacqueline and what this was going to do to her . . .

"What happens now?"

"Do you agree to marry me?"

"As you keep saying, I don't have any choice, do I?"

She bared her teeth at him. "Say it!"

"I'll marry you, damn it," Robert said.

Lucinda laughed. "That's not a very romantic proposal."

"You said you didn't believe in such twaddle."

She came closer to him and reached out to touch his cheek with her fingertips. His face was as solid and unmoving as stone.

"You could at least kiss me. This is quite a momentous occasion."

Robert reached down to the floor and picked up the cane he had dropped earlier. Bracing himself on it, he pushed himself to his feet. For just an instant, he thought about how easy it would be to raise the heavy walking stick and club her with it. But that really *was* insane, and as his stomach twisted in self-revulsion, he knew he could never do such a thing. Even contemplating it made him sick.

"I won't kiss you," he said. "Get out."

"But we're still getting married?"

"That's what I said. I don't go back on my word."

"Are you *giving* me your word?"

He hesitated for a second before making it official, but then he nodded. There was nothing else he could do.

"All right," Lucinda said. "You won't be sorry about this, Robert."

"I'm already sorry about it."

"You'll see, it won't be as bad as you think it will." She sounded almost eager now, almost like a girl who had just received a genuine proposal of marriage from a young man who loved her. "I can make you happy. I can."

Robert doubted that, but he didn't see any reason to argue the point with her. It would just be a waste of time.

She came up on her toes and brushed her lips across his cheek. "In time you'll forget," she whispered. "You'll forget how this all started, and all that will matter is that we're a family."

That would *never* happen. She had drifted off into some fantasy world. But again, telling her that wouldn't accomplish anything.

"Good night," she said.

"Be careful when you leave," he said coldly. "You wouldn't want anyone to see you. Think of the scandal."

A flash of anger crossed her face, but it went away quickly. "You'll see," she said again, and then she opened the door, checking the hallway before she slipped out of the room and eased the door closed behind her.

All Robert saw as he stood there balancing on his cane was his life stretching out in ruins before him. Trapped in a loveless marriage, raising a child that wasn't his, living with a woman he couldn't stand, whose mere sight made his flesh crawl despite her surface beauty . . . that was what he had to look forward to for years and years. The rest of his life, in fact, because he knew that, once he married Lucinda, there would be no getting away from her. She would never allow that.

And as for Jacqueline . . . he had worried how she would react when she found out he planned to return to the Hampton Legion. What was she going to do when she found out that he was going to return as a married man, with a baby on the way?

WHEN ROBERT awoke the next morning, after a night of troubled sleep, for a few seconds he thought that he must have dreamed the encounter with Lucinda. Surely nothing so bizarre could have been real. The very idea that she would force him to marry her because she was pregnant by Cam was too ludicrous to believe.

But then, with a certainty that sent a chill through him to the very core of his being, he realized that it hadn't been a figment of some disturbed dream. The conversation had really happened.

Robert buried his face in the pillow and groaned as if he were in mortal pain. His body wasn't, but his soul was. He wanted to stay where he was and never crawl out of the bed. That way he wouldn't have to face the situation. He could pretend it didn't exist. That was impossible, of course. The problem wouldn't go away just because he ignored it. With a sigh, he forced himself out of bed and began to dress.

By the time he limped downstairs, he had steeled himself to confront Lucinda. He had to find a chance to talk to her alone and persuade her to give up this crazy idea. She would never be happy being married to a man who didn't love her. She'd had plenty of other suitors over the years. After all, she was a beautiful woman from a wealthy family. Surely one of her former beaus would be glad to marry her and raise the coming child as his own.

But most of the eligible young men in Charleston had gone off to the war, he reminded himself. Still, he had to give it a try. He couldn't just give up and go along with what Lucinda wanted. That way lay disaster.

When he reached the bottom of the staircase, the first person he saw was Diana. She smiled asked, "Can I give you a hand, Robert?"

Not unless you can talk some sense into your sister-in-law, he thought. But he said, "No thanks. I'm getting around pretty well these days. My leg stiffens up occasionally, but it doesn't bother me all that much."

"I was just about to have some breakfast. Come along with me?"

"Of course," he said with a smile. In truth, the delicious aromas drifting from the dining room would have had his mouth watering if he hadn't been so preoccupied with the problems of Lucinda and her condition. He supposed he ought to eat, to keep his strength up if for no other reason, so he linked arms with Diana and walked toward the dining room. He asked, "Has Allard already gone to the shipyard this morning?"

"Yes, he usually leaves quite early, at the same time his father does. They're very devoted to their work."

"And neither of them wants the other to get there first and get ahead."

Diana laughed. "That may have something to do with it. They are rather competitive."

"Allard, especially."

"He's . . . ambitious," Diana said. "I tell myself that's a good thing."

"I'm sure it is. He'll go far, Diana. I've always known that."

"If he doesn't get distracted by the lure of adventure."

"He's still here, isn't he?" Robert pointed out.

"Yes, but sometimes I see this look in his eyes . . . I think he's longing to be elsewhere, probably out at sea, fighting the Yankees again."

"A man thinks he wants a lot of things that he really doesn't," Robert said. "I know my friend. He's happy being here with you."

"I hope so. I truly hope so. I know it would be better if we . . . if we were able to start a family . . . Has Allard spoken to you about that?"

Robert felt something uncomfortable stirring inside him. He had known Diana for quite a few years, but this was not the sort of thing he felt at ease discussing with her. "Not really," he said.

"I sometimes feel that I've been a terrible disappointment to him."

"Oh, I don't believe that at all. He loves you, Diana. Nothing could ever change that."

"I hope you're right."

They walked into the dining room and found Katherine and Lucinda there. Robert stiffened at the sight of Lucinda, but she just smiled at him and didn't say anything.

What really shocked him was that Jacqueline was sitting at the table, too, wearing a neat and attractive traveling outfit. She greeted him with a bright smile and said, "Good morning."

"Uh, good morning," he managed to respond even though he was taken aback by her presence. He glanced at Lucinda and saw that the smile curving her full lips was exceedingly smug. "What are you doing here, Jacqueline?"

She blinked in surprise at the blunt question, but the smile remained on her face. "I thought you and I could go on a carriage ride this morning. Since you're a soldier, you might like to see all the preparations that have been made."

Bless her heart, he thought, *she was really trying.* Too bad it was all for nothing.

For a moment he thought about telling Lucinda to go to hell. But then he saw the malice glittering in her eyes and knew that if he reneged on their agreement, all her hatred would be turned against Cam. He couldn't allow that. So he forced himself to say, "I'm sorry, Jacqueline, but I don't think I feel up to that."

"Oh." She looked crestfallen, and he hated to think that he was the cause of it. In the final analysis, *he* wasn't to blame, of course—Lucinda was. But he couldn't explain that to Jacqueline. He wanted to postpone that awful moment for as long as possible.

Perhaps Lucinda sensed that, and her feral instincts told her this was a good time to strike. Whatever the reason, she said, "Anyway, Robert is going to be busy this morning. We have a lot to discuss, don't we, darling?"

"What?" Jacqueline's head jerked toward Lucinda, then back toward Robert. "Darling?" she repeated. "What in heaven's name is she talking about?"

"Oh, he hasn't told you?" Lucinda purred before Robert could say anything. "Isn't that just like a man?"

"Lucinda . . ." Robert began warningly.

The look she flashed toward him was like a pair of daggers, but it came and went so fast that only he saw it. Then, still smiling, she said, "There's no need to be shy about it, Robert. Everyone will have to know sooner or later, and the sooner the better as far as I'm concerned." She lifted her chin proudly as she went on, "Mother, Diana

. . . Jacqueline . . . I'm very pleased to tell you that Robert has asked me to be his wife, and I've accepted his proposal."

The three women couldn't have looked more shocked if Lucinda had dropped a writhing rattlesnake in the middle of the dining-room table. They weren't the only ones who were surprised. A crash sounded from the door to the kitchen, and when Robert looked that way, he saw Ellie standing over the shattered remains of a bowl of oatmeal.

Katherine collected herself first. "Why . . . why, that's just . . . that's just very surprising."

Diana clutched Robert's arm. "Is it true?" she demanded. "Have you lost your . . . I mean . . . are you really considering . . ."

Jacqueline stood up slowly, her back straight. "I don't believe it," she declared. "Robert, tell Lucinda that she's mistaken. Tell her that you couldn't possibly marry her. *Tell her!*"

His voice sounded hollow and distant in his ears as he said, "It's true. I'm going to marry Lucinda."

"And as soon as possible," Lucinda said. "I think we'll have the ceremony right here in the house, with just the minister and family present."

Katherine shook her head. "I never dreamed . . . I just never dreamed . . . We have to tell your father and Allard about this. Malachi will be . . . stunned."

Jacqueline turned to Robert and held out a hand toward him. "Please," she begged. "Please, Robert. This can't be. You and I . . . we were going to be married, when the war is over . . ."

"Things change," Robert choked out.

"We fell in love," Lucinda gloated, "but we kept it a secret from everyone. Now we can't keep it to ourselves any longer. We want to be husband and wife for all the world to see."

"Noooo," Jacqueline wailed.

Robert wanted desperately to put his arms around her, to hold her and tell her it was all a lie, that he didn't love Lucinda and would never marry such a cold-hearted shrew.

But he couldn't do that because it would mean ruining his brother's life. Robert had never thought of himself as being particularly noble, and he'd never had any interest in being a martyr. But sometimes things happened that people couldn't control. Circumstances forced them to travel paths that they never would have chosen for themselves. All he could do now was to let this tide of madness carry him and hope to make the best of it, although he sensed that there really was no "best" in this situation.

Jacqueline took a step toward him. He thought she was going to try to hug him, but instead her hand flashed up and cracked across his face. "You bastard!" she grated. "How can you do this to me?"

Robert's face stung. That was all right. He embraced the pain. He deserved it. He said dully, "I'm sorry, Jacqueline. I never meant to hurt you."

"Well, you did. You have. And I . . . I'll never forgive you!"

With tears rolling down her cheeks, she rushed out of the dining room. Diana called out to her and hurried after her.

"Oh, my," Katherine said shakily. "Oh, my."

And Lucinda just smiled.

"ARE YOU sure you want to go through with this?" Allard asked as Robert stood in front of a looking glass and made a last-minute adjustment to the silk cravat he wore.

"Of course." Over the past few days as the hurried preparations for the wedding were made, he had dulled his emotions, refusing to let himself think about the utter ruin he had made of his life. He just hoped that saving Cam was worth it.

So far, Cam was sullen and angry about the whole thing. He had no idea, of course, that Lucinda was pregnant with his baby. All he knew was that his brother was marrying the girl he was smitten with. He had refused Robert's request to be his best man, leaving that job to Allard.

"I still have a feeling that there's something about this you're not telling me," Allard persisted. Like Robert, he was dressed in an expensive suit with a swallowtail coat. They were in a small anteroom off the ballroom of the Tyler mansion, where the wedding ceremony would take place shortly.

"There's nothing to tell," Robert said. "Your sister and I are in love, and we're going to be married. You'll soon be my brother-in-law as well as my best friend."

"Well, it's as your best friend I'm speaking right now." Allard inclined his head toward the door. "You can be outside before anyone knows what's going on, and there's a saddled horse waiting by the shed for you. I've seen to that."

Robert frowned in surprise. "You'd help me run away from your own sister?"

"I don't know what she's done, but I don't believe for a second that you're marrying her because you love her. Get out while you can, Robert. Go back to the Hampton Legion now. You're better off fighting Yankees on a bad leg than marrying my sister."

Robert laughed humorlessly and shook his head. "I can't do that, Allard. I've given my word, and I intend to keep it. You should know something about that."

"I do," Allard said, "but I thought you'd given your word to Jacqueline."

Robert's breath hissed between his teeth. He would have preferred that Allard not mention Jacqueline. He hadn't seen her since that awful morning a week earlier. She and her parents had left Charleston that very day and returned to Four Winds. Since the wedding was private, the Tyler family hadn't been forced to send an invitation to them, which would have surely been refused graciously. Things always had to be done graciously, no matter how much pain and anger and tragedy were involved.

"I'm going through with this," Robert said stubbornly, "and nothing you can say or do will change my mind."

"Well, at least I tried," Allard said with a sigh. "Are you ready?"

Robert took a deep breath and nodded. That was a lie, of course. He would never be *ready* for this. But like a battle, the time for it had come, and it couldn't be avoided.

With Allard at his side, Robert left the anteroom and walked into the ballroom to face the Tyler family, the minister, and in just a few moments . . . his bride-to-be.

PART THREE

"They were going to look at war,
the red animal—
war, the blood-swollen god."

—*Stephen Crane*

CHAPTER SIXTEEN
Return to the Legion

"CAP'N, YOU'RE A SIGHT for sore eyes, and I ain't lyin," Sgt. Norm Doolittle said as Robert shook hands with him. "It just ain't been the same without you in command."

"From what I hear the legion acquitted itself very well at the battle of Second Manassas a few days ago," Robert commented. "You were right in the thick of the fighting."

"Yeah, but that ain't necessarily a *good* thing," Doolittle said dryly. He pointed to a scabbed-over gash on his forehead. "That's where I got this. Some Yankee officer tried to slice my head open with his saber . . . right before I blowed his guts out."

It was September 4, and the Army of Northern Virginia was encamped just south of the Potomac River, between White's Ford and the town of Leesburg. On the far side of the river was Maryland, and that was where General Lee was headed. A few days earlier, the Confederates and the Yankees had clashed for a second time along the banks of Bull Run, near Manassas, and again the Southerners had emerged triumphant, routing the Union army under the command of Gen. John Pope. Lee was turning out to be a leader who was not content to rest on his laurels. His next move was to be nothing less audacious than an invasion of Maryland.

The military situation had come a long way in the two months that Robert had spent recuperating—and getting himself married. After being on the defensive during the long, grueling Peninsula campaign carried out by McClellan, the Confederates had gone on the attack. Their success at Second Manassas had emboldened Lee. His men needed supplies, so he was going to let the Yankees in Maryland furnish them while at the same time demonstrating in the general direction of Washington DC. Lee envisioned that a negotiated peace would be the best outcome of this war; an outright military victory by the South was unlikely. Many people in the North, including some leading political figures, had only lukewarm support for the war at best, and some of them openly opposed it. This foray into Maryland would put pressure on the Yankees to craft a settlement with the Confederacy that would put an end to the war. Failing that, a successful campaign might also make it more likely that Europe would finally take a hand in the conflict and bolster the Confederacy.

Robert had picked all this up from fellow officers in the camp as he looked for Company E. He'd had to move quickly to catch up with the army before the campaign started. He had left Charleston the day after his wedding to Lucinda, catching the first of several trains that took him to Richmond, and there he was able to catch on with a group of reinforcements headed for Leesburg, where the army had concentrated after the clash with Pope along Bull Run.

If anyone thought it was strange that he had hurried back to duty only one day after his wedding, nothing was said about it. Robert would have left the same day if he could, but Lucinda had insisted they spend at least one night together. That way, when the baby was born, it would be at least possible that the child had been conceived on the wedding night. No one would really believe that, but they would at least pay lip service to the lie.

In reality, Robert never touched Lucinda. He had sat up in an armchair in the hotel room where they had gone after the ceremony, smoking cigars and nipping at a flask of brandy while she slept. He had left in the gray dawn without waking her.

Later that morning, as the train stopped briefly at Mount Holly,

Robert gazed out the window, down the street of the little settlement, at Tobias's blacksmith shop. He was tempted to get off, rent a horse, and ride out to Four Winds, where he would force Jacqueline to listen as he explained the whole terrible thing to her. She would understand and forgive him, and even if they could not be together the way they had hoped, at least from now on, they could be friends . . .

That was all sheer fantasy, of course. For one thing, Tobias had surely heard what had happened in Charleston, and the freedman wouldn't let him take a horse and certainly wouldn't offer to drive him to the Lockhart plantation. And if Robert had somehow managed to get to Four Winds, he wouldn't have been able to talk to Jacqueline. Everett Lockhart would have taken a bullwhip—or a shotgun—to him, and deservedly so considering the pain he had caused Everett's daughter.

So, knowing it was hopeless, Robert had stayed on the train, and a short time later it had pulled out of Mount Holly and rolled on northward, carrying Robert away from the woman he was married to—and also away from the woman he loved.

Sergeant Doolittle looked at Robert's cane and asked with a frown, "Are you sure you're up to bein' out here, Cap'n? Maybe you should've stayed put a while longer where you were."

Robert smiled. "I couldn't do that. I missed the company too much." He didn't say anything about wanting to get away from his wife. He didn't even mention getting married. That was none of Doolittle's business, or anyone else's in the army, for that matter. Robert went on, "What's this I hear about General Hampton not being in command of the legion anymore?"

"It's true," Doolittle said with a sigh. "The army's done been reorganized. We're part o' General Hood's division now, and Colonel Gary's in command o' the brigade. Seems like a pretty good officer. They call him the Bald Eagle, or so I hear tell. You can see why he got the name too. Fella's noggin is a mite shiny."

Robert clapped his sergeant on the shoulder and laughed. Despite everything that had happened, it felt good to be back with the legion.

"Who's in charge of the company?" He hoped the man wouldn't mind relinquishing command, whoever he was.

Doolittle scratched his head. "Well, right now, I reckon I am. When they did their reorganizin', a lieutenant name of Stanton was put in command and made an actin' cap'n. Not a bad fella, but a mite reckless. He got a foot o' Yankee steel in his guts down on Bull Run, so he didn't make it. Since then, I just been hopin' you'd get back. I sure didn't want 'em to make me an actin' lieutenant or anything like that."

"Don't worry, Sergeant," Robert told him. "You're safe from that fate."

The hour was growing late in the day. Campfires were beginning to be kindled. Lee wasn't making any attempt to conceal his army. That was pretty much impossible. One couldn't move tens of thousands of men and all the horses, wagons, and guns that went with them without raising a ruckus. Robert had no doubt that Yankee scouts were opposite them on the other side of the Potomac.

Lee *wanted* the Yankees to know what he was doing. That was the only way to draw them out and perhaps prompt a showdown. At the very least, the thrust into Maryland would distract the Yankees and keep them from trying to mount another offensive at Richmond.

As Robert was pondering that, Doolittle said, "No offense, Cap'n, and don't get me wrong, I'm sure glad to have you back in command, but how are you gonna keep up with us? You can't march across Maryland with that bum leg, and I ain't even sure you could ride a horse that far, if'n you could get hold of one."

"I'm hoping to catch a ride on one of the supply wagons," Robert said. "I can get around just fine for short periods of time, so fighting shouldn't be a problem."

Doolittle rubbed his jaw for a moment and said, "Again, no offense, Cap'n, but you might've been better off stayin' down home for a while longer, until that leg o' yours healed up completely."

"I'll be fine," Robert snapped, unable to suppress the irritation he felt at the sergeant's attitude. He knew Doolittle was just worried about him, but the man didn't realize just how badly he had needed to leave Charleston. The alternative—staying there with his new *wife*—was unthinkable.

LATER, ON the evening of September 4, the Army of Northern Virginia moved out, fording the Potomac at White's Ford and crossing over the river into Maryland. Although it was hardly a perfect solution, Robert found a place to ride in one of the wagons in the supply train. Doolittle could keep the company in line during the march, and if there was trouble, Robert could reach them fairly quickly. Still, he felt some frustration at being separated from his men. If his leg continued to get better, he planned to get his hands on a horse so he could stay with his company.

For three days the column marched through Maryland. Robert had to admit they weren't an impressive-looking bunch. Their uniforms were dirty and ragged and haphazardly patched. A few of the men still had boots or shoes, but most were barefoot as they trudged along the dusty country roads and through the peaceful farming communities. Still, their spirits were high, and they laughed and shouted and sang as the inhabitants turned out to watch them. They had beaten the Yankees time and again, and they were ready to whip the enemy some more.

Many of the Marylanders had a general sympathy with the Confederacy, but they hadn't felt strongly enough about the cause to secede from the Union and join their Southern brethren. Lee was hoping to recruit some reinforcements from among them. But the civilians just watched impassively as the soldiers passed through, neither celebrating nor trying to hinder the passage. Robert saw the message plainly on the faces of many people. They just wished this war would go away and leave them alone. It had little to do with them, and they had crops to get in.

Lee called a halt to the march and concentrated his army at the town of Frederick, in western Maryland. Farther west, and running north and south, was a high, rugged ridge known as South Mountain. It stretched for miles, all the way to the Pennsylvania border. It was cut by gaps in only a few places.

South Mountain was one of the keys to the plan Lee hatched while the army was halted at Frederick. The wily commander would move his forces west of the ridge and then use it to shield them from the Yankees as they raced northward into Pennsylvania, where they would forage for food and supplies in the rich farm country there. At the same time, Lee would undertake the daring maneuver of splitting his army, a tactic that had worked for him before, even though it carried some terrible risks.

Lee's hope was that, after a successful invasion of Maryland and Pennsylvania, his army would be able to withdraw down the Shenandoah Valley. But to accomplish that, the Confederates had to overwhelm the Union garrison at Harpers Ferry, the entrance to the valley, and hold the town until Lee's army got back. The task of capturing the strategic town fell to Thomas J. "Stonewall" Jackson, who would attack the Yankees there from three directions at once, utilizing not only his own division but also those of Gens. Lafayette McLaws and John G. Walker.

While Jackson was taking care of Harpers Ferry, the rest of the army would march through the gaps in South Mountain and turn north, with Gen. James Longstreet leading the swift march to Hagerstown, only a few miles from the Pennsylvania border. If everything went according to plan, Jackson would capture Harpers Ferry and then rendezvous with Longstreet at Hagerstown, reuniting the army for its thrust into Pennsylvania. Lee detailed these plans in a document called Special Orders No. 191. With everything in place, the Southern troops pulled out of Frederick on September 10, heading west across South Mountain and through Turner's Gap.

If everything had worked perfectly, Lee's daring plan might have succeeded. But somehow, in a manner never fully explained, a copy of Special Orders No. 191 went astray, and the Confederates had the bad luck to have it fall into the hands of General McClellan, recently restored to command of the army formerly commanded by Pope. Little Mac now knew that his enemy's forces were split up and highly vulnerable to an attack. All McClellan had to do was to rush his army across South Mountain and fall on the Confederates before they knew what was happening to them.

Luckily for Lee and the rest of the Army of Northern Virginia, McClellan was incapable of doing anything in a hurry. He knew he needed to attack, but still he waited.

That gave Lee's cavalry chief, Jeb Stuart, time to discover from a sympathetic Marylander that McClellan was privy to the details of Special Orders No. 191. This was a disaster in the making, and Lee could no longer afford to think about invading Pennsylvania. With a small force still in the vicinity of Boonsboro, just west of the ridge, Lee had to try to save his army from destruction, and to that end he sent riders galloping after Longstreet, who was on his way to Hagerstown with two divisions, and to Jackson, who was closing in on Harpers Ferry, with orders for them to concentrate their troops at Sharpsburg, a small town on Antietam Creek, west of South Mountain. To give them time to get there, Lee and the men available to him would have to hold the South Mountain passes and prevent the Yankees from pouring through in pursuit. It was quite a challenge, but they had no other option. They had to succeed or see their army destroyed.

By the morning of September 14, John Bell Hood's division—including the Hampton Legion—was well on its way up the road to Hagerstown, marching briskly. Hood himself was no longer in command, though. He had been relieved of duty because of a lingering controversy. Following the battle of Second Manassas, Hood had argued that his command was entitled to claim some fancy new ambulance wagons that had been captured from the Yankees. He had insisted so vigorously, in fact, that other commanders had been offended, to the point that Lee was forced to relieve Hood of command and place him under arrest, so that he traveled at the rear of his division rather than at its head.

The whole thing seemed ridiculous to Robert when he heard about it. It sounded to him like the generals had been squabbling like a bunch of children, and Lee had had to separate them to break up the fuss. But it made no sense to deprive a division of its trusted commander while the army was in enemy territory and about to venture even farther into it.

Robert was on horseback now. More than a week of riding in the supply wagon had given his leg time to heal, and now he no longer needed a cane to get around. He expected that he would be sore after a day in the saddle, but there was only one way to find out.

The sudden pounding of hoofbeats made Robert rein in and turn to peer back along the column. He saw a courier galloping hard past the long line of marching men. Curiosity made him want to call out to the man, but he knew the courier wouldn't stop or even pause in his mission. The man raced past him.

Well, if it was something important enough to affect the entire division, he would know about it soon enough, Robert told himself.

A short time later Colonel Gary, along with several members of his staff, came riding toward the rear of the column. Gary reined in and traded salutes with Robert. "Captain Gilmore, turn your men around," the Bald Eagle ordered. "We're on our way back to Boonsboro."

"Yes sir." Robert had had a chance to speak to Gary several times during the advance through Maryland, and he knew that the colonel was a serious, capable officer.

"The Yankees are on their way through Turner's Gap, and I'm told that Harvey Hill has his hands full holding them back. We're going to give him a hand."

"Yes sir," Robert acknowledged. He knew that Gen. Daniel Harvey Hill's troops, along with Stuart's cavalry, served as the rear guard. If the Union army had caught up to them at the gap through South Mountain and were giving them a fight, it didn't bode well.

Colonel Gary hurried on, and Robert called to Norm Doolittle, "Turn 'em around, Sergeant! We're goin' back where we came from!"

"Yes sir!" Norm Doolittle responded eagerly. "Sounds like a fight abrewin', sir."

"I imagine it's already come to a boil," Robert said.

The fighting had started early that morning as riflemen from Hill's command, posted in Turner's Gap, had opened fire on the long line of blue-clad troops snaking up the National Road toward them. The skirmish had rapidly escalated into a real fight, with the Confederate defenders in the gap clinging tenaciously to their positions even though they were heavily outnumbered. Despite the gallantness of their efforts, they wouldn't be able to hold on without help.

It had been a couple of weeks since the men of the Hampton Legion had seen any action, and longer than that for Robert. As they hurried back toward Boonsboro, they had an extra spring in their step. They were accustomed to victory, and they saw no reason why this should be any different, despite the fact that McClellan had a larger, better equipped, and more rested army. The size of a soldier's heart was what counted, and nobody had bigger hearts than these valiant Southerners.

Even though they were hurrying, it was more than ten miles to their destination. The middle of the day came and went, and still the troops hadn't reached Turner's Gap. The rugged bulk of South Mountain was visible in the distance, and at times Robert thought he saw clouds of powder smoke floating and heard the crackle of rifle fire and the dull boom of artillery. But that might have been his imagination.

Always before, when he had gone into battle, his thoughts had been of Jacqueline. Now he thought of her again, but much to his disgust, he couldn't help thinking of Lucinda too. If anything happened to him, she would be a widow. That would probably be fine with her. She could put on a show of mourning for her lost husband and get everyone's sympathy, but she wouldn't miss him. He had done what she wanted—he had married her and given her baby a father, even if it was in name only—and now she no longer had any need of him.

But if he died, what would Jacqueline do when she heard about it? Would she cry? Would she mourn for him?

Robert couldn't answer those questions, and that uncertainty gnawed at him. Maybe it would be better if he didn't come out of this battle alive. After the stunning, terrible turn that his life had taken, what reason did he have to cling to an existence that promised to be nothing less than miserable?

Then he reminded himself that he had a duty to his men. He had to lead them, and that included staying alive if he could. The chances of all of them coming through the battle would improve that way. He pushed aside any thoughts of being deliberately reckless just because he had been trapped into a loveless marriage. Taking that way out just wasn't something he could do.

Late in the afternoon, Hood's division reached Boonsboro and moved through the village straight for Turner's Gap in the ridge that loomed darkly ahead of them. By now, Hood himself was in command, his arrest suspended for the time being by Lee. Lee might have to follow military protocol most of the time, but when he was going into battle, he needed his best commanders in the field. Robert heard the shouts of acclaim from Hood's men, most of them battle-hungry Texans, as the general rode toward the front. The men of the legion joined in the shouting as well. Even though Hood had replaced their original commander, Wade Hampton, they had fought under him at Second Manassas and knew what sort of general he was—a fighter.

Now Robert could definitely hear the sounds of battle and see the thick patches of gray smoke clogging Turner's Gap and the smaller Fox's Gap a short distance to the south. In places the battle had spilled out onto the ridge itself, although mostly it was too rugged for combat except in the area of the gaps themselves. Those bottlenecks kept the fighting contained to a certain extent, but the difficulties of the terrain also meant that the clashes within the gaps were especially fierce. The Confederate commanders kept pouring men into the gaps, trying to keep them plugged, and the Yankees kept hitting them again and again, trying to break through.

Company E trotted up the National Road and into the gap. Artillery shells burst close by, and bullets were already ripping through the air close enough for their whistling sound to be heard. Robert swung down from his saddle, knowing that he might never find the horse in the confusion after the battle. But he had to be on the ground with his men.

Hill's subordinates were placing the reinforcements as they arrived on the scene. A colonel with a bushy mustache grabbed Robert's arm and shouted, "Take your men up on that knoll, Captain, and for God's sake, hold it!" He waved toward a small rise of ground topped by a few trees, just north of the road.

"Yes sir!" Robert responded. He turned to call, "Sergeant Doolittle, advance to that knoll and have the men dig in!"

"Follow me!" Doolittle bellowed at the company. As he started up the slope, a bullet came out of somewhere and plucked the floppy-brimmed hat off his head. Doolittle didn't pause as the hat went sailing away with a hole in its crown. He kept moving up the hill.

Robert wasn't far behind him, waving the men on. As they came to the top of the slope, he saw a large number of blue-clad troops emerge from some trees about two hundred yards away. As the Yankees started forward, Robert shouted to his men, "Get down and open fire!"

The soldiers sprawled on their bellies at the crest of the rise and began firing at the advancing Yankees. The Union troops stalled momentarily as several of them fell to the volley, but their commanders rallied them and sent them charging toward the knoll. Robert drew his pistol. The range was still too great to use the sidearm, but the gap between blue and gray was narrowing quickly. Robert's men reloaded and fired again, and more of the Federals dropped. The Yankees were beginning to return the fire now, and bullets sliced through the tree branches and thudded into the trunks.

Robert went to one knee to make himself a smaller target. He drew in a deep breath and tried not to get too much powder smoke in his lungs. Quickly, he took stock of his condition. None of his Malvern

Hill wounds hurt at the moment, or if they did, he didn't notice them. He was confident that he was in good fighting form.

The Yankee advance stopped short of the bottom of the knoll. The ones who were still on their feet pulled back, leaving behind their unlucky comrades who had fallen to the accurate rifle fire of Robert's men. During the lull, Robert rose to his feet and walked along the line, checking on his men. "Anybody hurt?" he asked Doolittle.

"A couple o' fellas got scratched," the sergeant replied. "Nothin' serious."

Robert nodded, pleased by the news. Company E had been through enough battles so that it no longer had a full complement, and he didn't want their numbers shrinking even further.

A glance toward the Federal line told him that the Yankees were attacking again, their ranks bolstered by reinforcements. This was an even larger group coming toward the hill. "Everyone get ready!" he called. "Here they come!"

He felt a cold finger along his spine as he realized that he and his men were outnumbered this time. But they still held the high ground, he told himself. They would fight hard and repulse this attack.

"Damn it!" Sergeant Doolittle cried out. Robert swung around to see that one of the men who had been beside the sergeant was now sprawled on the ground, blood pumping from a wound in his throat. The soldier's bare feet drummed against the ground as he died. Doolittle looked up at Robert, waved at the ridge looming above them, and called, "That shot came from up there!"

Robert lifted his head toward the heights. There were Yankees up there, and now they were beginning to rain lead down on the Confederate defenders. Robert saw men clad in gray and butternut running across the wooded slopes as they moved to counter this new threat, but in the meantime the Confederates in the base of the gap were in greater danger than ever before.

There was nothing his men could do about that, Robert told himself. It was up to other troops to turn back the Yankees on the slopes. His company's job was to hold the road and the area alongside it.

"We've got plenty of Yankees right in front of us to shoot at!" he called to them. "Open fire!"

Smoke and fire geysered from their rifles. The powder smoke was so thick that Robert couldn't make out the Yankees for a moment, but when it began to clear, he saw that although some of them had fallen, most were still on their feet and still charging toward the knoll.

A cannon roared in the distance, and a second later a shell slammed into one of the trees on top of the knoll, blowing it to kindling. The Yankees had brought an artillery piece to the edge of the woods to soften up the Confederate defense.

His stomach suddenly clenched. It had been an artillery round that had almost killed him before, and now he didn't know if he could stand up in the face of another barrage like that. He knew he wasn't a coward, but he couldn't deny that fear gnawed savagely at his guts. He wanted to turn and run . . .

But he didn't. Instead he called calmly to Doolittle, "Sergeant, have our best marksmen concentrate their fire on that cannon at the edge of the woods!"

"Yes sir!"

Robert wasn't sure where he found the reserve of strength to remain calm while panic was nibbling at the edges of his brain. But find it he did, and for the next few minutes, as more artillery shells raked the hilltop, he directed the fire of his men toward the Yankee gun crew. One thing about South Carolina boys—they were damned fine shots. When four of the gunners had fallen to sharpshooter lead, the survivors hauled the gun back into the trees.

Meanwhile most of Robert's men were still raking the Yankees advancing on foot across the open ground in front of the knoll. More than a dozen Federals were down now, but others kept coming. The leading edge of the attack reached the foot of the slope. Robert knelt and opened fire on them with his pistol, aiming and firing carefully so as not to waste ammunition. He emptied the pistol, and three of the rounds found their targets. Robert began to reload.

"Bayonets! Bayonets!" Doolittle shouted.

The Yankees were halfway up the hill and coming on fast. A ragged volley from the defenders dropped a few of them, but then the others were in the faces of the Confederates. The Southerners lunged up from the ground to meet them. Bayonets clashed. Rifles smashed together. Men yelled and hollered in each other's faces from a distance of less than a foot as they struggled for their lives.

Robert's pistol bucked in his hand again and again. He saw one of the shots strike a Yankee in the face at point-blank range, saw the man's features disappear in a hideous smear of red. When the hammer clicked on an empty chamber, Robert jammed the pistol back in its holster and yanked his saber from its scabbard. He parried a bayonet thrust with it and slashed the blade across the Yankee's face in a wicked backhand stroke that left the man screaming and blinded as blood poured into his eyes. Robert shoved him away.

Then the Federals began to retreat down the hill, the back of their charge broken. Company E had held its position again. Robert's men reloaded quickly and peppered the fleeing bluecoats with some farewell shots to speed them on their way. Robert leaned against a tree with most of its branches shot away and huge holes gouged out of its trunk. His chest heaved as he tried to catch his breath.

Doolittle came over to him. "You all right, Cap'n?" he asked.

Robert nodded. "I think so. Casualties?"

"Two men killed and a couple more wounded. I reckon we got off pretty light."

"It may not yet be over," Robert cautioned.

Doolittle waved a hand toward the western horizon. "Sun's about down. I don't s'pect the Yankees'll feel like fightin' much longer."

Robert turned his head and saw that Doolittle was right. Only a thin bulge of red on the horizon remained of the sun. The evening shadows would begin to gather within minutes. And the Yankees, except on rare occasions, had little stomach for fighting in the dark.

To tell the truth, Robert felt the same way. He looked around Turner's Gap, aware now that the firing on the hillsides above them had come to a stop too. "We held, didn't we?" he said.

"Looks like it," Doolittle agreed. "For today, anyway."

Today was enough, Robert thought. Today was all anybody had, blue or gray, Confederate or Yankee.

"We'll hunker down here," he said, "until somebody tells us to do otherwise. Detail somebody to brew up a little coffee."

"Yes sir," Doolittle acknowledged with a grin.

Robert took off his hat and ran a hand over his head. He had come through this battle. His "loving wife" back in Charleston wasn't a widow—yet.

BY THE morning of September 15, the Confederate forces had all been withdrawn from Fox's Gap, Turner's Gap, and Crampton's Gap. The way was open for McClellan to cross South Mountain. But the battles of the day before had bought Lee the time he needed to regroup his army. He had received word that Jackson's attack on Harpers Ferry had been successful. The Confederates controlled the town. Not only that, but Jackson had left a small force behind to occupy Harpers Ferry and was even now racing toward Lee with the rest of his troops. The balance of Longstreet's divisions, which had reached Hagerstown, was on the march as well, returning to Sharpsburg, where Lee had issued the order to converge. Before McClellan could catch up, the divided Army of Northern Virginia would be whole again.

The invasion of Maryland and Pennsylvania might not have gone as planned, due to the unforeseen mishap of Special Orders No. 191 being discovered by the Yankees, but something good could still come out of this. In the back of his mind, Lee had wanted a showdown, an all-out fight between his army and McClellan's, the biggest battle of the war so far. Maybe, if it went well, it would be the final battle of the war. And it would be fought near Sharpsburg, where the Confederates began to form their line along and west of the little stream called Antietam Creek.

CHAPTER SEVENTEEN

The Bloodiest Day

ROBERT DIDN'T HAVE A scratch on him after the battle at Turner's Gap. It struck him as ironic that he seemed to have a guardian angel protecting him, now that he didn't care all that much whether he lived or died.

September 15 was spent withdrawing from South Mountain across Antietam Creek to Sharpsburg. That evening Hood's brigade, including the Hampton Legion, received orders to move north along the Hagerstown turnpike and camp across the road from a small, white-frame church, the sanctuary of a sect called Dunker or Dunkard. Robert didn't know anything about that particular denomination. All he knew was that he was grateful for the chance he and his men had to get a little rest before the impending battle. McClellan was slowly moving his army across South Mountain and toward the Confederates. Robert expected that the next day would see the two armies clashing again.

The morning of September 16 was peaceful, though, except for the occasional artillery shell lobbed from long distances by the Yankees. The blasts worried Robert, but he tried not to pay attention to them. If one of those shells was fated to land on him, so be it.

There were woods to the west, at the company's back, and across the road, just north of the church, a broad cornfield stretched toward another line of trees. During the afternoon, Robert stood with Norman

Doolittle and stared across the cornfield. It reminded him of home and brought back poignant memories of working in the fields on the farm.

Both men sipped the bitter brew of grain that passed for coffee. Doolittle said, "Looks like a pretty good corn crop over yonder. Wonder who it belongs to?"

"Someone who'll probably never get to harvest it," Robert said. "Before this is over, it'll probably get too trampled and shot up to amount to anything anymore."

"I purely do hate to see a good crop go to waste." Doolittle shook his head sadly.

Robert smiled. "Go get yourself a few roasting ears, Sergeant. Or it'll just go to waste."

Doolittle grinned and trotted across the road. He returned with his arms full of corn to shuck and roast. Robert remembered doing that, too, and he felt another pang of homesickness in his chest.

What was he doing here? His family didn't own any slaves, had never owned slaves. It was foolish for him to be risking his life to preserve the "peculiar institution." But no matter how much the Northerners insisted that slavery was the only reason for the war, Robert knew that wasn't true. He was here because he firmly believed that the states were not required to submit fully to the federal government. They had entered the Union freely, and they ought to have the right to leave freely, if that was what the people wanted. "We, the people . . ." was a mighty noble phrase, but this war would decide whether or not it had any real meaning or if it was just a sham, a hollow promise that a power-hungry federal government had no intention of keeping.

The Yankees had demonstrated their arrogance by invading Virginia in the first place. They could yap like noisy little dogs all they wanted about how they were just trying to free the slaves, but what they really wanted was to keep the South subservient. Robert had heard enough talk among Malachi Tyler and his friends and business associates to know that the growing ties between the Southern states and the British industrialists scared the hell out of Yankee businessmen. Any notions that the South had about becoming more self-sufficient had to be nipped in the bud, and nipped hard. That was truly why the North had gone to war. All the high-flown rhetoric aside, everything came down to money, and that knowledge left a taste in Robert's mouth even more bitter than that of the mock coffee.

Late that afternoon, a breeze of excitement rippled through the camp. Rumors spread that the Yankees were about to attack. Hood appeared a short time later, and his arrival confirmed the speculation. The men began forming a line of battle along the turnpike.

The Hampton Legion was positioned at the far left end of the Confederate line, well north of the church. Robert glanced down the road at the whitewashed building a quarter of a mile away as he stood with the men of Company E. There would be no psalm singing today, but there were probably quite a few prayers being mouthed silently as the soldiers marched through the cornfield.

Enemy fire erupted immediately from the woods on the east side of the field. Rifle volleys raked the Confederates, and field guns were rolled forward to belch flame and smoke. Grapeshot tore into the gray-clad soldiers, who by now had broken into a run and were shouting defiance as they charged. The Rebel Yell filled the air.

Robert's saber was in his right hand. He waved it over his head as he urged his men on. Suddenly, something—probably a bullet—hit the blade with such force that the painful impact shivered all the way up Robert's arm, even as the saber's grip was torn out of his hand. Caught up in the attack as he was, he couldn't stop to look for the fallen weapon. All he could do was keep running toward the woods. He drew his pistol as he neared the trees.

All along the line, Hood's men exercised restraint. They didn't fire until they entered the woods. The Yankees had pushed ahead all the way to the edge of the old growth, so the fighting was suddenly being carried out at close quarters, in many cases hand to hand.

Robert leaned against the trunk of a tree, grimacing as a bullet slammed into it just above his head and sprayed bark splinters into his face. Some of them scratched his skin and stung, but none of the splinters struck him in the eyes. He drew a bead on a Yankee soldier who was reloading about ten yards away and pulled the trigger. The man had just glanced up, wide-eyed with fear as he desperately rammed ball and wadding down the barrel of his rifle. Robert's shot took him in the chest and knocked him backward. His legs kicked high in the air, and then he fell limply. Robert shifted his aim to another soldier and fired again. This shot struck the man in the hip and turned him half around, but he caught his balance and limped toward Robert, yelling as he poised his bayonet for a thrust. Robert shot him in the chest.

The fighting was fierce all around him, a mad swirl of blue and gray among the late afternoon shadows under the trees. When Robert's pistol was empty, he didn't take the time to reload it. He holstered the weapon and snatched up a rifle that had been dropped by some unlucky Johnny Reb or Billy Yank. The stock was sticky with blood, but Robert gripped it tightly and went to work with the bayonet.

Bloody and intense as it was, the fight didn't last long. The afternoon was too far advanced for that, and the light was waning. After less than an hour, the Yankees pulled back through the trees, and the Confederates moved back across the cornfield to resume their position around the church and along the road. Darkness fell with nothing decided—except the deaths of the men who had fallen in the woods and the cornfield.

"What'd I tell you, Cap'n?" a weary, begrimed Norm Doolittle asked him that night as they hunkered beside a small fire and gnawed on stale pone. Reinforcements had come up and allowed those who had taken part in the battle to pull back into the woods west of the turnpike so that they could rest and cook their meager rations. "That poor ol' cornfield got the hell shot out of it this evenin'."

"And that was just McClellan's way of probing our line," Robert said. "That's probably where he'll start coming at us again tomorrow. I'm afraid that cornfield's in for a lot worse than it got today." And so were the men of the Hampton Legion, he thought grimly.

Robert slept little that night, perhaps a couple of hours. And that slumber, as it so often was for him, was haunted by dreams of two women: the one he didn't want and the one he couldn't have.

Maybe, once the child was born, he could take steps to get Lucinda out of his life. Divorce was uncommon and difficult, but not unheard of. Such a thing would cause a great scandal, of course, but that didn't worry him. His own reputation mattered little to him. And once the child was born, Lucinda would lose her power over him. After that, she would no longer be able to threaten to expose Cam as the child's real father. No one would take such a claim seriously.

Yes, Robert mused as he sat with his back against a tree, his hat pulled down over his eyes, halfway between sleeping and wakefulness, a divorce might just be the best course of action. It wouldn't enable him to get Jacqueline back—nothing would ever do that, he feared—but at least he wouldn't be forced to spend the rest of his days with the woman who had ruined his life.

He was jolted out of his drowsy reverie by the sudden crash of artillery fire in the distance. Explosions followed quickly as the shells began to land along the Confederate line. After a night of relative quiet, the Yankees had started another bombardment, and that was bound to be the precursor to yet another infantry attack. Robert scrambled to his feet and called, "Sergeant Doolittle, get the men up! Up!"

Around him, the still-weary soldiers of Company E pulled themselves upright and began fumblingly checking their rifles and powder and shot. It was not yet dawn, but the rising of the sun was close enough so that a dim gray light filled the sky and filtered through the trees. Tendrils of fog rose from the ground and curled around the men. It was an eerie, disheartening moment that made Robert's heart pound in his chest. Doom seemed to hang over all of them. He wondered if the Yankees in the distance felt the same way.

No orders had come for them to move out, so all they could do was stand there, waiting while the artillery barrage continued. The shells were falling close but not directly among them. That could change at any time, though, and without any warning. With each blast, the ground trembled under the soldiers' feet, most of which were still bare and no doubt a little chilled in this cool, foggy predawn.

Robert wiped the back of his hand across his mouth. He was hungry—like the rest of his men, he'd had little to eat the night before—but he wasn't really aware of the emptiness in his belly. He sniffed. His nose was running a little. He hoped he wasn't coming down with the grippe. Then a bleak smile touched his lips as he realized that in all likelihood he didn't have to worry about getting sick. The looming battle would be a sure and permanent cure for the ills of many of these men.

The artillery barrage eased, but that wasn't necessarily a good sign. It just meant that the Yankees were ready to push up their infantry. Mere moments later the crackle of rifle fire intensified. Most of it sounded like it was coming from farther north along the Hagerstown turnpike, on the far left flank of the Confederate line. McClellan might be damned slow to move, but he was an able tactician when he finally got his army started. That area was where the defensive line was the weakest and where there were fewer physical obstacles to an attack. Farther south along the line, Antietam Creek itself served as a barrier to the enemy, and there were also several hills the Confederates could try to hold, as well as a sunken road that would provide cover for the Southern riflemen. Up here, though, the terrain was mostly open fields, broken only by occasional clumps of trees such as the one where Robert and his men waited along with the rest of Hood's brigade.

When the shooting started in earnest, Robert took out the pocket watch he had bought in Richmond just after he had been released from the hospital. The watch had survived the skirmish the day before and still ticked steadily. Despite the fog and the early morning gloom, it was light enough for him to be able to read the time—two minutes past six o'clock.

He waited tensely for another five minutes or so, listening to the sounds of battle several hundred yards up the turnpike. Those sounds didn't seem to be coming any closer, so Robert said to Doolittle, "Sergeant, tell the men to fix themselves some breakfast if they want."

"You reckon we got time, Cap'n?" Doolittle asked dubiously.

"We haven't been called on yet," Robert said. "There's no telling when or if we will be."

"I reckon so." The sergeant turned to the troops. "All right, boys, you heard the cap'n! Kindle some fires and get the coffee boilin'!"

Amazingly, the fighting remained static as the sun rose. The fog was still thick, but it had a golden glow to it now. The early morning scene might have been tranquil and beautiful if not for the terrible racket of the battle going on.

Doolittle brought Robert a cup of the grain coffee. He sipped the hot, bitter stuff and felt it bracing him. The sergeant handed him a biscuit as well, but Robert gave it back. "I don't think I can eat right now, but thank you," he said quietly. "I'll have something later."

"Yes sir, me too." Doolittle tucked the biscuit inside his shirt. "Just save this here fella for a snack later."

The men talked quietly and nervously among themselves as they huddled around the fires, their words sometimes drowned out by the crash of artillery, this time from their own guns. When the battle had been going on for almost an hour, they began to hope that they wouldn't have to fight today.

Then Hood and his staff officers arrived, and the general announced, "We've been summoned to go to the relief of General Lawton. Form up into battle lines, men."

Alexander R. Lawton's brigade had relieved Hood's brigade the night before, after the fight in the woods east of the cornfield, along with a brigade commanded by W. H. Trimble. Now, from the sound of Hood's words, Lawton's men were in trouble, and Robert didn't doubt that Lawton and Trimble had taken the brunt of the Federal attack.

Leaving their fires, the soldiers hustled out of the woods and onto the road, turning north and trotting toward the fighting. It was hard to tell the clouds of powder smoke from the fog, but Robert thought most of the smoke hung over the road itself and the area just east of there. He hurried along, pistol in hand, his empty scabbard bumping against his leg. He never had found the saber, which had probably been broken by the shot that knocked it out of his hand.

Hood was in the vanguard of the advance. He was not the sort of commander to issue orders from the rear of any fight. The men of the Hampton Legion followed closely behind him, so Robert was near enough to hear Hood's heartfelt exclamation of surprise and dismay when they came upon the shattered remains of Lawton's command. Lawton himself had been seriously wounded, but he was still trying to rally his men as they struggled in the cornfield with the Yankees.

"Form a line!" Hood bellowed as he wheeled his horse around and waved an arm to direct his men into place. "From the road to the woods! Form a line and advance!"

Bullets whipped around the heads of the men as they formed ranks. The Hampton Legion was on the left end of the line, beside the turnpike, and Robert and Company E anchored the very end. The rest of the legion and the rest of Hood's Texas Brigade stretched out to the east, reaching all the way to the woods on the far side of the field.

"Advance! Advance!" came the order, and Hood's men started forward. At the same time, what was left of Lawton's command began to fall back. Wounded men, covered with blood and barely able to stand, stumbled through the ranks of Hood's brigade, Hood's men parting briefly to let them through and then closing ranks again. The wounded who couldn't walk tried pathetically to crawl. Robert's heart went out to them, and he wanted to stop to help them, but of course he couldn't. The enemy was straight ahead and had to be dealt with.

The dead simply lay where they had fallen, and horror crawled coldly through Robert's veins as he was forced to step on some of them.

The corn stalks had been flattened in the fighting, and now only rough stubble was left. It was hard on the bare feet of the advancing men, and they began to leave bloody footprints behind them. They never slowed, however. The hail of bullets in the air became thicker. Men grunted as lead thudded into flesh. The wounded stumbled and fell while the others kept going. Smoke filled the air, along with cries of pain. And then there were the Yankees.

The blue-coated figures loomed up out of the fog, screeching like misbegotten demons from some hell born of self-righteousness and delusions of grandeur. Robert emptied his pistol into them as he stumbled forward. Steel rang against steel as bayonets clashed. He went to a knee to reload and then rose up again. A Federal officer on horseback spurred at him, tried to ride him down. Robert twisted, brought the pistol up, and blew the Yankee out of the saddle. Stepping over to him, Robert wrenched the pistol out of the dead man's hand. He checked the loads and saw that only one chamber was empty.

With both hands filled, he strode through the devastated cornfield, firing right and left, each pistol rising as he squeezed off a shot, only to pull it down again as he fired with the other hand, back and forth, spewing death and destruction, untouched by the storm of lead all around him, blessed—or cursed—by the luck that protected him.

Jacqueline, he thought as the right-hand gun clicked empty, and then again, *Jacqueline,* as he fired the final shot in the left-hand gun. Screaming hate, a Yankee soldier charged him, bayonet held low to gut him. Robert threw the left-hand gun in the man's face, blood spurting as it pulped his nose. The man stumbled, his charge ruined. Robert batted the rifle with its attached bayonet aside and swung the gun in his other hand, feeling the solid thud as it met the man's head. He drew back his arm and battered the Yankee again and again, driving him to the ground, striking with the gun until the man's skull was shattered and misshapen and his brains were leaking out into the dirt of the cornfield, the blood mixing with all the blood that had already been spilled. The dust and dirt churned into crimson mud.

And through it all, somehow the heavily outnumbered Confederate line held. Not only held, but advanced slightly, through the cornfield and into the woods bordering it, and along the turnpike that the Yankees had intended to use as a highway to the destruction of the Army of Northern Virginia. The sun rose higher and burned off the fog as the battle raged, but it could do nothing about the thick clouds of stinging powder smoke that hung over the bloody ground.

Robert fought like a madman, snatching up fallen sabers and rifles and wielding them until they were knocked from his hands. His hat was gone, long since fallen and trampled underfoot. Whenever he was able to stop and catch a breath, he realized that his leg hurt badly, but when he looked down he didn't see any blood except that which had splattered on his uniform as other men died. It was the old wound that ached, not a fresh one.

Those lulls never lasted long, not more than half a minute or so, and then the fighting resumed. He had no idea how long he and his men struggled with the Yankees in the cornfield. It seemed like days but was probably no more than an hour, two at most. The morning was still fairly new.

Gradually, as more and more men began to fall around him, Robert realized that some of the rifle fire was coming from a different direction. Over the din of battle he heard shouting from the east and looked in that direction. The Yankees, with their seemingly endless supply of troops to throw into the fight, had finally broken through the Confederate line to the right of Hood's position. That meant Robert and his comrades had been flanked, and now they faced enemy fire from two directions. In this chaos, the command structure was shattered, and Robert knew that if he waited for orders to pull back, he and all of the men left alive in his company would be slaughtered before those orders ever came.

"Fall back!" he yelled hoarsely. "Company E, fall back!"

He caught hold of men he recognized and thrust them toward the rear. Stumbling over bodies that seemed to be lined up in neat rows, he found all the men of his company that he could and told them to retreat. In front of all the others was Sergeant Doolittle, wrestling with a burly Yankee. As Robert staggered toward them, Doolittle finally managed to drive the butt of his rifle against his opponent's skull, smashing the Yankee to the ground.

"Sergeant, fall back!" Robert shouted at him.

Doolittle turned and started toward him, but the sergeant had taken only a couple of steps when he jerked suddenly. Blood flew from his right arm as a bullet struck it. Doolittle cried out and stumbled toward Robert, who managed somehow to catch him before he fell. "Hold on, Norm!" Robert shouted. "Let's get the hell out of here!"

He positioned himself on Doolittle's left side and got an arm around the sergeant's waist. Doolittle was bleeding heavily from his wounded arm and seemed to be only half conscious. Robert hauled him along, and eventually they broke into an unsteady run.

It wasn't until he realized that his feet were pounding along the hard-packed surface of the turnpike that he knew they had made it out of the cornfield. Through bleary eyes, Robert spotted the church ahead on his left. Confederates in full retreat streamed into the woods west of the church. Robert headed in that direction with Doolittle. They had to get away from the Yankees so he could wrap a bandage of some sort around the sergeant's arm and try to stop that bleeding.

The church had been damaged, its walls heavily pocked by bullets. A few larger holes showed where it had been hit by artillery fire. Robert and Doolittle were passing it when something struck Robert's left ankle a heavy blow. The impact knocked his leg out from under him, and he toppled to the ground, taking Doolittle with him. Robert's whole leg was numb, but as he rolled over he looked down and saw blood welling through a hole in his boot. He had been hit like General Hampton during the Peninsula campaign, but there was no surgeon handy to tend to Robert's wound.

He had to get up and move before the pain hit him. His life depended on it, and in all probability so did Sergeant Doolittle's. Rolling onto his hands and knees, Robert pushed himself upright, dragging his wounded leg after him. He hobbled over to Doolittle, bent and got hold of the sergeant under the arms. Doolittle had passed out from losing so much blood and was dead weight now. Robert grunted loudly as he lifted Doolittle and began dragging him toward the trees.

Some of his men saw him coming and ran out to meet him, taking Doolittle from him. Pain roared up Robert's leg and almost knocked him off his feet, but he managed to hop on into the woods before he collapsed. He leaned heavily against a fallen log, panting for breath for a moment before he was able to call out, "Bind up that wound in Doolittle's arm! Get that bleeding stopped!"

His own boot was full of blood by now. He gritted his teeth against the agony that gripped him, and then a half-hysterical laugh forced its way out of his mouth. For a while there he had almost started to believe that there was some sort of mystical shield around him, protecting him from harm so that he could go back to a miserable life in Charleston with an unwanted wife and a child that wasn't his own. That prospect seemed a lot more unlikely now. If he didn't bleed to death, he would probably die of blood poisoning. He knew about the field hospitals, knew their reputation as abattoirs. He would never make it out alive.

"Jacqueline . . ." he murmured.

That thought of her and the sound of guns were the last things he knew as darkness claimed him.

HOOD'S BRIGADE, battered and mostly out of ammunition, remained in the woods west of the Hagerstown turnpike the rest of that day as bitter fighting raged up and down the five-mile-long line that traced Antietam Creek. From the north end—where the valiant defenders blunted the first Federal thrust of the day—to the middle—where Confederates died by the hundreds in the bloody pit of the sunken road—to the south end—where the battle finally turned at what came to be known as the Burnside Bridge and the Yankee attack was turned back once and for all—men fought and died. By the end of the day, when the battle ended at last in a stalemate, with the Confederate and Federal positions still roughly what they had been early that morning, nearly five thousand men had died, and more than twenty thousand more were wounded or missing. Many of the wounded later died from their injuries. Never before in the history of the divided nation had so much blood been spilled on a single day. It was raw carnage, unfettered slaughter.

But Robert Gilmore knew nothing more of it than his part until that evening, when consciousness slowly came back to him as he lay on a cot in a church in Sharpsburg that had been converted to a temporary hospital, like many of the other buildings in the settlement. He let out a groan and tried to move, but a hand came down on his shoulder to hold him still. Robert gave a little shake of his head and forced his eyes open. The hand resting on his shoulder was big and knobby-knuckled, with hair bristling on the backs of the fingers, and the whole thing was covered with dried blood. Blood was caked under the fingernails too. The stains extended as far up the man's arm as Robert could see. His sleeve was rolled back to the elbow.

"Take it easy, son," a deep voice rumbled. "You're safe now. No Yankees here."

Slowly, Robert turned his head to look up at the man. He saw a lined and weathered face and gray whiskers. "You're . . . a doctor?" Robert rasped.

"No, a minister. This is my church." The man waved his other hand, which was as bloodstained as the other. "I've been pitching in to help the surgeons. Ralston's my name, Joseph Ralston."

Robert closed his eyes. He couldn't feel anything below his left hip. "My leg," he said. "Did they take my leg?"

"No, son. It's just bandaged up mighty tight."

Robert heaved a sigh of relief. He had a horror of being less than whole. Death might have been better. And it probably would have come to that, since the surgeons were mostly butchers, hacking off limbs left and right, and most of the men who had amputations performed died anyway.

"They probably would have taken it off," Ralston went on, "if not for that sergeant of yours."

Surprise made Robert open his eyes. "S-Sergeant?"

"The one with the wounded arm," Ralston said with a nod. "He regained consciousness after the two of you were brought in. The surgeons were going to put you on the table and take your leg, but Sergeant Doolittle stopped them." Ralston shook his head sadly. "He wasn't able to persuade them to leave his arm, though. It had to go."

"Is . . . is he all right?"

"He's alive." The minister shrugged. "Beyond that, it's in the hands of the Lord."

"The . . . the battle?"

"It's over, at least for now. I don't know what the morning will bring. Both sides . . . it was awful, just awful . . . so many men dead . . . I hate to say it, son, but it's times like this that make me question my faith. How can the Lord allow such things to happen? How can both sides be so convinced that right is on their side that they can kill and kill and kill . . ." Ralston stopped and took a deep breath, let it out in a long sigh. "It's enough to make me believe that man is not as far above the animals as he likes to think he is."

Right now, Robert didn't care about philosophy or theology or how far above the animals man might be. He was alive, and that knowledge carried with it an unexpected sweetness. He was lying in a place of worship that was now filled with the stench of death and the moans of wounded men instead of prayers and hymns, and his own future was uncertain at best. But his heart still beat, and his blood still flowed in his veins, and despite everything, that felt good.

"If you'd like, I'll write a letter to her for you," Ralston said.

"Who?" Robert asked.

"Your wife. Your sweetheart. I wouldn't be knowing which she is, only that you kept calling her name while you were passed out. Who is she, son? Who's Jacqueline?"

"The woman I love," Robert murmured.

And for now, the thought of her and the knowledge that he was alive were enough for him to cling to as he closed his eyes and drifted off to sleep.

CHAPTER EIGHTEEN

Visitors to Charleston

"THE ANKLE WAS SHATTERED by a Yankee bullet,'" Allard read from the letter, "'but the doctors believe I will be able to walk again once it heals. When I am well enough to leave the hospital, I will come to Charleston forthwith. Your obedient servant and friend, Robert Gilmore, Captain, Hampton Legion.'"

Lucinda sniffed angrily. "He writes to you but not to his own wife."

That's because he doesn't love you, my dear sister, Allard thought but wisely kept the thought to himself.

"Poor Robert," Katherine said from her chair by the fireplace. The whole family had come into the parlor after dinner, and Allard had read the letter that had arrived that day from Robert. She commented, "It must have been awful for him and for all those other poor boys, just awful."

Malachi grunted and rattled the newspaper in his hands. "What's bad is that all those men died, and Lee didn't accomplish what he set out to do. I tell you, I don't know if he's the right man to be leading our army or not. He ran back from Maryland with his tail tucked between his legs, and what has he done since then except sit and lick his wounds? Meanwhile Lincoln issues his damned proclamation and says he's going to free the slaves! I'd like to kick that damned ape, if he wasn't so blasted tall. I don't think I could reach his backside with my foot!"

"Malachi!" Katherine scolded. "I don't like to see you get so stirred up. It's not good for you."

"Don't worry about me," he warned. "Worry about the Confederacy. It's going to hell in a hay wagon!"

Allard wasn't sure the situation was quite that bad. True, Lee's invasion of Maryland had turned out to be a failure, but he had escaped with most of his army intact, though heavily battered. Six weeks had passed since the battle near Sharpsburg, and during that time Allard had read all the newspaper accounts of the great, epic conflict and had heard it discussed extensively by his father, his father's business associates, and the workers at the shipyard. He knew that the Army of Northern Virginia had remained in place on the battlefield for a day after the combat, risking another attack while they prepared to withdraw back across the Potomac. But McClellan had acted cautiously, as always, and hadn't moved until it was too late to prevent the Southerners from crossing the river. Allard now knew from Robert's letter that his friend had been badly wounded and had been carried out of Maryland in an ambulance packed with other injured men. It had been a hellish journey to Richmond for Robert, Allard was sure.

He had worried a great deal about his friend and former classmate at the Citadel. Knowing that the death toll had been exceedingly high in the battle, Allard had feared that Robert was dead. When weeks had gone by without any word from him, that fear had grown. Today, when he had broken the seal on the letter and seen Robert's handwriting, a tremendous sense of relief had washed over him. That relief had been tempered by learning of Robert's wound. There was no way of knowing how long he would be laid up while he recovered from the bullet-shattered ankle.

A cold autumn rain fell on Charleston that night. It was the sort of night when Allard would really enjoy snuggling in a warm bed with his wife. He looked at Diana, who was knitting, then felt a pang of regret as he glanced at his sister. Lucinda was the one beginning to show a rounded belly that indicated she was with child, while Diana, who had been married for almost a year, was as slim as ever. Both she and Allard had begun to worry that she was barren. Diana's mother had had only one child, and that had been a difficult birth. Maybe Diana was fated not to bear any children at all.

Allard's eyes narrowed as he looked again at Lucinda. She insisted that Robert was the father of her child, that conception had occurred on their wedding night, but Allard didn't believe that for a second. For one thing, her condition wouldn't be visible by now if that were the case, and for another, he knew his sister and her morals—or lack of same. He had thought it through, and the whole thing made more sense now. Robert never would have abandoned Jacqueline Lockhart and married Lucinda unless he had been forced somehow to do so. The one thing Lucinda would have been able to hold over Robert's head was Cam's well-being. And Allard knew quite well that Cam and Lucinda had been carrying on during the spring and summer.

That baby inside his sister, Allard thought indelicately, was Cam Gilmore's. But there wasn't a damned thing he could do about it. He couldn't prove it, and if he accused Lucinda of blackmailing Robert into marrying her, she would deny the charge. Besides, it was too late to change things. Robert and Lucinda were married, and Jacqueline would never forgive Robert for that. Any stirring of the pot would be pointless.

And Robert, despite his relative youth, was a grown man, a seasoned military veteran. He had made up his own mind, and if protecting his younger brother was worth that to him, Allard had to respect that decision. Still, it was hard, knowing that Robert was in for a lifetime of unhappiness.

Meanwhile, Katherine and Diana knitted garments for the baby that was on the way. Not Lucinda, though. She was so satisfied with herself at being with child that she couldn't be bothered to do anything but preen.

The sudden rapping of the lion's-head knocker on the front door made everyone glance up in surprise.

"Who in blazes can that be on a night like this?" Malachi asked. Then he raised his voice. "Thomas!"

"I'm gettin' it, Marse Malachi," the elderly butler said from the foyer as he shuffled toward the door.

Allard tucked the letter from Robert inside his coat and stood up. He went to the foyer, curious who the caller might be. He wasn't expecting who he saw when Thomas swung the door open. A short, burly figure in a major's uniform stood there, water dripping from the brim of his hat.

"Major Pinckston!" Allard exclaimed, recognizing his old professor of mathematics and artillery from the Citadel—and his father-in-law.

Stafford Pinckston smiled and shook as much of the moisture as he could from his hat and greatcoat as he stepped into the mansion. "Allard," he said. "It's good to see you, lad."

Allard didn't have a chance to say anything else. Diana had heard him call out her father's name, and she now rushed from the parlor to throw herself into the major's arms, heedless of his wet clothing. "Daddy!" she cried.

Pinckston embraced her. "Diana," he said, his voice choked with emotion. "It's so wonderful to see you. I came here straight from the train station because I couldn't wait to see you any longer."

Katherine and Malachi hurried out of the parlor as well, but Lucinda stayed behind. Allard and his parents stood back patiently, waiting while Diana and Pinckston held each other. It had been more than a year since they had seen each other. Their only contact had been through letters. Finally Pinckston stepped back a little and rested his hands on Diana's shoulders and looked her up and down.

"It seems like you were just a little girl the last time I saw you," he said, his voice thick with emotion. "And now look at you. You've turned into a beautiful woman. A married woman, at that." He took her chin in his hand and smiled. "Am I going to be a grandfather any time soon?"

Diana blushed prettily. "Really, Father," she said.

Pinckston chuckled. "Never mind. That'll come soon enough." He turned to Allard and extended his hand. "My boy."

Allard took the major's hand, and Pinckston pulled him into a rough hug, slapping Allard on the back with his other hand. "You've been treating my daughter well?" he asked with a mock sternness.

"Of course he has," Diana said. "Allard and I are very happy."

Pinckston then hugged Katherine and shook hands with Malachi.

"Welcome back, old friend," Malachi said. "Have you returned to Charleston for good?"

Allard saw the hope leap into Diana's eyes at that question. It was dashed quickly, though, as Pinckston shook his head and said, "I'm afraid not. I have two weeks' leave, but when it's over, I'll be heading back to the army. There's talk that we'll be going into winter quarters soon, perhaps near Fredericksburg."

"Oh, I hope so," Katherine said. "It's bad enough having to wage a terrible war without having to fight in the winter too."

"Well, we'll fight when the Yankees want to fight, I suppose."

Katherine took Pinckston's arm. "Come into the parlor and sit down, Stafford."

"I'll probably get your furniture wet if I do," the major protested.

"Goodness, don't worry about that! It's only a little water. It'll dry."

All of them went into the parlor, where Pinckston said hello to Lucinda. He didn't seem surprised by the visible evidence of her condition, so Allard supposed that Diana had written him of the news of her pregnancy. He knew she had told him about Lucinda and Robert's being married. She had read part of one of Pinckston's letters to Allard, in which the major had expressed his astonishment. It had taken him by surprise, as it had everyone else.

The major sat down on one of the divans with Diana beside him. Malachi instructed Thomas to bring their new guest some brandy. "I expect you could use a drink to warm you up on a night such as this," Malachi said.

Pinckston put his arm around Diana's shoulders. "Just seeing my girl again has warmed my heart and soul," he said.

Nothing was said about Tamara Pinckston while the six of them visited for the next hour or so. Malachi and Pinckston talked a little about the war—the major had command of a battery that had taken part in all the major actions of the past year—but Katherine wouldn't let them dwell on the subject. Pinckston came from a fine old Charleston family and was acquainted with all of the city's leading citizens, so most of the talk centered on them.

Finally, Pinckston put his hands on his knees and said, "I suppose I should be going."

"But you've just gotten dry," Katherine protested. "You don't want to go back out in that miserable downpour and get soaked again, Stafford."

"You can't suggest that I stay here, Katherine?"

"Well, why not? We have plenty of room, after all."

"I have a home of my own," Pinckston pointed out gently.

What no one wanted to mention was that the stately old Pinckston family home had been closed for more than a year, with only a caretaker staying there. Otherwise, it had been deserted since the major had gone off to war, his wife had moved back in with her parents, and Diana had been living with the Tylers, first as a guest and then as a member of the family.

"Stafford, I'd take it as a personal favor if you'd be our guest while you're in Charleston," Malachi said with uncharacteristic gentleness. But then he added with a withering glance at Allard, "It would be quite a refreshing change to have someone around to talk to who knows a few things about life."

Allard felt a flush of anger, but he suppressed it for Diana's sake. He knew she wanted to have her father stay too.

"Well . . . I suppose I could," Pinckston said. "I ought to check on the house while I'm here, though, to make sure that it's being kept up properly. But that can wait for another day."

"Thank you, Father," Diana said as she took hold of his left hand with both of hers. "It'll be good to have you here."

"Well, this has certainly been a fine welcome," Pinckston said, smiling around at everyone in the room, even Lucinda. "Thank you all."

Diana hugged him again. This was the happiest Allard had seen his wife in a while. Maybe the major's visit was a good omen, coming as it did on the same day that Allard had received the letter from Robert and discovered that his old friend had survived the awful battle in Maryland. And Allard, with the superstition of a born sailor, held the firm belief that a fellow should take all the good omens he could get.

LATER, IN their bedroom, Allard watched Diana brush her long red hair as she sat at her dressing table. She looked beautiful in her nightdress, and the motion of her arm as she brushed her hair was graceful and sensuous in a way. Allard felt longing stir within him. He moved behind her and rested his hands on her shoulders.

She lifted her eyes so that she could look at him in the dressing-table mirror. "It was so wonderful to see Father again," she said.

Allard was glad that the major had come for a visit, too, but that wasn't really what he was interested in at the moment. Still, he didn't want to be impolite, so he said, "Yes, it certainly is. I know you're glad that he came to Charleston, and that he agreed to stay here." He started to slide his hands down from her shoulders, intending to slip them into the bodice of her nightdress. "But now—"

She set the hairbrush down and turned suddenly on the chair, seemingly unaware his intentions. "Allard," she said, "there's something I haven't told you."

That took him by surprise. As far as he knew, Diana always told him everything, especially when something was bothering her. From the serious look in her green eyes, whatever she had on her mind now was indeed bothersome. So he put aside the frustration he felt and asked, "What is it?"

"I had a letter . . . from my father's commanding officer."

Allard's eyebrows rose. "From the commander of his artillery brigade, you mean?"

"That's right. Colonel Stephen Lee. He expressed a great deal of concern about . . . about my father."

"I don't understand that," Allard said, shaking his head. "Major Pinckston seemed just fine to me tonight."

"What Colonel Lee said was that Father has become . . . reckless. He's been taking too many chances with his life and the lives of his men. There have been several instances over the past year when his battery came under heavy fire, but he ignored orders to withdraw and later claimed that he never received them."

"Well, your father has a history of being quite a fighter," Allard pointed out. "He was decorated for his service during the Mexican War, you know. You might even say he was a hero."

"Yes, of course, I know that," Diana said. "But this goes beyond the usual valor. From what Colonel Lee said, it sounds like . . . it sounds almost like Father is *trying* to get killed."

That sounded unlikely to Allard. "Why would he want to do that?"

"Because of Mother," Diana replied, her face growing hard and angry.

Allard knew he would be treading on dangerous ground if he ventured further into this conversation. Diana was still angry with her mother for what she had done over a year earlier, but at the same time, she still loved Tamara Pinckston. Carefully, he said, "I never did fully understand your mother's actions."

"I'm not sure *she* fully understands them. All I know is that she is disappointed with the way her life has turned out, so she blames that on Father and takes her anger out on him. But it's not his fault. He's the same man he was when she married him. She knew he wasn't rich anymore, even if some of his family does still have money."

"Money isn't everything."

"Easy to say when your family has always had plenty of it," Diana said. Then she quickly reached out and caught hold of his hand. "Oh,

I didn't mean to sound like that, Allard. I know you've never really cared about such things." She laughed, but without much humor. "You'd be just as happy being a penniless pirate."

"Well, maybe not penniless . . ." he said with a smile.

"At any rate," Diana went on, "Colonel Lee said that he was going to send Father home on leave, and he asked me to try to find out if something is bothering him. I think . . . I think he doesn't want to live anymore because my mother left him."

"Even if that's true, there's nothing you can do about it."

"I wouldn't be too sure about that."

Allard frowned. He didn't like the sound of something that was in Diana's voice. "What do you mean?" he asked.

"My parents need to clear the air between them. Maybe then they could settle their differences."

"If your father wants to see your mother, he knows where she is."

Diana shook her head and said emphatically, "He would never go over there. Never. He would see it as crawling to her, and he's too proud to do that."

"Well, I don't see any other solution."

"Mother could come here."

Allard said doubtfully, "I don't know your mother all that well, but I don't think she would do that."

"She might if she didn't know Father was here." Quickly, before Allard could interrupt, Diana rushed on, "If your mother invited her for dinner and didn't say anything about my father being here . . ."

"My God," Allard said, "you're positively diabolical."

She punched him on the hip. "Don't say that. I just want to help my mother and father to be happy again. And I don't want my father taking foolish, needless chances with his life. You can understand that, can't you, Allard?"

"Of course," he said. "I was just joking. I know you have only their best interests at heart."

But despite that, he wasn't sure her plan was a good idea. He might not have a lot of worldly experience, but it seemed to him that forcing two people to care about each other when they didn't want to was nearly impossible. Still, he wasn't going to say that to Diana. Not here and not now. Instead he smiled warmly at her and said, "Why don't you come on to bed now?"

She returned the smile. "Do you have *my* best interests at heart, Allard . . . or just your own?"

"Both," he said as he took her hand. "Definitely both."

"OH, I don't know, dear," Katherine said with a dubious frown. "It seems rather presumptuous, don't you think? And Tamara might never forgive me if I kept something like that from her."

"If you tell her that my father will be here, she'll never come," Diana said. "But if you invite her to dinner without mentioning it, she'll accept. She loves going out to dinner."

"Don't we all?" Katherine said with a sigh. "But no one entertains like they used to since the Yankees put that dreadful blockade in place. I don't know what they were thinking."

They were thinking that it would help them win the war, Allard told himself. The purpose wasn't to inconvenience Charleston society. But it wouldn't do any good to point that out, so he kept it to himself.

"Please, Mrs. Tyler," Diana said. "If there's any problem, I'll take all the blame."

"Oh, I'm sure there'll be plenty of that to go around." Katherine sighed. "All right, dear. I'll do as you ask. But really, you have to start calling me Katherine."

Diana hugged her. "Thank you, Katherine. If this works, I'll be forever in your debt."

Katherine patted her on the back and laughed. "You can pay that debt by giving me a passel of grandchildren to fuss over and spoil, dear."

She didn't see Diana wince at that comment—but Allard did. He caught his wife's eye and gave her a slight shrug. His mother hadn't meant anything by it, and she didn't know how worried Allard and Diana were about that subject.

"We'll have to keep it from my father, too," Diana cautioned. "He would never come downstairs if he knew my mother were here. She hurt his pride too much."

"Just leave it to me," Katherine said. "I'll handle everything." She laughed again. "This is exciting in a way, almost like being in a play."

Allard stood up from the breakfast table. He had remained at home later than usual this morning because Diana wanted him to be on hand in case she needed any help convincing his mother to go along with the plan. But it bothered him that his father was already at the shipyard. He wanted to get down there so he could be a part of the work that was going on. If Malachi was going to force him to stay in Charleston and help run the family business, then Allard intended to play a valuable part in the effort. He didn't go down there just for show.

As he put his hat on, he said, "I'll leave it to you ladies to work out the details."

"Don't say anything to your father," Katherine warned. "Malachi is a wonderful man, but sometimes not, ah, the soul of discretion."

Allard bit back a laugh. The idea of Malachi Tyler—blunt, opinionated, "say whatever he thought and back it up with the threat of a swift kick in the rear" Malachi Tyler—being discreet was more than humorous. It was ludicrous.

"All right, Mother," he said. He went to Diana, bent over, and kissed her on the forehead. "I'll see you this evening."

She caught hold of his hand and squeezed it. "Thank you, Allard."

He nodded, smiled, and left.

The rain had stopped, but the weather was still chilly and blustery. In the foyer, Allard shrugged into an overcoat, tugged his hat down tighter on his head, and reached for the door. He pulled it open. And startled the man standing just outside.

"Cap'n!" Allard exclaimed.

Barnaby Yorke grinned and said, "Aye, lad, 'tis me, all right. Did you see me comin'?"

"No, I had no idea." Allard seized his hand and pumped it eagerly. "Come in, come in."

Every time Yorke returned from Nassau with another cargo of much-needed supplies, he paid a visit to the Tyler household. Katherine had tried to persuade him to stay while he was in Charleston between voyages, but Yorke had insisted on staying in a room he rented in a house near the waterfront. Given the way his mother felt about the captain, that was probably a good idea, Allard thought. Not that anything would ever happen between them, of course, but Katherine seemed unable to keep herself from making a fuss over him, and that always annoyed Allard's father.

It had been more than a month since Yorke had last departed, and Allard had started to worry about him. A normal voyage shouldn't have taken more than two weeks. But there wasn't really any such thing as a normal voyage to Nassau, because the circumstances were always different. Sometimes running the blockade was more difficult than other times, and often the speedy little cutter couldn't sail a straight course to the Bahamas but was forced to go a circuitous route to avoid Yankee patrols. Those circumstances meant that every voyage was a little different than the one before it.

Even knowing all that, Allard worried. So he was greatly relieved to see Yorke. He took the captain's arm and led him to the dining room. "Look who's here," he announced as they entered the room.

Katherine's face lit up as she saw him. "Barnaby!" she said. She came to her feet and hurried over to embrace him. Allard thought the hug was a little harder and lasted a little longer than it might have if his father had been here.

Yorke disengaged himself and gave Diana a hug as well. "Both you ladies are as beautiful as ever," he said. "Makes an old sea dog glad to come into port ever' now and then."

"How's the *Diana*?" Allard asked.

"Sleek and swift as ever," Yorke said. He patted Diana on the shoulder. "Just like her namesake here."

Diana blushed. "You're a shameless flatterer, Captain Yorke."

"And why should I be ashamed o' something I'm so good at?" he asked with a grin.

"Does Malachi know you're back?" Katherine asked.

"Aye. I sent for him as soon as we docked so he could go over the cargo. When he told me Allard was still here, I decided to come on and say hello. He didn't need me there, and I know he'll do a fair inventory o' the cargo. One thing you can say about Malachi Tyler, he's as honest as the day is long."

Allard wasn't surprised his father had stayed at the dock. Malachi might not like Yorke being around Katherine, but he wouldn't let that distract him from business.

"I was about to start to the shipyard," Allard said. "Do you want to come with me?"

"If you don't mind, lad, I'd just as soon stay here a while and visit with your ladies. A fella gets mighty lonely for female companionship when he's out at sea for weeks at a time."

"Is that why you always pay a visit to Doña Graciela's when you're in Nassau?" Allard asked with a grin.

"Allard!" his mother exclaimed. "We don't talk about such things in this house."

"Sorry, Mother," he muttered.

"Anyway," Katherine went on, "I'm sure this Doña Graciela's place can't offer the same sort of down-home hospitality we can."

"Certainly not," Yorke said, and he shot a warning glance at Allard to tell him to hold his tongue.

"Have you had breakfast?" Katherine asked. Without waiting for an answer, she went on, "I'll tell the cook to prepare something for you."

"That'll be just fine, Katie," Yorke said. "And plenty o' coffee, if you've got it."

"Of course! Diana, come with me. We have plans to make." She sent a meaningful glance toward Yorke. "Now that the captain is back in town, we'll have to have a small dinner party to celebrate."

Diana caught on right away. "Yes," she agreed. "That's a wonderful idea, Katherine." The two of them bustled out of the dining room. Katherine was clearly happier than she had been in quite a while— since the last time Yorke was in Charleston, more than likely.

Allard headed for the front of the house again, saying, "I'll see you later, Cap'n," but Yorke stopped him by taking hold of his arm.

"There's something I have to talk to you about, lad," he said quietly, and Allard could tell by his tone of voice and the look on his face that he was worried. Yorke had done a good job of hiding it until now, but something was wrong.

"What is it, Cap'n?"

"I need a big favor of you, lad."

"Anything, Cap'n. You know that."

"Best not be so quick to promise that," Yorke advised. "Hear me out, but don't say anything about it yet to your ma or that pretty wife o' yours."

A bad feeling stirred inside Allard. "What is it you want me to do, Cap'n?" he asked, worried that he already knew the answer.

"I know you gave your word, lad . . . but the next time I sail for Nassau, I need you to go with me."

CHAPTER NINETEEN

Guests for Dinner

ALLARD STARED INTO YORKE'S craggy, bearded face. That answer had been exactly what he didn't want to hear. But if that was the case, he asked himself, why had he felt an undeniable surge of excitement when Yorke had made his request?

He tried to ignore that feeling. "Cap'n, you know I can't do that. I promised my father I'd work at the shipyard with him. More importantly, I promised Diana I wouldn't go to sea again."

Yorke grimaced. "I know, and I wish I didn't have to ask this of you. But I need your help. You remember Señor Valencia?"

"Of course," Allard said, recalling the suave foreigner they had met at Governor Haworth's house.

"You remember he paid us half the money for carryin' those guns to Charleston on the *Ghost?*"

"Yes."

"Well, those guns wound up on the bottom when the poor ol' *Ghost* sank."

Allard nodded. "I know. But that wasn't our fault. The Yankees sank us. Let Valencia blame them for his loss."

Yorke rubbed his bearded jaw and nodded. "That's what I told him when he braced me about the money he'd paid us and demanded it back. Valencia knew he was runnin' a risk when he loaded those guns on the ship. There ain't any guarantees in this business. I would've been within my rights to tell him to go climb a stump. But since I'd put most o' the money in the bank in Nassau, I gave it back to him."

"Then I don't see what he has to complain about."

"That was only half the value o' them guns. And now, it seems that his partners, whoever they are, are puttin' pressure on him to replace the other half o' what they were worth."

"That's crazy!" Allard said. "They had to know the risks too."

"That's what I told Valencia. And I told him I didn't have that kind o' loot to turn over for no good reason. Then he said his partners would take ownership of the *Diana* in exchange for the debt."

Allard felt a flush of anger. "It's not a legitimate debt," he said. "We were never paid that money, and anyway, the guns were lost because of an act of war. Like you said, Cap'n, there are no guarantees."

"I couldn't agree with you more, lad . . . but on our way back here from Nassau, we had a run-in with another ship. The fellas on it tried to make us heave to so we could be boarded."

"Yankees?"

Yorke shook his head. "Not hardly. This ship wasn't flyin' no flags."

"Pirates," Allard breathed.

"Aye," Yorke said, "and my guess is they were workin' for either Valencia or whoever his partners are. When I wouldn't give 'em the *Diana*, they decided to just take her."

"The bastards! Obviously, you were able to get away from them."

"We got off a lucky shot with one of our guns and took down their mainmast. It was touch and go for a while there, though."

Allard shook his head and said, "It's bad enough you've got to worry about the Yankees without having to dodge pirates too."

"Aye. It was almost like I was back in the South China Sea with ol' Black Nick again. And as much as I admired your grandpa, I don't particularly want to go back to those days."

"Well, something has to be done about this," Allard declared, "but I don't see how I can help, especially by going to Nassau."

"Haworth has some influence over Valencia, and I was hopin' he might be able to persuade the Spaniard to rein in his partners. But he's a mite leery about takin' sides unless I can make it worth his while."

"He wants a bribe?"

"Not money," Yorke grimaced. "He wants *you*, for his daughter."

Allard was stunned. He could only stare at the captain in amazement. Finally, he said, "Winifred? He wants me for Winifred? That . . . that's insane! I'm *married*. I'm in love with Diana."

"I know, lad, I know," Yorke said in low, worried tones. "I thought maybe if you went and explained the situation to her yourself—"

He stopped suddenly as the door to the kitchen opened and Katherine and Diana reappeared. "Oh," Katherine said. "I didn't know you were still here, Allard."

Yorke put an arm around Allard's shoulders. "The lad and I were just catchin' up on old times," he said heartily. "I'd best not keep him from his work any longer, though." He added to Allard, "We'll talk some more later. Go on with you now, son."

Allard didn't want Diana to see how upset he was, so he forced himself to nod and smile. "Yes, we'll definitely continue this conversation later, Cap'n." He went over to Diana and gave her a kiss on the cheek. "I'll see you this evening."

As he went out of the dining room, he gave Yorke a meaningful look that the women couldn't see. Behind him, he heard his mother say, "Sit down, Barnaby. Your breakfast is almost ready."

ALL DAY long at the shipyard, Allard was distracted by the events of the morning. It was difficult to keep his mind on his work when he was still so shocked by what Yorke had told him.

The one thing he knew was that he couldn't sail to Nassau and romance Winifred Haworth just because Yorke was in some sort of trouble with a shady character like Augustin Valencia. He would do anything he could to help sort out the situation, short of that, but he couldn't break his word to Diana.

Late that afternoon, he was in his office, staring into space and mulling it over, when his father stormed and slapped some papers on his desk. "Did you authorize this payment for lumber?"

Allard looked at the invoices for a moment before he nodded. "The amount seemed reasonable."

"Reasonable? For God's sake, boy, this is thirty percent more than we usually pay!"

Malachi's face was flushed with anger. Allard reined in his own temper as he said, "The war has affected prices, Father. Good lumber is harder to come by, and therefore more expensive."

"Don't tell me about the damned war! This blunder of yours is going to cost us hundreds of dollars!"

"It's not a blunder," Allard said stubbornly. "I looked into it before I authorized this purchase. This is the best price we could get."

Malachi snatched up the papers and with a wrench of his hands tore them in half before throwing the pieces back down on Allard's desk. "The best price an incompetent young fool like you could get, maybe! But I never would have agreed to this. You should have spoken to me about it first, Allard. I know I gave you the power to authorize such purchases, but I see now that was a mistake! I thought you had actually gotten a little sense in your head!"

Allard's guts tightened, and his hand trembled a little as it clenched into a fist. He had sailed on a privateer, a ship of war. He had been in combat. He had been wounded. And he had killed men. He was a man, not a little boy, and his father had no right to treat him like one. Keeping his anger under rigid control, he began, "Father—"

"Bah!" Malachi interrupted him. "I don't want to hear any of your feeble explanations. You don't sign any more purchase orders, you hear me? You don't do anything except . . . except double-check the entries in the ledgers. You *can* do simple addition and subtraction, can't you?"

"Of course, but are you saying I no longer have the authority—"

Malachi leaned forward, thrusting his fists on the desk. "You don't have the authority to use the privy unless I give it to you," he thundered. "And I'm not sure you're smart enough to handle that!"

He straightened, turned, and stalked out, leaving Allard sitting at the desk, white-faced and trembling with rage.

If it weren't for Diana, he *would* go back to sea, he told himself. If his father was going to treat him like this, Malachi didn't deserve to have those promises honored.

An ignorant, incompetent boy . . . that was all he would ever be in his father's eyes, Allard realized. And it was a bitter realization indeed.

BY THE time he arrived home that evening, he was still furious. Malachi had avoided him since their confrontation, but that hadn't assuaged the anger Allard felt toward his father. He knew he had to put that aside, though, at least for the time being. There were other, more pressing problems to be dealt with. Such as Captain Yorke and his dilemma.

Yorke came out of the parlor as Allard was giving his hat and coat to Thomas. He said, "There you are, lad. I been waitin' for you—"

Before Yorke could say anything else, Katherine emerged from the dining room. "Allard, I have to speak to you—"

And from the top of the staircase, Diana chimed in, "I'm glad you're home, Allard. I need—"

"Stop it, all of you!"

The words flew out of his mouth before he could suppress the exclamation. Instantly, the others looked hurt, and he wished he had somehow clamped his lips shut. But all he could do was say rather limply, "I'm sorry, but I can't hear you if you're all talking at once."

Diana reached the bottom of the stairs, so he turned to her. "What was it you wanted to talk to me about?"

"I just thought you ought to be the one to ask my father to come to dinner tomorrow night," she said, still looking and sounding offended. "But if that's going to be too much trouble for you . . ."

"No, no trouble at all," Allard said quickly. "But won't he be here anyway, since he's staying with us?"

"Not tomorrow night. He plans to have dinner with some of his colleagues at the Citadel. And tomorrow night is the only night my mother will agree to come!"

Katherine said, "That's what I wanted to talk to you about, too, Allard. You and Stafford always got along well while you were at the Citadel. Perhaps you can persuade him to postpone his get-together with his cronies and join us instead."

"Well, I can try," Allard said. "Major Pinckston and I were never all that close, though. If he won't agree to come to please you and Diana, Mother, I can't imagine that I'll be able to make any difference."

Katherine patted him on the arm. "Just try, dear."

"I will," Allard promised. He turned to Yorke. "Now, Cap'n, you and I have some unfinished business . . ."

"Nothin' that won't wait," Yorke said. "I'll be here for a week or more before startin' back to Nassau. Plenty o' time for us to get together and hash over old times."

Yorke's eyes looked worried, though, and Allard knew the captain didn't like having the threat hanging over his head. But they couldn't discuss the matter around Diana and Katherine, so Allard just nodded. "Is the major here?" he asked. "I'll go talk to him right now."

"He's upstairs in the blue guest room," Katherine said.

"He just got back from checking on our house," Diana added.

"I'll see what I can do," Allard said. He started up the stairs.

A few moments later, he rapped lightly on the door of the guest room. "Who's there?" the major called.

"It's Allard Tyler, sir."

"Ah. Come in, Allard."

Allard opened the door and found Pinckston standing in front of the bureau, wiping his face with a towel. His eyes were rather red, though, and Allard realized with a shock that he must have been crying. The thought of the bluff, hearty artillery officer ever crying seemed so foreign to Allard that he could barely comprehend it. He remembered Diana saying downstairs that the major had been over at the family home this afternoon. Perhaps that visit had stirred up some painful memories and made him recall that once he and his wife and their daughter had been a family—although, given Tamara Pinck-ston's state of mind, probably not a particularly happy one.

But Pinckston wasn't going to admit to any sort of emotional dis-tress. Instead, he said, "I'm glad you're here, Allard. You and I need to have a talk." He gestured toward a comfortable armchair.

Allard sank into the chair while the major sat on the edge of the bed. "What did you want to discuss, sir?"

"As you know, I always thought you were an excellent cadet. You were just a boy, though, and I must admit, I was a little worried when I found out that you and Diana were to be married."

"I can understand that. You knew me only as a student."

Pinckston nodded. "Yes, and I can see that you've grown up a great deal in the past couple of years. Still, I'd like some assurances that you're going to be able to take proper care of my daughter."

"I would do anything for Diana, sir," Allard said emphatically. "She means the world to me."

Pinckston said, "And to me. I'm glad to hear that you're working at the shipyard. That's a fine profession for a young man."

Allard's jaw tightened. After the way his father had blown up today, he wasn't sure anyone could say that he was working "with" Malachi. He had been stripped of what little power he had, and now Malachi had him doing tedious chores that any bookkeeper could do, and probably better. Instead of being groomed to someday take over the shipyard, as he had expected, he was no more than a flunky. But that wasn't the sort of thing that Major Pinckston wanted to hear right now, so Allard just nodded and waited for his father-in-law to go on.

"I expect as time goes on, you'll want to move out of here and have a place of your own?"

"Yes sir. It seemed best, though, and simpler, what with the war going on and all, for us to stay here for the time being."

"Perhaps you'd like the house where Diana grew up."

That offer, if it was such, took Allard by surprise, enough so that his eyebrows rose. "But that's your house, Major," he said. "I'm sure that after the war—"

"After the war, I'll be selling it, if you and Diana don't want it." Pinckston added wryly. "Assuming that I live through the war."

"Oh, I'm sure you will."

"But that will never be my house again," Pinckston went on as if he hadn't heard Allard. "I realize now that I can't live there. It holds too many memories for me, memories that I wouldn't want to relive every day for the rest of my life."

Allard leaned forward and clasped his hands between his knees. "You don't want to make any important decisions right now, Major," he said. "We don't know how things are going to turn out with the war, and . . . and things can always change."

"Some things can't," Pinckston said flatly. "Some roads, once you go down them, you can never go back."

"I don't believe that—"

"Believe it, my boy. Take the word of someone who's older and a lot more experienced than you."

Allard drew in a deep breath. This conversation had been illuminating, but it hadn't gone at all the way he had intended. Nor had he come close to solving the problem with which his wife and mother had charged him.

"Sir, the real reason I came up here was to see if you would join us for dinner tomorrow night."

"I'm sorry, but I already told your mother that I'm having dinner with some of the instructors from the Citadel. You remember them, I'm sure." He named off several professors.

"Yes, of course, but couldn't that wait for another night? My mother has her heart set on tomorrow."

Pinckston frowned at him. "Why is this so important? It seems to me that one night would be just as good as another—"

"It's not so much my mother," Allard blurted. "It's Diana."

"What does Diana have to do with this?"

"She . . . has something she wants to say." Allard's brain raced furiously, trying to come up with a plausible excuse. "An announcement she wants to make."

"An announce—" Pinckston stopped short, his bushy eyebrows rising and his mouth forming an O of surprise. He came to his feet. "Are you saying what I think you're saying, son?"

Allard forced a weak smile. "I really can't say anything else, sir. It's, uh, not my place to do so."

Pinckston held up his hands and said, "You don't have to say anything else." He grabbed Allard's hand and shook it vigorously. "By God, this is wonderful news, wonderful news. I couldn't be happier."

"But . . . I didn't really tell you anything."

The major closed one eye in an exaggerated wink. "That's right. You didn't tell me a thing. Don't worry, I'll act properly surprised when the time comes."

"So you'll be there?"

"For something this important? Of course I will! My other engagement can wait."

Allard nodded in relief. Diana and his mother would be happy now. Their plans could continue. And he'd had to mislead Pinckston only a little. The major had jumped to an unwarranted conclusion mostly on his own.

Pinckston still had hold of Allard's hand. He worked it loose and said, "Thank you, Major. I'll tell them."

"All right, my boy. And until then, mum's the word, eh?"

"Yes sir. Mum."

Allard left the room as quickly as he could, pausing in the hall outside the major's door to heave a small sigh of relief. That had been an ordeal he didn't want to repeat any time soon. Of course Pinckston was going to be upset when the planned dinner announcement didn't go as he expected it would, but there was nothing Allard could do about that.

Diana met him at the bottom of the stairs. "Did he agree to come?"

"Yes, I was able to talk him into it."

She put her arms around him and hugged him. "Thank you, Allard. I knew you could do it." She paused. "What did you tell him?"

He had hoped that she wouldn't ask him that. "He expects you to announce that you're going to have a baby."

Diana stared at him. "What!"

"I had to tell him something. And to be honest, I didn't actually say that's what was going to happen. He just sort of took it for granted."

"But Allard—"

"Don't worry about it, Diana. Once he comes in and sees your mother sitting there, he'll forget all about the other."

"I suppose you're right." She gnawed at her lower lip for a moment. "Still, I hate to disappoint him."

"Let's just concentrate on bringing about a reconciliation between your parents."

"Yes, you're right, of course." She kissed him. "Thank you, Allard. What would I ever do without you?"

He thought about Yorke's problem and the solution the captain had proposed, and he said, "Let's hope you never have to find out."

RELATIONS BETWEEN Allard and his father were strained that evening and the next day at the shipyard, but Allard didn't bring up the argument and neither did Malachi. But Malachi didn't give him any important work to do, either. So Allard knew his father was still angry and mistrustful of him.

He wanted to get through this dinner before he had any sort of confrontation with Malachi again, though, so he kept his own resentment under control. He could only handle one potential crisis at a time, he thought wryly as he kept busy with the mundane chores Malachi assigned him.

At the end of the day, Allard headed home, taking care to leave a short time after his father did. He didn't want Malachi thinking that he was shirking. When he arrived, he found that Diana's mother was already there, sitting in the parlor with Diana and Katherine. Tamara

Pinckston greeted him warmly, hugging him as she said hello. Given the Tylers' standing in the community, she had been glad for Diana to marry Allard.

"I'll go upstairs to change and be right back down," he told his mother, but Katherine shook her head.

"I'll send Thomas up to let you know when dinner is ready," she said. "There's no point in you coming down until then."

She seemed to be trying to tell him something, and after a second Allard understood. He was supposed to make sure that Major Pinckston didn't come downstairs until everything was ready for him. If he and Tamara realized the other was there before dinner was about to get under way, either or both of them might bolt.

Allard nodded. "Of course, Mother." He pecked Diana on the cheek and then went quickly upstairs, heading straight for the major's room.

Pinckston answered Allard's knock with a bright, "Come in."

Allard just stuck his head in the room. Pinckston was only half dressed and was still shaving. "Evening, Major," Allard said. "Ready for the big night?"

"Almost." Pinckston grinned in anticipation of what he thought was going to happen.

"I'm going to change, and I'll be back in a minute," Allard went on. "We'll go downstairs together, all right?"

"That's fine, lad. I'll wait here for you."

Allard nodded, glad that the major was cooperating, even though he had no idea what he was really cooperating in. Allard went on to his room and wasted no time in cleaning up and trading the suit he had worn to the shipyard for a nicer, more expensive one.

When he returned to the major's room, Pinckston was just putting the finishing touches on tying his cravat. Allard hoped the delay wouldn't be too long. Things could get awkward if his father-in-law started gushing about the announcement he expected Diana to make this evening.

Thankfully, Thomas rapped on the door only a few minutes later, and when Allard answered the summons, the butler said, "Miz Katherine says y'all can come on downstairs now, Marse Allard."

"Thanks, Thomas." Allard turned to Pinckston. "Ready, Major?"

Pinckston smiled. "Ready as I'll ever be, my boy."

They walked to the head of the stairs and started down. Allard didn't see his father anywhere and figured Malachi was already in the dining room with the others. He would have been surprised to see Tamara Pinckston, no doubt, but he would go along with whatever his wife wanted in a case like this. Malachi wasn't the sort to involve himself in anyone's emotional entanglements.

"Are you excited, Allard?" Pinckston asked as they reached the closed doors to the dining room.

"More nervous than anything else, sir," Allard answered honestly.

Pinckston chuckled. "Well, you'll get over that."

I wouldn't be so sure, Allard thought as he reached out and opened one of the doors. "After you, sir," he said.

Pinckston nodded and strode into the dining room. Allard stepped in behind him and eased the door shut, leaning against it and hanging on to the knob so the major couldn't flee without trampling over him. Of course, Pinckston was burly enough to do just that if he wanted to.

Instead, he stopped short, staring at the table where Tamara sat at Malachi Tyler's left hand. Katherine was to Malachi's right, with Lucinda beside her. Diana sat to her mother's left, with an empty chair between them. Tamara must have assumed that Allard was going to sit between her and Diana. Now, though, she stared in shock at her husband, who returned the stare for a long second and then exclaimed angrily, "My God! What's going on here?"

Diana got nervously to her feet and said, "Come sit beside me, Father." She gestured toward the empty chair between her and Tamara.

"No!" Tamara exclaimed. "Stafford, what are you doing here?"

Pinckston drew himself up stiffly. "I could ask the same of you."

"I'm here to have dinner with old friends," Tamara said coldly.

"Well, so am I." Pinckston paused. "And to hear my daughter announce that she and her husband are expecting a child."

"What!" The gasped exclamation came in unison from Tamara, Katherine, and Malachi. They couldn't have timed it more perfectly if they had practiced together all day.

"There's no baby!" Diana said quickly. "That was just a ruse to get the two of you to sit down and have dinner together like a couple of civilized people. You're never going to be able to work out your problems if you never see each other."

Pinckston said, "There are no problems to work out. Your mother left me, Diana. She made her feelings perfectly clear."

"You made *your* feelings perfectly clear, Stafford," Tamara said in a voice like ice, "when you insisted on remaining in your teaching position at the Citadel. Your lack of ambition was intolerable, but I stood it for as long as I could."

"My work there was important," Pinckston shot back, "and so are my duties now with the army!"

"The only reason you're off fighting in that war is because you refuse to face up to the way you've failed your family!"

Allard exchanged a glance with Diana. This wasn't going well at all—but he had never really expected it to. Diana had been much more optimistic about that possibility than he.

"Mother, Father, please," she said. "Don't argue. Just sit down and try to have a civil dinner—"

Pinckston interrupted her with a snort of contempt. "I'll not sit down at a table with that woman ever again."

Tamara came to her feet and said coldly, "Nor do I have any desire to share a meal . . . or anything else . . . with that man." She turned to Malachi. "I'd appreciate it if you'd have my driver bring my carriage around, Malachi."

Clearly not wanting to take sides—or even have anything more to do with this debacle—Malachi looked to his wife for guidance. Katherine said, "Tamara, Stafford, I'd take it as a personal favor if you would both just sit down." She gave a strained laugh. "Surely you can both stay and have dinner."

Pinckston and Tamara shook their heads in stubborn refusal.

Allard knew that his mother and Diana didn't want to abandon their goal of getting the feuding couple together again, but it was beginning to look as if their effort was doomed to failure.

Diana wasn't ready to give up, though. She said, "I'm sorry I lied to both of you, but you have to understand that I did it only because I love you. I want to see you both happy again."

"Too late for that," her father said curtly. "My only happiness now lies in killing those damned Yankees."

Tamara sniffed. "I see that you're as crude as ever, Stafford."

That might have provoked yet another round of insults, but instead, at that moment, Thomas came into the dining room and tugged urgently at Allard's sleeve. "Marse Allard," he said, "they's a problem out in the hall."

Allard didn't see how there could be a bigger problem out there than there was in here, but he said, "What is it?"

"Cap'n Yorke, sir."

In the strain of the confrontation between the Pinckstons, Allard hadn't even noticed that Yorke wasn't there. Of course, Yorke didn't take all his meals at the Tyler mansion while he was in Charleston, so there was nothing unusual about his absence.

Allard was about to step out of the dining room and see what Yorke wanted, when the captain himself appeared in the doorway. He said, "Sorry to interrupt your little party, Katherine, but I could use a little help here."

His right hand was clutched to his left arm. Blood welled between his fingers, trickled down his arm, and dripped to the polished hardwood floor of the dining room.

CHAPTER TWENTY

Nassau Again

N O, I NEVER GOT a good look at the bastard," Yorke said as the doctor finished binding up the deep knife slash in his arm. The captain was sitting in Malachi's study while the physician worked on him. "The fella came out of an alley and cut me before I knew what deviltry he was up to. Went for my throat, but I got my arm up in time to block the knife. 'Fore he could try again, I got my derringer out o' my pocket and let him have both barrels in the face."

"You killed him?" Allard asked in a hushed voice.

"Seemed like the thing to do at the time, seein' as he was dead set on carvin' me up. I'm just glad there was only one of 'em."

"Does the law know what happened?" Malachi asked harshly.

Yorke shook his head. "No, I got out of there before anybody showed up to check on the shots."

"Good," Malachi said. "Then there's no need to involve the authorities in this."

Allard looked at his father in surprise. It wasn't that he didn't agree with Malachi; bringing in the law seemed an unnecessary complication. But he hadn't expected Malachi to feel the same way.

"It's too important for the *Diana* to continue running the blockade," Malachi went on. "We can't afford to take a chance of having you locked up, even though you clearly killed that man in self-defense. Just a common cutthroat out to rob you, no doubt."

Allard's first thought was that the attempt on Yorke's life was connected to the trouble he was having with Valencia and the foreigner's mysterious partners. Yorke must have felt the same way, because when Malachi made that comment, the captain gave him a quick, meaningful glance.

It was a mistake, though, because Malachi noticed the exchange and frowned. "What's going on here?" he snapped. "You two know something that I don't?"

There seemed to be no avoiding the subject now. Malachi was like a bulldog; once he got his jaws locked on something, he didn't let go. Yorke sighed and said, "This might be tied up with some other trouble we're havin', Malachi."

"What trouble? Nobody's told me about any trouble except for that blasted Union blockade. Damn it, the *Diana* is my ship, too! If there's some sort of threat to her, I have a right to know about it."

"Aye, that you do," Yorke agreed. "It's like this, then."

For the next few minutes, he filled Malachi in on the situation, explaining the demands that Valencia had made, both for himself and on behalf of his partners, and also how he had tried to get Governor Haworth to intercede, only to have the governor make a demand as well.

That seemed to surprise Malachi more than anything else. He glared at Allard and demanded, "What does this girl want with *you*? What did you *do* down there, damn it?"

"I didn't do anything!" Allard said. "I swear. I never led her on or anything like that. She simply got it in her head somehow that she . . . well, wanted me."

Malachi grunted skeptically. "Well, there's no accounting for taste, I suppose." He clasped his hands behind his back and frowned. "Obviously, you can't go back to Nassau and woo this girl. You already have a wife . . . even if there's *not* a child on the way yet." He shook his head. "By the way, that was a terrible trick to play on Stafford."

Allard shrugged. "I had to get him to dinner some way. Mother and Diana were counting on me."

"Yes, I know what it's like to have to keep the womenfolk happy. Their little plan didn't work, though, did it?"

In fact, the plan had been a spectacular failure. In the confusion that resulted from Yorke's bloody arrival, both the major and his estranged wife had taken their leave—Tamara back to the Oaks while the major went downtown to a hotel. Diana had gone upstairs crying. Allard had wanted to go after her, but at the time, Yorke had still been bleeding . . .

"Getting back to the other problem," Malachi said, "what are we going to do about it?"

"I don't plan on turnin' the *Diana* over to a thievin' scoundrel like Valencia," Yorke said.

"Of course not. But based on what you've told me, he and his associates must be to blame for the attempt on your life. Valencia probably thought that, if you were dead, I could be bullied into giving him what he wants." Malachi gave a short, humorless bark of laughter. "The man is sadly mistaken in his assessment of my resolve."

"Aye, Malachi, you can be a stubborn son of a . . . gun," Yorke said.

"Do you really think Governor Haworth could help, if he was willing?"

Yorke shrugged. "He could make it mighty difficult for Valencia to operate out of Nassau, if he wanted to. With Haworth on our side, Valencia wouldn't have much choice but to back off."

"All right, then," Malachi said with a nod. He turned to Allard. "You've got to go to Nassau."

"What!" Allard practically yelped. "You want me to . . . to leave Diana and . . . and go to Winifred . . ."

"Don't be a damned fool," Malachi said with a withering glare. "You're not going to leave Diana. Well, you *are*, but only long enough to go to Nassau, talk some sense into that other girl's head, and persuade her father to help us. You can handle *that*, can't you?"

Allard stared at his father, wondering if Malachi had lost his mind. What he proposed was madness. In the first place, it would break Diana's heart if he went back on his word to her. And in the second, what guarantee was there that he could convince Winifred and her father of anything?

And yet, as Allard thought about it, the idea began to make a kind of bizarre sense. If Winifred heard from his own lips that he was married and deeply in love with his wife, she might give up whatever designs she had on him. And if he could win Winifred over, surely her father would be willing to help him and Yorke.

Despite all the drawbacks, there weren't any other options that Allard could see. They had enough to worry about with the Yankee blockade. They couldn't afford to be threatened by smugglers and pirates and would-be killers too.

"I'll talk to Diana," Allard said grudgingly. "But I can't promise anything."

"Don't worry about Diana. She'll understand," Malachi said. "Besides, she's too upset and worried about her parents right now to be overly concerned about *you*."

Allard wasn't so sure about that, but he could try.

"YOU . . . YOU want to go to sea again?" Diana said haltingly. "You want to go back to Nassau to see that . . . that girl?"

When he had returned from his voyage to Nassau the previous year, Allard had told Diana about Winifred Haworth, but he hadn't gone into detail about her efforts to seduce him. In fact, he chose not to mention that part of the story at all. The omission, however, came back to haunt him, because now he had to tell Diana the whole story—all of it. If she were going to agree to his taking on the task his father and Yorke had set for him, she was going to have all the details first.

Her eyes were still red from crying about the dinner fiasco and the renewed, still bitter argument between her parents. He knew she believed that all she had accomplished was to make things worse, which meant that, when her father returned to the army, Stafford Pinckston would likely be more reckless with his life than ever.

And now Allard was dumping these additional troubles on her. He felt miserable about doing such a thing, but as she listened, he explained as best he could the dilemma facing everyone involved with the ship that bore her name.

"So you see," he concluded, "I have to convince Winifred and her father to be reasonable—"

"And what if you can't?" Diana interrupted. "Are you going to just take this woman to bed and be done with it? Or will you have to marry her?" Her voice grew chilly. "Perhaps those island girls don't mind a man having two wives."

"Winifred's British. She's not from the islands. And I'm not going to marry her or do anything else with her, for God's sake! I just have to talk some sense into her head."

"And if you can't?" she said again.

He shrugged. "We'll deal with that situation if it arises. But you should know, Diana, there is no way I would ever betray the love you have for me or the love I have for you."

She glared at him, sniffled a little, then finally said, "I believe you. But I still don't want you to go." She held up a hand to forestall his next argument. "I understand. I know it seems you *have* to go. But I don't have to like it."

He ventured cautiously, "You mean you agree?"

"What choice do I have? Your father is right. Something has to be done, and it appears you're the only one who has a real chance of succeeding." She caught hold of his hand. "But if you betray me, Allard Tyler, don't bother coming back to Charleston, because there won't be anything waiting for you here."

"That will never happen," he vowed. "Our marriage is safe."

She smiled faintly. "And don't get your head blown off by the Yankees on the way there or back, either."

"It'll never happen," he said. "You don't have to worry about *that*."

THE *DIANA* sailed three nights later, slipping out of the harbor in a thick fog. The gray paint on the ship's sleek hull blended in perfectly with the writhing tendrils of mist. There were a few tense moments when a Union ship was seen about a hundred yards away. Even though the lookouts aboard the blockade-runner were aware of the Yankee vessel, the reverse wasn't true. After that near encounter, the way was clear, and the *Diana* was soon far out to sea, clipping along at a nice rate.

Allard was regarded as a passenger this time, not a crewman, although he was perfectly willing to help out where and when he was needed. He spent most of his time at the railing, enjoying the way the *Diana* sliced cleanly through the water. The weather was clear and the winds were fair most of the time, although the ship did have to run through one squall. As it pitched and heaved during that storm, Allard discovered that his months on land had cost him his sea legs, at least to an extent. His queasy stomach was extremely glad when the storm passed and they were back in relatively calm water again.

Once, Yorke jogged to the southwest to avoid a ship in the distance. Odds were that this other vessel was not a Federal patrol boat, but Yorke wasn't taking any chances. That slight delay meant that four days passed by the time the *Diana* came in sight of the two low, green humps on the horizon that were New Providence and Andros islands.

That evening they were close enough for Allard to make out the harbor at New Providence Island and the picturesque town spread out on the shore of it. When he used Yorke's telescope, he could even see Governor's House and Fort Fincastle atop the small hill overlooking the harbor. He felt an odd stirring inside, a mixture of dread and anticipation. Nassau was a beautiful place, and even though he had been there only a short time, he craved the fragrant air, the constant music, and the sense of peace and tranquility that lingered over the island.

There were times, though, when those perceptions were false, as he realized when he recalled how he and Yorke had been attacked in the street that night. That was before the agreement with Valencia regarding the shipment of guns, so Allard didn't see how the two things could be connected, but the memory still made him uneasy. Like the serpent in Eden, violence could easily lurk in the beauty that was Nassau.

The ship docked as the sun was setting. In the hold was a cargo of cotton bound for the mills in England. Unloading it could wait until morning, and once the hold was empty, it could be filled again, this time with goods that had been brought from Liverpool on British ships and unloaded in Nassau to be picked up by the blockade-runners. Neither side was strictly in violation of international shipping laws—although the Yankees didn't see it quite that way. Federal ships carefully left the British vessels alone, however, even though their captains knew what was going on. So far, the British had stayed officially neutral, and no one in Washington, from Lincoln on down, wanted to do anything to tip that delicate balance. A British invasion from Canada would likely spell doom for the Union. It was what the Confederates had been hoping for, but so far it hadn't happened.

A carriage pulled up on the dock as Allard and Yorke were disembarking from the *Diana*. Governor Haworth's butler, as short and red-faced as ever and wearing a bowler hat, climbed out and approached them. He took the hat off his mostly bald head and bowed.

"Good evenin', gents," he said as he straightened and replaced the bowler. "Governor Haworth was informed that your ship was approachin' the harbor and sent me to tell you that he expects you both for dinner this evenin'. In an hour, shall we say?"

Yorke nodded. "Aye, that'll give us time to make ourselves presentable. Tell the governor we'll be there."

"Thank you, Captain." The butler bowed again and climbed back into the carriage, which rolled away briskly.

"Well, that didn't take long," Yorke said to Allard. "We wanted to talk to Haworth as soon as we could. Looks like he's anxious to settle things too." He clapped a hand on Allard's shoulder. "No time for a visit to Graciela's. We'll just have to clean ourselves up as best we can on board ship."

Allard was nervous as he washed, shaved, and dressed in clean clothes. Even though he had come all this way to meet with Winifred Haworth, he was nervous about the impending encounter. If it didn't go well, not only would he not help solve the problems facing him and his father and Yorke, he might make the whole thing worse. Despite the tropical setting, he sensed that he would be on thin ice tonight, and he would have to tread carefully.

"Ready, lad?" Yorke asked as they met again at the gangplank.

Allard nodded. "I suppose. I wish it hadn't come to this, but since it did . . ."

"You have that pistol o' yours?"

Allard touched the reassuring weight of the Colt Navy holstered butt-forward on his left hip. "Yes. I just hope I don't need it."

Both of them were very alert as they walked through the streets. As always, the town had a holiday atmosphere about it. Allard didn't let himself be taken in by that, however. He was ready for trouble.

They reached Queen Anne's Staircase and started up toward Governor's House. No one else was on the carved stone steps. Allard thought this might be a good place for someone to jump them, but they reached the top without incident and followed the flagstone walk to the mansion's entranceway.

The butler let them in and took them to the dining room with the french doors that opened onto the terrace where Allard had first met Winifred. Neither the governor nor his daughter was there at the moment. The butler asked, "A glass of port, gentlemen?"

"I could do with a drink," Yorke said, and Allard nodded. He wanted to remain clear-headed tonight, but he didn't think a glass of wine would muddle his brain too much.

The butler brought the drinks to them and left them standing in front of the french doors, looking out at the night and sipping their wine. Within a few moments, footsteps sounded behind them. Governor William Haworth said, "Your timing is impeccable, gentlemen."

Allard stiffened in surprise when he saw that Augustin Valencia was with the governor. The Latin chap was as sleek and well dressed as always as he smirked at them.

"Eh?" Yorke sounded as surprised as Allard felt. "What's Valencia doin' here, Governor?"

"Señor Valencia is here at my request. The problem between you has to be cleared up tonight. There's no longer any time to waste."

Yorke bristled with anger. "There ain't no problem, because this fella's got no right to make any claim on my ship! Who ever heard of a smuggler wantin' a guarantee of delivery?"

Haworth smiled faintly and shook his head as he said, "Unfortunately, Captain, it's no longer a matter of Señor Valencia's claim alone. It's mine as well."

Yorke and Allard both stared at the man for a long moment. Allard was utterly confused, but Yorke's puzzled expression suddenly cleared. "Ah," he said. "I reckon I see now. Valencia's got just one partner . . . you, sir."

Haworth smiled and inclined his head in acknowledgment of Yorke's statement. Allard's confusion began to clear. He said, "You're the one who's been trying to get his hands on the *Diana?*"

"She's as fine a ship for blockade-running as I've ever seen," Haworth said. "She'll be worth a fortune before this war is over . . . which I can tell you right now, gentlemen, won't be for a long time. I know your precious Confederacy is counting on military and diplomatic aid from England, but I promise you, it's not coming. Too many people there are already getting rich from the situation the way it is."

"Supplying the blockade-runners, you mean," Yorke said.

"Exactly. But if Augustin and I own that ship of yours, we can cut out one step in the process and make even more money."

Anger blazed up inside Allard. He said, "You'll never get your hands on the *Diana!* My father will never agree to turn her over to you."

"Oh, no?" Valencia said. "Not even to save the life of his only son?" He slid his hand inside his coat and brought up a pistol.

Yorke's big hands clenched into fists. "You damned blackguards, both of you! Your daughter's not still interested in the lad, here. You just wanted him in Nassau so you could hold him for ransom!"

"That ransom being the ownership papers for the *Diana,* yes," Haworth agreed. "Well, what do you say, gentlemen? Young Mr. Tyler's life . . . both of your lives, actually . . . in exchange for that ship?"

Allard stood there tensely, his gaze fastened on the gun in Valencia's hand. He was aware of the weight of the Colt on his hip, but he didn't think he could use it before Valencia would shoot him down. In an attempt to stall for time, he asked tightly, "Does Winifred know anything about this?"

"Very little," Haworth replied.

"How do you think she'll feel when she finds out you used her to steal the *Diana* from us?"

Haworth's smile didn't waver. "I think I know my daughter better than you do, Mr. Tyler. As long as it means she'll be able to continue living in fine style, she won't care what I do."

Remembering Winifred's rather loose morality, Allard knew that Haworth was right. He glanced at Yorke, but the captain's face was set in hard, expressionless lines. He had no idea what Yorke planned to do. He didn't want to let Haworth and Valencia get away with their underhanded scheme, though.

"It is a good thing my men did not succeed in killing you the first night you came to Nassau, Señor Tyler," Valencia said unexpectedly. "I had no idea at the time you would ultimately prove so valuable to us."

"*You* were responsible for those men jumping us that night?" Allard asked.

"Of course. I saw the way the lovely Winifred looked at you, and I do not mind admitting that I was jealous. My Latin blood, you know. I had my sights set on that oh-so-charming girl. And I am a man who gets what he wants."

"But not at the expense of profits," Haworth snapped. "As you said, it was lucky these two got away unscathed that night."

Allard felt like kicking himself. He had never fully trusted Valencia, but he had considered the governor to be a distinguished, well-educated diplomat. Haworth might be well educated, but at heart he was a common criminal, the same as Valencia.

"Well, gentlemen," Haworth went on, and Valencia lifted his pistol for emphasis, "what will it be?"

Before Allard or Yorke could answer, the door of the dining room burst open, and a red-faced man who was short of breath, as if he had run all the way up Queen Anne's Staircase, hurried in. Allard recognized him as Cyril Judkins, the harbormaster.

"Governor!" Judkins said excitedly. "Governor, a Royal Navy ship just docked! Its commander and a couple of his officers are on their way up here!"

"Do you know why?" Haworth asked tensely.

Judkins bobbed his head up and down. "I overheard them talking about it. They're coming to take you into custody, sir!"

"Damn it!" Haworth said as he paled. "Obviously the Crown has some inkling what I've been doing here, after all."

Valencia looked frightened enough to pass out. "What are we going to do?" he asked. "Should I shoot them?" He gestured with the pistol toward Allard and Yorke.

"I should say not! We need them now more than ever. You take them out the back way and work your way around to the harbor. The *Diana* will be putting out to sea again tonight. Do you know the fishing village called San Remo on the north side of the island."

Valencia nodded. "I know the place."

"Winifred and I will give those officers the slip and meet you there tomorrow morning. From there . . ." Haworth shrugged. "Well, I suppose we shall sail where the wind takes us."

"But our money! We cannot leave without our money!"

"I have a chest full of gold. I'll bring it to San Remo with us."

Just like the pirates they were, Allard thought. They kept their plunder in a treasure chest.

Judkins clutched at Haworth's sleeve. "What about me, Governor?"

"No one knows about your involvement with my illicit activities, man. Just keep your head about you, and you'll be fine."

Judkins nodded. He pulled a handkerchief from his pocket, took his hat off, and used the cloth to mop his face and balding head. He started to turn away.

Valencia stepped behind him and slammed the pistol against his skull, just above the ear. The harbormaster dropped like a stone, and Valencia raised his gun again, obviously intending to batter his brains out. "He knows too much about our affairs to live," Valencia muttered.

For the first time since he'd drawn the pistol, his attention had strayed from Allard and Yorke. Allard's hand darted under his coat and his fingers closed around the butt of the Colt Navy. As he drew it and eared back the hammer, he said loudly, "Don't move, Señor!"

"You, either, Governor," Yorke added as his derringer slid from his sleeve into his palm. He leveled the small, two-shot pistol at Haworth.

The two conspirators both froze. Haworth's lips drew into a snarl. "I'll make you both rich men if you help us," he said. "If you don't, I'll see you both dead."

"I reckon your days o' makin' threats are just about over, mister," Yorke said.

From behind them, Winifred's voice said coolly, "Not quite, Captain." The words were followed by the metallic click of a gun being cocked.

Allard looked over her shoulder and saw that she had come through the french doors from the terrace. She had a small pistol in her hand, and she looked like she knew how to use it. Judging from the determined expression on her face, she wouldn't hesitate to do so, either. The muzzle of the gun was pointed between Allard and Yorke, so she could shift her hand a fraction of an inch and gun down either of them.

But not both, Allard thought. Not both.

"Are you going to drop your weapons, gentlemen, or am I to be forced to fire?" she asked.

Valencia didn't give them a chance to answer. He screamed, "Kill them! Kill them now!" and twisted up out of his crouch, bringing his own gun around as he did so.

"No!" Haworth shouted, but now that Valencia's sudden move had snapped the tension, it was too late to stop what was happening.

Allard jerked to the side as the gun in Valencia's hand spouted flame. He fired instinctively, aiming at the man's cream-colored suit, then he cocked the Colt and pulled the trigger again as the first .36-caliber slug slammed into Valencia's body and drove him back a step. Allard's second shot found its target, too, and another crimson flower bloomed on the breast of Valencia's shirt. He dropped his gun and staggered to the side, then fell to his knees and pitched forward.

"Winifred!" Haworth screamed. He rushed forward.

Yorke stepped aside to let the crooked governor pass, but he kept his derringer trained on Haworth anyway. Allard turned, too, and saw to his shock that Winifred had dropped her gun and stumbled back onto the terrace. They found her leaning against the stone railing, both hands pressed to her belly. Allard's eyes widened as he saw the blood leaking between her fingers. Valencia's single stray shot had struck Winifred.

"No!" Haworth cried. "Oh, dear Lord, no!"

As Allard watched in horror, Winifred's eyes rolled up. She sagged backward, farther over the railing, and then toppled over it, falling out of sight. Haworth screamed and fell to his knees, clutching the railing.

Yorke shook his head and then walked over to Valencia. He hooked a toe under the man's shoulder and rolled him onto his back. Allard could tell by the Latin's sightless stare that he was dead.

The white-haired butler, as imperturbable as ever, despite the bloody tragedy spread out before him, ushered three Royal Navy officers into the room. "Governor Haworth?" one of them asked briskly.

Yorke pointed to the sobbing man on the terrace. "Yonder," he said. "But I don't reckon he's the governor any more, is he?"

"No, indeed," the British officer replied. "He's under arrest for crimes against the Crown."

Allard didn't think Haworth cared about that right now. In one savage moment, everything had changed. Haworth's plans were ruined, and his daughter was badly wounded, perhaps even already dead. All because of his own greed.

"Cap'n," Allard said to Yorke, "I hope we don't have to stay in Nassau very long. I'm ready to go home."

PART FOUR

"Things fall apart;
the center cannot hold."

—*William Butler Yeats*

CHAPTER TWENTY-ONE

A Winter's Day

CAREFULLY, ROBERT CLIMBED DOWN from the buggy. He had recovered from his Malvern Hill wound; the only time his right leg ever pained him was when the weather was cold and rainy, as it was today. But his left ankle, although it had healed enough to support his weight, would never be the same again. It would always be stiff. He would walk with a bad limp and require a cane for the rest of his life. He could move fairly quickly when he had to, but any strenuous activity left him sore and even more hobbled the next day. He would certainly never be fit for combat again. Yet he had not resigned his commission. He still hoped there would be *something* he could do to help the cause.

But now, he had personal business to take care of, so his first stop was at Four Winds, the Lockhart plantation. Reluctantly, Tobias agreed to drive him out from Mount Holly after Robert had said, "All right, I'll walk, then, if you won't help me."

"I'll be damned, Captain, if I don't think you'd try," the freedman had said with a shake of his head. "Hold on, I'll hitch up the buggy. Ain't gonna do you no good to go out there, though. Miss Jacqueline ain't gonna talk to you. Prob'ly her folks won't even let you see her. Can't say as I blame 'em, neither, the way you broke that poor little gal's heart."

Tobias hadn't said another word to him on the way out to the plantation. He hadn't needed to. The words spoken back in Mount Holly haunted Robert as the buggy rolled through the mist under brooding, overcast skies.

During the weeks he had been in another Richmond hospital, he had kept up with the war news. Following the army's failed foray into Maryland that had ended along the banks of Antietam Creek, both sides had spent several months jockeying for position, finally clashing again when Union Gen. Ambrose E. Burnside, now in command of the Army of the Potomac, having replaced McClellan, decided to cross the Rappahannock River at Fredericksburg. Lee had moved to block Burnside, and the result had been a crushing defeat for the Yankees as the Confederates, ensconced on the high ground just west of the river, mowed down the troops that Burnside unwisely threw against them. The victory had raised spirits all across the South, spirits that had fallen after the failure of the Maryland campaign. Now there was once again talk in Richmond of forcing the Yankees to negotiate a peace settlement. In less than a year there would be another presidential election in the North. If the Confederacy could keep the pressure on long enough, it was highly likely that the factions supporting a negotiated end to the war would be able to turn Lincoln out of office.

Robert hoped that someone, somehow, would be able to bring the war to a peaceful conclusion. He wished it had never begun in the first place. But the pain he and so many others had suffered could not be for nothing. The South couldn't just give up.

But now he was more concerned with personal matters than he was with sweeping, national concerns. He stayed informed about the condition of Sgt. Norm Doolittle, who, against the odds, survived the amputation of his right arm. Doolittle had actually recovered faster than Robert, and the sergeant had been mustered out of the army and sent home to South Carolina, back to his family. Doolittle couldn't read or write, but he had found someone to write a letter to Robert for him, and in it he reported that he was doing pretty well. He was back on his farm with his wife and children, and his wife was already expecting another baby. Obviously, losing an arm hadn't diminished Doolittle in other ways, and Robert was glad for the man who had become a friend as well as a comrade in arms.

Robert had also received a few letters from Lucinda while he was in Richmond. He was surprised by their tone. She seemed genuinely worried about him. He had supposed it would be all right with her if he died in battle. That would allow her the sympathy due any woman widowed by the war. But instead she expressed a wish that he would recover from his wounds and said that she was looking forward to seeing him when he was well enough to come to Charleston. If nothing else, Lucinda Tyler—Lucinda Tyler Gilmore, that is—was a complicated woman, never easy to figure out. She also mentioned that her pregnancy was proceeding well—as if he would care about that.

But to his surprise, he found that he *did* care. The child was innocent. It knew nothing of how it was conceived or the circumstances of its "parents'" marriage. Cam was too immature to be a father in anything except the biological sense; maybe it was a good thing, after all, that this child would have Robert to help raise it. Maybe some good could come of this sordid situation.

Still, the thought that Jacqueline hated him gnawed at Robert. He wanted to talk to her one last time, to try to make her see that he wished things were different between them. He wanted to know that she was able to put everything that had happened behind her and get on with her life, so that she would have at least a chance of finding happiness with someone else. She was a beautiful, intelligent woman. She would have no shortage of suitors, especially once the war was over and the young men came home again.

Christmas 1862 had come and gone. More than two years now since the Ordinance of Succession. Almost two years to the day since the *Star of the West* had tried to sail into Charleston Harbor and been turned back by the guns of the Citadel cadets—Robert and Allard among them. And after stopping briefly at the Gilmore farm to see his family, Robert was now on his way to Charleston to be reunited with his wife. But not without a brief detour to Four Winds.

All those thoughts flashed through his mind as he limped onto the gallery of the great plantation house and approached the door. Resting his weight on his cane, he grasped the knocker and rapped it sharply.

The Lockharts' butler answered the summons a moment later. The man's eyes widened in surprise as he recognized Robert. "Captain Robert Gilmore to see Miss Jacqueline Lockhart," he said anyway, even though the servant knew perfectly well who he was.

"Yes suh, Cap'n. Come in," the butler said as he opened the door wider. "You jus' follow me, an' I'll tell Miss Jacqueline you here."

He took Robert's hat and led him into the parlor. As Robert sat down in an armchair, the butler offered him a drink. Robert shook his head. He wasn't interested in anything except seeing Jacqueline. This wasn't exactly a social call. It was more urgent than that. Robert felt instinctively that a great deal was riding on what might be said here today.

A soft footstep in the doorway made his head lift. A smile touched his lips, and he opened his mouth to tell Jacqueline hello.

But the words never came out, because it wasn't Jacqueline who stood there. It was her mother, Priscilla Lockhart, and the expression on her face was as cold and hard as ice.

"What are you doing here, Robert?" she asked without any pretense of politeness.

"I came to see Jacqueline," he said. "I need to talk to her."

Priscilla's mouth tightened into an even thinner line. "I was afraid you'd say that. It's impossible. She doesn't want to see you."

"Does she even know I'm here?"

"No. All the servants have firm instructions to notify *me* if you ever showed up, not Jacqueline. And not her father, either. Everett's not even here today. He's gone to a neighboring plantation to discuss business with its owner." Her tone became more scathing. "So don't expect him to sympathize with you and come to your aid just because you're a wounded soldier."

"I don't expect anything of the kind," Robert said. "I desire only an opportunity to speak to Jacqueline, even if just for a few minutes."

"You'll not get it," Priscilla said flatly. "You're no longer welcome here, Captain. Jacqueline wants nothing to do with you, and neither do I. Go to Charleston . . . to your *wife*. She's the one who needs you now."

Robert frowned. What did Priscilla mean by Lucinda needing him? Of course, it could have been simple angry rhetoric, but he had the feeling there was more to it than that.

He brushed that worry aside as he pushed himself to his feet. "If you won't tell Jacqueline I'm here, I'll go find her for myself. She has to hear what I have to say."

"Nothing you could say would be of the slightest interest to her." Priscilla pulled herself up to her full height. She was unusually tall for a woman, statuesque and undeniably beautiful—or she would have been had her eyes not been blazing with hatred. "I make no secret of the fact that I never liked you, Mr. Gilmore. I never considered you good enough for my daughter. But I never believed you would do such a terrible thing to her, either. I thought you loved her, even though you were wrong for her."

"I did love her," he said, his voice thick with emotion. "I *do* love her, still. I always will."

"Too late," Priscilla said simply. "Much too late."

Robert limped toward her as she blocked the door. "Get out of my way," he said.

She turned and made a gesture. Two men suddenly appeared behind her. They were white, tall, broad-shouldered, and muscular, with harsh, rugged, merciless faces. Robert recognized them as two of the plantation's overseers.

"Leave quietly and peacefully, or these two men will give you a thrashing and throw you back in Tobias's buggy," Priscilla said. "You may not believe me, Robert, but I wouldn't want such a thing to happen to one of our gallant Southern soldiers, even you. But it will, unless you leave now. I'll do anything to keep you from ever seeing Jacqueline again. You'll only hurt her."

Robert seethed inside as he came to a stop and stood there, staring in disbelief at Priscilla and the two men. They would carry out her orders, and he knew it. He knew as well that he would not stand a chance in a fight with these two. Even if he hadn't been wounded, the odds probably would have been too much for him to overcome. And he was unarmed except for his cane.

"I beg you to reconsider, Mrs. Lockhart."

"No. Leave now, or I won't be responsible for what happens." She smiled in triumph. "And either way, you won't see Jacqueline."

There was nothing he could do. He sighed and said, "I'll leave."

Still smiling, Priscilla stepped aside, as did the two brutal-looking overseers. "Good-bye, Captain Gilmore," she said with finality.

As he limped past them, Robert thought for a second about whipping his cane into the face of one of the men and then trying to deal with the other one, but he discarded the idea as futile. He thought about shouting for Jacqueline and trying to let her know that he was here, but even if he was successful and she came downstairs, she would have to witness him being pounded to a pulp by the two men—because he was sure Priscilla would order such a beating if he defied her wishes. He didn't want to put Jacqueline through that ordeal.

So he took his hat from the butler and hobbled to the front door. The butler moved ahead of him and opened the door for him. Robert limped out without looking back.

Tobias was waiting in the buggy. Somewhat to Robert's surprise, the freedman got down and helped him climb up into the vehicle. As Tobias stepped up to the seat and settled down on it, his great bulk making the buggy shift on its thoroughbraces, he said, "You didn't get to talk to Miss Jacqueline, did you?"

"No," Robert said bitterly. "Her mother saw to that."

"Could'a told you as much, if you'd alistened. You'd have more luck chargin' the whole blamed Yankee army all by yourself than you would tryin' to get past Miss Priscilla." Tobias flicked the reins. As the buggy rolled through the curve of the drive and into the lane leading back to the main road, he asked, "What you gonna do now?"

"Go to Charleston, I suppose. I have people waiting for me there."

My loving wife, he thought.

ROBERT SENSED that something was wrong as soon as Thomas opened the door of the Tyler mansion. "Marse Robert!" the old man exclaimed. "Thank th' Lord you're here!"

Thomas took his hat, but the servant's movements were automatic, his attitude distracted.

"What is it?" Robert asked. "What's wrong?"

"It's Miss Lucinda . . . she done took sick a few days back, and she ain't gettin' no better."

Robert's breath hissed between suddenly clenched teeth. If Lucinda was seriously ill, did that mean the baby was in danger, too? Of course, it did, he told himself. He didn't know much about medical matters, but that was just common sense.

And he was worried about Lucinda, too, not just the baby, he realized. Considering the things she had done to ruin his life, he would have been within his rights to hate her and be glad to hear that she was sick, but he found that he couldn't do that. He asked Thomas, "Has a doctor seen her?"

"Yes suh. Says he's doin' ever'thing he can for her."

Robert wondered fleetingly if Priscilla Lockhart had known that Lucinda was ill. That might be what had prompted her comment about someone in Charleston needing him. The Tylers and the Lockharts were old friends; he thought that Katherine Lockhart might have sent a message to Priscilla telling her about Lucinda's condition.

"Who's with her now?"

"Her mama and Miss Diana, suh. But I know she'd be mighty pleased to see *you.*"

Robert nodded. "I'll go up right away." He started toward the staircase but paused as he reached it. "Is Allard here?"

"No suh. Marse Allard's done gone to sea with Cap'n Yorke."

That took Robert by surprise. He knew that Allard had promised both Diana and his father that he wouldn't sail with Yorke any more.

Obviously something had happened to change that situation, but what it was, Robert had no idea. Allard hadn't written to him about it.

He nodded and went on up the stairs, dread mounting with him as he climbed. He had spent hours thinking about how terrible it was going to be if he were shackled by marriage to Lucinda for the rest of his life; the possibility that something might happen to her had never occurred to him, nor had he pondered what his reaction to that might be. Guilt welled up inside him. There had been plenty of times when he hated Lucinda. But he didn't want her to die.

He told himself to stop thinking like that. People fell ill all the time without dying. She would recover and be just fine. He remembered, though, how sickly she had been at times over the past couple of years. He wasn't sure she had the strength to fight off a serious illness.

He reached the hall and started toward Lucinda's room when someone whispered behind him, "Marse Robert!"

Stopping and turning, he saw Ellie coming out of one of the rooms. The housemaid's face was taut with strain. "Ellie, what is it?" he asked.

"Oh, Marse Robert, I'm sorry!" she choked out. "I never meant for this to happen, I swear I never did!"

Robert's chest tightened. "Are you talking about Lucinda?"

Ellie nodded. Tears shone in her eyes.

"Ellie, what did you do?" Robert found it hard to believe that Ellie could have had anything to do with Lucinda getting sick, but that's the way the housemaid was acting.

"I . . . I brought her that drug, that opium. She made me, Marse Robert. Said she'd have me whipped if I didn't get it for her. So I did it."

Robert reached out with his free hand and grasped her arm tightly. "You gave her opium? When?"

"Last . . . last winter, when she was so sick."

The horror inside Robert eased a little. He'd thought that Ellie meant she had given the opium to Lucinda recently. "Why in the world would she want the stuff?"

"Because you'd gone off to the war, I reckon, and she missed you. Miss Lucinda, she's loved you for a long time, Marse Robert."

He shook his head. "No. That's not possible. If she loved me, why did she carry on so with my brother?"

"Don't you see, suh? It was because she couldn't have *you*." Ellie wiped the back of her hand across her cheek as one of the tears spilled out. "And then, after that business with the baby—"

Robert's hand tightened on her arm again. "What baby? The one she's carrying now?"

Ellie looked miserable as she shook her head. "No suh. The first one. The one she got rid of. She made me fetch old Aunt Susie to help her take care of it."

This shadowy upstairs hallway with its chilly drafts now seemed to be spinning crazily around him. He struggled to grasp what Ellie was telling him. "You mean . . . she was with child before . . . by Cam . . ."

"Yes suh. And I know Marse Cam got to be the father o' this baby, too, but I ain't told nobody. I never said nothin' about it to nobody, I swear. It was hard standin' by, watchin' what she was doin' to you, but . . . I figured that was the way you wanted it, since you went along with her."

Robert released her arm and raised his hand to his face. He covered his eyes and let everything he had just learned soak into his brain.

"After you went off to the war," Ellie whispered, "and after she got rid o' that baby, Miss Lucinda made me fetch that opium for her, and she got sicker an' sicker from the stuff. And Lord help me, I got it for her because I was scared of her, but that wasn't the only reason. You're a good man, Marse Robert, a fine man, and I . . . I'm a mite fond o' you myself—"

"Don't say that, Ellie," he choked out. "For God's sake, don't say that."

"It's true," she insisted. "And I thought that if nothin' happened to her, sooner or later Miss Lucinda would find a way to get you for herself, and I didn't want that to happen. So I got that drug for her and even though I know I'll burn in hell for it, I sort of halfway hoped it'd make her sick and she'd forget about you."

And maybe even die from it, Robert thought, but he didn't level that accusation at Ellie. It was too late for such things now.

"Now she really is sick," Ellie went on in a tortured voice, "and it's all my fault—"

"Wait a minute," Robert said as he lowered his hand from his eyes. "You said you gave the opium to her last winter. None since then?"

Ellie shook her head. "No suh. She stopped all that when she . . . when she started seein' Marse Cam again. And then, a couple o' months later, she was in the family way, and she started tryin' to take good care o' herself again."

"So you didn't have anything to do with whatever is wrong with her now. You couldn't have."

"Yes, I did," Ellie said. "If I hadn't helped her get that drug all them months, she would'a been stronger. She'd'a been able to fight off the fever that come on her."

"You can't know that," he said, even though he had been thinking earlier that Lucinda's weakened condition in the past might have affected her in battling this illness. That was still possible, of course, but he didn't want Ellie blaming herself for what happened to Lucinda. "You haven't told anyone else about this, have you?"

She shook her head. "No suh. Didn't trust nobody but you."

"Good. Don't say anything. You're not to blame. Do you understand me?" If Malachi Tyler knew about this, he would probably have Ellie whipped within an inch of her life, and then he would sell her. Robert didn't want that to happen to her.

"But Marse Robert—"

"Don't say anything!" Robert repeated. If Ellie had contributed to Lucinda's illness, that sin was between her and her Creator. Bringing it into the open now would serve no purpose. Robert had other concerns. He turned toward the door of Lucinda's room and said, "I've got to see her."

Ellie stood there in the hall, wringing her hands, as Robert knocked softly on Lucinda's door. A moment later, Diana peered out, her face wan and drawn. Her eyes widened when she saw him.

"Robert!" she exclaimed. She pulled the door open wider, stepped out, and threw her arms around him, hugging him tightly. "Thank God you're here!"

"It's . . . bad?"

Diana stepped back a little and nodded. "Very bad. She came down with a fever almost a week ago, and nothing the doctor has tried has helped it."

"The baby?" Robert whispered.

Diana just shook her head. "Still alive, the doctor says. But if Lucinda doesn't pull through . . ." She didn't have to go on.

"Can I see her?"

Diana took his hand. "Yes, of course. She's been asking for you. She didn't know you were coming, of course. You should have sent word that you were on your way . . . No, never mind. You didn't know she was sick."

With Diana holding his hand, he walked quietly into the sickroom. Katherine Tyler sat in a chair close beside the bed, leaning forward to wipe her daughter's face with a wet cloth. She looked up at Robert, and a weary smile appeared on her lips. "Oh, Robert," she said. "I'm so glad to see you." She set the cloth aside, came to him, and hugged him.

"Is she awake? Does she know what's going on?"

"Sometimes. If you just talk to her, dear, I . . . I think she'll respond."

Robert went to the bed and sat down in the chair. Lucinda's head was propped up on pillows. Her blonde hair hung in limp tangles around her flushed face. Her eyes were closed, her arms lying loosely outside the covers. Robert glanced at the shape she made under the covers, the prominent bulge of her condition easily visible. He knew, logically, that Cam was the father of that baby . . . the second child, Robert now knew because of his conversation with Ellie, that Cam had conceived within Lucinda. But somehow he felt a connection beyond that of uncle by blood with that new, endangered life. He swallowed hard and reached out to take Lucinda's slender, fragile hand in both of his.

"Lucinda," he said softly. "Lucinda, it's me. Robert. I'm here."

For a moment he thought she hadn't heard him. But then, with just the tiniest flicker, her eyelids began to open. As they lifted, her blue eyes tried to focus, failing for a second before they finally found his face. They looked at him with surprising power, and her dry, cracked lips moved. She whispered, "Robert . . ."

"I'm here," he said again. "I won't leave. I'll be right here by your side while you get better, Lucinda."

"Robert . . ." she breathed again. "Too . . . late."

"No, you're going to be fine," he said stubbornly. "You're too strong to let this sickness beat you, Lucinda. Listen to me. You've always been strong, always known what you wanted and how to get it. You can overcome this, just as you've overcome everything else."

She tried to smile. "No . . . never got . . . what I really wanted . . ." She found the strength somewhere to tighten her fingers on his. "Until now . . . until it was . . . too late . . ." He was about to tell her that she couldn't give up, when she murmured, "Almost . . . too late . . . but not quite."

"That's the spirit," Robert told her. "Just keep on—"

She seemed not to hear him. It was taking all her strength just to hang on and tell him what she wanted him to hear. "Not too late . . . for our child."

What could he say? She knew the baby wasn't truly their child. Or did she? In her feverish state, she might believe that their marriage was real, not a sham, and that the baby was really theirs. He couldn't say anything to deny it, not here, not now.

Her eyes closed for a moment, and he thought she had slipped back into unconsciousness, but then they opened again and peered at him. "Promise me . . . ," she said. "Promise me . . ."

"Anything," he said, and at that moment, he meant it.

"Raise . . . our baby . . . love him . . . help him . . . grow to be a fine man . . . like you."

"Lucinda—"

Her hand squeezed his with incredible strength. *"Promise me."*

"I promise," he said. There was nothing else he could do.

The lines of strain on Lucinda's face eased a little. She breathed a long sigh. "Everything . . . will be all right . . . now," she murmured as she closed her eyes.

She didn't say anything else. Her fingers fell away from Robert's, and for a second he thought she was gone. But her chest continued to rise and fall at a rapid but steady rate. She was sleeping again.

Robert sat beside her for several more minutes, then stood up and joined Katherine and Diana, who stood near the door, watching anxiously.

"Isn't there anything that can be done?" he asked them.

Katherine laid a hand on his arm. "I think your being here is the best medicine she could have, dear. The doctor will be by later, and until then, we'll just keep her comfortable and keep hoping and praying."

Robert nodded.

"You look exhausted," Katherine went on. "Would you like some coffee? something to eat?"

Robert nodded numbly. "I suppose that's a good idea."

"I'll sit with Lucinda," Diana offered.

"Thank you, dear," Katherine said. "Come along, Robert."

They stepped into the hall, and Katherine eased the door shut behind them. Robert glanced along the hall, glad to see there was no sign of Ellie. He hoped that she heeded his advice and kept her involvement in Lucinda's troubles to herself.

Before they reached the staircase, Malachi Tyler appeared at the top of the steps. Robert was shocked at how gray and haggard the man looked. He supposed that worry over Lucinda had robbed the man of some of his vitality. Malachi had always had a softer spot for Lucinda in his heart than anyone else in the family.

"How is she?" he asked quickly. "Has there been any change? Is she any better?"

"Maybe a little," Katherine said, "now that Robert is here. She woke up enough to speak to him."

Malachi grunted and held out his hand to Robert. "Glad you're here, son. How's that ankle of yours?"

"Mended as well as it's going to, sir. I can still get around, so I'm grateful for that."

"Yes, so am I. Maybe it'll make a difference, your being here—"

Diana jerked open the door of Lucinda's room while they were standing there. Fear shot through Robert as he saw the alarmed expression on her face.

"You'd better send for the doctor right away!" she said.

"Oh, my God!" Katherine cried, her hand going to her mouth. "Lucinda's taken a turn for the worse?"

"Not exactly," Diana said. "I think she's about to have the baby."

CHAPTER TWENTY-TWO

Casualties of War

S WEAK AS SHE was, how was that even possible? Robert asked himself. She was barely clinging to life. How could she find the strength to bring a new life into the world? Maybe that was all the strength she had left. Maybe his being there had given her just the hope she needed to do this one last thing. And he had promised her that he would raise the child as his own. Maybe that had something to do with it too. Maybe she was trying to give him one last part of herself.

Those thoughts whirled crazily through his head as he stood in the hallway outside Lucinda's room with Malachi Tyler. Katherine and Diana were inside with Lucinda, along with the cook, who was something of a midwife among her people. Another servant had been sent to fetch a doctor as quickly as possible. Meanwhile, the three women were doing what they could for Lucinda.

"The child can't possibly live," Malachi said in a hollow voice. "It's too small, too young."

That would have been true had the baby actually been conceived on Robert and Lucinda's wedding night. In reality it was several months older than that. A child born prematurely seldom survived, but this one might have a chance.

Him. Lucinda had referred to the baby as a boy. How did she know that? She couldn't possibly be sure. But Robert wasn't going to discount the idea that some sort of maternal instinct had told Lucinda she was carrying a boy. Stranger things had happened. Given her background, he never would have thought that Lucinda had any maternal instincts to start with. And yet, during his brief conversation with her, her concern for the baby had been evident. He thought, not for the first time, that Lucinda Tyler was a mystery that might never be solved.

A rattle of hurried footsteps on the stairs made Robert and Malachi swing around. They saw a bearded man in a tweed suit reach the top of the staircase and start toward them. Robert didn't know him, but Malachi said, "Thank God you're here, Doctor. It appears that my daughter is trying to have her baby."

"That shouldn't be possible," the physician muttered. "I must go in and have a look." He patted Malachi's arm. "Be strong, my friend."

Malachi jerked his head in a nod. He didn't look very strong at the moment. In fact, he looked like he was almost on the verge of collapse himself.

The doctor went into Lucinda's room. Robert and Malachi waited tensely. Only a few moments passed before the door was jerked open, and the doctor looked out with a surprised expression on his face. "Tell your servants to bring clean sheets!" he snapped at Malachi.

"She really is having the baby?" Robert asked, knowing already in his heart what the answer would be.

"She's trying," the medico responded grimly. "But it's going to be damned dicey."

Malachi hurried downstairs for the clean sheets. The doctor ducked back into Lucinda's room and shut the door. Robert was left standing by himself to ponder everything that had happened today. First, his failure to see Jacqueline, then his return to Charleston and the discovery that not only was his wife perhaps on her deathbed but also that he might be a father, at least legally, before this day was over.

For the first time, he was almost glad that he had been wounded. Grasping his cane tightly with both hands as he leaned on it kept him from trembling quite so much.

THE OVERCAST afternoon turned into a gloomy, early dusk, followed by a night that settled over the city like a dark blanket. A raw chill came with it and wormed its way into the Tyler mansion, where it seeped into Robert's bones. Both legs ached, and the discomfort finally grew so intolerable that he had to ask one of the servants to bring a chair into the hall so that he could sit down while he waited outside the door of Lucinda's room.

He heard an occasional cry of pain along with the mutter of low, urgent voices. He couldn't even begin to imagine what was going on. Having been raised on a farm, he knew about the biological facts of giving birth, but intellectual knowledge went out the window when the process became personal. He tried to tell himself that he didn't love Lucinda, that the child she was trying to bring into the world wasn't his, so he shouldn't be so concerned. He was able to convince his mind of those things. But not his heart.

To his surprise, he found himself praying for both souls in danger behind that door. His life would be much simpler if neither Lucinda nor the baby survived, but that thought only filled him with cold dread. Yes, he loved Jacqueline; he always would. No, he didn't love Lucinda—not really. But he couldn't bring himself to hate her for what she had done to him. He realized now how lost and alone and terrified she must have felt to do the things she had done. She had been trying to save her life the only way she knew how. That just made her human, not evil, as he had supposed. No one could truly know what he or she would do in a given situation until such moments were actually encountered. Being in combat had taught him at least that much.

So he sat and waited and hoped and prayed. And finally he heard a cry from beyond the door that was different. A thin, irritated wailing that told him a new life had been rudely awakened and dragged kicking and screaming into this world. His head jerked up at the sound, and he pushed himself to his feet and leaned on his cane as he faced the door, waiting for it to open.

That took several more minutes, endless minutes, but at last the knob turned and the door swung open. Diana stood there, looking drained and exhausted, but she held in her arms a tiny bundle wrapped in a soft blanket. She smiled and said, "You have a son, Robert."

Tears welled from his eyes. He shook as he never had before going into battle. In that moment, as he looked at the red, wrinkled face of the tiny, blanket-wrapped creature, he realized that war was really a trifling matter. *This* was what was really important in the world. And it was bigger and more exhilarating and more terrifying than any mere clash of arms could ever be.

"Do you want to hold him?" Diana asked softly.

Robert swallowed and shook his head. "I . . . I don't think I can right now. I'm shaking too bad. I'd drop him." He tried to look into the room. "Lucinda . . . ?"

Diana's smile went away, and still holding the baby, she turned slightly so that Robert could see past her to the bed, where the doctor and the cook stood by pensively and Katherine sat in the chair with her head down, pressed against Lucinda's arm, as her back rose and fell with her sobs.

"I'm sorry, Robert," Diana whispered.

More tears rolled down his cheeks. How could he feel this way? *He hated her!* Why was he crying? *She had ruined his life!* Why did he feel like something had just broken inside him?

He reached out with a trembling hand and moved a corner of the blanket aside so he could see the baby's face a little better. The little lips pushed in and out; the forehead below the wispy fair hair wrinkled in a frown.

"Lucas," Robert said. "His name is Lucas Malachi Gilmore, after both of his grandfathers."

Diana nodded. "That's a fine name. I'll take care of him . . . if you want to go in."

He had no choice. Something compelled him to enter the room. He limped to the other side of the bed and reached down to take Lucinda's left hand. The fingers were cool and limp. He looked at her face, which was calm now. Death had smoothed all the lines of pain and struggle. There was a certain beauty in death, the poets said, and in that moment, Robert saw it in Lucinda's face. She was at rest. Her lifelong fight against whatever demons had haunted her was over. Somehow Robert knew that her sins had been forgiven, and if the Lord could be that merciful, her husband could do no less.

"Don't worry," he murmured, hoping that she could still hear him. "I'll see to it. Our son will be fine."

THE FOG was thick as the *Diana* steamed swiftly toward the South Carolina coast. Just the right kind of night to run the blockade. If there was a Yankee patrol boat out here, the skipper wouldn't be able to see his hand in front of his face, let alone the sleek, gray cutter gliding through the water.

Allard stood tensely on the bridge next to Yorke. This was only the fifth time he had been aboard a ship slipping past the blockade, and he was still nervous about the whole thing. Yorke seemed to be perfectly relaxed, though. He said, "We'll be back in Charleston before you know it, lad. I'm sure you're anxious to see that pretty, redheaded wife o' yours again."

Allard nodded. "Yes, I am, Cap'n, and I hope you won't be disappointed when I say that I've finally had my fill of the sea."

"Oh, I ain't disappointed," Yorke said with a chuckle, "but I ain't sure I believe you, either. The lure o' the sea has a way o' sneakin' up on a man. He may think that he's through with it, but likely there'll come a day when he starts to long for the feel o' the wind and the spray and a deck under his feet."

Yorke could believe that if he wanted to, Allard thought, but he was convinced that, in his case, it wasn't true. The unexpected violence and tragedy in Nassau had soured him on the experience from now on. Winifred Haworth was dead, and Allard couldn't bring himself to believe that she had deserved that fate, no matter how complicit she was in the illegal activities of her father and Augustin Valencia. William Haworth, former governor of the Bahamas, and Cyril Judkins, the harbormaster, were on their way to England in chains by now, to answer for their crimes. While it was true that many men in England were getting rich from smuggling goods to the Confederacy, Haworth and Valencia had gone beyond that, dealing also in theft and murder. The cargo of rifles that had precipitated the crisis for Yorke and the Tylers had in fact been stolen by Valencia's men in the first place. The Crown might turn a blind eye to the smuggling, but these other crimes couldn't be ignored.

Well, it was all over now, Allard told himself. A new governor and harbormaster had taken the reins of power in Nassau, and the blockade-running between there and various Southern ports would continue—but without Allard's involvement.

The fog wrapped around the ship seemed to muffle all sound as well as impede vision. When a ship's bell suddenly sounded to starboard, it was heart-stoppingly close. Allard tensed even more as Yorke gripped his arm.

"Yankee cruiser," Yorke whispered in his ear. "But they don't know we're here. They're just tollin' that bell to warn others like 'em where they are."

Allard knew that on nights like this, the blockaders would be out in force. But that strategy often backfired because they just got in each other's way. Their captains had to worry about ramming a friendly vessel in the fog.

Yorke chuckled softly. He had already pulled a cord connected to the engine room, signaling a full stop of the engine. The *Diana* cut through the water in complete silence, except for the faint hiss of the sea against her hull. An in-shore breeze filled the sails and kept the blockade-runner moving.

The Yankees might suspect that a ship was out here, but they wouldn't be able to tell that by listening for its engines. Nor could they see their intended prey in this fog. Allard's breath came quickly, shallowly, but he believed they would glide past the blockaders successfully. A moment later, he found out just how wrong he was.

A whoosh shattered the silence suddenly. He had to fling his arm up to shield his eyes as a rocket arced over the bow of the *Diana*. The flare attached to the missile cast a brilliant light over the sea.

"Damn it!" Yorke burst out. "Hard aport!"

The helmsman spun the wheel to veer the little cutter away from the Union cruiser less than a hundred yards to starboard. The rocket's red glare lasted only seconds, but that was long enough for the Federal gun crews to spot the blockade-runner and draw a bead on her. Flame gouted from one of the cruiser's guns, then another and another fired.

Allard heard the splash as the first shell missed, but a second later, the deck shivered under his feet and a grinding crash from amidships filled the air. At least one of the shells had struck the vessel. Somewhere a man yelled, "Look out! The mast!" and there was another crash, then screams. The shot had toppled one of the masts, and at least one man had been caught under it when it fell.

"All ahead full!" Yorke bellowed into the speaking tube. The engine still had steam up, so it wouldn't take long to get it running again. But even that short time might be too long.

More blasts roared from the big guns on the cruiser. Cannonballs slammed into the sleek little cutter.

One of the crew raced up the ladder to the bridge and reported in a shout, "We're holed, Cap'n! Takin' on water!"

"Man the pumps!" Yorke shouted as he shouldered the helmsman aside and took the wheel himself. As he spun it, he said to Allard, "We're runnin' straight for shore! That's our only chance now. If we can go aground before we sink, we might be able to salvage part o' the cargo!"

The hold of the *Diana* was loaded with goods, split pretty evenly between military and civilian supplies. Every bit of it was vital to the

Confederacy, so he had to try to save as much of it as he could. The ship itself was probably lost, Allard thought, but there was nothing to be done about that. Blockade-running was a dangerous profession, after all. No captain, no matter how skilled, could beat the odds every time. Not even Barnaby Yorke.

"I didn't expect the Yankees to be smart enough to start usin' rockets and flares," Yorke said as he tightly gripped the wheel. "That'll make things harder on us from here on out," he added, assuming they were going to survive this encounter. But what else could he do? Allard asked himself. Yorke wasn't the type to give up without a fight.

The deck vibrated under Allard's feet as the engine valiantly struggled to keep the cutter moving toward shore as water poured into the hold. Behind them, another rocket sizzled into the air, and the brilliant illumination from it burned through the fog. The cruiser's guns pounded out another volley. None of those shots found their target, but it didn't really matter. The damage had already been done.

Allard was suddenly thrown off his feet as a final round from the cruiser slammed into the *Diana*. He landed so hard that the breath was knocked out of him, and for a moment all he could do was lie on the deck and gasp for air. Finally he lifted his head and looked around. In the fading glare he saw Yorke lying a few feet away, half propped against the wheel, which was still intact. Something about the captain looked so odd. It took Allard a few seconds to understand. Then he realized that a long, jagged piece of a plank from the deck was protruding from the captain's midsection.

The light was gone then. Allard scrambled onto hands and knees and crawled across the deck toward Yorke. His hands slipped in something wet and sticky, and he knew it was Yorke's blood, spreading in a pool around the captain. He touched Yorke's coat and put his arms around the man.

"Cap'n!" he called desperately. "Cap'n!"

Yorke stirred a little. "L-lad," he breathed. "Save the cargo . . . if you can."

"To hell with the cargo! I have to do something to help you—"

One of Yorke's hands found Allard's leg and closed on it tightly. "Forget about . . . me," he gasped. "This splinter's gone . . . through an' through . . . I can feel it comin' out . . . of my back. It's done for I am."

"No, Cap'n," Allard shouted stubbornly.

Yorke's hand squeezed convulsively. "The cargo!" he said. "That's what . . . you've got to save! Don't let . . . the Yankees get it . . . or this ship."

"All right," Allard promised. "I'll do my best."

"All anybody . . . can do." Yorke shuddered. "Tell Katie . . . tell Katie I always . . . always . . ." His head slumped against Allard's shoulder, and a final tremor went through him.

Hot tears sprang into Allard's eyes. He didn't try to hold them back. As they rolled down his cheeks, he gently lowered Yorke's body to the deck. The wheel spun above them, out of control. Biting back curses, Allard grabbed hold of it, pulled himself to his feet, and groped for the speaking tube. "Give me everything you've got!" he called down to the engine room. "And keep the pumps working as long as you can!"

The *Diana* was wallowing now, and Allard knew she couldn't stay afloat much longer. But he thought he could hear the roar of breakers up ahead. He didn't know exactly where they were on the coast, but they couldn't be too far from Charleston. Yorke had been making his final approach to the harbor when everything had gone to hell.

Allard's vision blurred, but not from tears. He realized that blood was running into his eyes from a gash on his forehead. He hadn't noticed he was hurt until now. He used the back of his hand to wipe away as much of the gore as he could. The *Diana* forged on toward the shore. The Yankee cruiser was probably giving chase. He vowed that he would burn the *Diana* and all of the cargo before he would let those bastards capture her.

Then the cutter lurched violently, throwing Allard off his feet again. He heard the massive, grinding, scraping sound and knew that the ship had gone aground.

Once again, he had come home.

THE OVERCAST remained, which was appropriate for a funeral. Under those gray skies, Lucinda Tyler Gilmore was laid to rest in Magnolia Cemetery, with her family and representatives from many prominent Charleston families there to mourn her passing. Capt. Robert Gilmore stood beside the grave with his infant son cradled in his arms, wrapped securely in blankets against the chill. Robert's face was haggard but stonily emotionless. He had cried all the tears he had. Now he had to look forward instead of back, and part of that involved saying good-bye to Lucinda.

Malachi's face seemed to be carved out of granite, too, but Katherine sobbed openly and miserably. So did Diana and many of the other women at the funeral. Finally the service was over. Robert bent carefully, picked up a handful of freshly turned dirt from the mound of it beside the grave, and dropped it on the coffin. The sound of the dirt striking the lid was one of the most awful things Robert had ever heard.

Then, at last, he was able to turn and walk away, carrying the child with him. Slowly, the others made their way from the grave as well, trudging back toward the carriages lining the narrow roadway through the cemetery.

At first Robert thought he was imagining things when he saw the bedraggled figure with the bloody bandage wrapped around his head walking stiffly toward them. Then he stopped, stiffened, called out, "Allard! Allard, is it really you?"

Behind him, Diana screamed, "Allard!"

She rushed past Robert as Allard broke into a shambling run. Husband and wife came together, embracing and kissing as they clutched desperately at each other. Robert walked up to them, still carrying Lucas, and finally, as Allard hugged Diana, he looked over her shoulder and asked Robert, "Is it true what they told me at the house? Lucinda . . . Lucinda is gone?"

Robert nodded. "I'm sorry, Allard. I know the two of you weren't close, but still . . ."

With an arm around Diana's shoulders, Allard nodded. Tears shone in his eyes. He nodded toward the bundle in Robert's arms. "And that . . . ?"

"He's your nephew. Lucas, meet your Uncle Allard." Robert heard the note of pride in his voice and was glad it was there.

The others came up to join them—Katherine and Malachi, Cam, Tamara Pinckston and her parents, Everett and Priscilla Lockhart—but not Jacqueline. She had stayed behind at Four Winds.

Cam was crying too. He had been furious with Robert for marrying Lucinda, and he probably would have been insane with anger had he known that the baby nestled in Robert's arms was actually his. But he would never know. Robert had made that promise to himself. There was no good reason for Lucas to ever know the truth about how he had come to be. Robert felt bad about it—it was never a good idea to build a life's foundation on a lie—but that was better than trusting a baby to an irresponsible scoundrel like Cam.

The reunion in the cemetery was a mixture of happiness and sadness. Diana and Katherine were thrilled that Allard had returned, although the bloody bandage around his head was mute testimony to the fate of the blockade-runner. Allard hugged everyone, shook hands with his father and Robert and Cam. Then Malachi finally asked, "Where's Yorke? What happened to the ship?"

"We ran into a Yankee cruiser as we were approaching the harbor," Allard said. "Cap'n Yorke thought we could slip past them in the dark and the fog, but they were using flares and spotted us."

"Flares!" Malachi frowned. "Those blasted Yankees are getting too ingenious."

"We took several hits from their guns," Allard went on. "A mast was knocked down, and they holed us below the waterline. The engine and the pumps were still working, though, so Captain Yorke made a run for shore. We got there ahead of the Yankees—barely—and ran aground on James Island. Some of our troops from Fort Johnson were close by, and they reached us in time to help the crew drive off a Yankee boarding party. Most of the cargo was saved, and the ship can be repaired."

"Yorke's a fine sailor," Malachi said grudgingly. "I'll give him that much. Where is he, with the ship?"

Allard nodded dully. "Yes, he's with the ship . . . but he didn't bring her ashore. I did. Barnaby Yorke is dead." The words hung in the empty air for a moment, their import even more grim because of the surroundings. Then Katherine Tyler let out a scream that was cut off abruptly as she fainted and slumped to the ground.

THE SOUND of loud, angry voices drifted into the parlor of the Tyler mansion from upstairs. Allard, Diana, Robert, and Cam sat there, mostly in brooding silence. One of the servants was taking care of Lucas. A downstairs maid had had a child recently and was still suckling it, so she had been given the job of being a wet nurse to Lucinda's baby.

"What's going to happen now?" Cam finally asked. "Are they going to fight all night?"

Allard shrugged. "That's between them. I get the feeling that there are a lot of old grudges and wounds, and Cap'n Yorke's death has brought them all out."

Diana reached over, took his hand, and squeezed it. He summoned up a shadow of a smile. He still felt numb about the whole thing. In only a little more than twelve hours, he had nearly lost the ship, almost lost his life, and saw Captain Yorke, his friend and mentor, die in his arms. Then he had arrived home to find that his only sister was dead too. And he hadn't even had a chance to say good-bye to her. For all the clashes they'd had over the years, for all the angry words and cold silences between them, he still loved her. It was hard to believe that Lucinda was gone.

But she had left behind a baby, a beautiful, healthy baby. Even in his stunned state, Allard had been able to look at little Lucas and realize that he was only a month premature, at most. That meant either Robert and Lucinda had been together earlier than anyone had known or . . .

He looked at Cam, who was clearly oblivious to the truth. He hadn't had a chance to discuss the situation with Robert, but if Robert wanted to maintain the facade that he was Lucas's father, that was all right with Allard. Robert would be a good father. Allard seriously doubted that Cam would ever grow up enough to fulfill the responsibilities that came with parenthood.

Meanwhile, the battle royal between Katherine and Malachi Tyler continued. Allard had suspected for a long time that there had been something between his mother and Captain Yorke. He hadn't really wanted to know the truth, and he certainly wasn't curious about the details. But his parents knew what had happened, and obviously it was a bone of considerable contention between them.

They would work it out, Allard told himself. They had to. There had already been more than enough tragedy in the Tyler family. There had to be a limit to what one group of people who loved each other could endure. Didn't there?

IN THEIR bedroom, Malachi and Katherine faced each other angrily. Her eyes were red-rimmed from crying, and she still dabbed at them from time to time with a lacy handkerchief. "I don't expect you to understand," she said to him.

"Oh, I understand, all right," Malachi said. "I understand all too well. You're upset because your lover is dead."

"Barnaby wasn't my lover!" More tears sprang to her eyes.

"He was at one time," her husband accused, his voice cold with suppressed rage now instead of hot with fury.

"Oh, all right!" Katherine burst out. "What's the use of denying that? I confessed that to you years ago! And you said you forgave me!"

"That was before Yorke came back."

Katherine reached out and put a hand on his arm. But he jerked it away from her, and she flinched as if he had struck her instead.

"Please, Malachi," she pleaded. "I swear to you, nothing happened between Barnaby and me . . . except . . . except long ago . . . the times you already know about, when we were young and hadn't been married long—"

"Is Allard really my son?" he cut in. "Or was he fathered by that seagoing scoundrel?"

She stared at him. "How can you say such a thing?" she cried. "Of course Allard is your son! Just as Lucinda was your daughter." Anger came back into her voice. "Or have your hurt feelings already made you forget that we buried our oldest child today, Malachi?"

He grimaced, pain etching lines into his face. "I haven't forgotten," he said. "Nor have I forgotten that you betrayed me with Yorke all those years ago, either. How am I to know that you didn't do it again, after he came back into our lives?"

She laughed humorlessly. "You could try trusting me. You could trust your wife, who loves you very much."

Slowly, Malachi shook his head. "I wish I could, Katherine. I really wish I could."

She balled her hands into fists and trembled from the power of the emotions coursing through her. "You bastard!" she said in a low, ragged voice. "Why won't you listen to me? Why won't you believe me? Yes, I was upset when I heard that Barnaby is dead. But I was upset because he was a dear old friend, that's all. He wasn't my lover. He hasn't been my lover for more than twenty years!"

Malachi's face was gray with strain. His breath hissed between his teeth as he slowly shot back at her, "No matter what you try to say now, it can never change anything that happened. You and Yorke . . . You and Yorke—"

Katherine's hands shot out and gripped his arms as rage welled up inside her again. "Yes!" she cried. "I don't deny what happened all those years ago! Do you want to know the details, Malachi? Do you want to know how Barnaby comforted me when you were never home, when you were always working day and night at the ship-yard?" She shook him. "Do you want me to tell you what it felt like to be naked with him in our own bed? Do you want to hear how wanton I was? But it didn't mean anything, damn you! It didn't mean anything except that I was lonely. And when I realized how wrong it was, I put a stop to it, to everything. And I never, never did anything like that again! I love you, Malachi. I've always loved you. And if I could go back and change the past so that I never hurt you, I would! I would! But I can't!" She collapsed against his chest, tears flooding from her eyes. "I can't, I can't . . ."

For a long moment, he stood there, holding her, his arms stiff at first, as if they held her against his will, then softening as one hand moved up her back, under her hair, rubbing the back of her neck. He murmured, "Katherine . . ."

"I'm so sorry," she said between sobs. "I'm just so sorry. I can only plead for forgiveness so many times."

"It's . . . all right." She felt him stiffen again as some sort of jolt went through him. As if it took a great deal of effort to get each word out, he went on, "I forgive . . . you . . . and hope that . . . you'll . . . forgive me—Ah!"

She jerked her head up, knowing that something was terribly wrong. "Malachi!" she cried as she saw how ashen he was. As she stepped back in sudden alarm, he pressed a clenched fist to his chest and stumbled forward a little. Then he fell to his knees.

She screamed, "Malachi!"

"Katherine . . . Kate!"

Agony contorting his face, he fell forward, doubling over against the pain that must have filled his entire being at that moment. She kept screaming his name, but she knew it wasn't doing any good.

He couldn't hear her anymore, and never would again.

DRAWN BY the screams, Allard—followed closely by Diana, Robert, and Cam—burst into the room and found Katherine sitting on the floor with Malachi's head pillowed on her lap. His father's body was sprawled limply on the rug next to the bed. Allard knew that he would never speak to Malachi again. And he knew that he had been wrong. Evidently there *wasn't* any limit on tragedy.

CHAPTER TWENTY-THREE
Winds of Change

L UCAS SEEMED TO LIKE the slight rocking motion of the train, judging from the way he had slept quietly in Robert's arms since the locomotive had pulled out of the depot in Charleston. Of course, it hadn't been all that long, and the train now slowed to a stop at the station in Mount Holly. He looked down into his sleeping son's face and hated to disturb him. But it couldn't be avoided. Life held a great deal of disturbance, and Lucas would have to learn that sooner or later.

For the first six weeks of the boy's life, Robert had worried constantly that the fact Lucas had been born prematurely would cause him to be sickly. But Lucas was the picture of robust health, and the doctor had pronounced him to be in fine shape, certainly strong enough for this short trip with his father.

When the conductor announced the Mount Holly stop, Robert stood up, cradling Lucas in one arm while using his other to pick up a small carpetbag. He moved awkwardly, because he still had to use his cane with that hand too. Robert and Lucas disembarked from the car.

"Y'all stayin' long, Captain?" the conductor asked as he stood on the platform, keeping an eye on the passengers who were disembarking and those who were boarding the train.

"I don't know," Robert said with a shake of his head. "I truly don't know."

Junie, Lucas's nurse, had made the trip, too, and now she climbed down from the open car where slaves rode and came along the platform to take the baby from Robert. He told her to follow him and limped down the street toward the blacksmith shop.

Tobias saw him coming and walked out of the squat building to meet him.

"Hello, old friend," Robert greeted the freedman warmly.

"Lord have mercy," Tobias said as he looked past Robert. "Who's that child?"

"My son," Robert said with a smile. "Lucas Gilmore."

Tobias used a blunt fingertip to move the blanket aside a little while Junie held the baby. "Would you look at that?" he said. "That is one fine-lookin' boy, Cap'n."

"Thank you. I think so too."

Tobias turned back to Robert, a frown of concern beginning to appear on his face. "What are you doin' here, Cap'n? It ain't that I'm not glad to see you, but—"

"But I don't have any business around here anymore, is that what you were about to say?"

Tobias's massive shoulders rose and fell in a shrug. "Can't see as you do," he said bluntly.

"Well, I have to prevail on you once again to take me out to Four Winds. Just one more time," he added quickly as Tobias started to shake his head. "I have to talk to Jacqueline, and after that, I'll never bother her again, if that's what she wants."

"What Miss Jacqueline wants don't matter. It's what her mama wants, and Miss Priscilla ain't gonna let you anywhere near that gal."

"We'll see about that," Robert said.

Tobias looked at him for a long moment, then finally shook his head. "You're in one o' them moods again, ain't you, Cap'n? You're fixin' to tell me that if'n I don't take you to Four Winds, you'll walk ever' step o' the way, only you'll have that baby with you this time."

"I hope it won't come to that," Robert said, "but if I have to . . ."

Tobias sighed and reached for the cord that tied his thick black-smith's apron around him. "Just you wait a minute, Cap'n, and I'll hitch up that ol' buggy hoss o' mine."

A short time later, Robert was seated next to Tobias as the vehicle rolled toward the Lockhart plantation. Junie sat behind the seat with Lucas in her lap.

Robert meant what he had told Tobias—this was the last visit he would pay to Four Winds if he couldn't speak to Jacqueline and convince her that he still loved her as much as he ever had, still wanted to marry her and spend the rest of his life with her. Yes, things had changed, no doubt about that. Lucas's mere existence was proof that things were no longer as they once had been. But that didn't mean nothing would ever be the same again. There still had to be a shred of hope in life.

And the events of the past two months had taught Robert that there was no time to waste. Life was fleeting. Robert had learned that from his experiences in combat, where a man could be alive one second and dead, his brains blown out, the next. But the lesson had been brought home even more by what had happened in Charleston one cold, gloomy twenty-four hours in winter. In that time, Lucinda had died and Lucas had been born, Barnaby Yorke had been killed by the Yankees, and Malachi Tyler had been felled when his heart gave out. All three deaths had been unexpected, although in Yorke's situation it was well known that blockade-running carried its own dangers. But no one could have predicted the fever that struck down Lucinda or the spasm in Malachi's chest that had killed him. At least, according to Allard, his mother and father had made peace with each other, to a certain extent anyway, before Malachi's passing. But even so, Robert didn't know how Katherine was holding up. The poor woman had suffered three terrible losses in short order. Robert wasn't sure he would have had the strength to go on if he had found himself in those circumstances.

And so, carrying the lesson in his heart that some things just couldn't wait, he returned to Four Winds, determined not to be turned aside this time, no matter what.

It was a beautiful day, Robert thought as Tobias turned the carriage into the drive leading to the plantation house. Still cool, but the sky was clear and breathtakingly blue, and there was just a hint of warmth in the breeze that blew, a hint that spring was on its way and another winter would soon be gone.

Tobias brought the buggy to a halt in front of the door. Leaving Junie and Lucas in the vehicle, Robert climbed down and started toward the door. It opened before he got there. The same servant who had greeted him on his previous visit stood there, a worried scowl on his face. Obviously, someone had seen the buggy coming up the drive.

Before the servant could speak, Robert smiled and said, "You might as well go tell Mrs. Lockhart that I'm here."

"Done sent for her already," the butler said. He glanced over his shoulder. "An' here she come now."

He stepped aside, and Priscilla Lockhart appeared in the doorway, as beautiful and regal as ever. "What are you doing here, Captain Gilmore?" she asked coldly. "I don't want to be impolite to one of our gallant soldiers, but you know you're not welcome here."

"I've come to see Jacqueline," Robert said. "I want her to meet my son."

Anger blazed in Priscilla's eyes. "You'd throw your foul actions right in her face like that? I swear, Captain—"

"Don't call me that," Robert cut in. "I'm not a soldier today, not an officer. I'm just Robert Gilmore, and I want to see the woman I love."

Priscilla's upper lip curled in a sneer. "A fine one you are to be talking about love! Your *wife* hasn't been in the grave even two months yet. That's hardly a proper mourning period."

"That wasn't a proper marriage."

Priscilla nodded toward the buggy and said, "The baby in the arms of that sable wench says differently, Robert."

He controlled his anger with an effort. He intended to tell Jacqueline the truth, but only her. She deserved to know what had really happened. He knew he had to bare his soul to her if he was to have any hope of reconciling with her. But it was no one else's business.

"Please, Mrs. Lockhart," he said. "Just let me speak to Jacqueline alone for a few minutes."

"No. I'm sorry for your loss, Robert, I truly am. But I intend to see to it that you never speak to my daughter again."

He sighed. He had wanted to avoid any unpleasantness, but he could see that wasn't going to be possible.

"I'm sorry, too, Mrs. Lockhart, but I'm afraid I'm going to have to insist that I see Jacqueline, whether you like it or not."

He took a step toward the door. Priscilla drew herself up in the opening and glared at him with a determined look, as if she would fight him herself if she had to. But a sudden drumming of hoofbeats from the lane made him stop and glance over his shoulder. He saw the two overseers who had done Priscilla's bidding on the earlier occasion pull their lathered mounts to a stop. Far back down the lane, a small black boy dressed in the livery of a house servant trotted after them. Clearly, Priscilla had sent the boy to fetch help as soon as she knew that Robert was coming. And that was probably as soon as the buggy had been spotted approaching the plantation.

"You need us for somethin', Miz Lockhart?" one of the burly men asked.

"Yes," Priscilla said. "See that Captain Gilmore gets in that buggy and goes away. If he doesn't want to cooperate, *put* him in the buggy and get it out of here."

The men grinned in anticipation as they swung down from their saddles. They cuffed back the broad-brimmed hats that shaded their faces and started toward Robert.

Tobias stepped down from the buggy behind them. "Hold on," he said. "Don't much like the looks o' this."

One of the overseers glared at him. "Keep your mouth shut and stay outta this, you black bastard. I've whipped the hide off your back before, and by God, I'll do it again!"

Tobias drew himself up angrily and clenched his big hands into hamlike fists. "I ain't no slave no more, Mistuh Garrett, and you can't talk to me like that. I'm a freedman now."

"Your skin's still black." The man reached for the whip that was coiled and hung from a strap on his belt.

"Tobias!" Robert said sharply. When the blacksmith looked at him, he shook his head. "Stay out of this, Tobias," he went on. "I appreciate what you're trying to do, but I don't want anybody else to get hurt."

Tobias hesitated. "You sure, Cap'n?"

"I'm sure," Robert said.

Tobias shrugged and stepped back. The second overseer sneered. "Looks like you got lucky, boy," he said.

"One o' these days, Mistuh Warner, maybe we see 'bout that."

The white man glowered and was about to say something else, but his companion plucked at his arm. "Come on, we got a chore to do. Maybe when it's over, we'll tend to that darky's needin's."

"Yeah."

The two men split up, Garrett going to Robert's left, Warner to the right. Robert moved to the edge of the gallery, aware without looking around that Priscilla Lockhart still stood watching in the open doorway.

Let her watch, he thought. If it was a show she wanted, he intended to give her one.

"You gonna leave peaceable-like, Cap'n?" Garrett asked. "We don't wanna hurt one of our boys who ought to be off fightin' the Yanks, but we'll do it if we have to."

Robert's country drawl, which had been submerged by his months in Charleston and in the army, slipped back into his voice as he said, "Only ones who're gonna get hurt are you two peckerwoods."

That stiffened the overseers with anger. Warner was closer. He growled an oath and lunged at Robert, reaching for him with big hands.

Robert stepped aside, moving surprisingly quickly for a man with a stiff ankle, whipped his cane around, hooked the handle around

Warner's ankle, and pulled. Warner was already a little off-balance, and the unexpected maneuver sent him tumbling off his feet. He crashed to the floor of the gallery.

Robert whirled toward Garrett and jabbed the tip of the cane into his midsection. Garrett grunted in pain and doubled over. The cane came up and cracked down sharply on the back of Garrett's neck. He joined his companion in sprawling on the gallery.

These two men had spent the war disciplining slaves on the plantation. They were strong, no doubt about that, but they were slow, almost lumbering. Robert had worked hard during the past weeks, strengthening not only his bad ankle but also the rest of his body. His muscles were like rawhide now, and although his injuries hampered him, he had learned to compensate for them. Most of all, he knew what it was like to fight for his life. That was exactly what he was doing here. And he was fighting for Jacqueline.

Priscilla looked surprised and worried that Robert had knocked down the two overseers with such seeming ease. Robert knew that the fight wasn't really over, though. Garrett and Warner were already picking themselves up. Robert moved down the steps and went part of the way toward the buggy, giving himself more room to maneuver.

"You lil' sumbitch," Garrett said as he started toward Robert. "Throw that stick down and fight fair!"

"You want a fair fight, I'll take a hand," Tobias called from beside the buggy.

Robert motioned him back. "No, Tobias. I have to do this myself."

Warner was on his feet again too. Inside the buggy, Lucas began to cry, a thin, plaintive wail. Warner said, "What the hell is that? A little pickaninny? Been gettin' you some dark meat, Cap'n?"

Rage welled up within Robert, but he controlled it, knowing it wouldn't do him any good to lose his head. He said, "You gonna talk or fight, you tub of lard?"

Warner snarled and leaped at him again. Garrett moved at the same time, and when Robert stepped aside from Warner's charge, he moved into range of the big fist that Garrett swung. The punch slammed into Robert's jaw and knocked him back. He lost his balance and went down, and Warner whooped gleefully, ready to rush in and stomp Robert half to death.

Robert managed to hold on to his cane, and he met Warner's charge by bringing the heavy walking stick up sharply between the overseer's legs. Warner screamed in agony as he practically impaled his privates on the cane. He doubled over and collapsed.

That gave Garrett time to swing a kick that landed on Robert's wrist and knocked the cane loose. It went spinning away and landed out of reach. Robert rolled desperately to avoid a second kick. He came up on his hands and knees and tried to push himself to his feet, but he couldn't move fast enough. Garrett laced his fingers together and clubbed both hands down into the small of Robert's back. Robert couldn't hold back a cry of pain as the blow drove him down onto his belly.

A kick sank into his side, sending more shards of pain through him. Forcing his muscles to respond, he rolled again and flung up his hands, grabbing Garrett's foot as the overseer aimed yet another kick at him. Robert heaved, sending Garrett toppling over backward. That respite gave Robert a chance to snatch up his cane. He threw himself on top of Garrett and pressed the length of wood across the man's throat, bearing down on it. If he put enough weight on the cane, he could crush Garrett's throat, maybe kill him. Robert didn't want to do that, but nothing was going to stop him from—

"Robert!"

The cry made him ease up on the cane and lift his head. He saw Jacqueline in the doorway, struggling to get past her mother. Priscilla was considerably taller and heavier than her daughter, but Jacqueline shot past her and ran across the gallery.

She stopped short as Garrett slammed a punch into Robert's head while he was distracted. Robert was knocked to the side. Garrett's muscular weight came down on top of him, and the overseer's hands locked around his neck. Now he was the one in danger of having his throat crushed. He was the one in danger of dying.

But not for long, because only a second later, a fury in silk and crinoline struck the overseer. Jacqueline slammed her little fists against him, shouting, "Let him go! Get off him, you bastard!"

She wasn't big enough to do any damage to Garrett, but her attack flustered him and made him ease off the pressure on Robert's neck. He gulped air into his lungs. Priscilla arrived on the scene. She danced around, pulling at her daughter, saying, "Jacqueline, stop it! Stop it, I say! Come away from there!"

There was no telling what might have happened next if a loud, angry voice hadn't demanded, "What the devil is going on here?" Everett Lockhart went on to order, "Garrett, let go of Captain Lockhart right now! Get off of him. And Jacqueline, stop hitting Garrett!"

Everett had to wrap an arm around his daughter's waist and pull her away from the fracas. Garrett stood up and stumbled back a step from Robert, wiping a hand across his face as he did so. He looked at Everett and said, "Warner an' me was just doin' what the missus told us to, boss."

"That doesn't surprise me," Everett said coolly. "What's wrong with Warner?"

Garrett sniffed. "Got walloped in the, uh . . ."

Everett waved a hand. "Pick him up and get him out of here. Both of you, get back to the fields."

"Yes suh."

Everett was still holding on to Jacqueline. He released her, and she ran to Robert's side, falling to her knees so that she could help him sit up. "Are you all right?" she asked, her eyes wide with worry.

He nodded. "Yeah. A little . . . out of breath, that's all."

"Your ankle . . . ?"

"Still stiff as ever," he said with a grim smile, "but other than that, it's fine."

Priscilla said angrily, "Everett, you don't know what's going on here. I wish you hadn't interfered—"

"If I hadn't ridden up and seen a brawl going on practically on my front porch, Robert might be dead now," Everett said. "I'm not that fond of the boy anymore, but I don't want one of my men to be responsible for his death." He added, "Jacqueline, get up and leave him alone."

"I tried to tell her that," Priscilla said. "She wouldn't listen to me."

With both of them still sitting on the ground, Robert caught hold of Jacqueline's hand. "I have to talk to you," he said quickly before her parents could continue browbeating her. "It's important. Please. Just five minutes."

She frowned at him and then punched him hard on the shoulder, harder even than she had been striking Garrett. "Why should I?" she demanded. "You hurt me, Robert. You broke my heart. Why should I listen to you?"

"So you'll know the truth," he said. In the buggy, Lucas let out another cry. Robert nodded in that direction. "So you'll know why I did what I did."

For the first time, uncertainty appeared in Jacqueline's flashing eyes. "I know why you did it. You . . . you got Lucinda with child, and then you had to marry her. That sort of thing . . . happens sometimes."

"Jacqueline, please," Robert said in a half whisper. "Five minutes—alone."

She drew in a deep breath and let it out in a sigh. "All right."

"Jacqueline, no!" Priscilla cried.

Everett reached down, took hold of Jacqueline's arms, and lifted her to her feet. He turned her so that he could look into her eyes. "Is this what you really want?" he asked.

She hesitated, only for a second, then nodded.

"All right." Everett released her and extended a hand to Robert. "My daughter is willing to give you a chance. I won't do any less."

Again, Priscilla wailed, "Everett, no!" but the others ignored her.

With Everett's help, Robert stood up. He brushed himself off, picked up his cane, and then held a hand out to Jacqueline. "Why don't we walk around to the gazebo?"

Emotion stirred in her eyes, and he knew she was remembering the other time they had talked in the gazebo. Again she hesitated. Then, slowly, her hand came up, and her fingers slipped into his. "All right," she said. "But Robert, whatever you have to tell me . . ."

"Yes?" he said when she didn't go on.

"It had better be awfully good."

SHE GAVE him five minutes, then five more. Finally, she looked at him and said, "You did it to save Cam?"

"At first. Lucinda would have ruined his life, one way or the other. I don't like to speak ill of the dead, but you know what she could be like."

Jacqueline nodded. "You said 'at first.'"

Robert smiled solemnly. "Yes, but then I started to think about the child. He hadn't done anything wrong. His father was a fool, and his mother was . . . well, I don't know what exactly Lucinda was. I never really figured it out. But the child wasn't to blame for anything his parents did. I started to feel like . . . he needed me. And then, when I got back to Charleston and Lucinda . . . died . . . and I saw Lucas for the first time . . . when I held him for the first time . . ." Robert's voice was soft but thick with emotion. "My heart went out to him, Jacqueline. That's all I can say. No matter how the circumstances came about, I looked at him . . . I looked into his eyes . . . and in that moment he *felt* like my son, and I felt like I was his father. I still do. I think I'll always feel that way."

"Oh, Robert . . ." She put her arms around him and hugged him, and he could tell she had been deeply touched by his story. But then she drew back and said, "What are you going to do? The war is still going on, and you're in the army. Even if you weren't, you can't raise a child on your own. You're just a man."

"I couldn't agree more," he said, smiling again. "That's why I'm hoping that . . . my wife . . . will help raise him."

She began to breathe more heavily. "Robert, are you asking me—"

"I am," he said. "I love you, Jacqueline. I always have. I always will. Maybe I should have told Lucinda to go to hell. I don't know. I did what I thought was the right thing at the time. Maybe it wasn't, because it hurt you so badly, but . . . in a way . . . maybe it was, because I have Lucas now. But my life . . ." He had to pause as emotion almost overwhelmed him. "My life will never be complete without you. I love you, Jacqueline. Marry me. Be my wife and my lover and the mother of all our children, Lucas and all the ones to come. Marry me."

"My God," she whispered. "My God. I . . . Robert, I don't know what to say."

"Just say yes."

A long, heart-stopping moment went by. And then she smiled. "Yes."

With tears welling in his eyes, he pulled her into his arms. They kissed and laughed and embraced and kissed again. And then they laughed as they heard Priscilla exclaim, "Oh, dear Lord!"

"I'm as surprised as you are, dear," Everett told his wife, "but, for a change, I think we're going to have to trust Jacqueline."

Robert and Jacqueline turned and saw her parents walking toward the gazebo. Behind them came Tobias and Junie. The nurse still held Lucas. He had stopped crying and was gurgling happily now. A pudgy arm stuck out of the blankets and waved in the air.

Robert slipped an arm around Jacqueline's waist, held her close, and said, "He wants to meet his new mother."

"And I want to meet him, too, because he's your son," Jacqueline said. She looked up into Robert's eyes. "Our son . . . but remember what you said."

"What's that?" Robert asked.

With a twinkle in her eyes, Jacqueline said, "That Lucas is only the first of many babies we'll have, you and I."

Late One Evening . . .

ALLARD LEANED BACK IN the chair, closed his eyes, pressed the balls of his hands against his temples, and tried to drive away for a moment the image of all the papers spread out on the desk in front of him.

His father's chair. His father's desk. And here he was in his father's study, trying to do Malachi Tyler's work. The shipyard was vital, not only to his family, but also to the Confederacy. It had to be kept functioning.

And the responsibility for that had fallen squarely on Allard's shoulders. There was no one else to do it. His mother knew nothing about the business. And she was barely holding herself together these days after the devastating losses she had suffered.

Of course, Allard had suffered those losses too. His sister was gone, his father was gone, and the man who had been his best friend—other than Robert Gilmore—was gone too. One had been taken by war, the other two by natural causes. Which proved, once again, that war, for all its horrors, wasn't the real danger. The real danger was living in the first place.

Allard lowered his hands, opened his eyes, and sighed. He had been poring over the shipyard's accounts all evening, after a full day of working in the office and out in the yard itself. The numbers weren't going to be any different in the morning, he told himself. And he was tired and wanted to spend some time with his wife before they went to bed.

Still, he hesitated, splashing a little brandy into a glass from the decanter on a corner of the desk. He sipped the liquor and thought about everything that had happened recently. Perhaps the most shocking development was that Robert and Jacqueline were engaged to be married. The engagement was highly improper, of course, and as Lucinda's brother, Allard knew that he ought to be offended because Robert was marrying again only a couple of months after her death. But he couldn't bring himself to be that upset about it. He wanted Robert to be happy, and besides, Lucas needed a mother. At one time, Jacqueline Lockhart had been about as flighty and shallow as a girl could be, but she had grown up in the past couple of years. They all had. Jacqueline and Diana, Robert and Allard . . .

But not Cam, of course. Cam was still . . . well, Cam. Allard wasn't sure anything would ever change him. He was still at the Citadel, but from the stories Allard heard, Cam was usually one small step away from trouble. That was probably the way it would always be.

Allard tossed back the rest of the drink and thought about Captain Yorke. A deep hatred for the Yankees still burned inside him because of Yorke's death. Allard knew that men died in war, and in one way of looking at it, the crewmen of the Union cruiser had only been doing their duty to enforce the blockade. They had their orders and had to carry them out, like soldiers everywhere. But knowing that didn't make Allard hate them any less. Somehow, someday, he would find a way to strike back against them. A way to make them pay.

But not tonight. Tonight he was ready to put the work and the worries—and the hatred—aside for a while and spend what was left of the evening with his wife. He set the empty glass on the desk, stood up, and blew out the lamp.

A few minutes later, he came into their bedroom and found Diana sitting in a chair but already wearing her nightdress. She was working on some knitting, but she set it aside when Allard came in. Standing up, she came to meet him, slipping comfortably and familiarly into his arms. Their lips met. Allard stroked her body, relishing the feel of her warm, firm flesh through the thin fabric.

"I've missed you," he murmured as they broke the kiss.

She laughed softly. "You just saw me a little while ago."

"That doesn't matter," he said. "Whenever we're apart, for however long it may be, I always miss you."

"I hope you always will," she whispered.

They kissed again, passion mounting. Allard was ready to take her to bed. He slipped down one shoulder of the nightdress so that he could run his lips along the sweet smoothness of her skin . . .

Then his gaze fell on the knitting she had set aside on the small table next to the chair. He frowned as he realized she was making some sort of tiny garment, like it was for a . . . baby . . .

"Diana," he said, his voice suddenly thick, "what are you knitting?"

She looked into his eyes, smiled, and said, "Allard, I have something to tell you."

9 781681 629322